THE
DOME OF THE
GUARDIANS

MICHAEL K. ANDAM

authorHOUSE®

AuthorHouse™
1663 Liberty Drive
Bloomington, IN 47403
www.authorhouse.com
Phone: 1 (800) 839-8640

All names, characters, places, and incidents are completely fictional.
Any resemblance to actual events, locales, or persons,
living or dead, is entirely coincidental.

Published by AuthorHouse   06/01/2017

ISBN: 978-1-5246-9451-7 (sc)
ISBN: 978-1-5246-9450-0 (hc)
ISBN: 978-1-5246-9469-2 (e)

Library of Congress Control Number: 2017908453

Print information available on the last page.

Any people depicted in stock imagery provided by Thinkstock are models,
and such images are being used for illustrative purposes only.
Certain stock imagery © *Thinkstock.*

This book is printed on acid-free paper.

Because of the dynamic nature of the Internet, any web addresses or links contained in
this book may have changed since publication and may no longer be valid. The views
expressed in this work are solely those of the author and do not necessarily reflect the
views of the publisher, and the publisher hereby disclaims any responsibility for them.

Acknowledgements

To my parents, Kenneth and Jane Andam, I dedicate this book. Thank you for not only being my spiritual mentors, but also my biggest fans. To my wife, Brittany, thank you for your love, patience, and support. To my siblings, Felix, Kenny, and Kobe, thank you for being great examples and for opening opportunities for me to become the man I am today.

A special thanks goes to Tammy Morse, Chelsea Tolman, Rebecca Maxfield, Leah Brazee, Bruce and Rose Marie Boston, Steve and Collette Astle, Kathleen Christensen, Kenneth Boggs, and the many wonderful contributors who saw me through this book and who provided support, read, offered comments, and assisted in the editing, proofreading, and design. I am highly indebted to Karen Trifiletti for working to improve the text considerably and for providing golden suggestions to improve this book as a whole.

Last but not least, I would like to express my gratitude to all my cousins, nephews, nieces, uncles, aunts, friends, mentors and fitness enthusiasts in the United State, Ghana, and all over the world who love and support me in all of my endeavors and achieving my dreams.

—Michael K. Andam

Preface

In the beginning, Earth was created as a living sphere. Its purpose was to serve as the stage where man would act out the story of his life. Each person born would be given the opportunity to fulfill a certain role, a destiny, in this grand, dramatic work during his or her time on this stage.

A set of laws governs the role of each mortal actor. Adherence to these laws determines whether or not an actor's final scene will end triumphantly. They will either leave Earth with the promise of great reward and eternal joy, or the disappointment and despair of knowing that they lived beneath their potential, having squandered that time with things less noble and worthy.

The master planners of the theater are constantly watching, directing, and hoping for the success of each actor. Each reaps according to their ultimate desires and intentions. Each striving mortal being will inherit a degree of glory beyond our present conception. Other earthlings, however, who intentionally reject light and truth, will live selfishly and prefer vanity, deceit and impropriety over goodness. Those who do so and who refuse to change or consider their ways will not reach the highest degree of glory otherwise attainable. These are they who fall easy prey to serious pitfalls and worldly or pagan distraction and who choose never to change course. All individuals will falter; faltering is natural. It is those who apply the grace given by the Master Planners who will pick themselves up, and find failures and foibles redeemed. These are they who will grow in glory until the perfect day. Moreover, no one is left unaided. Since earthly trials and challenges can be overwhelming at times, special messengers who are well versed in the rules are sent to assist the actors throughout each scene of their life's act. They often enter and leave quietly as they fulfill their assignments. Biblical records are replete with these acolytes such as the Samsons, the Gideons, and a host of other valiant messengers and prophets who challenged and subdued the dictators and detractors of their time. Other kings and warlords, such as Leonidas of Sparta, have also come to defend against evils like slavery and anarchy.

These messengers are present in our day as true prophets. Regrettably, we often do not listen to their warnings or heed their counsel. As a result, many perish. Other valiant ones endowed with special gifts are sent to assist the prophets in teaching truths and defending the oppressed. These lionhearted men and women work in our midst every day. Their mission, by divine decree, has been hidden from man—until now. The time has finally come to reveal to the world the true identity of these protectors. They are the rescuers from evil, and defenders of truth. They are the Wackida.

It is my hope that in the not-too-distant future, your personal sphere will be one of those destined for a rescue operation of the Wackida. As this story unfolds, you have a decision to make: Your decision is whether or not to believe— in the Wackidas and your divine heritage and calling or in life's random origin and destiny. The choice is yours. Skeptics, remember the valiant men of the past. Think of their sacrifice and their indelible footprints across our world. Even if you have no more than a desire to contribute to the peace, stability, and welfare of this world, I urge you to cultivate that. Dare to dream that there is potential within you far greater than you could ever imagine and maybe, even dare to live up to it.

Introduction

The incessant dream of the gentle-hearted has been to live in a society where peace rules the land and where love reigns in the hearts of men—a society in which all would be keepers of one another and dwell harmoniously with nature throughout their lives. For centuries, this dream has been forgotten by many. Our planetary abode has been torn apart by evil, pride, war, and greed. As a result, our people have been denied the peace and tranquility that we yearn for and so desperately need.

A ray of hope shines through this seemingly endless fog. Stories kept alive through the generations tell of mighty warriors of valor who have championed the fight for peace. These defenders fled the storms of wickedness, vanquished evil, and courageously led their fellow men to safety and refuge. They created havens where peace and love dwelled in every heart, where people looked to each other as brothers and sisters, and where nature offered up its blessings in abundance. Every gift, blessing, and harvest was cherished with thanksgiving and shared with all—no one went without. Pride, envy, covetousness, and greed were all unknown.

Over time, as one generation succeeded another, these legendary stories gradually lost their luster. They were soon brushed aside as imaginative projections from the minds of dreamers. Humankind lost faith in achieving Utopia in this life, or ever again.

During my childhood years, I read a number of these stories about mighty humans of valor and was filled with admiration for their acts of bravery. Not only did these heroes fight against sheer wickedness and evil dictators in order to free the oppressed, but many of them had to face formidable opponents of an invisible but knowable realm. They were intractable opponents that possessed the power to control the forces of darkness and keep people in submission; dark, evil forces that struck great fear in the hearts of men, and who ruled entire communities without mercy. These forces of evil turned humankind into slaves who were forced to perform horrible, dehumanizing, and almost impossible acts that turned them into beasts of burden.

The agents of these dark powers ruled with an iron hand— wielding whips with which they lashed at humans to do their bidding, and threatening them with torture and pain. None would dare raise a voice of opposition. None would dare rise in protest or make an effort to escape the sickening abuse. All people bore their burdens of oppression with heavy hearts, void of hope for relief—that is, until the day the men of valor appeared. These heaven-sent warriors came to rescue the captives and lead them to a safety. It was thrilling to read such wonderful stories, and I often felt that I was part of the rescue team. At other times, I imagined that I was the rescuer myself. These stories were true to me, at least as a child, and kindled my desire and hope that someday a rescuer would emerge to aid the suffering masses of our planet.

As I grew to manhood, I discovered for myself how twisted, fallen, and demented our society had become. Evil forces, black magic, and deceptive enchantments plagued the people and destroyed the freedom of humans. The evils I'd read about in pivotal, ancient, historical accounts as I grew up, had become a grim reality in the world I lived in. Most of my peers had become enchanted by the allure of the dark arts. I watched, muted, as virtue and integrity were losing the battle in my associate's lives, and as the dark forces took a stronger hold on the minds of the youth. In my mind, I could foresee what the future would hold for us if nothing was done to stop the spread of this disease—if no champion were to come to our aid in this age, to rescue and teach the true path to everlasting peace and happiness. If no deliverer would come, and if none of us would be emissaries, the darkness would overpower and snuff out what was left of the world's goodness.

Even though my peers succumbed to temptation, I always felt a natural distaste for the dark arts and recognized them as the scourge of humanity. I could see through the facades and cloaked evils capturing and enslaving the minds of the innocent. Because of my upbringing, I saw the illusionary impressions of good masquerading and thinly veiled. I had learned early on to discern between good and evil. I'd been taught to see, to reverence light and lift, and to abhor oppression. For a time, I had not really known what oppression was like, except vicariously.

One day, my life was suddenly and unexpectedly changed by forces more powerful than I ever imagined existed. I encountered experiences even more thrilling than the exciting stories I read as a youth. I was tutored and led on a journey to discover the secrets of the universe. I was prepared, called, and given the title, *Wackida*, or "rescuer from evil." I became equipped with special weapons and abilities to combat evil and to destroy wicked humans that yielded themselves to serve as mediums to the evil ones.

I accepted my election willingly when my duties were revealed to me, and I have been conditioned to serve. I have been permitted to reveal my mission. I do this in hopes that those who learn of my journey, my battles and triumphs performed in genuine love for all, will come to recognize the great love of the masters of our universe. By every expedient means, they are ensuring our welfare and eventual triumph in hopes that we might earn the greatest of all rewards in store for the faithful—life eternal! This is my goal for all. This is my story.

CHAPTER 1

The Beginning

My name is Magnus Muller. I was born on the sixth of July, in the year of our Lord nineteen hundred and forty-two—during the emerging science-technology revolution, and sixteen years before the breakthrough that led to the invention of the integrated circuit, also known as the microchip. I was raised in a little community six miles west of the township of Kennymont on a hill located in the southern part of Felixburg County. My parents were well-to-do and highly respected in our community. They had four children: two girls, and two boys. I was the second child born to my parents after the birth of my elder sister, Janet. My brother, Jason, was the third child, and our favorite sister, Katelyn, was the last.

My parents were both raised in the suburbs of the small town Sierramond—one of the industrial settlements in Felixburg County. Life was not easy for the poor settlers in Sierramond. Most of the youth did not have the benefit of education, and my grandparents on both sides, who were neighbors at the time, worked hard to provide a good education for my father and my mother. My parents attended the same institution from childhood through high school. Father was very fond of Mother, but he left Sierramond after high school to attend college in Tangieum—a township over a hundred miles away. After pursuing a degree in engineering and metallurgy, he returned five years later to Sierramond to take a job with a small copper mine in the community, and was thrilled to discover that his childhood sweetheart had still not married. They readily rekindled their friendship which soon turned into a sweet courtship. Within a year, they were married and began a joyful life together.

Father and Mother worked tirelessly to attain a good status in life. They were loving parents who did all that was necessary to make a happy home. We did not lack the necessities of life but were brought up to eschew pride and to esteem humility and charity.

Academically, Jason proved to be the brightest of the children in our family. He was more technically oriented than the rest of us, and pursued his studies with a diligence that pleased my Father. He and I were very close, and regularly spent time together discussing his various academic endeavors. Katelyn, on the other hand, loved the arts. She especially took to poetry, music, and dance. She often thrilled us with her performances, and we all considered her to be very gifted, except for Janet. We all adored Katelyn. Jason and I felt Janet, our oldest sister, was envious of Katelyn. Janet did not feel as comfortable expressing herself as Katelyn did, and did not seem as confident and involved in her studies as the rest of us. Although we accepted and loved Janet as a sister, Jason and I preferred to keep out of her way to avoid her sulky mood and the tight tension in the air when she was around. Then there was me. Because of my poor health and small physique, I preferred to spend most of my time reading. I was an average student, and did well enough to get by. What I loved to do most was spend hours reading wonderful stories about heroes who would go on thrilling adventures. These heroes would use their physical strength and strong moral values to fight against evil and protect the innocent. I often found myself daydreaming about one day becoming just like the heroes in my books.

We were a happy family. We lived in a mansion near the western outskirts of our community, on an estate that was less than a mile from a beautiful beach with calm waters that we called Serena Beach. One could see for miles past the tall walls of our property. The rows of gently rolling hills and vast fields were dotted with sweet-scented blossoms and soaring shade trees. Stretching nearly twenty miles to the north sprawled a dense forest, and, to the east, nestled in the hills, lay the modest homes and tidy streets of our nearby community.

Between our property and Serena Beach, lay a paved road that stretched southward from our iron gate through clumps of thick bushes, then gently turned eastward towards a cluster of small homes. It then led to an overlook of large, well-cultivated farms between the settlement and the forest of tall trees. The road continued through the main township of Kennymont, until it finally snaked northward to link up with the major highway that led to the populated settlements in Felixburg County.

Our community life as a family was wonderful. My father often took us to Serena Beach with our friends and their parents for picnics on the weekends. We would spend almost the whole day at the beach with my family and friends before retiring to our home late in the afternoon. We loved wading and kicking in the water as the gentle waves rolled and broke into a myriad of glittering white bubbles on the shore. We were regularly called by our father or neighbor's booming voice, warning us to stay close to the shoreline anytime we unintentionally swam toward much deeper water. There were times when we would go shell hunting along the beach as far out as Camilla Cove. We would compare shells to see who had found the most beautiful of the day, and Father was always the best judge.

Occasionally, Father would gather our family to the town hall or the park to participate in activities organized by community leaders. Sometimes it was a food festival; at other times it was a welfare service project or a sporting competition. Such activities brought us together as a community to build relationships, work together, laugh, sing, and enjoy the precious things that mattered in life. Mother was well known for her ice cream, and the children would flock, to sample the homemade vanilla and strawberry flavors.

Sometimes the family would spend evenings outside on our front porch. It was an extended porch constructed around the second story of our three-tiered mansion. We could listen to the faint cries of a variety of creatures that lived in the forest and the hills as they prepared for the night after a busy day. As the sun sank over the hills on the western horizon, its reddish glow made the distant mounds look like they were on fire. As the sun kept creeping down, the sky would slowly turn gray and meet the darkened forest and hills, creating silhouettes of the trees that resembled ghostly armies of giants. The impending invasion of these imaginary giants sent chills down my spine.

Sometimes after our outings, during a full moon, we would retire to the southern side of the porch to watch the sea. I was fascinated by the illuminated waves crashing gently onto the shore. In the quiet of the night, I could faintly but distinctly hear the beautiful sound of the sea. Flashes of very bright light would occasionally come from further up the shoreline. They were peculiar lights, and were unlike anything I'd seen before. When I asked my father what they were, he told me they were electric eels playing games.

There was never a night of absolute silence. Typically, the faint, distinctive sound of the crashing waves was interspersed with sharp cries and squeals made by nocturnal hunters and their prey as they fought for survival in the vast wilderness.

My childhood was a happy one, and I was full of energy and love for everything around me—my parents, my siblings, our neighbors and friends, and nature. All of the experiences I had in my youth created within me a strong desire to grow up faster. I was excited for the day that I would have my freedom to explore the outdoors and embark on an adventure. I believe my father observed this insatiable curiosity in me, and warned all of his children, especially me, to never venture outside the walls of our estate unaccompanied. There was a deep-rooted superstition about undefined territory in nearby communities. This stemmed from oral legends of the deep forests. Many people avoided the forests because of mythical accounts of diabolical beings believed to roam deep within it. According to the legend, these beings are restless spirits who harbor resentment toward the living. Apart from their grisly appearance—including long, grimy knotted hair; odium eyes; pug nose; raspy voice; and serrated teeth—they also have a tendency to bewitch and control those who come under their spell. One rumor claimed that, these beings are both shape and gender changers.

My father, as our family's protector, was concerned about us being exposed to any form of danger, even though he did not fully believe the legends. Unlike the others who took them seriously, he felt they were created to discourage residents from venturing into the unknown. All the same, he took all necessary precautions to ensure that we stayed safe within the walls of our estate or in the populated communities nearby. Since he was often away from home on business, my mother became the one largely responsible to keep us close. Since education was of the utmost importance to my parents, my siblings and I were enrolled in a high-performing primary school in Kennymont. Due to the distance, we had to be transported every day to school and back by our butler, Henry Walder. We were often joined by some other youth in our neighborhood who attended the same school. We made a lot of friends, and regularly studied together in the small local library on the weekends. Henry had taught school for years prior to becoming our butler, so he assisted us and our nearby friends with our school assignments. This was especially important to Father, as it was often necessary for him to be away on business.

In school, I took a special liking to my schoolmate, Jennifer Madna, the daughter of the local baker. We became very close friends, and always sat together whenever we went to the community library. My mother and father were good friends with the Madnas and often invited them to our home for dinner. I could tell that Jennifer liked me as well. She always preferred to sit with me and talk during our breaks at school instead of joining the other girls. Because of this, a jealous bully named Lucas would often pick on me. Although I had my physical limitations, I wasn't afraid. There were times when I was tempted to fight Lucas, but he was a lot bigger than me, and I did not want to lose a fight in front of Jennifer. Even more than that, my instincts and upbringing cautioned me to never be an aggressor, but to seek peace. Jennifer and I chose to distance ourselves from Lucas when he would start taunting and calling me names.

I graduated from high school when I was sixteen, and plans were made for me to continue my education at Cliffsville College. It was very sad parting with Jennifer. I had become so fond of her and wished that someday, after my education, I could ask for her hand in marriage. We promised we would remain faithful to each other and agreed that it was best for me to focus on my education, so I could earn enough income to raise a future family. Then, we could talk more seriously about marriage.

Though I loved academics, my yearning for adventure nearly grew into obsession in my early years of college. In my spare time, I would read the memoirs of other adventure-seekers and their bravery and tenacity as they sailed through unknown waters, climbed and conquered high mountains, and explored forbidden forests. I yearned for the opportunity to follow their pursuits, and become immortalized alongside them. I decided that exploring the hills and forests close to my home, despite the legends and myths, would be my starting point. I felt it would be a test of courage to prepare me for future adventures. The urge to explore the unknown was incredibly strong, especially during my visits back home, but I was careful to keep my excitement and desires to myself. Outwardly, I conformed to all the rules and directives given me by my parents in order to avoid suspicion. My thoughts and plans were never betrayed by my behavior or demeanor.

I turned eighteen in the summer of my second year of college, and at the end of the semester, I returned home for summer break. As soon as I arrived, I was informed that my father, who was now working as the chief executive officer of a chain of copper mines, had been called away on unexpected business to attend to a problem in a mine from the Tyresecourt township about two hundred miles from our home. He, my mother, and my sister, Katelyn, who was now in the fourth grade, had left for Tyresecourt, and were expected to be home in two weeks. After having been home for a day, I received word that they were extending their stay through the end of the month.

My sister Janet had gotten married the previous year, and was traveling abroad with her husband. My brother, Jason, was also gone; he lived with my Aunt T'ana in Terrelmont Cove while he attended a prestigious technical institution, Dashonam Institute, located in the twin settlement of Skylerburg and Davisyork, about a mile from Terrelmont Cove. He was a full-time student at Dashonam. Living with my aunt saved money and a long commute.

I looked forward to spending time with Jennifer when she returned home for her own summer break, but that was still another week away. With my sister off and married, and my brother away at school, I was home alone with only our butler, the cook, and the gardener. Though I was now a fairly healthy young man of about five feet four inches in height, I was still slight in stature, with a hardly noticeable limp in my left leg caused by poor childhood health. Because of this, my parents still regarded me a frail and vulnerable child who needed close supervision. They issued strict instructions to the household staff to take good care of me during the period of their absence. I was truly given the best care, but I soon became bored, and once again, anxious for adventure.

My curiosity about the forest and hills grew day by day, and I felt a strong desire rising within me to explore them. Over the next few days, a plan for an exploration trip began to formulate in my mind. I'd convinced myself that an adventure such as this would prove that I could overcome my physical limitations. I dreamed of walking stealthily among the tall forest trees and climbing to the crests of the hills. Admittedly, thoughts of my father's frequent warnings throughout my childhood echoed in my mind. The thought of disobeying him pricked my conscience and hindered my confidence, but I shook off the uneasy feelings. I rationalized simply: I was eighteen, therefore I was old enough to make my own decisions. I talked myself into believing it was the right thing to do, and began to plan my strategy.

Secretly, I began to gather the few things I would need for my upcoming adventure: a flashlight with spare batteries, a sleeping bag, some candles, a machete, a pocketknife, a bow with a quiver of arrows, a pistol, some canned food, fresh fruit, and a few other items. I stuffed everything into a large knapsack and determined how I would slip out of the house early the following morning. The servants in the house did not have the slightest inkling about my intentions. I had bid them goodnight, and went to bed early. I figured that I would be gone for about three days, and would be home before my family returned from their trip.

Before I retired to bed, I called Jennifer. We talked of our excitement over our imminent rendezvous, and we made plans as to places we'd go and people we'd see during the summer. I hadn't intended to tell her my secret, but I couldn't keep it to myself any longer. I ended up telling her, but not before making her promise to keep it a secret. I knew she would be upset, and as I had anticipated, she began to cry and begged me not to follow through with my plans. I reassured her that I would be safe and back home before she returned the following week. After many questions, and some last futile attempts at making me stay, she finally resigned to the fact that I was determined to explore.

I woke up at about four o'clock in the morning, and after a quick wash, I strapped on my knapsack, picked up the bow and arrows, and slung them over my left shoulder. With loaded pistol in one hand, and the machete in the other, I slipped quietly out of the house. By the time I left, it was five o'clock in the morning. I was sure none of the servants would be awake for at least a couple of hours. I made my way quickly to the gate and sat under the big fruit tree close to it. I waited until the birds started chirping and singing, announcing that it was about five-thirty. I quietly opened the iron-gate, slipped out, and closed it behind me. I began walking on a westward dirt path for a while before heading north to the forest.

Despite the legends, during my eighteen years of living in the community, there were never reports of wild animal attacks on the residents who worked on the farms at the edge of the forest. I convinced myself that there was nothing to fear. Nonetheless, I remained cautious as I walked towards the looming trees, clutching the loaded pistol in my right hand, heading straight into the expanse of the virgin forest. I walked briskly and confidently until I was out of sight from any member of the community. I chose a secluded spot, and sat on a small outcrop of rocks to wait for daylight. The scene that greeted my eyes, as the sunlight filtered through the dense foliage of the tall trees, was breathtaking. As far as I could see, there was very little undergrowth. It was apparent that during the forest's development, there had been competition for sunlight, and the tall trees won the contest. All the weaker trees and smaller shrubs had died off. The few pockets of undergrowth that did manage to survive did so because of the patches of sunlight that filtered through the foliage.

I tentatively entered the forest and chose my path carefully, leaving physical markers on the ground and identifying landmarks to help me retrace my steps home, should I be destined to leave the forest and its mystery behind. There was always the chance. Though I kept telling myself that there were no wild animals living in this part of the forest, and that I did not believe any of the undocumented tall tales about the virgin lands, I was still deliberate as I tread my way through the forest. I planted my feet as quietly as possible. My senses were on high alert, and I kept darting my head toward the slightest noise.

Although my progress was very slow in the first hour, my confidence grew as time passed without incident. Along the way, I saw a few harmless squirrels, rabbits, birds, and deer—certainly nothing that looked even remotely dangerous. At one point, I realized that I had come so deep into the forest that I'd lost track of the direction back to the mansion. I swallowed my fear, re-assuring myself that I could retrace my path using the signs I had left along the route.

After hiking for several hours, I heard a faint sound in the distance, similar to the sound of a bubbling spring. I eagerly changed my course to follow the sound, hoping to find fresh water. I felt a deep sense of joy when I came upon a stream flowing gently with a rich variety of shrubs growing along its bank on either side. I dipped my cupped hands into the clear stream and tasted the sweet, refreshing water. I noticed the shrubs were quite thick in some areas along the banks, and I was thrilled to see that some bore edible, sweet berries that were familiar to me. I felt encouraged, having discovered the water that the animals relished. I moved upstream in an attempt to locate the source of the flowing water. The sound intensified until, at last, going around a thicket of shrubs ahead, I stumbled upon a sizable deposit of rock from which the water flowed. The water appeared to be bubbling from out of an underground spring, which flowed out in thick rivulets from the rock bed—nature's own way of calling me to herself. By this time, I was feeling tired, hungry, and in need of a safe place to rest.

I climbed the rock to a higher elevation while keeping an eye out for any poisonous reptiles or spiders hiding in the crevices. I came to a flattened, ash-gray, almost crystalline, spot on the rock on which to sit, that gave me a clear view of part of the forest floor. I then climbed a little higher and arrived at a large scoop in the rock, shaped like an oblong dish. It was spacious and a perfect place to rest. From this elevation, I could see that this outcrop was part of a much larger rocky terrain that stretched for miles. I ate and lay down to rest for a while. I estimated, from looking at the position of the sun, that it was probably one or two o'clock in the afternoon, which meant that six or seven hours had passed. Up to this point, I'd felt enthusiastic about my exploits, but now that the sun was starting to set, and the cold was starting to set in, my courage began to waver. I began to regret my decision to leave despite the warnings of my father. *What have I done? How will the servants react when they notice that I'm gone? What will my parents think when they return home and I'm missing? I was foolish to think that I could do this alone!* I imagined a search party being organized to look for me, and I began to feel a sense of guilt and shame for my selfish actions.

I thought about abandoning my plans and rushing back home, but my obsession and curiosity overruled my resolve to return. *If I start back immediately, I still wouldn't make it back before nightfall. It would make more sense to wait until morning, after a good night's sleep. That will give me at least one night to look around and see what I can find.* That thought alone boosted my confidence and reaffirmed my determination to satisfy this relentless hunger for adventure. With renewed conviction, I settled into my new nook to snatch a few uninterrupted hours of rest. I woke up with a start and was surprised to find that it was completely dark. The darkness was like a dense fog except for the faint skyline defining the path of the winding stream ahead of me. I didn't have any idea what time it was, and I didn't dare switch on my flashlight for fear of night predators. I certainly didn't want to provoke an unwanted encounter.

For the most part, it was quiet, but occasionally the silence was broken by loud squeals and scurrying noises coming from the forest floor and the fluttering of nocturnal birds or bats above. A conjured-up vision of vampire bats sent chills down my spine and sent me groping for my sleeping bag. I pulled the cover over my head, slipped onto my other side, stuffing some padding between me and the rock, hoping to disengage until the sun came up. Just as I was drifting off, I saw a faint yet steady glow of light appear in the trees far off from where I lay. The light was coming toward me, and I watched as it drew nearer and nearer, growing bigger in size and brightness. Fear began to take hold of me and left me paralyzed on the ground. Trees blocked the source of the radiant light. It continued to move toward the rocky ledge where I was lying, and I could just make out two personages, definitely human, moving alongside each other. They appeared to be conversing, but I was hardly paying attention to the conversation because these two humans were floating instead of walking, and the light emanating from them was purer and more exquisite than anything I had ever seen or could even begin to describe.

The personages stopped at the foot of the rock, several feet away from me, and continued their conversation in a gentle foreign language. I could see and hear them clearly now. They were two males, with shiny white, close-cropped hair and shortly trimmed beards. Their countenance was magnificent to behold. They talked among themselves for a while, and then resumed their journey, passing me, until they were out of sight. I stayed motionless, and tried to comprehend what I had just seen. My mind was racing with questions: *Were the legends true? Who were these strange beings, and what were they doing in this forest?*

Clearly, they were human, but they'd spoken a language I'd never heard before. In fact, they appeared to be of a higher species of humanity—more intelligent and emanating a love and wisdom that drew my soul toward them in an unprecedented way. *Had they see me?* Whether they had or not, I was compelled to seek after them. Somehow, we were connected. I was so preoccupied with my thoughts that I didn't notice their return, until the glowing light was as close as fifty yards from me. I watched them effortlessly retrace their path and disappear into the woods from which they had earlier emerged. Sleep had fled my tired body, and I lay wondering how long it would take before daylight would permit me to progress. Luckily, about an hour later, the melodies of songbirds announced that the sun was about to rise. The chirping also reminded me that I had been missing from home for twenty-four hours. I climbed down from my elevated rock lodging as the sun filled the forest with its welcoming light. I quickly cleaned myself and ate some fresh fruit from my pack. This rocky ledge had served me well. I decided to use it as a base camp so I could return to a familiar place before nightfall, as long as I remained in the forest. After picking some berries to supplement my food stock, I strapped my pistol in its holster around my waist. With my machete in my right hand and bow and arrows slung over my left shoulder, I started out to trace the path of my strange visitors.

It took a few hours to get through the trees before I finally emerged onto a rocky terrain that extended for miles. It dawned on me that this terrain could be linked to the rocky ledge that now served as my campsite. I hiked northeast for a while, trying to trace the path of the unknown, illuminated beings, and ended up going west, circling back to the rocky terrain. In the distance I could see rolling hills. I had a view of these exact hills from the porch of our home. I realized that I was close to the western border of the forest, which had taken me nearly six hours to reach. It was past noon, and I needed to hurry to get back to my outpost before nightfall.

I abandoned my earlier route and opted to follow the rocky terrain southward in hopes of locating my camp. It turned out to be an intelligent gamble. I could now move faster. As I moved along the terrain, I saw a few reptiles as they scurried and slithered into crevices, but my journey continued on without incident. After several hours of walking at a brisk pace, I was relieved to hear the familiar sound of the brooklet faintly in the distance. I soon arrived at my camp and was able to wash and eat before dusk. I slipped into my sleeping bag just before total darkness engulfed the forest. My body was weakened from the day's activities, and I soon fell into a deep slumber.

During the night, I had a strange dream that I was being chased by men mounted on huge flying reptiles that breathed fire. They were similar to the mythical dragons that I'd read about in some of my books as a child. One of the reptiles effortlessly uprooted a small tree with its tail and hurled it at me. As the tree hurtled toward me, I was jolted awake by a sharp, severe pain in the side of my head. I must have jerked my body while dreaming and hit my head against the rock. I lay awake for a long time, trying to soothe my headache with some balm I'd thought to add to my supplies. Finally, the balm finally took effect, and the pain gradually eased. Just as I was dozing off again into a fretful and uncomfortable sleep, I noticed the bright glow from the night before coming from the same direction. As the light came closer, I noticed that there were three illuminated beings this time. Again, they stood at the same spot as the night before. The three talked for a while, then rapidly floated by the rock, along the bank of the stream, and out of my sight. They returned by the same route until they disappeared into the forest, just as the two had done the night before.

Intrigued, I woke up early the following morning and started on my quest to learn more about these mysterious beings. Now that I was getting familiar with the route, it took me only a few hours of brisk walking to arrive at the spot on the westward side of the forest that I had reached the previous day. I moved a little bit higher up the rock to survey and determine the direction I should go. Suddenly, about six yards from where I had stopped, I saw it. It was a large reptile, a cross between a chameleon, an *Agama agama* lizard, and some type of alien creature. It was the size of a small alligator but had webbed feet and long, curved claws that looked like razor-sharp talons. Its body was flat, and it had an oblong, hideous head, set with a pair of reddish protruding eyes that could rotate in all directions. It had two protruding flabby lobes of outer ears and some sort of antennae-type sensors where nostrils should have been. A bright yellow line stretched from below one earlobe across the snout and to the other ear. The upper and lower jaws were covered and separated by a pair of lips. The neck was decorated with a reddish muffler, and at its posterior end, its long body narrowed to a pair of long, helical tails. It seemed a live encounter with the mythical dragons I had seen in my dream only hours before. If such strange creatures like the one I was witnessing really did exist, then maybe the dragons from the stories were not a myth after all. Maybe they truly did exist.

Suddenly, the protruding eyes of the small monster rested on me. For an instant, a bolt of fear ran through me, and I was sure it was going to attack. But, instead, it gradually changed color and took on the guise of the rocky terrain. I would never have seen this strange creature if it had seen me first and adopted this perfect camouflage. I fixed my eyes on it for a long time, partially out of curiosity, partially out of caution. After realizing that it had been spotted, the creature suddenly darted away at an incredible speed for its size. Now that I was certain it meant me no harm, I followed it at a reasonable distance, keeping at least a hundred feet between myself and the creature. I followed it down a gentle slope and watched it vanish into a crevice in the rock. I cautiously drew closer to the spot where it had vanished and examined the crevice. I could not believe how a creature of that size could have vanished into such a shallow opening. I searched around the area, looking for a possible hole that it could have run into, but found none.

The creature had vanished into solid rock. As I took a step forward, I suddenly felt the rock beneath my feet give way. A sizable trapdoor, cleverly disguised to blend in with the rock's surface, had opened under me, and I began falling down a smooth, steep underground tunnel. I panicked as I saw the trapdoor swing and snap shut above me. Instinctively, I made a frantic effort to grab onto something in the dark, but the walls were too smooth. The tunnel was nearly a vertical fall, and at the speed I was falling, there was no preventing it. Less than a second later, I felt my body launch into airspace. As I fell, my thoughts suddenly turned to Jennifer. *Will I ever see her again?* The next moment, I hit something and blacked out.

CHAPTER 2

The Sacred Dome of the Guardians

How long I was out, I could not tell. I became aware of myself submerged in a glass casing filled with some kind of fluid. I instinctively clenched my lips shut to stop the substance from filling my lungs. When I couldn't hold my breath anymore and was forced to gasp, I found that I could somehow breathe comfortably. In the next instant, still astonished, the area around me burst into light, which grew brighter and brighter until everything was enveloped in blinding white. The fluid around me began to swirl into a small whirlpool and was almost instantly sucked from the casing through a drain in the glass floor. The case dissolved, and I fell down, blinking rapidly and struggling to see past the glare of the incredibly bright room.

As my eyes began to adjust to the light, I could see that the room I was in was very large, close to the size of a stadium dome. The floor was coated with a material that looked like refined gold— if it wasn't real gold, then it certainly was as beautiful. The dome seemed to be empty except for what appeared to be doors, or curious panels, evenly arranged around the inner edge of the dome. The walls were about fifty feet high and sloped inward at the top, leaving a space through which the sky could be seen (later I learned that it was an illusion—the "sky"

I saw was merely artificial and designed to portend that the dome was on the earth's surface).

After realizing that I was alone in my new surroundings, I started to walk around and take a closer look at this strange and beautiful place. I simultaneously noticed that my body felt very different than it had before. I walked over to one of the walls sealed with reflective surface and was startled and confused by what I saw. My corpus, the body I'd lived with since birth—stunted, imperfect, hindered—was now more beautiful than I could have ever hoped to imagine. The limp in my left leg was gone. I was bigger and more muscular, and I felt great power and incredible strength surging through my body. I now stood at about six feet five inches tall, and my once sparse and dull hair had grown thick and long. It was now black as a raven, with a touch of sheen. I could see farther and with more detail than I ever had before. My ears were picking up the sounds of small gusts of wind from across the massive dome. These changes were strange but not unwelcome. I was happy considering the physical advantages I now possessed. I was in coveralls of a greenish hue, which hugged my body, leaving only my forearms and head exposed. I stared down at my perfected forearms and hands, in awe. I stood in bewilderment at my transformation.

My mind started to race as it rehearsed, in vivid detail, what had happened from the moment I left home to the time I fell down the concealed tunnel. *Where am I? How long have I been unconscious? Where are my things—my pistol and my other weapons?* I had no idea if I was dreaming again, if my senses were playing tricks on me, or if I was hallucinating as a result of the terrible fall. *This cannot be real!* I thought to myself. I tried to make myself wake up but soon knew that I was, indeed, a very conscious Magnus Muller, now in a body that was new and yet somehow familiar. Then the thought struck me: *I can breathe underwater just as easily as I can the air. There must be more changes to my anatomy than I am aware of. I need to find out what has happened to me.*

As I began to step toward one of the panels on the wall of the dome, the three radiant superhumans that I'd seen in the forest appeared before me. They looked even more brilliant in full light than they had in the dark forest, and their eyes spoke compassion and wisdom. My emotions ran the spectrum in what seemed like a nanosecond—from panic, to bewilderment, to confusion, to wonder, to peace. Their gentle smiles and gestures assured me that they meant no harm. I had nothing to fear. It seemed they were speaking on a level unknown to man. My thoughts transferred easily to them, I could tell, and theirs to me, without a spoken word. As I observed them, I noticed that instead of floating this time, their feet were touching the golden floor. All three now had a flat pair of sandals made from what looked like the same gold, with three woven gold straps, two of which fastened into place over the tops of their arches and the third around the ankles. It was locked in place by a golden buckle on the side of the ankle.

Even in my newly enhanced body, I felt inferior to these beings. Then one of them began to speak to me in my native tongue. "Hello, Magnus. We are Guardians, selected by the Creators known as the Supremos, who organized the universe eons before your physical planet was created. They looked upon the wide expanse of space and its rich stock of unorganized matter and counseled with each other before organizing it under eternal laws—as an abode for the perfection of the universe. With these same pre-existent materials, solar systems, planets, and other heavenly bodies are also being organized into galaxies. Living souls are also being formed and assigned to live on selected planets. By obedience to irrevocable eternal laws, these creations may then be guided to attain perfection. Among these numberless creations is your planet."

My feelings of inferiority were eclipsed when it seemed they might have been magnified in the face of Perfection personified. The tenderness of voice, a love more perfect than any I'd known, captivated and calmed me. It produced in me an unbidden and seemingly undeserved feeling of acceptance, inspiring me to greater heights than rebuke ever could. The words the first messenger spoke and the knowledge he was imparting to me were new, yet they seemed strangely familiar. It was as if I were hearing truths I'd known all along but had forgotten. It was effortless to trust and accept everything he was telling me.

He continued, "We are charged with the responsibility to oversee and nurture the growth and development of your planet and its inhabitants through its given period of existence to the day of fullness and perfection. The plan for your planet, and other selected ones of its kind, is to populate it with humans imbued with intelligence, and to provide them with eternal laws whereby they can progress and grow in knowledge and wisdom. These humans, including you, Magnus Muller, are creative beings endowed with the power and the potential to develop and attain this knowledge and wisdom; you've the potential to become exalted, and to live forever, helping to prosper and perfect other universes, by virtue of One who showed the way."

The Guardian went on to explain that I, like all other offspring, was originally a spirit essence, organized from very fine matter and filled with intelligence. I was taught and trained with love as a spirit being until I had attained adulthood in the "First Phase" of my life, prior to mortal birth. This was an amazing concept to me: to consider that I had already attained adulthood in a previous phase of my life. I had no recollection of any previous phase of life as a spirit being, and yet I believed and eagerly clung to his every word.

"In the Second Phase of your life," he continued, "you were clothed with a replica of your spirit body from the elements of your planet, which was formed through the process of physical birth. You have been given the freedom to choose whether or not to live by the universal law of perfection. The plan of happiness sets forth these laws of eternal progression. One day, all followers, adherers to the same, will be initiated into the Order of the Supremos." The Creators who addressed me were neither selfish nor covetous in sharing their power, desire, and storehouse of spiritual riches. They desired that all may be guided with love and without compulsion, to attain that cherished status. They clarified that this was our transcendent and earthly purpose.

The Guardian went on to explain that I and everyone else were taught the law, among other essential lessons, when we were just spirits, but the plan required that at birth, a veil should cover our minds to make us forget our previous existence. The known law was, however, permitted to linger in our subconscious mind so truth would resonate with us when we heard it again in this life. Special spirits that proved to be fully committed in pre-existence, known as Agents, were foreordained to be born in selected ages. We, who are here now, are among them. These Agents were clothed with power and authority to teach the law on their home planets. Thus, the process of obtaining perfection was executed. As a result, intelligence, spirit, and coarse matter in the universe continue to be transformed from their unorganized state into organized, humans, animals, plants, planets, solar systems, and galaxies, and from their organized state to greater levels of intelligence and potential.

This same messenger paused in his explanation, looking directly into my eyes to make sure I was comprehending. "The obedient intelligences," he said, "are being given the knowledge and power to assist in these exalting, creative duties." A spark of hope lit within me. I sensed he was talking about my own obedience as an intelligence, and I was consumed with a hunger to learn more.

He continued, "Each inhabited planet in our galaxy has Guardians assigned to oversee its progress. They are not to interfere in the affairs that transpire on the planet but are permitted to counsel and assist the Agents where necessary. Their main assignment, however, is to prepare, train, and guide someone who has been selected and foreordained to live for a thousand-year period, to fight deception and evil, and to help the inhabitants choose to live the perfect law of the universe."

My excitement rose within me. I sensed I was on the verge of experiencing an adventure beyond anything previously imagined.

"You, Magnus Muller, were appointed to this duty ages before you were clothed with your physical body. Your birth on this planet and in this era was foreordained, and your ancestral line has been carefully chosen and monitored. Through it, you have imparted to you the genetic characteristics that will enable you to acquire courage, strength of character, and other qualities you'll need for this special assignment. Your love of nature, your preoccupation with adventure, and your desire to find truth and knowledge are traits that you inherited and were selected to guide and to bring you here to learn of and accept your mission as an Agent. Having reached eighteen years of planetary life, you are now ready. You acted without compulsion to indicate your readiness for your assignment. We were aware of your location in the forest, and knew your curiosity would convince you to try and find out who we were."

I marveled at the power the Guardian possessed to know my thoughts. *Could he read my mind?* As soon as the question arose in my head, he immediately began to answer. "To answer your question," he said, "each human is able to see and relate to another by virtue of a life wave that emanates from the brain and overlaps the similar waves of other living beings. This wave connects with the universal life waves that operate in each galaxy. All living things are endowed with this gift and power. Even simple forms of life, such as plants and animals, have these life waves. Humans possess the power to control the range of their own life waves according to their desire. However, those humans who are inexperienced with the process can have their life waves withdrawn involuntarily from interacting fully with other life waves, depending on their mood. An individual's life waves can be voluntarily or involuntarily withdrawn so as to not overlap fully with any other person's life waves. If you voluntarily initiate the withdrawal, your focus repels all other persons' life waves around you from overlapping with yours, and you appear invisible to those around you. On the other hand, when you are fully relaxed and peaceful, your life waves spread farther to overlap with many other life waves. If it overlaps with those of someone you know very well, a thought about that person comes into your mind, and is often reflected in your reality. You are already recalling times when such has happened in your life. You are also wondering, *"Why now?"* When you were released from the biosynthetic machine, we were present, but you could not see us until we desired you to."

My every thought was open to them like a book. I realized that every life memory and experience was somehow etched into my being. My soul was like a text. The Book of Life was real, but not in the way I'd imagined it. I was thrilled to learn about the life waves of the universe. It explained several mysterious experiences I had had during my life, which were now no longer a mystery. It all was becoming so clear to me.

This Spirit of Spirits continued to impart knowledge to me. "Nature," he said, "has a vast amount of information hidden to the uninitiated, but you, Magnus, have been endowed with the power to access this information whenever you desire. You will come to learn and recognize truths as fast as you seek answers. Whenever a question comes up in your mind, it is our duty as Guardians to give or guide you to the answer. We may reveal it to you as an intuition or as a direct message in your mind, or we may help you discover it through what you experience. All will depend on how well *you believe what you know but do not see.* The world may teach you differently—it will teach you that it all will depend on *how you believe what you see.* Remember these things."

"The first knowledge you will receive is foundational to all future knowledge. It is gaining a full comprehension of all events in every age of your planet's existence. You will gain this knowledge by receiving a memory upgrade. Each event will flash before your eyes and be imprinted on your mind and memory, and you will come to know them as if you had been there when those events occurred. You can recollect them at any time just by focusing your mind on a particular date or event."

Something clicked. How often I'd yearned for a photographic memory to capture tomes at the library at once, to learn at an exponential rate, to absorb more than I felt I could in this restricted sphere, and with limited senses. It was just a hint, an echo—of what was truly possible. I could hardly believe what my ears were hearing. This was a dream come true.

My other-worldly instructor paused for a moment, giving me a chance to ponder and assimilate. Then he continued, "The changes you have observed in your body, including increased strength and adaptability, are deliberate. These changes are in place so that you may effectively fulfill your important assignment. Remember that the success of a person in this life depends on how willingly and successfully he lives in total obedience to the prescribed laws. That success brings everlasting happiness. You have wondered why you and others may be born with physical limitations if perfection is the ultimate goal for each of us. This is a worthy question. Each person has a purpose and a tailor-made laboratory of experience prepared for them. Those with disability are merely tested differently than those without. At the same time, they serve as instruments to test the compassion and love of those who live among those born with challenges. Your childhood limitations have helped you gain humility and compassion for others, as you recognize. You have passed your test and are now endowed with a set of superior powers and a strong body.

"Mental communication is the only medium through which we are permitted to offer you guidance and assistance when you start your assignment," he intoned with a look of seriousness. "We may teach and counsel you but will never compel you to perform, or perform on your behalf, any physical activity pertaining to your planet. The Guardians are assigned only as a resource to Agents and Rescuers who have been ordained and have been born on that home planet."

As soon as the question arose in my mind as to how these supreme beings had earned their Guardian status, he began to answer, "We were born on other planetary orbs, much like yours, and have successfully passed through your phase of existence. Through obedience to the laws which were given, we have developed and have been accepted for final initiation into the Order of the Supremos. We have gone through extensive preparations toward our initiation. Our last assignment is to serve as Guardians until this planet has gone through its ordained period of existence and has attained perfection. As Guardians, we assist the Agents and the Wackida in every millennium as they influence others to live to qualify for their ultimate reward."

The next questions that came to my mind were these: *How long have I been here? What has happened to my body?* The answers came instantly. "Over a period of forty-five years from the day you fell through the secret portals of this dome, according to the time reckoning for this planet, your body has been modified through supernatural genetic engineering to enhance the natural features you inherited through your ancestral line in order to complete your preparation for your assignment."

"Forty-five years?" This realization shook me. My mind began to race as I tried to comprehend the significance of what he was telling me. What had become of Jennifer… my family? Were my parents still alive? Would I ever see them again? My heart sank, imagining the grief and despair they must have gone through after my mysterious disappearance. With the realization that I would very likely never see my friends and family again, my curiosity as to the purpose of it all intensified. I quickly drew my focus back to what the Guardian was patiently waiting to tell me. I sensed that he couldn't continue without my full attention and my desire to learn.

"A chip is implanted within you which is a very sophisticated, biological replica of the chip invented several years after you were born. By the time you were eighteen, there had been an accelerated development in information processing on your planet. In the last forty-five years that you've been in the Dome, technology has advanced. Significant discoveries have been made in all fields on this planet. These discoveries and inventions came through enlightened and intelligent beings. Scientists have accelerated the use of this planet's resources and have made discoveries through inspiration, to organize simple matter into complex innovations. As Guardians, we have the ability to organize simple matter into complex biological machines. The memory machine is one of these innovations, and the biosynthetic machine is another."

I was intrigued with his advanced scientific knowledge and his ability to create complex machines from simple matter. The Guardian quickly recognized my desire to gain more knowledge concerning the functioning details of these machines. "These machines function and perform on the same basis as the plants you are familiar with. Some perform like the lesser unicellular creations, such as the bacterium or the amoeba that have been programmed to asexually reproduce by duplication of its nucleus and then splitting into two daughter organisms. Others perform like the more complex multi-cellular creations that are able to grow and reproduce by gametes and respond to external environmental stimuli until they have filled their purpose." I felt an increasing love and gratitude for this Guardian who loved and cared about me enough to consistently grant my request and provide additional knowledge at each moment of inquiry.

He continued, "Because the forces of good and evil are ever-present, the master of evil, Xoedikus, is hard at work influencing the minds of the weak to embark on the creation of things to propagate evil. Xoedikus was one of the most beloved and brilliant children of the Supremos. His potential for greatness was marked. He had a large following and was greatly admired, but as his renown grew, so did his pride. Arrogance filled his heart, and so was born a plan of his own—a plan meant to replace the wise and loving plan of the Supremos. But when presented, his plan was rejected. Hatred and anger filled his heart, and he and those who followed him swore to forever defy the Supremos, their ageless plan, and all who supported it.

"Pride gave birth to sin and sin to evil, and Xoedikus became the master and the lord of all that was dark and iniquitous; thus was born the opposing force to light. Consenting and submitting to the will of the Supremos, to be led along the ageless pathway, is the only way to obtain peace and spiritual growth in this life, and perfection in the life to come. The loving Supremos desire this for as many of their offspring as would live by the universal law of perfection. Fortunately, their love and mercy also provide help for those who are misled by Xoedikus to find their way back, as you will learn in due time. Your mission is to find those who are lost and guide them back to the path once more.

"You will see and discern these things in due course. The ultimate creative ability that will be imparted to those who earn the status of the Order of the Supremos is the power to organize and populate planets with living things, and to serve, provide for, and sustain their offspring." Although I did not fully understand what he was telling me, I trusted that in due course I would gain a full knowledge of my creative abilities and their purposes.

"On your arrival here, you were put into the biosynthetic machine, which was programmed to modify your physical frame and enhance your features to equip you for your planetary assignment. For forty-five years, you were kept in a suspended state while your body was going through biosynthesis. The machine provided you with oxygen and nutrients while you went through a gradual, controlled body modification. You have already observed that your physical frame has increased in size and strength far beyond any living being or animal destined to live on your planet in this age. Your skin is composed of tiny, almost imperceptible and impenetrable plates that resemble scales, which will insulate and protect you. You will be immune to the effect of the elements found here. You can escape fires and snowstorms, walk through freezing temperatures or boiling waters, withstand any natural element or synthetic chemical compound, and no weapon from Earth will be able to harm you.

"Your skin has the ability to absorb unlimited amounts of energy from whatever environment you find yourself in—water, sunlight, fire, or the open air. This will be your source of energy during the period of your assignment. You will occasionally feel hunger. Food will be necessary as a source of nutrients to replace your newly modified cells so that they will not age with time. Any aged cells in your body will be absorbed and replaced with perfect daughter cells, which will cause the aging process within you to come to a standstill. Your vision, sense of hearing, and sense of smell have been highly enhanced, with increased sensitivity to match your newly heightened mentality, and give you an advantage over all beings that may try to harm you. You are not yet exalted, neither are you mortal. You are in an intermediate state of translation. You are a translated being."

He paused, giving me a chance to absorb and reflect upon these changes. While pondering, I wondered about the particular details of the physical change that allowed me to survive while immersed in fluid. He smiled, as if he was pleased with my inquiring mind, and was happy to pass on the knowledge according to my desire to receive it.

"You will notice that the flesh covering the inner layers of your lower jaw, just beneath your tongue, now has a rich layer of blood capillaries embedded in a layer of interconnected micro-channels that open externally just below the inner part of your lower jaw via sixteen embedded, miniature, cellular pumps with expandable exit holes, eight on either side of your lower jaw. These modifications allow you to breathe underwater. You were able to extract oxygen from the fluid you were immersed in while you were in the biosynthetic machine. The pumps function the way gills function in fish, causing your epiglottis to reflexively flip shut and seal off access to your lungs as soon as water touches those under your tongue. Whenever you are submerged in water, or any fluid for that matter, the liquid is directed by the miniature pumps to flow through the convoluted micro-channels and over the woven rich layer of blood capillaries under your tongue for oxygen extraction. It then exits through the expandable outlets under your jaw. In an oxygen-deficient environment, you will adapt and respire just as the facultative anaerobes do." I moved the tip of my tongue to feel for these miniature pumps and was surprised that they were hardly noticeable. I lifted my hand under my jaw to feel for the expandable outlets but had to put quite a bit of pressure on my jaw before I could feel them. I was somewhat relieved that they were not noticeable.

As I lowered my hand, I glanced down at the green coveralls I was wearing. "Even your outfit is extraordinary," my instructor continued. "The coveralls with the green hue are designed to withstand any impact or shock to your body. They can also grant you partial invisibility, as you are now able to blend with your environment as you desire. Eventually you will learn to control and use the natural, more perfect method of drawing the life waves close to your head to achieve total invisibility. A tiny, highly sophisticated physiological brain has been linked with your central nervous system to allow you to naturally control all the additional modifications made to your body. Your planet's microchip design is an inspired, inanimate replica of this tiny brain. Though your spiritual essence cannot be modified because it is your personality, your persona, you have been given a boost in spiritual power and to your physical frame and strength. You have available to you, in times of need, enhanced reflexes and spiritual weapons which you will come to know about in the course of your lessons and studies.

"Your greatest spiritual weapon is, however, your mind. Most importantly, you are endowed with the ability to instantly discern events that transpire at your destined location. Your gift of discernment will also enable you to know of events which will require your intervention. You will be provided with a spectacular mode of transportation to your assigned area, when needed, to work and to prevent any calamity that is not permitted by the Supremos, or to intervene in the calamity at just the appropriate time. You will need to learn of the dimensional, kaleidoscopic realms within your planet and the forces that control and oppose the plans of the Supremos. In the course of your interaction with these worlds and realms, you will learn to use some of your added abilities to master control of your senses and emotions."

My mind rang with uncertainties. *Was I really the best person to be appointed to an assignment of such magnitude? Would I ever again live a normal life?* I knew I would never, in my current state, enjoy the companionship of a loved one, or the happiness and satisfaction of marrying and raising a family. I would probably never have friends to share moments of sorrow and joy with, as I did with Jennifer, because of the need to keep my identity secret. *Where would the joy of living a thousand years among society be, if I would be unable to associate with my fellow humans?* My faith in my role in this plan began to ebb, and I felt myself begin to sink into despair. Just at that moment, a soft, soothing voice intercepted my negative thoughts. It was a female voice. I raised my head and was surprised to see seven more Guardians standing with the previous three. Five of them were female and wore robes similar to those of the men, except that a gold-plated belt adorned their waistline to enhance their beautiful, shapely bodies. They each wore their long, silvery-white hair braided into a bun and pinned at the nape of the neck with a beautiful golden pin. They wore sandals similar to those of the men. These women were stunningly beautiful. Angels stood before me.

The soothing, comforting voice spoke tenderly. "My son, ever since planets began rolling into existence, the Architects, who hold the keys of the universe and guide each galaxy in its evolution, have applied the same process and principles to nurture your planet toward its destined potential as it has all other exalted planets. Much of this work goes unseen by mortals. As you have learned, spirit beings born to Earth are given the expression of their identity in physical bodies and are offered the opportunity to learn and grow through structured institutions, such as marriage and family, tribes, and countries. Each institution is bound together by traditions, faith, and religion, and a common hope and aspiration. It is in these mediums that the epitome of love, honesty, hard work, sacrifice, and loyalty are learned and perfected, yielding unspeakable joy." I knew her words to be true as I reflected on my own family institution, with our traditions and our common hopes and aspirations. I truly felt a fleeting sense of happiness in my heart when I thought of my earlier life with my family, especially realizing now I may never see them again.

"Evil exists in this world. The master of all evil, an ambitious, rebellious spirit offspring, was once destined for your planet to acquire a physical body. But he was denied this experience and was barred from progressing due to his pride and rebellion. As a spirit, he still operates, and in his anger and jealousy of your potential, he is working to derail humans off the true path of happiness and onto the path of misery that he knows well. Without evil, which is an opposing and essential component of the eternal plan, goodness cannot be discerned, understood, and appreciated. Opposition is crucial to our progression, and the Supremos have wisely given humans the power of will to choose good over evil. Humans who are prideful or domineering in attitude, who desire power and wealth above anything else, all against the dictates of their conscience, are easily enticed to be instruments and agents in the hands of this evil being. Often, they are drafted into the opposing armies, to enforce dominance and inflict subtle forms of wickedness upon those that oppose, thereby destroying their victims and their potential happiness."

I wondered, *Why should the rebellious offspring, Xoedikus, be so intent on destroying us? He made his choice knowingly, and we had the right to make ours. Does he entice us with wealth and power just to win us over to increase his forces, to demonstrate his power to influence, or to satisfy his prideful ego?* Once again, the answer was almost instantaneous. "The evil one is envious. He envies humans, who have earned the right to be born and acquire physical bodies because of their faithfulness, and he envies the inheritance promised to the faithful ones. He knows his days are numbered, and he only wants to mislead more people to suffer with him in the end—and he is succeeding. My son, without Agents and the special messengers who are willing to be the instruments in the hands of the Supremos to counter evil and guide humans to voluntarily live by the perfect law of the universe, the plan of the Supremos cannot succeed. This is the pattern applied to all planets that have successfully fulfilled the measure of their creation and have been perfected and exalted. It is your turn to fulfill your destined duties and earn your reward. Your sacrifice will be great, but your reward will far exceed the greatest of all joys that humans can ever experience. It is a great honor to be the elect for this assignment in this millennium."

I felt honored to be chosen and empowered to influence my fellow sojourners to stay on the right course. But a fear began to rise within me, the fear of being rejected because of the strange modifications made to my physical body. *Would I appear to be a freak among them?*

By this time, I was growing accustomed to this new telepathic form of communication. "You are a handsome specimen of manhood, and there is no outward, easily perceptible modification that will tell you apart from other humans. You may mix freely in society anytime you choose, and wear normal clothing as you wish, but you must ensure that your true identity is never revealed. Remember, you are not the first to be elected for this assignment on your planet. Others have been chosen and have worked most effectively in earlier millennia. Your planet is advancing toward its perfect state, and it is your turn to help save as many people as you can from the influence of evil—to negate the triumph of the evil forces over them. This Sacred Dome has been in existence since the creation of your planet, and we were assigned to this planet in its formative years. Our work will be complete when your planet, and as many of its inhabitants as will choose to work with the good forces, have been perfected."

I was relieved to hear my physical changes would not be easy for others to detect, but still, thoughts of ending up as a lone crusader were dissonant ones. They sent my mind longingly back to happy days as a child with my parents and siblings. I remembered the security I felt and the great lessons taught in our home. I often saw in the eyes of my parents that unfading gleam of love for each other and for us as they showered us with affection, ensuring our comfort and happiness. I remembered this with fondness and wished I could relive those moments. Hearing my counselor's gentle but firm voice, I suddenly awoke from my daydream as she continued.

"We need to impress upon you that the greatest institution in all eternity that humans have been blessed with and that has been made accessible to all humans, primitive and developed, is the institution of marriage and family. It is upon the pivot of marriage and the family that the progression of humans hinges and rotates. The family unit is the medium in which true love is able to flourish and grow to elevate humans to spiritual heights. An understanding of its importance and its eternal and sacred nature will cause humans to cherish and nurture it with commitment and dedication. True love and dedication are what make the family unit and the human race succeed.

"The opposing throng knows this, and for that reason, families have been the target of persistent attacks by the evil one and his minions in all generations. Take note of the fact that marriages and families are the building blocks of societies and nations. A peaceful community or nation is only a reflection of the cooperative coexistence of those who value and cherish the family unit—not only their own, but their neighbors' as well. You were surprised to see our team made up of an equal number of males and females. Gender has existed all through eternity, and the eternal law requires the unity of the two in a loving, eternal marriage to mutually support each other, raise and train offspring, and impart the same recognition and support to other families in order to successfully journey through life's probationary period and to earn the greatest gift of life—together."

The truth, as she spoke, distilled into my soul, and I felt overjoyed with the possibility of being reunited with my loving parents again. I began to reflect: *Had we as a family satisfied the conditions for being reunited?*

"We are an example of what humans can become as couples who are obedient to the universal law of perfection. Not one of us could have attained this status alone, without our spouses, even if we were totally obedient to all the other laws individually. As you can see, the law of eternal marriage holds great importance. However, you must come to understand that there are those born naturally with uncommon characteristics or feelings, which are not in conformity with the accepted norm as outlined in the divine law. Should such people be shunned by society because their natural feelings do not conform to the norm? Is it by any fault of their own that they are born that way? No. They are children of the Supremos and are equally loved by them. Such people are given to our societies to test the tolerance, compassion, love, and the ready support that we are required to offer them. We all have our different tests and obstacles, but the Supremos will grant us our reward regardless of our physiological and psychological constitution, provided we strive to learn and live the law. As we seek our heavenly parents in prayer and with singleness of heart, they promise to give us the motivation and courage to overcome all things. Hatred, evil people, and evil acts divert and derail the most sacred institution in the eternal scheme of things."

This was new information to me, as I had never known of anyone who was faced with these struggles in my community as a youth. I, on the other hand, had a desire to be with Jennifer, and I had hopes of marrying her someday. I felt a tinge of sadness and disappointment as I realized Jennifer most likely would have her own family by now and our plans to be married could never be fulfilled. *How could I ever be loved and marry with my impending assignment to be done in secrecy and my modified structural state?*

I saw a gentle smile brighten the pretty face of the being speaking to me. "Do not worry," she said. "It has been foreordained that a suitable and loving partner will be born and raised in the last century of your service to humanity. You will naturally be attracted to each other and will live in love and succeed together. She will come to know your true identity, but she will never betray your trust. With her, you will be blessed to create a family that will bring joy into your life."

She touched my forehead with her right forefinger, and suddenly, a vision was opened to my mind of a lovely girl with dark brown hair and olive skin. She was remotely familiar. Her eyes beamed with intelligence and wisdom, and she carried herself with an air of perfect comportment, bravery, and confidence. She was fascinating, and I was instantly drawn to her.

"She will be your wife, and an image of her will constantly be in your memory to spur you on until the day you will be united with her."

I felt her love for me so strongly; it was as if I could reach out and touch her. I gained a renewed confidence in my assigned mission, and my previous worries and disappointments faded away.

"You are now free to explore the Dome, but you are not ready to enter any of the panel doors. These will open when you touch the wall and will close when you touch the same spot. When you have satisfied your curiosity, you will receive your final instructions in preparation for your assignment."

I took my first step toward the wall of the Dome and was surprised by the effortlessness of my movement. I was almost gliding; I felt swift-footed and very light, as though gravity had very little effect on me. By now, having weighed all the odds, I had already made the decision to accept my foreordained assignment with full purpose of heart, but I was curious what would have happened if I hadn't chosen to accept the assignment, *Would they have relieved me of these responsibilities? How could I fit into society now, with my family scattered or dead after this long period of time?* My schoolmates and friends would be about sixty-three years old, and I still didn't look a day over twenty! I had most likely been given up for dead and was only a shadow of a memory in the minds of my family by now. *Would they even recognize me if they saw me? Would I recognize them?* In my mind, it wasn't a difficult decision. My choice was between becoming an outcast in society or faithfully fulfilling my destined duties.

"You have made the right choice," came the sudden remark from my guide. "All of the selected humans do ultimately accept their assignment and faithfully fulfill them to expectation. Each is given the title of Wackida, which means 'rescuer from evil.' With your acceptance, it's time to start the preparations for your sacred duties."

I felt a little apprehensive, wishing I had more time to explore the Dome.

"There will be enough time to learn of the Dome's secrets when you begin your assignment. As for now, you'll be taken to a special chamber to undergo conditioning in which you will receive and store a summary of events that have transpired from the time of the birth of your planet to the present day."

With this announcement, the Guardians dissolved out of view, leaving only one male Guardian, who appeared to be the leader. He led me toward one of the Dome walls and touched a panel door which then opened into a chamber stocked with strange machines. I glanced into a mirror that was positioned by the entrance and paused briefly to look at my reflection. For the first time since my transformation, I saw my face. I was clean-shaven and looked handsome with my thick hair and deep brown eyes. Truly, there was nothing visible to tell me apart from an ordinary person. I was happy with what I saw. He waited a moment for me to take in my transformation, and then beckoned me to lie down on what appeared to be a sofa, which he called the memory station. I was immediately sucked in and buried in the strange material until only my face was left free. I felt a powerful electrical current pass through my spine, through each vertebra, until it reached my brain. This was followed by a strange tingling sensation at the base of my neck. The vision of the life of our planet and its inhabitants started registering in my memory. It was so vivid in my mind's eye that I felt as if I were there watching the events unfold. The panorama was swift enough to educate me on Earth's entire history in the same time that an average person could read a history textbook.

I saw civilizations rise and fall. I saw periods of war, strife, and great destruction by the natural elements of water, tornadoes, earthquakes, and volcanic eruptions. But despite these calamities that rocked the planet, there were periods of peace and prosperity, with adventure, learning, and great discoveries. I saw my ancestral line of great men of valor and power. Some were adventurers, some discoverers, some diviners, and some researchers of the mysteries of life. The vision eventually brought me to our age, and I saw in greater detail my parents, their birth, and the lives they led during their youth: their marriage, the birth of my siblings and I, and all of the events thereafter until the present time.

I learned what had happened in my home after my disappearance. Henry, our butler, had contacted my father about my disappearance from home the very morning I left. My parents had returned the following day and had questioned Jennifer to see if I had told her anything. Jennifer had become anxious and despondent when I failed to return at the time I had promised. She was overcome and finally broke down and informed my parents of my secret resolve to investigate the hills and forest for a few days, despite her plea to convince me to change my mind.

My father begged a group of courageous men to find me and bring me back home. They started the search on the third day, the very day I fell through the concealed trap door into the Dome. For three days, they disregarded the stories and legends that had instilled fear in the hearts of the villagers. They ventured into the forest and hills to call out my name, turned over rocks and fallen trees, and waded through streams and caves to find me. They searched relentlessly until they finally discovered my camp. After a week of fruitless efforts and receding hopes, I was presumed dead, and the search was called off.

My father was given a dream in which a messenger informed him that all was well with me and that I had been called to a special duty. He told my poor mother about the dream and did all that he could to console her, but she would not be comforted. I watched as she cried for the remaining years of her life, until she died at the age of seventy-eight. She never recovered from the shock of my disappearance and the misery of my pronounced death. My father, on the other hand, was still alive at ninety-two years of age. My sister Janet, now sixty-five years old, had three children, two boys and a girl. Unfortunately, her marriage ended in divorce when her children were still young. Jason finished school a couple of years after I was presumed dead and moved to work abroad. He eventually married and had three girls. At the age of sixty-one, he was now preparing to voluntarily retire from civil service. My baby sister, Katelyn, graduated from college and went on to pursue a successful career in acting. Now she was fifty-nine and had two sons. I was glad to learn about what happened after my disappearance, but I grieved over my mother's broken heart. Oh, how I wished I could have shown her that I was alive and well before her passing, before she even shed one tear on my behalf! Even though it was my destiny to be in this place, I was still angry with myself for my inconsideration toward my loving mother, for my decision to run off into the forest all those years ago. I could only hope that she was now resting in the heavenly realm with an absolution of peace and happiness, knowing that I would one day be reunited with her. Jennifer, my faithful childhood sweetheart, had wept and waited sadly for two years in the hope a miracle would bring me back, since my body was never recovered. After two years, though, she gave up hope and moved on with her life. As suddenly as the current flowing through my spine and brain had started, it stopped. I was released from the folds of the protoplasmic sofa with a rich memory of events that had transpired over generations of our planet's existence.

I sat on a chair close to the memory machine, musing over my experience. The memory of my birth and upbringing clung tenaciously to my mind. I had taken it for granted and had never known until now how deeply my mother loved me. The trauma she endured during my birth and her sacrifice to nurture me as a physically handicapped baby harassed my memory. She tended to me with loving care, regularly taking me to the hospital for treatment because of my infirmities. Those tender moments she shared with me as a young child and throughout adolescence, and the faith and positive thoughts she implanted in my mind to boost my self-esteem, built my confidence and brightened my perspective so that I could triumph over my challenges.

All of this came to me as I sat pensively by the memory machine. I felt the pain and disappointment of failing her, of not giving her the joy of knowing her efforts had not been in vain. But I was too late. I now understood the news of my death was such an emotional blow to her that she could not come to terms with the loss for the remainder of her life. I missed her so much and hoped that someday I would be given the opportunity to be reunited with her and to enfold her in my arms, apologize for the pain I had caused her, and express my great love for her.

My guide, tracing my thoughts and emotions, waited patiently for me to regain my composure before he spoke. He then gave me my final instructions: "You are now ready to embark on your educational voyages. You have been given the ability to memorize languages quickly. It is important for you to understand that on your journey, you cannot carry any weapons—none other than the powers of your mind and body, that is. With those powers, you can overcome any challenge you meet. Your focus on a specific challenge will activate the powers within you to counter any threat. However, do not be deceived by all that you see. Your emotions will be tested to their fullest extent. We cannot interfere, but we will mentally connect with you and instruct you when you need it most and you diligently seek for our help."

He pointed to a panel on one of the walls and instructed me to go over and touch it when I was ready to start the first voyage. He then dissolved from my view. I cautiously moved to the panel and hesitated briefly before gingerly lifting my hand to touch it. Again, doubt began to flood my mind as I wondered about my ability to succeed. Though my mind was ready, I still lacked the confidence to plunge headlong into the unknown. After a few seconds, I mustered up enough courage, sucked in a deep breath, and placed my hand on the panel.

CHAPTER 3

The Pits of the Damned

I n one swift motion, the panel opened before me, and I gazed into a long, misty corridor. As I stepped inside, the panel quickly slid into place and snapped shut behind me. This was my first test, my first mission. I was at the end of my reason and instruction. I concluded, instinctively, that, moving forward with faith was my best option. I began moving quietly toward a faintly lit corridor. I had hoped that my memory bank and power to discern would clue me in on what to expect, but it did not happen as I thought it would. I realized that my new environment, this unfamiliar place, was not a functional part of the physical realm of our planet. I had only been educated on one of the realms of the history of my own earth—there was another real and powerful invisible realm pertaining to Xoedikus and his followers. As I steeled myself for possible entry, I reminded myself of the cause and commission.

My duty was to protect the cause of the physical world and the spiritual forces acting for the benefit and progress of its inhabitants. I was to protect my fellow humans from the evil plans of Xoedekus, the rebel child of the ageless rulers of the universe. He was out to destroy my brothers and sisters, and I had to negate his plans. It dawned on me that what I was about to experience was not only to test me and teach me to use my new abilities, but to expose me to the unseen worlds within my planet—and therefore learn about them.

I had been walking warily along this eerie cobblestone corridor, fully alert and ready to react to any threat of danger, when I felt the floor beneath me shift and heave a little. A piece of the rocky floor ahead of me suddenly swung downward as though it were on a hinge, exposing a long flight of stairs leading into a dark subterranean cavity. I knew that I was going to have to go down that stairway whether I liked it or not, so I jumped down onto the first stair. I was getting used to panels snapping shut behind me, so I wasn't surprised when the hanging sheet of stone sealed off my point of entry with an echoing thud.

The darkness was so thick that I was forced to stand still and wait. Terrifying thoughts of slipping and falling through endless pits of darkness flashed through my mind. I realized that this was similar to the way I had felt when I fell in the forest forty-five years before. However, I was sure that this time, any falling into pits would not have such pleasant outcomes. The darkness was getting to me, and I needed to focus. As I strained to see the flight of stairs, I felt my eyes suddenly adjust their focus to what seemed to be something akin to night vision. I could see the narrow stairway before me had high, rough walls on either side. Relieved by this adaptive response, I continued on down the long stairway much less apprehensive, and finally, after descending for what seemed like miles, I stepped off of the last stair onto the floor of an oval chamber.

Ahead of me loomed a large gate cut out of stone, supported by an endless number of pivotal hinges. The gate seemed to be the only outlet from the oval chamber, so I moved toward it. As I reached out to touch it, it opened slowly on its creaky hinges, and I stepped inside. Not surprisingly, it shut behind me. Ahead were a series of similar but smaller gates. Each one shut behind me as I passed through. As I ventured further into the depths of this dark place, I heard fearful, soul-wracking sounds, similar to the wailing of wounded animals, except these sounds were human. The intensity of the wailing increased with each gate, it was nearly deafening.

After passing through the seventh gate, I arrived at what looked like a long, unending chamber. It resembled a prison that stretched far into the distance and which, at first glance, seemed unoccupied. I was prompted to look down and fought a sense of repulsion and incredulity I'd never known. Thousands and thousands of humans looked up at me from deep within the vast pit in which they were imprisoned. They were tightly cramped together underneath sealed stone gratings. They were the source of the howling, moaning, and swearing that I endured through my walk to this awful place. Theirs were the agonizing lamentations of the mentally morbid and the hopelessly dejected. Their faces were sad and drawn in grimaces of absolute pain and suffering. Their red, tearless, pleading eyes begged for mercy. They yearned to be rescued from this torment. I was overwhelmed with pity and sadness for these people from my Earth, my brothers and sisters. I couldn't imagine anyone deserving such a horrid fate!

Then, a quiet voice in my mind said, "Look more closely at them." As I looked closer, I began to see who they really were. "These," the voice continued, "were those who willingly accepted the evil one and became his representatives in the flesh. They were the wicked ones who destroyed all things, who committed acts of unspeakable evil. They became hardened and merciless through obedience to the commands of the evil one. They fought the preceding Wackida and killed the Agents of their age. These were the people who were tutored in wickedness and empowered through their master to deceive and mislead others off the true path of happiness, with the intent of damning their souls to an everlasting doom. They spent their probationary period on Earth willfully violating all the good laws taught to them, continually seeking false rewards. Even in death, though they plead for deliverance, their natures remain unchanged. Given the chance, they would continue their previous endeavors. So now they must reap the just reward of their labors."

"Their great misery is the knowledge that they have come short of the glory that others enjoy. A vivid memory of what they could have become if they had lived by the universal law of life, which they chose to reject, is the source of their misery and torment. The torment of disappointment in the mind of man is as detailed and exquisite as burning in an eternal lake of fire and brimstone. Their anguish is therefore an agony, and regret for their choices produced their present state of everlasting suffering." This mental torture in the spirit was far worse than physical suffering in a lake of fire and brimstone. This I knew just by looking into the eyes of the wicked that writhed beneath the grates.

"Now," the voice prompted me, "focus on a face in the dungeon." I singled in on the face of one man. I could recollect the face from the history of mankind I'd accumulated in the memory machine. I knew who this man was. Then, suddenly, my mind was sent to the time he lived on Earth. I saw him being born to loving parents who were in the logging industry. He was their only child, and his parents adored him very much. They gave him the best education that could be had in that part of their world. I saw how he was nurtured with affection, and taught the laws of morality. He was christened Godwin, trained to be a gentleman, and taught how to live a good and honest life. He took over his aging parents' business and was doing very well. He lacked nothing in his day, yet as a young man, his yearning for more wealth morphed into greed for more money, power, and fame. This goaded him to embrace evil to reach his goals. He formed a gang of thieves and murderers, and with them he raided, stole, murdered, and maimed thousands of people.

He became a renowned drug dealer, and his organization sold drugs to young, innocent children, turning them into addicts and taking away their livelihoods. He personally executed anyone who tried to stop him or any rivals who intruded on his business endeavors. He bribed government officials and law officers to turn a blind eye. He could not be touched by the law. His parents eventually died from disappointment, grief, and shame. He didn't even bother to attend their funerals. For years, he ruled the underbelly of his city with an iron hand and instilled fear in the countrymen who lived around him. He became the evil king of everything around him and gave an appreciable measure of triumph to the evil forces. But his reign of terror couldn't last forever. He was stricken with a debilitating disease, which contributed to his decline. He was abandoned by his fair-weather colleagues, who pretended to admire him but hailed his exploits for their own gain. His master, the evil Xoedikus, also abandoned him to deteriorate in health and suffer until his death. Now he was here, his evil-tainted spirit essence captured by the master he served so well, to earn his eternal reward.

I shifted my focus onto another man who was in this hell. I saw the life he led as the captain of a slave ship centuries ago. I saw how he captured humans from the coasts of Africa and sold them into slavery in the Americas. Executioner, as he was called, was ruthless and wicked, having no respect for human life. He chained the people he captured in the cargo hold of his rat-infested ship for days on end without enough food or water. He whipped and flayed open the naked backs of any captive who groaned out of hunger or misery. Any man, woman, or child who seemed very sick or weak was thrown overboard. Most of them drowned, but some managed to keep their heads above water until they were devoured by sharks.

I saw him as he amused his shipmates by chaining up weaker slaves by their feet on the deck of the ship. He threw buckets of water on their bare, brutalized bodies and left them exposed to the freezing weather while his crew watched them shiver uncontrollably until their death. He took pride in his name and his business. I saw how he greedily relished his ill-gotten blood money from the capture, torture, and sale of innocent people. He was arrogant, completely oblivious to all who saw him for the monster that he was. At the age of forty-six, as his ship was on its way back to Africa to enslave more people, a terrible storm hit the high seas. He lost his life, as did all his wicked crew members.

A prisoner with very long hair was next to catch my eye. She may have been pretty during her Earth life, but evil is eventually revealed in our countenance and demeanor, once it forms our character. I wondered what had earned her this hellish ordeal and focused on her past life in mortality. I was shocked to see her begin life as a poor, abandoned young woman. Her parents had died of a plague when she was thirteen, and her relatives had abandoned her because of her stigma as potential carrier. She lived in the ruins of a dilapidated house and begged on the corner of the street near the home of a very old gentleman, a widower, for her survival. Her condition touched the heart of this kind, childless gentleman who lived alone in the community. Out of pity, he took her under his roof, adopted her as his daughter, and provided her with the necessities of life.

Her name was Ingritude, and she blossomed into a beautiful woman who caught the eye of every eligible bachelor in the community. This rich gentleman counseled her to be careful of a particular suspicious, sweet-tongued young man she was intimately associated with. He knew the young man had previously had some skirmishes with the law and was very rude to his aged parents. She was not very happy with her benefactor's advice. She sulked, until one night she succumbed to pressure from her male friend to get rid of the "nosy old man." Ingritude and her boyfriend suffocated the old gentleman in his sleep, then searched the house and stole a substantial amount of his jewelry, expensive paintings, and money. She went into hiding with her lover that very night. After some time, the hunt for her subsided, and they secretly fled the country to escape the reaches of the law. Ingritude never felt remorse for taking the life of the old gentleman who had been kind to her in her time of great need.

With her charm and the wealth acquired from the sale of the jewelry and the paintings, she established a brothel where many young women were enticed into prostitution. Her whorehouse was well patronized, and the lives of the young women were ruined. Some years later, her accomplice in the crime got his hands on a substantial part of her wealth and deserted her. He went to a distant city and married another woman. Ingritude sought information until she was able to learn his address. She hired assassins to trace and kill him and his new wife for betraying her. The job was carried out, and while she was on her way to a secret rendezvous to pay off the assassins, she had a fatal accident, losing her life at the age of forty.

It became evident that the prisoners confined in these hellish dungeons lived like beasts during their probation on Earth. My pity for these people was quickly replaced with revulsion and disgust. These weren't even people to me anymore. They were subhuman beasts who had earned their punishment.

I looked past the swarms of faces, and I noticed sentries holding tridents, clad in black. They had seen me and were keeping their distance. Occasionally, a sentry would stab the hands of prisoners who managed to climb up and reach through the stone gratings over their heads. These sentries were members of the group who chose to serve the evil one and rebelled against the Supremos in the beginning. I could discern that, after ruling this planet for centuries, they knew they were approaching the close of their evil reign. They knew from past experience to leave a Wackida alone.

As I walked from dungeon to dungeon, I came to appreciate the wisdom and justice of the law-givers. These prisoners were truly lost souls who had once tasted the goodness of the law given, but had blatantly turned against it. These humans had indeed been the devil's advocates and deserved the reward they'd so diligently worked for. Captive spirits of the dead were being led in chains by evil sentries who were assigned to work within society on earth. These sentries were those who enticed and tempted humans to condemn and violate the true law and to become their captives upon departing the physical realm. After seeing the wretched fate of those who had succumbed, I was now more determined than ever to battle them to the fullest. I vowed to fight, to vanquish them, and to rescue as many souls as I could from their wiles and feigned promises during my millennium of service.

This series of dungeons stretched for miles, and each was full of humans who were wailing and ranting and gnashing their teeth. The noise was unbearable. Thankfully, I was instructed to climb up another stairway before reaching the end of the prisons. I had seen enough of the fate of those who were condemned to the Pits of the Damned.

I hurried up the flight of stairs for a distance of about a half mile, arriving at another wide expanse that stretched for miles. This area, unlike the pitch-black pits, was very dimly lit. As I gazed around, taking in my surroundings, my eyes rested on more people milling about. Those on this level, however, were not confined in dungeons but were permitted to move around. They moved in a steady pace, as if in a trance. Their faces were withdrawn, and their heads were bent down as if they were searching for something. Their countenances reflected disappointment, loss, and confusion. Their attire identified the periods in which they lived. Occasionally, they mumbled some words and a whimpering cry escaped their lips. None ever sat down to rest or made an effort to find the way out. They behaved more like sleepwalkers. These were not as forlorn as those in the Pits of the Damned. I stood searching my mind for a possible explanation to their state. *What did they do to deserve a life in this gloomy place where none rest or converse, but where each is busy doing nothing but pitifully pacing up and down, mumbling and crying out?*

Once again, the voice in my mind offered an explanation.

"You are in the realm of the proud, the greedy, the selfish, the drunkards, and the drug addicts who would not listen to the soft voice of their conscience and would not repent and change their ways, even after the message of the universal law of perfection had been taught to them. These were the arrogant, the self-centered, the adulterers, the liars, the thieves, the cheats, and the swindlers in their day. They were taught the law but rejected it and disregarded the warning of the Agents, whom they often persecuted and looked down upon with disdain.

"They chose to follow false priests and to live the carnal laws, but neither had they committed any act of murder, profaned the truth, or blasphemed the sacred name of the Supremos. Life seemed fulfilling to them as they amassed wealth by exploiting others. They showed no sympathy to anyone and never paid attention to the needy, the widows, and the fatherless who continually cried to them for help. Their offenses ranged from indifference to human suffering to selfishness, gluttony, debauchery, and adultery. They are now in the Realm of Failure."

Their countenances varied according to the gravity of their offenses. They were as numerous as the sands upon the seashore and were blind to anything beyond the realm in which they were confined. Some appeared to be unsure about their changed condition and environment. For whatever reason, there was no need for sentries to guard them on this level. I cast my eyes around to see if any of those close to me were aware of my presence, but they seemed oblivious. They were mostly preoccupied with sadness and anger; they paced back and forth, lamenting and protesting their earned confinement. Here, they yearned for but were deprived of things they had enjoyed in their former lives on the planet.

"They also have a torturing memory of what they could have become had they chosen to live the perfect law that was offered them," the voice continued. "Even laden with regret, they were still as stubborn and unrepentant as they had been in the flesh."

I lingered a little longer. What else could I learn? I cast back my memory to access their days on the planet and the sort of life they had led in their probationary period there. What I saw was not at all pleasant. They were indeed a recalcitrant lot—strong-headed and unrepentant in both character and conduct. During this revelatory moment, I received instructions to move away from them to a spot about two miles from the staircase that reached up from the Pits of the Damned to this level. I arrived there, and, to my surprise, saw a spiral metal staircase descending to my location. I moved toward it. As soon as I stepped onto the first stair, it moved up in a carousel, lifting me over half a mile to another level. As soon as I stepped off the topmost stair, the area beneath me sealed off. I then understood why the occupants of the level I had just left appeared to be making no effort to find a way out of their abode: there was no outlet for the guilty and the deliberate violator or rejecter of the saving laws taught them by the Agents.

The light at this level was brighter, not quite as dark as it was on the level I just left. Some of the occupants of this level were very well organized, and their existence appeared to be relatively more tolerable, though their demeanor still portrayed sadness. I noticed straightaway that these were men and women of nobility and fame who had lived in various centuries. They were properly outfitted in clean, decent clothes, their fashionable attire depicting the periods in which they had lived. Their mannerisms also reflected their good upbringing and good education. Among them, I recognized popular religious leaders of the recent past as well as centuries long ago. Their robes of office revealed the era in which they lived. Also in the throng were kings, queens, lords, princes, and princesses, in addition to those who had been acclaimed as great inventors and warlords, there were many who had exhibited great courage as they ventured into uncharted waters or unexplored territories, discovering lands, artifacts, and laws of nature—things that have been of great benefit to humankind. All could be identified by the crowns on their heads or by medals pinned to their robes or other insignias of honor conferred in life, which they still wore with pride. Among them were some of the humans I had admired so much in my youth, some of whom were my ancestors. Learned men in both the arts and the sciences were here, as well as some of the great musicians and other artists who had graced the planet and been immortalized in our history books. *Why were they here?* They had used their talents well, I thought.

I also noticed with surprise that those who had married were separated from their spouses, who occupied the same spiritual realm. My stored memory of the events of the ages in which they lived clearly indicated that most of them were happily married in their lifetime and had been faithful to one another. What I was seeing was totally at variance with what the female member of the Guardians had told me about married couples. *What about the love and happiness they had shared together? Did it end with their death? What about the challenges shared in bringing up their children with love and discipline, their moments of intimacy and appreciation of each other? Were all these done in vain?* I was fed immediately a sad but logical explanation.

"These are men and women of nobility and great acclaim, who did wonderful service to their countries and the planet at large, as you have observed. But they did not live fully by the universal laws of perfection. They considered some aspects of the law restrictive to their freedom and did not abide by them. They gloried in their achievements and success and loved to be praised and worshipped. Their superficial acts of kindness were performed for all to see so that they could bask in the respect and praises of humans. They showered love and extreme care on their own children, but selfishly did not care for the welfare of others. They performed acts of kindness occasionally and openly, but without true love as the motive. Their hearts were empty of concern for the welfare of the needy and the underprivileged. They loved to be given the high seat at gatherings and to be the toast at important functions—the center of attention in public places. This pride blinded them to the true purpose of life, which is love unfeigned and unconditional service to all beings, and with all glory being given to the creators of all things."

Among the people on this plane were also those who were so preoccupied with research and so engrossed in their work that they were oblivious to the needs and events around them. They had neither time nor desire to pay any attention to anything going on around them during their mortality. All these had been taught the law but did not have time to listen well, let alone accept it, appreciate its tenets, and live it fully. And there were still others here who had been taught the true laws in their purity but had yielded to the craftiness of men and rejected the truth. They accepted, instead, the counterfeit laws taught by the detractors of truth, because these counterfeit laws suited their lifestyle and satisfied their egos. Also here were those who were of the noble class that had fanatically held on to the laws as interpreted and imposed by uninspired humans in religious leadership positions. They would not even listen to, let alone accept, the true version of the law, but claimed for themselves, because of their social status, the right to persecute and ostracize the Agents, as well as any who defected after receiving a testimony of the true laws.

On this same level, but isolated from these nobles who had lived on the planet, was another group, classified as the heathens and the uncultured. I was surprised and wondered why and how these heathens, some of whom had been regarded as savages, had qualified to inherit this part of the habitation after they departed from life. I was confused, and though I had understood well all that had been taught me by the Guardians, I could find no reason to justify their presence here, even after reviewing the life they had led through my spiritual memory bank.

"These heathens did not have the law taught to them during their probationary period on the planet," I was assured by the voice in my mind, "but they were true to the dictates of their conscience. They were born into the traditions and customs of their forebears, and faithfully held on to these practices throughout their lives. If they violated any of the universal laws of perfection, it was done out of ignorance and through their belief in the traditions they had inherited. Unlike them, their noble counterparts had lived in civilized, enlightened eras and had the privilege of the influence of the Agents and the Wackida but had not fully embraced the warning."

I saw the wisdom of the Supremos in assigning these humans who were ignorant of the law to this level of existence after their probation on the planet. Of the three levels that I had been privileged to visit, this level, the Community of the Noble and the Ignorant, was far more tolerable than the two I had visited previously. The heathens on this level were numerous and kept away from the abode of the nobles and the enlightened, though there was no physical barrier or restriction separating them. I came to comprehend that spirits are drawn to and attract those of the same levels of light or darkness, and that everyone remains in the level in which they, by prior choices, have become used to. In terms of my question about the singleness of married couples in this realm, the Guardian explained that this was so because the couples consummated a contract of marriage based on the period of their mortal lives only. A higher law and marriage was required to allow their love and relationship to continue in eternity.

Those who appealed only to the civil law by choice and not out of ignorance, would continue to live as individuals afterward. Those who appealed to the civil law in ignorance, could be taught differently and be united in the heavenlies. "The true universal laws of perfection taught the approved procedures that would enable a couple's union to last forever, because progression after life could be achieved and fulfilled only through a lasting, loving matrimonial relationship," the voice explained. "The religious leaders in past centuries who were not inspired or authorized by the Supremos relied on their human intelligence and judgment to formulate ceremonial procedures and, thereby, corrupted the perfect procedures in the laws that were taught by the true Agents and the Wackida. They instituted a man-made system that had not the power to bind the couple for time and eternity. This corrupt law has eroded the understanding and euphoria of true marriage and its eternal purposes. Its adoption by the ignorant generations after them has resulted in unprecedented selfishness, impatience, and intolerance in a relationship that was designed to be eternally sweet and fulfilling.

"Selfishness, often developing into greed, anger, and hatred, has given birth to evil conducts that have led to a high rate of spousal abuse, divorce, or even murder in ages past as well as in current times," the voice continued. "Some females, out of greed, marry without love. They seek out wealthy partners and find flimsy excuses to divorce. They trump up false charges and manipulate laws to lay claim to undeserved wealth and property. Some males equally pretend and marry without love just to gain access to their spouses' wealth. Others betray each other. The worst effects and results of the inconsiderate nature of humans and the destruction of the sacred institution of marriage are felt by the young children in these broken homes. These innocent offspring are exposed at a young age to very harsh living conditions and, often, the need to struggle for survival. They are denied parental love and the caring example of parents that is so critical and crucial for molding them. Most often, the conditions after the divorce impose upon them hardship that denies them decent lives and the ability to cope with their situation in a decent and positive manner. Because the lives of their parents affect them psychologically, they are regularly influenced by their peers to submit to antisocial activities, which gradually mold them to become truants or rebels, envious of all who are doing well. Many—save those whose remaining parent is faithful to the law and Supremos— grow up filled with hatred because of their misfortune and become wicked, merciless criminals in the societies in which they live." "In order to survive," the voice added, "these latchkey children often embrace crime. Criminality becomes a means of obtaining unearned wealth or a way of unleashing their caged anger on society, or an attempt to receive recompense for the failures of their selfish and irresponsible parent(s). The acts of such divorced couples, those motivated by greed, often resulted in the destruction of their children's lives. Such parents will earn their just rewards according to the irrevocable laws of the universe. Others who divorced by necessity—those who were victims of betrayal or abuse by their spouse'—are released from their circumstances and promised a new and everlasting opportunity for eternal marriage. They are given power and grace to raise their children according to the laws of the universe."

I had received education on the purpose and the requirements of true love and marriage, and I had seen the practical results in the success of the five couples from another planetary body who had been appointed as Guardians for our planet. I remembered what they told me when I first saw the females among them. It was all so logical to me now, so true. I was deeply engrossed in these reflections when I noticed faint spots of light approaching from the distance. As they reached my range of vision, I recognized them to be men and women attired in clothing similar to those of the Guardians. For some reason, though, they were not nearly as bright as the Guardians.

They came in pairs of the same gender and were very numerous. When they finally reached me, they introduced themselves as the Tutors. My quizzical nature was soon satisfied. I learned that some humans with good hearts who resided in this abode of the Noble and the Ignorant had been inadvertently deceived and confused about the true nature of things on earth and the real plan of happiness. The craftiness of their fellow beings denied them the opportunity to learn about the saving laws. Others, such as those regarded earlier, the heathens, never had the opportunity to be taught the universal law. According to the mercies extended by the Supremos, an opportunity was extended to them to be taught in their present sphere, and to either accept or reject the perfect law of marriage and other related laws. A few in the Realm of Failure who were not taught the law and did not live by the dictates of their conscience as well were also being taught. Those found repentant and worthy would be given the opportunity to prepare to leave for a higher and more pleasant arena for further growth. This would happen when other requisite conditions for their progress were met.

I inquired about their level of success, and they replied that most of the nobles and the learned were unresponsive to their teaching, but they occasionally encountered a few who humbled themselves and embraced the message with full purpose of heart. Over two millennia ago, when the program was initially instituted by the Supremos, only a few of the residents in the community of the Noble and the Ignorant and the Realm of Failure had advanced. They had been more successful with the heathens who had accepted the new message readily and wholeheartedly in their post-mortal spirit state. These heathens from all races expressed deep regret and remorse for their earthly ignorant conduct. Most of them had manifest genuine love for their spouses and children, and for all other humans, as expected by the Supremos, during their tenure on earth.

The Tutors informed me that I had learned all I needed to learn here and directed me to go in the direction from which they had come to continue my education. I was about to leave when I saw a familiar figure approaching. It was my mother! I desired so much to hug her and explain what had happened to me and apologize to her for the pain I had caused her, but I was restrained by two of the male Tutors. She appeared not to be perturbed or surprised at seeing me here. She smiled and waved at me as if she knew the truth about my disappearance. She was led by two smiling female Tutors to continue the lessons on the laws. My mom was receiving the lessons! It was gratifying to know, and I had hopes that my ancestors were also receiving the lessons in their realms.

I reluctantly moved in the direction the Tutors had shown me, emotionally subdued by this encounter. As I paced along, I reflected on the experience I'd encountered in the Community of the Noble and the Ignorant. Here I had learned more fully of the love, mercy, and justice of the Supremos. Every human was precious to them, and they provided opportunities for each human to be taught the saving laws, either in their period of probation on the planet or after the demise of those who did not hear the truth during their lifetime. This arrangement compensated for any deficiencies in the laws of the countries or the communities in which each human was born and brought up—creating an equality of opportunity for all humans to hear and accept or reject the universal law of perfection. This included, in particular, those who were born and raised in countries where the teachings of the universal law of perfection were strictly forbidden or banned by national laws in their lifetime.

As I moved further away from the Community of the Noble and the Ignorant, I encountered terrain that was rugged and strewn with pitfalls. There were areas that emitted a substance like thick smoke. It was black and blinding. In my frustration to find a path through these pitfalls, I decided to go back to the abode I'd left a moment ago. I saw the blinding smoke thicken ahead of me. The fear of falling into a pit almost paralyzed me. At that moment, the voice in my mind intervened and seemed to dislodge my fear, while gently reprimanding me for my mistrust of the Tutors who had shown me the way. I was instructed to focus on my mission, train my emotions to resist fear and other such distracting feelings, while cultivating courage. I was directed to focus with faith on my objective, and I was promised that all would be well.

My focus and attitude changed, and my eyes were opened to see a lighted pathway. I walked along this pathway until I arrived at the edge of a deep chasm. It seemed bottomless, and it was so wide I could not see the other side of it. How to cross the chasm was a mystery to me, as it stretched as far as I could see on either side of my path as well. It appeared to be unending. However, I remembered the voice's admonition to resist doubt and to focus positively. After all, the Tutors had come from this section of the abode, so there surely had to be a way across the chasm and on to the beyond.

My focus on a solution to cross was instantly rewarded; I noticed a long rope bridge about ten yards from where I stood. I quickly walked to it and stepped on it. I walked very light-footed but steadily on the swinging rope bridge to the other end. It was a long crossing. The moment I stepped off the bridge onto the other side of the chasm, the area before me burst into a marvelously lighted terrain of exquisite beauty. Ahead of me lay a bright, beautiful city of great splendor. I turned to look back only to find, to my surprise, that the chasm and the rope bridge were nowhere in sight. *Why had I not seen the terrain and the city from the other side or during my crossing? How is it that I can now not see the chasm or the rope bridge over which I just crossed to this side?* I raked my mind for an explanation and received an answer almost immediately.

"The glorious city before you is called the City of Light. It is hidden from the view of all who dwell on the darkened side of the chasm until they are permitted to cross over. This occurs only when they accept in their hearts the perfect law of the universe taught them by the Tutors, and once they have been judged and justified by the Supremos. The terrain of pitfalls, the thick blinding smoke, and the wide chasm prevent the unrepentant from attempting to cross over, while the rope bridge becomes visible only to those who are approved and authorized to cross safely. Even then, the city is revealed only after successfully crossing the rope bridge and stepping on the grounds beyond the chasm. You, as the Wackida being prepared for this century, have been permitted to see the bridge and cross over so that you can learn of the worlds, realms, and habitations within your planet and gain testimony of the truthfulness of all things to motivate you in the assignment ahead. The Tutors, as you have seen, were authorized to cross over from here to the other side to fulfill their important duties. There is constant renewal, as you have seen, for the faithful and the honest after death, because all are engaged in the glorious work of the Supremos until Earth fills the full measure of its creation."

I moved on. Now, I was to learn about events in the City of Light.

As I cast my eyes around, I saw rows upon rows of healthy, beautiful, sweet-scented flowers of intensely different colors and species planted all around me and stretching all the way to the shining city. I noticed, to my surprise, that some of the flowering plants naturally bore flowers of different colors on the same branch. Between the rows of flowers were pathways laid with white stones that looked like polished granite. They were arranged to form beautiful mosaic designs and shone in the light, creating a radiant landscape. As I approached, the intensity of the light increased. A great iridescent wall stretched across my path to encompass the city, yet I could not see through it. I could, however, see the tops of high buildings above the wall. I arrived at a gate of transcendent beauty. It opened the moment I stopped in front of it and closed without a sound behind me.

CHAPTER 4

The City of Light

In the broad expanse before me lay the most beautiful city I had ever seen or could have dreamed of. I could see columns upon columns of white buildings interlinked by wide streets paved with a substance that looked like bronze. The buildings were tall, and each had a number of floors, but there appeared to be neither windows nor doors for entry. The roofs were made of the same iridescent material as the outside walls and were in a shape similar to the Sacred Dome. In front of each column of buildings were a variety of decorative trees that I'd never seen before on our planet. The trees were healthy, firm, and symmetrical, indicative of a perfect and grand Designer.

I was fascinated by the perfection and beauty of these trees. They each appeared to have a full complement of leaves, and the smoothest, most unsullied trunk and branches. Their growth was perfect, requiring no pruning, unlike the shade trees at the mansion back home. I did not, however, see any fruit-bearing trees in the city. I also noticed there were no shadows cast by either the buildings or the trees, suggesting that the source of the light was not a sun, which rises and falls. My mind went back to the Tutors I'd seen at the third level of outer darkness. I knew they were sent to that gloomy lair from this beautiful city. Yet, here, I expected to see some worthy inhabitants on the streets. The city appeared to be rather empty.

How can this be? I thought. *How can I gain the knowledge I was sent here to acquire with no one available to lead me?* Gratefully, the answer came as a firm and clear voice in my mind.

"You will now be educated to understand this world and how it has been designed to operate. All humans, as you may have already observed, after shedding their physical frames in death, are brought as spiritual selves to this or one of the other levels of existence in the world of spirits, according to their deeds and their obedience to the universal law. These spirits are admitted to this world as adults, even if they were a child or a youth at the time of their departure from the physical realm. This is because each human grew to adulthood as a spirit and was educated to acquire a high level of knowledge before birth onto their planet.

"You have learned about the first of the major divisions in the spiritual world that reigns invisible around your planet, and its three levels of light or glory, intelligence, or truth.

"Did you take note of the fact that the amount of darkness in each of those levels did not vary, and that you did not see any vegetation in that section of this world? The vegetation you encounter in this terrain is designed to decorate and beautify and, therefore, exists only on this side of the chasm that has perpetual light. It is an expression of what is to come when the spiritual and the physical worlds of your planet unite forever in glory. When it becomes exalted, darkness shall be removed into its place forever. White light dispels darkness, and for that reason, the Tutors can go and teach the heathens only with their light deliberately shielded to make the intensity very low and bearable. The inhabitants can tolerate only the amount of light which they themselves possess. They then, once taught, may grow in that light if they choose. In the evil of evil sphere, darkness perpetually reigns, just as light perpetually reigns in this ultimate city known as the City of Light, the Abode of the Faithful.

"I see that you are curious as to why you have not seen any fruit trees or crops in this realm. A spirit dwelling here does not need food but is constantly sustained on universal energy. You will not, therefore, find water or food in any part of this world that you have been permitted to visit. Note also that there is no air or temperature or humidity effect. Everything, including the plants on this side of this world, is sustained by the universal energy, which is the same energy that provides sensory experience of any kind. The natural senses of sight, hearing, touch, and smell are active and enhanced in this realm by virtue of the universal energy."

The instruction felt so natural, and my spirit, so at home here. "You have been taught enough for the moment. It is time to explore," the voice instructed.

I moved toward the first row of buildings and realized that I was almost floating, and again it felt as if gravity didn't exist here. I stepped out onto the bronze street. New questions arose: *What types of vehicles were used here for transportation if there was no air, water, or even gravity?* After all, the construction of paved streets seemed to be an indication of the use of some kind of vehicular transport, though I had seen the Tutors float close to the ground in the same way I'd seen the Guardians do in the forest.

Instead of a brief explanation, the voice taught me about centuries' worth of technological advancements.

"The inhabitants of these realms do not need the metal and plastic contraptions known as cars, ships, airplanes, and so forth. The creation of these items was inspired by the Supremos to teach humans on the planet to utilize the materials available to create things that were useful to them. Vehicles were thus created on the planet as a means of conveying human physical bodies or heavy goods quickly from one area over some distance to the other.

"It started with the use of animals for transport, then the creation of the wheel, then the coach pulled by horses, followed by the engine powered by oil derivatives or steam. The creation of the engine, electricity, and other mechanical innovations led to the creation of other complex, sophisticated means of transportation, such as the airplane, the train, the ship, the submarine, spacecraft, hovercraft, and others.

"This technological revolution also inspired the discovery of various waves through which radio, television pictures, and other communication messages are transmitted. Waves have been in existence since the creation of the planet but were reserved for human discovery, as inspired by the Supremos, to be used to further the progress and enlightenment of man, to the glory of the Supremos. "Humans are given the glory for the advancement in technology. However, there exist more advanced galactic photonic tactile waves that carry great, inexhaustible energy. They will be revealed at the appropriate time in the history of the human family to solve all energy problems. The sun's unlimited energy will be harnessed with specially designed tracking satellites and conveyed *via* the galactic photonic tactile waves to Earth, to be picked up by every mechanical device that is equipped with a special kind of photonic cell receiver anywhere and at any time on the planet. This will occur in the concluding chapters of the planet's lifetime.

"The unity of the developed nations to pull resources together to design, build, and share this unlimited energy with poorer nations should be anticipated; if performed, it will open the doors for the realization of our potential to be one another's keeper—to share our talents and gifts of creativity for the benefit of the whole of the human race.

"The earlier successes in creation from existing materials will inspire humans to acquire the skill to tap their inherent gifts to create more complex things from existing materials during these concluding decades of the planet's physical life, in emulation of the creative abilities of their eternal parents. The occupants of the City of Light may travel to any place, at any pace or rate they desire, by light through mental focus, but only within the realms permitted. This is the mode of travel for beings of light, whether as spirits or resurrected beings. A resurrected being is one who has passed through mortality into the realm of spirits, and who regains their body in perfected form."

The voice proceeded to teach me things relating to the energy of inanimate objects, plants, and animals and how they fit into the eternal scheme of things. Animals that have been loved and well cared-for and have responded positively to the love of whom they served shall be with their masters to dwell happily together forever. Animals also have spirit essences and are sent to serve their earthly probation and to faithfully fulfill their destined duties on planets through birth.

"Animals also have a selection of universal laws which govern their existence and are influenced by conditions created for them. Those of higher species have their language. They can, learn, having a measure of spiritual intelligence, and are imbued with sensory attributes enabling them to respond favorably to the feelings and righteous desires of their masters. Those of lower species tend to fulfill their purposes as they serve in the food chain, which is essential to growth and progress of life.

"Plants also have spirit essences and are on your planet to fulfill their destiny. Their purpose includes providing food and raw materials for medicine, promoting health and shelter, and acting as agents for the purification of the air. They are also providers of comfort, as they serve as shade trees and bear flowers to beautify. They were made to live in a partial symbiotic relationship with humans. All these were given for the benefit of humans.

"All living things that have been prepared and adapted by the all-knowing Supremos to live eternally with humans in their approved final states of existence, will abide here. Once all born and reared on this earth have passed the portals of mortality and reached their eternal abode, the earth itself will also undergo a marvelous transformation and rest from its labors. It will become a celestialized orb and achieve its own perfection." I saw in my mind's eye the role of all nature, including what we deemed inanimate, in the eternal scheme of things as perfectly planned by the Supremos. I came to further understand and respect nature, and to appreciate and look upon all that we have been given as a great blessing. Each gift was part of a carefully preconceived program that was essential to and supportive of our growth and development toward perfection. Humans have oftentimes referred to whatever existed around us simply as "natural," without realizing the spiritual creation and planning process that preceded what we see and avail ourselves of—the physical creation.

I thought of the general destruction of ecosystems worldwide. I thought of the unnecessary killing of animals for sport and trophies. I thought of industrial waste dumped into our bodies of water that polluted and killed the living things in our oceans, rivers, lagoons, and lakes. I thought of the indiscriminate cutting down of trees in our forests, especially on the banks of our water bodies, and the resultant drying out of rivers and lakes, and the gradual conversion of vast stretches of arable land to deserts. I thought of gaseous pollutants emitted and negligently discharged by industrial organizations, causing acid rain, destroying our planet's protective ozone layer, and bringing about global warming with its attendant adverse weather and environmental changes. I understood that with the manufacturing culture would come industrial waste, but wondered why we hadn't thought sufficiently ahead to make provisions to include the proper management of these deadly by-products and toxic waste. I saw then how inconsiderate and destructive humans had been in the management of the planet and life forms that the Supremos had lovingly given us. Selfishness and greed had twisted our thinking and clouded our reasoning, causing us to seek and grab all that we could without thinking of reserving some of these resources for future generations.

I had nearly reached the edge of the first row of buildings when a panel unexpectedly opened and revealed an entrance to the building. From the entrance, emerged two male personages who were dressed as Tutors but were of a far brighter countenance. They had been waiting to receive me. They beckoned me to follow them and led me into the building. The long hallway was divided by a transparent, soundproof pane that resembled glass. Numerous occupants were organized into two parallel streams of learners, separated into study cells by the same clear material.

On one side were the males, and on the other side were the females. Tutors of the same gender taught the groups of ten students in each cell. Interestingly, the students in the first few cells, though clothed in white, varied in the brightness of their countenances. They were all focused on their lessons and seemed to be totally oblivious to our presence. I turned to my guides for an explanation. They both smiled at me, and then one of them spoke.

"All the spirits who satisfied the law and qualified for exalted living are received into this side of the spirit world after they temporarily shed their physical frames and undergo a life review. Joining them are the departed who lived in the developed world and had good hearts but never had the privilege of being taught the universal laws of perfection in life. These are they who accepted the law here after passing through the portal of death. (As you see, we never really die. We just enter a new space in a new condition.) In addition to these, are the ones who were counted as heathens and were ignorant but willingly received the universal laws of perfection in this realm when Tutors were sent to help them. Here, they receive further instruction on the laws of truth, part of which they had lived on the planet as the universal laws of love or perfection by responding positively to the dictates of their conscience. They are taken through the laws that will enable them to live and perform the duties they qualify for the final perfected planet hereafter.

"As you might have noticed, the brightness of their countenances varies one from another according to the level of their knowledge and commitment to the laws during their probationary period on your planet. In the initial stages of their training, they are taken through the basic laws, and by the time they arrive at the respective level of spiritual tuition, their brightness increases correspondingly. It should be noted, however, that those who lived the law in life progress faster than those converted in this realm. In fact, the level of knowledge acquired in life determines the rate of progression in the next and one's final destination. Some won't go beyond this building, which has three more levels of study. The rest will go beyond, to other buildings you will soon learn of. A person's final level cannot be exceeded. They may minister to those below, but not rise above their assigned kingdom."

We walked the length of the long hallway along the side occupied by the males. It was a distance over ten miles, and each space was occupied by students viewing micro-projections of lessons they needed to learn. They needed also to listen attentively to their tutors. We climbed a short flight of stairs to the next floor to find an arrangement similar to the one we had just left, but this time the glow of the students was brighter and more uniform. The same pattern existed on the third and the fourth floors of this building, but at each level, the glow of the students increased in intensity.

My guides informed me that at the conclusion of the tutorials on the fourth and last floor, a set of deserving students would advance to another sector city where still higher laws of the universe were revealed.

"Those who are judged to have reached their full permitted potential, according to the lives they led during their probation and thereafter, are given special training to prepare them for the roles they will be required to play in the earth's winding up scenes. Though they will not earn the highest reward, they will willingly live and serve happily in that saved condition forever. Since the planet has not yet attained its full potential, some of these persons are sent out as Tutors to the third and second levels of the dark side of this world, to teach the billions there the universal laws of perfection, as you have already observed. They're a large company, so those who have reached the limit of their training are housed in the many buildings you see here. The most modest abode compares to a mansion on earth. While some are sent forth as Tutors of humans, others are assigned to train pets and other faithful animals to properly adapt to and live in the environment for which they qualify. There, they are reunited with their earthly, benevolent masters. Occasionally, they walk the animals on the paved streets and teach them the manners suited to their earned realm of existence.

"Others study and perform a variety of labors, which include the spiritual tendering of horticultural and agricultural plants. On the perfected planet, flowering plants will be tended and beautified, and flawless food crops with perfect nutrients will be grown and cared for. They will yield forever. Perfected humans may eat for enjoyment, though it will not be necessary, as their perfected bodies will be more refined than their earthly ones. Once attained, their spirits will never again be separated from their glorified body.

"You have learned all you need to know here. Continue along the bronze-paved streets in this direction past all the columns of buildings you see," the messenger instructed me, after he led me outside the building. "You will be admitted to another sector city to learn more."

With that final statement, my guides dissolved and vanished, and I was left alone, wondering what I was to expect in the sector city.

I walked briskly past a great number of buildings over a distance of about ten miles, until I passed the last building and arrived at the base of another high, transparent wall without a gate. I could neither see what was beyond the wall nor could I tell how to get to the other side. As I touched the wall upon arrival, however, I was instantly transferred to another city that was more beautiful than the one I had just left. Most of the buildings were smaller in size and more intricate and refined in architectural design. The streets were paved with silver and shone with an almost blinding radiance. The decorative trees were of other unknown species with deeper-than-mahogany trunks and more majestic limbs and leaves than those I had seen in the city I had just left.

I stood in awe at the marvelous scenery before me. Here, flowery trees and shrubs and creepers of all kinds grew in perfectly tended flowerbeds interspersed by lawns and pavements. The city was adorned with a beauty that exceeds our human ability to conceive. It was a glorious scene. I had learned to approach the first building in sight for assistance, so I moved toward it, and true to my expectation, two personages materialized before me. They greeted me pleasantly and beckoned me to follow them. They led me into the first building, which was organized in the same fashion as the one in the city I had just left.

I noticed that the population in this sector city was relatively smaller than in the other city and that there was a Tutor for every four students of the same gender, instead of for every ten.

"In this sector are those spirits who've graduated from the prior city. They will continue their training here," one of my guides stated. "They are to be taught other, higher laws which are reserved for only this sector and which they will be required to learn in order to enable them to perform their duties well hereafter. Those that deserve a still higher reward, according to the knowledge of the Supremos, are advanced from here to the final and highest sector for further instructions. Again, note that the majority of the buildings you see here serve as housing for those who advance. Now, there is nothing new to learn here. You must move on if you have no questions on your mind."

I realized that the Tutors appeared to be everywhere, though I had been informed that some of those who graduated from the first sector and did not qualify for advancement were sent out as Tutors. My guides responded before I could pose my question.

"There is a hierarchy of Tutors, just as you have in the levels of institutions on your planet. Those who cannot advance beyond the first sector you visited are assigned to the Community of the Noble and Ignorant and the Realm of Failure to teach the universal law of perfection. Those who cannot advance beyond this second sector are assigned to the first sector to teach the lessons appropriate to that sector and are also given some assignments particular to the realm they qualify to inherit.

"Those in this second sector are instructed by special Tutors who graduate freshly from the Final Sector for Potential Supremos, which is the sector of your next visit. The graduates from the Final Sector for Potential Supremos are taught all the laws that govern the universe and start their preparation to be initiated into the Order of the Supremos by teaching only what is necessary to entrants of this second sector. They are later given other assignments and are taught to organize simple spiritual machines. They then are assigned as Tutors Superior to teach new entrants to the Final Sector for Potential Supremos.

"Finally, as spirits, they serve and understudy those from other orbs who have been initiated into the Order of the Supremos to learn about the creation of other galaxies and planets. Some spirits serve as Guardians to guide a planet created by the Supremos to develop to its full potential before they are initiated into the Order of the Supremos. Most of these spirits, however, learn and permanently unite with their bodies at a time appointed by the Supremos. They are then assigned a realm to organize planets and populate them. Thus, the cycle of creation and perfection continues and renews itself endlessly. This is the work and glory of the Supremos and of each who follows the Supremos' order of life and liberty. Any further questions will be answered when you visit the Final Sector for Potential Supremos. Go in this direction, along this silver road, until you arrive at the base of the transparent wall." The two then dissolved and vanished from my sight.

After a distance of approximately five miles, I arrived at the base of the transparent wall. I touched the wall and instantly found myself in the final sector city. Before me was a glorious city of incomparable beauty. The city I left—exquisite in every detail and appealing beyond conception— was, now, by comparison only a shadow of this royal abode. The buildings appeared to have been built with refined gold, while the streets looked to be paved with the same material. The buildings' architecture was perfect, immaculate. Trees, flowers, lawns were manicured with scientific and yet artistic excellence. It was as if I saw art and science converge as one, and all truth coming together metaphorically in this sublime sphere. The whole city was serene, glorious, and royal. It was beyond majestic. If this was the final inheritance of the faithful to which level the former Wackida had been admitted, then I would use all my endowed faculties to fulfill my mission and earn it too. The visit to the sectors in the City of Light had kindled a spiritual fire in my soul, deepened my hope and passion to fight evil and bring as many as I could back to this heavenly place.

Two glorious personages met me here, but unlike my guides in the first and second sector cities, they were male and a female, a couple that had fulfilled the law of eternal marriage. Each was gorgeously attired and wore an intricately designed crown of gold on which was inscribed the eternal title of the couple. They welcomed me and led me into the first building, which was well furnished and occupied by only two couples. These were the trainers of future exalted couples. The golden city was only about three square miles, indicating that of the billions of humans permitted to serve their probation on the planet, not all had made it to the level of the Order of the Supremos and had qualified to be initiated to become co-creators in the universe. Those who desired to become like the Supremos, and accepted the eternal order of marriage when taught, and whose inevitable earthly mistakes were washed white by the Lighter of the City, entered this highest realm in the Eternal City.

I had been informed that my planet was in its last stages of development. Given that and the fact that who that had made it to the highest sector were so few as to be inhabiting only three square miles, then I needed to work hard to turn many more hearts to the perfect law of the universe before my term of service was over.

"Your education in this world has come to an end." The voice of one of my guides interrupted my train of thought. "You must return to the Dome to receive further instructions." My guides then led me outside the building. In the next moment, I found myself back at the point in the Dome where I had touched the panel. It was at this point that I became aware that I had left my physical body in the Dome and gone on the journey in spirit. How long I had been gone I could not tell, but I felt pangs of hunger for the first time since I started my journey— so characteristic of the mortal body. "Welcome back," said three of the Guardians, who were there to meet me.

They confirmed that I had indeed visited that spiritual world in the spirit. According to them, an invisible, limitless life cord connected my spirit self to my physical body at the navel and sustained it through a current of universal energy. Through this life cord, my physical body was kept alive to record all experiences encountered by my spirit essence throughout my journey. The breaking of this cord meant the final separation of the physical body and the spirit in what we term "death." I was told that though I had unlimited energy available to me, I needed to eat to replace worn-out cells in my physical body. They provided a plate of fresh seaweed salad including photo-nutrient rich hiziki, sea lettuce, sea palm, and dulse, along with a warm vegetable soup and kiwi-like fruit, with a natural sweetness and texture unlike anything I'd ever consumed for my sustenance. I was also informed that my journey had given me a firsthand knowledge and experience of the reality of the abodes earned by the wicked as well as the obedient as they transition from the physical planet to the spiritual. Before vanishing from my sight, they showed me the panel that would open to my next adventure, instructing me to start the journey when I was ready. After a little while, when I felt rested enough, I positioned myself at the front of the panel and touched it.

THE CAVES OF THE
DIMENSIONAL WORLDS

CHAPTER 5

First Cave

Instantly the panel opened, revealing a rock-bound tunnel. As I stepped inside, just as before, the panel slid into place and snapped shut behind me. Faith, now a close companion rather than unwelcome guest, invited me on. I walked slowly and deliberately forward through the poorly lit tunnel—effortlessly creating mental snapshots of everything in my path. After a short walk, the tunnel walls opened. I was met with a thick, murky, gray, impenetrable fog. One blink, and the fog dissipated and surroundings became pristinely clear. Our intelligent spirit bodies respond and adapt in ways our mortal bodies have forgotten. Discoveries like this provided tangible gifts of courage and fortitude, as soon as I acknowledged their Source. I could see ahead of me a vast bog, a bubbling, marshy stretch of land that was spewing forth some form of thick grey vapor. From all appearances, stepping into it would mean sinking. I considered walking along the edge to locate a solid pathway. Just then, the usual timely directive revealed that there was no solid path. I noted that it never came prematurely, or in advance of my exact moment of need. But neither was it ever a nanosecond too late. I needed to step into the bubbling marsh, and I would not sink—the dirt would not even smear my feet. I obeyed and as I did so, was amazed to see myself floating over the marshy land. I saw far ahead of me, beyond the bog, what appeared to be the silhouette of a mountain range. As I drew closer, I saw that they were in fact huge rocky caves. There were openings at the base of each mountainous outcrop. I began to hear an eerie moaning emitting from the mouth of the nearest cave. I continued forward. As I stepped inside, I found myself in what looked like a large chamber occupied by a number of dark-looking individuals clad in black attire. Each wore a headband fashioned like a coiled, live, spitting cobra ready to strike. Most of them had long black beards, and the areas around their deeply set eyes were sunken and gray. Their outer macabre vestments were matched by a pathetic, inner hollow emptiness. I could see that they were laboring around huge cauldrons mounted on stands with three legs of rocks, under which blazed red-hot fires. They appeared to be cooking something. *"What was this all about?"* The cauldrons you see hold a variety of products formulated to adversely affect humans. The first in the row contains a product whose formula generates an extreme craving for food. When ingested or released, it attracts the spirit of gluttony, creating a tremendous appetite and corresponding compulsion for its victims to eat ravenously. One needs a strong will to resist its power, and only a few humans are able to extricate themselves from its grip. Eating becomes the relentless passion of its victims; their prime focus in life becomes the gratification of this appetite.

"The second cauldron holds a brew that stimulates its victims to consume depressants in unlimited quantities. It confers upon them the spirit of avoidance: avoidance of pain, avoidance of sorrow, avoidance of conflict, avoidance of life. This formula propels its victims to seek out liquor, pills of varying shapes and sizes, that dull the senses and the zest for life. Those lured by its specious promises will seek the formula and its related counterfeits at all costs to satisfy their desire for it. Your planet is overrun with those grasped in the bonds of addiction, and this is one source of their problems. Once overcome by the cauldron's elixir, liberty is diminished, and the ability to satiate desire can only be met with more products. So Big Earthly industries, marketing the products, are only rewarded. And the cycle of dependency continues. Only a few humans are successfully rehabilitated. This concoction was developed after years of experimenting with cause and effect as the brewing and consumption of alcohol was introduced onto your planet. Since then, increased varieties and alternate substances with new addictive ingredients, became attractively advertised. Addiction to the liquor and like substances also results in under eating, emaciation, and sickness. Users often die from malnutrition, edema, and liver diseases and are usually sent to the Realm of Failure.

"The third cauldron contains a product that stimulates in humans the craving for drugs after the first intake. The immediate euphoria—counterfeit high—fuels a desire for continued use. Continued use promotes addiction. Victims caught in its web generally become lifelong drug addicts. They also tend to be violent thieves and murderers. As they are compelled by the uncontrolled reactions and demands of their acclimatized bodies to satisfy the craving for the drug, they are driven to do anything, even kill, to get money to purchase the product. The murderers among them end up in the Pits of the Damned. Unlike the contents of the first two cauldrons, which attract the spirits of vice, the contents of the third, fourth, and fifth pot are the actual drugs—cocaine, marijuana, opium, and other products which are made highly potent for this destructive purpose. These products are blinding and binding while they promise sight, new visions (hallucinations), and freedom from earthly pains or constraints.

"There are many more cauldrons in which are manufactured other mild yet destructive substances, including caffeine, additives, hormones, chemicals that are destructive to the body and its purposes. Many users develop cancer and associated diseases and thus destroy their lives. The planet, as it was created, contained all that was healthful and needful in abundance. Some of its stewards, however, in an effort to secure money and increase profitability, took shortcuts, created hybrids, added mercury-containing and hormone-filled products for humans to buy.

"You may wonder how these concoctions brewed in the spiritual realm could materialize on the physical planet. Are you aware that any product produced or created on your physical planet is inspired from the spiritual? Each item is first created spiritually, and laws governing its use for better or for worse are identified in the spiritual realm where it was created, even before humans are inspired to create it.

"While the Supremos inspire their children on the planet with ideas and favorable laws to create useful things, the evil one and his minions also identify negative laws to formulate and manufacture destructive behaviors. They inspire their equally evil converts on your planet to create them to infest and destroy lives. They also often take advantage of the useful things created with good intent by influencing their followers to apply negative laws to them and use them for evil purposes. The desires of the flesh, which are at variance with the desires of the spirit, are served instead. This gives the physical body prominence and the ability to suppress and dominate the influence of the spirit. Once the spirit is quenched, humans respond to the flesh—they become ruled by gluttony, addiction, and debauchery, to the great joy of the evil one and his minions. Human converts thereby become carnal and devilish."

While thus engaged, I became aware that most of the evil spirits in my presence had stopped their activities and were watching me angrily. They looked venomous and eager to confront me, yet something held them back. Then I noticed that my body's aura glowed brighter and brighter. As the intensity of the white light from my body filled the cave, I saw their anger turn to fear. The spirits started to flee from me. The next moment, they were hurled against the walls of the large cave, cowering and whining. Many of them lay motionless, as if they were dead.

"The evil cannot bear the presence of pure light," volunteered the voice in my mind. "It tortures and weakens them, and they will forever flee from it. It is an eternal decree." The voice further explained to me that spirits were all eternal and physically indestructible. Those that lay still had merely been momentarily drained of their strength by the light from my body. They would be restored to continue their work after I left that chamber in the cave. How I wished they could be stopped in the work they were doing, but I knew my work was not here. My assignment was to yet defend living humans and influence them from falling victim to the wiles of evil agents I was now observing.

I passed through the chamber with its rows of cauldrons, down a long corridor, and into the next chamber. Here were other rows of cauldrons with another group of evil spirit beings laboring at something. The light emanating from my body had by now totally receded, and I thought my entrance was unnoticed. I stood quietly observing these spirits and wondering what they were formulating here.

I was informed that this was the chamber of sensuality, where potions brewed acted on the mind to stimulate erotic desires of the body. The products promoted the destruction of virtue, leading humans to act lasciviously and commit a variety of sexual abominations. Like their counterparts in the first chamber, they relied on willing human agents, their converts, to manufacture their well-formulated potions. These spiritually created poisons were then translated into physical realities and advertised as performance enhancers. They promised speciously to promote satisfaction during sexual escapades. Their victims become hooked on the product, and on the deceptive sexual pleasures it claims. One promiscuous act leads to another, and none really satisfies, for none is according to the divine order. None are pleasing in the sight of the Supremos. Brothels spring up under its influence. Sex perversions, trafficking, and prostitution are some of its other effects. Pornography, polyandry, and bestiality all result from uncurbed sexual desires stimulated by the Big Industry which is backed by these dark spiritual producers.

A vision then opened to my mind, and I saw young, attractive women parading the streets and entertainment joints almost nude to advertise their bodies, hoping to attract the weak-minded to seek sexual gratification for a fee. I saw extreme hairdos and makeup applied to artificially enhance beauty and entice and lead susceptible humans down the road of everlasting doom. I saw young children and teens with eating disorders, trying desperately to transform their sacred body into something with airbrushed media appeal.

I saw extreme body mutilations displayed with pride as admirable fashion. I saw brothels where pornography was worshipped and sexuality was enhanced and admired. I saw acts of seduction, lust, and defilement in societies destroy the lives of the perpetrators and victims alike. I saw humans drawn by desire into perversions such as rape, incest, and child molestation. It was heartbreaking to see such acts carried out by humans who could have won favor with the all-loving Supremos and earned eternal happiness through obedience in this short but critical life. What was called good musical entertainment had been laced, in some cases, with choreographed suggestive dances that were extreme and that excited and aroused the sexual desires of both performers and spectators. The world had indeed gone carnal, sensual, and devilish, and this cave was the source. I had seen enough and desired that the vision be closed. Suddenly the vision was taken from my view.

"Remember, you need to learn of the methods used by these evil forces to capture their victims," the voice prompted. "For centuries, the evil forces have dealt with humans, learned of their weaknesses, developed many strategies, and mastered the art of deceit to influence and mislead humans to disbelieve the true Agents. These evil forces have thereby won their victims over to indulge in these perversions in the semblance of living happy lives.

"Those that demonstrate total commitment to such products and promises are enrolled and initiated as their instruments. They are taught dubious ways of acquiring wealth and are inspired to create and produce new products which are an improvement on the existing ones. By this method, they perpetuate their trade in a continuum from generation to generation. All the others trapped by such vices became addicted victims to the wares of the evil ones and waste away in their perversions. This is their demise and leads to incarceration in either the Pits of the Damned or the Realm of Failure, as determined by the gravity of their offenses.

"A few who have become aware of their deplorable state in life early enough and have desired to change, to gain freedom and extricate themselves from the hypnotic grip of these products and the destroyer, have been happily and sympathetically assisted by the Agents or Wackida of their time. After their conversion, the Agents taught them the perfect law of the universe and did all that was necessary to help them stay on track. Unfortunately, in most cases, only a few managed to stay on course and live an acceptable life in the eyes of our spiritual parents. Sadly, the majority of them, like pigs, returned to wallow in the mud and became worse off than they were before. Because they tasted the sweetness of the law of life, and knowingly rebelled against it, often profaning the name of their benefactors, they earned for themselves inheritances in the Pits of the Damned."

It was sad that a large number of humans had succumbed to carnality and sensuality by yielding to—instead of resisting—temptations to embrace the desires of the flesh. Once yielded, they became servants of the master they listed to obey—the master of mayhem. I shook myself out of my mental drift and realized I had moved about halfway through the chamber. On either side of me were the evil occupants cowering against the distant walls of the cave, their merchandise left unattended. They all appeared to be working with a group mind, or as if they were remotely controlled by their master, Xoedikus, who had led them in the rebellion against the Supremos. My encounter with those in the first chamber may have been conveyed to them, restraining them from attacking me. I walked past them without mishap and entered the corridor leading into the third chamber, with new anticipation.

I entered the third chamber and was not surprised to see more evil spirits bent over and busily working at smaller cauldrons. They stopped as if expecting me and started moving away, toward the periphery wall of the chamber. Once again, my curiosity was piqued. The voice quickly filled the void. The contents of the smaller cauldrons were unique. Most of these were released into the atmosphere and were received by osmosis, by inhalation or by way of skin receptors. Each of these products affected each human according to his or her constitution and spiritual strength. Their aroma was irresistible, and the molecules undetected by nasal nerves, and the skin's pores found the ingredients easy to absorb. Each molecular compound induced a decapacitating outcome. Clients' souls, cloaked by its influence, shrank in worthlessness, apathy, depression, slothfulness, despair, suicidal intent, mistrust, suspicion, and disbelief. Malicious motive accomplished: Imbued humans were stripped of their ability to focus and contribute their divinely endowed talents to foster the progress of the human race and the planet.

I moved on and entered the fourth and last of the chambers in the cave. Contrary to my expectations, there was not a single cauldron. Instead, evil spirits filled the chamber, from ceiling to floor. They were organized into groups, suspended in air or grounded, and each group held a different set of musical instruments. Each was occupied in creating different types of rhythms and lyrics to release to the inhabitants of our planet. I simultaneously and yet distinctively, heard types of music— metal, rock, classical, country, show tunes, pop, and beyond. I heard new categories of music—such as passion, nirvana, despara, and quaxin— as they were being conceived. While attuned to the classical, I relived my mother's soothing piano performance of 16th to 18th century classicists and hymns. As I listened to pop, I revisited musical jam sessions with inspired and talented youth, who composed uplifting score and lyrics. And as I heard the dis-synchronous, deafening, sense-depleting sounds in a motley group, my mind traveled to drug-enhanced performers in loud venues, seducing young audiences.

What else should I make of this?

"Remember, all existing materials, including sound, given to humans to create good things, can also be used to create evil things. Every use has a corresponding disuse or abuse. It all depends on who inspires the creator. As you can see, the evil one will never create anything that will be of benefit to humans. In fact, they can never truly create. All they can do is mimic, distort, or corrupt what naturally is or what humans can create. The music these evil spirits compile inspires—or "despires"— humans to be impulsive, erratic, and irresponsible.

"In primitive societies, music created and released is of several kinds. One form includes sounds that are intended to show respect for Mother Earth. Others are preparatory to inciting or preparing for war. Others are of purely evil intent. The latter involves the use of deep, throbbing drums and accompanying instruments that release sad, wailing sounds. Such music is then used by their priests to put people into a trance and to instill fear in the tribes, to control them and seduce them into performing ritualistic human sacrifices. These societies live in a condition of superstition and constant fear.

"In civilized societies, stringed instruments are increasingly common, though many other types are manufactured and applied. The music that is debilitating, created in the cave in which I stood, moves a certain direction to earth's young populus. Music of this nature is created in the spirit realm and released through agents who usually enter into a pact and sell their souls for fame, fortune, and success. These agents, under the pact, often reap for a contracted number of years. But popularity is fleeting. Often, perpetrators die suddenly and without warning. Their fans, often mesmerized by the product and influenced by the spirit realm, succumb to evil through suggestion. Your planet is gradually being annexed to the kingdom of evil by such strategies. Unfortunately, the rising generations come to accept seduction as a norm because they have no paradigm of the good life. It only takes one generation of abandoning the law for morality to dissipate and darkness to prevail. Agentive and prophetic voices of warning, at this stage, are readily dismissed."

I was instructed to leave the last chamber in this cave and enter the next cave, where I would have the opportunity to learn more about the methods of the evil one. I could sense there was more to be learned and braced myself to absorb all that I could so that I could fully know the forces with which I was contending. *Isn't it surprising that the evil ones could capitalize on the love of humans for music to enslave them and lead them to everlasting doom?* I thought. *Is there anything they can't do? Which segment of human activity don't they have the power to infiltrate?*

What should I expect in the next cave? What I did know was that the evil ones had no power over me, in spite of their rabid desire to tear me apart. I had attained only eighteen years of age when I was taken to be prepared for this assignment. I recalled my earlier ignorance about life's grand design and opposing forces engaged in determining the final outcome. I had now been exposed to the secret agenda of the evil one and knew the fate of those who fell to his tricks. I had seen the world in which they were now wasting away, experiencing suffering they had never known existed or had refused to believe in when in the flesh.

Fortunately, I had also witnessed the peace and joy of the departed souls who had accepted the saving plan provided by the all-knowing Supremos and had been loyal to the demands of the universal law of perfection—with its merciful provision for error and reconciliation. Many of the faithful had sacrificed all they had to share the law and testify of its sanctifying result, even at the risk of losing their lives. Some had, in their effort to rescue, been arrested, imprisoned, and starved to death, or killed by the sword or spear. Some were stoned or crucified or burnt at the stake or thrown into dens of wild animals to be torn apart. Some were decapitated or bound and drowned in the sea with a weight tied to their bodies, or dragged by horses on rough roads until their flesh was torn and mangled. As a youth, I had read about some of these atrocities in our history books. Until now, they'd seemed like fables. But now, they were more real than ever. The more I learned of the evil unleashed on humans in ages past, and how the evil forces were still at work making such horrid history part of our day, the more determined I became to fight and to save as many of the inhabitants of the planet as I could. I was very determined to learn all I needed to know to squarely meet my assigned duties. In spite of the extensive education I'd received in the world of spirits, I still felt inadequate to the task. The evil rebel and his hordes claimed millennia of experience and were highly organized in principalities and dominions all about us. They'd employed the most deviant and subtle tactics of spiritual warfare, and had a million barely detectable disguises. They had fought the Wackida and the Agents who preceded me over many generations.

It appeared that there was nothing they did not know about the vulnerability of humans—our weaknesses, our susceptibility and yearning to appease the desires of the flesh, our natural inclination to be covetous and selfish. Yes, they exploited them all, I mused to myself. But I also reflected on what they will never assimilate. They were incapable of comprehending man's endless potential for good and the great capacity for love that rested within each spirit on planet Earth. The stamp of the Imago Dei was on every soul. Each was made in the likeness of the Supremos, and had all the seeds of perfection in embryonic form. I knew and understood the true worth and nature of the human spirit, better than any sordid disembodied spirit ever could. That knowledge was power. And that power, divinely granted, would enable me to help save them.

Xoedikus and his hordes had never possessed bodies of their own and they never would. Because of their rebellion, they would never experience physicality nor have the opportunity to be fully human. Their progress was forever stunted, or "damned." They had lost the chance to become co-creators with the Supremos and to know full joy. The only way they could ever possess a body now was to temporarily steal and inhabit those of the weak-minded and non-believing. In other words, they could only live in borrowed bodies, despite their yearning to have their own. Oh, how they envied the mortals for this very reason!

Xoedikus, the master of evil, deceptively boasts of superiority. He takes advantage of the veil over the human's mind, preventing them from recalling his identity, rebellion, and inferiority. It has been the firm resolve of Xoedikus to frustrate the Agents and the mission of the Wackida. He uses lies to instill fear by keeping the truth from the mortals. He maintains advantage because humans only have the knowledge they've acquired here on earth to rely on and must trust in the teachings of their leaders, which is not always the easier choice. This causes them to lose faith at times and to stop listening to the quiet, inner voice that was given to them by the Supremos in order to guide them. This voice is always there to warn them against falsehood and to counsel them to listen to the Agents and the Wackida.

Had the humans not been clothed with the coarse physical matter required to inhabit the earth and their memories blotted out, they would see the inferiority of Xoedikus and his minions. Instead of falling susceptible to his snares, many would have thought back to the happiness they had had in their former home and would have shunned the wrongful desire to rebel. The hope of returning to their cherished abode could have buoyed them up whenever they faced extreme trials and unbearable challenges, if only they were permitted to remember.

Though seemingly cruel, forgetfulness was a merciful intervention imposed by the Supremos. Without forgetfulness, humans could never be tested. A child will likely do right if always in the presence of their parents. Likewise, with us. We needed mental and physical separation as part of a plan for us to gain knowledge and personal experiences through trials in the mortal state. This process planned to reward all obedient offspring. Through successful completion of their life's sentence on the earth, humans would finally enter into an exalted state—an experience the Supremos passed through themselves long ago.

By now I had reached the entrance of the second cave. I walked through a short corridor to the entrance of the first chamber and into the cave without any mishap.

CHAPTER 6

Second Cave

This new cave was distinguishable from the first in its organization and methods. The first chamber was occupied by spirits who had mastered the art of deception and imitation. Here, evil spirits inflated the notion of financial freedom, distorted the meaning of real prosperity, and set people on financial ferris wheels of greed. Essentially spirits here sought to influence hearts to unscrupulously seek material wealth at the expense of their neighbors.

Unlike spirits in the first cave, these actually worked through their earthly cohorts, or converts, by periodically taking possession of them. As they cohabited, like a virus does in a cell, the spirits overtook the cell's operative center and controlled the whole body through the nervous system. The human agent or victim becomes acutely aware of loss of power, but possesses no will or ability to retake control of his body. Observers may see him as one who flips between two personalities—like Dr. Jekyll and Mr. Hyde.

Once these victims taste wealth and become hooked on their extravagant lifestyles, the evil spirits withdraw. Their mission was duly accomplished. Their re-programming was enough to incite their client's relentless desire and quest for undeserved wealth. Each client would be promised continued sustenance if they would submit to the subliminal schema of the evil master. The evil spirits would then move on to possess another human body and repeat the cycle, increasing their converts.

Through these methods, they strategically gained many dedicated agents willing to obey all instructions from the evil one. Some agents who had attempted to violate the terms of the agreement had, in a rapid manner, lost homes and goods through strange fires. Others watched their startups and ventures collapse. Others faced seemingly unrelated but equally orchestrated types of misfortune, such as the strange deaths of loved ones. Even those who desired to break loose of the chains of lust and financial bondage, found it extremely difficult to do so, as now fear also held them hostage. Once the love of wealth became implanted and entrenched in a victim's mind through the practiced and mastered methods of these evil ones, greed became an obsession.

The occupants of this first chamber of the second cave were dressed in black, as those in the first cave. These evil ones, however, possessed strange, hypnotic, deep-set eyes which bore into your soul and spoke your destruction. As occurred in the first cave, they all stopped working when I entered the chamber. They had received no warning of my presence in their kingdom, to my surprise. *Why wouldn't others telepathically warn them?*

The voice in my mind offered an explanation.

"The groups in each of the two caves are endowed with the ability to transmit messages to others only within the bounds of their cave. Since the mode of operation in this cave is different from the former, there is no communication link between occupants of the first cave and the second cave. Among the subjects of the prince of evil, division had its advantage: it kept its subjects in check."

I realized that the occupants were not as numerous as I'd expected. It was explained that most of the wicked workforce was employed in geographical spheres around the humans.

"The spirits you find in the cave at the moment are those who have had to refine their techniques to enable them to go back to seek out other victims. It is also their custom to come together into this chamber every ten years by your planetary time to compare notes and share ideas for conversion and enslavement of victims, and to adapt these methods to the changing scenes on the planet. The spiritual warfare will go on unceasingly until the time your planet reaches full maturity. Then the Supremos will take charge and mete out to each individual a deserving reward according to the life he led and the laws he obeyed. At that time, evil itself will be bound for a season."

Suddenly, while engrossed in this tutelage, fiery darts flew at me from all directions. Before any could hit me, however, my body was instantaneously enveloped in a shield of fire which simply absorbed them, preventing any damage. A gust of white light suddenly burst forth from my body in waves, emanating in all directions, knocking out every evil spirit and filling the whole chamber with light. All the evil spirits were weakened and lay still as if they were dead. Not a spirit limb moved. This only bade me some time to determine my next move. I knew from my experience in the first cave that these spirits had only been stunned and would recover as soon as the intensity of my light dimmed.

I was instructed to move on, and as I was leaving the chamber, not one of the evil essences had yet recovered. I walked through them and continued through a short corridor into a second chamber. It was apparent, upon entry, that the occupants of this chamber had been alerted of my presence. They appeared not to be bothered by me, though. Interestingly, I saw some of them occasionally steal glances and move away from my path as I approached.

I learned that I was sent here to learn how to adapt to each habitat within the planet, and to prepare for the threats I would have to face. Here I'd also become more versatile in accommodating the defense mechanisms and auto-responses with which my new spirit body had been equipped. Gradually, I was discovering them, and learning not to resist them. I was about to learn about the first methods of occupants of habitat 1.

Those in this second chamber temporarily clothe themselves with the living bodies of animals and trees, through which they relate to and influence humans. Communities are converted in great numbers by fomenting fear and intimidation. Devotees are made rich through evil powers that often require human and animal sacrifices and other abhorrent practices. Greed attracts humans in vast numbers to throw caution to the wind and become devotees. By these processes, large populations fall under the spell of these evil essences, whose converts display wealth, dominate societies, and rule communities, often trampling upon the rights of people with disdain and impudence.

"Unlike humans, who have been blessed with the highest degree of earthly intelligence, the mammalian and other lower classes of animals possess varying levels of intelligence, some rudimentary, as designed by the Supremos. Each is given sufficient capacity and light to fill the measure of its creation. The bulk of the animal class operates by instinctive behavior endowed them by the Supremos. "By possessing the bodies of these animals and using them as creatures of evil, humans have been convinced to hate some of these innocent animals or view them as evil creatures. Superstitions around snakes, black cats, spiders, owls, magpies, bats, and a host of other outwardly unattractive specie are not uncommon. These are all part of the natural order, and each has its purpose in the divine economy. In fact, they are occasionally forced, like some humans, to serve as tools for the visible evil activities of these evil essences.

"The other group of living things used as a medium or an abode of these evil essences is trees. Select aged trees occupied by these stationary or spot-based evil ones became forbidden groves or forests ventured into by only the brave and the fearless. Strange noises and supernatural occurrences in and around these areas make them appear as abodes of evil and cast fear into the residents of the surrounding communities. This is more prominent in the primitive and the peasant farming communities.

"These simple people are often compelled to donate large portions of their crop harvest to the senior devotees of these deities to receive protection from evil under threat of misfortune. Occasionally, unexplainable but orchestrated incidents in these communities would buttress these claims and create panic and great fear, while the devotees of the evil essences fed fat on the crop that these poor simple peasants had toiled to produce. The deprived peasant farmers were then left to live in poverty and fear all their days."

I left the second chamber with the evil occupants rehearsing their act and wincing at every turn. I continued through another short corridor into a third chamber in the cave. Another group of evil spirits occupied this third chamber and were also rehearsing and practicing their art. I could not discern the purpose of their actions until the Personage whose Voice was my compass, clarified it for me.

"These that you see are stationed at chosen pre-determined earthly zones. They are known as spot-based evil spirits. But unlike their contemporaries in the second chamber, they house themselves in inanimate objects and are often more feared than their counterparts. They always work in teams led by a superior spot-based spirit.

"Each member in the team, however, has the permission to pose as the leader in the part of the realm he or she has been assigned to operate. They are trained to occupy selected rocky terrains, mountains, rivers, lakes, caves, bodies of water associated with shrines and superstitions around visions and healings. Many who are infirm on earth seek healing from the Supremos and Master Healer. However, as these spot-based evil spirits attend to them, they promise healing and vision through their own counterfeit power. They feign visions and appearances of former saints who lived on earth, and turn waters into bubbling springs with salts that appeal to the sense and superstitious mind. People flock to these places, and it becomes for the evil spirits, a perfect distraction from the divine. Consultations with otherworldly spirits are promised at these vacuous resorts. Hot springs abound which draw seasoned travellers, and newcomers to the world of spiritualism and its attendant spurious claims. Magicians find their way here and are sold into the practice for it is lucrative and growing. Many bring gifts and lay them at the feet of the shrines or healers, who profit thereby. Festivals are celebrated at great expense every year in their honor."

I left this chamber and was directed by the voice to enter a fourth chamber. *What more do I have to learn in connection with the sin of greed and covetousness in this cave?* I thought I had learned enough and needed no more lessons.

"You are wrong," the voice in my mind addressed me. "Continue into the fourth chamber of this cave and learn about something you have never thought of." I did as I was instructed and came upon a host of evil spirits who appeared to be writing or reciting prose from a book and making strange movements. I stood at the entrance for a while and watched them with surprise, unable to make out what the din was all about. Then it came to me. They were writing scripts and acting them out!

Cinematography and television, inventions inspired by the Supremos— were being compromised for evil. Pornographic films, suggestive advertisements for destructive products, lascivious prime time shows, politically correct but morally skewed programming, content and media that portrayed the triumph of evil over good were being planned for release through their agents onto the planet!

"The adversary has so many crafty, well-thought-out, and tested methods for shifting the focus and destroying the happiness of humans," the Voice explained. "He seizes his victims' moments of gloom and confusion to entice them to escape reality with fantasy. At first, the fantasies were wholesome, romantic, and clean, with pro-social messages. Over time, they became increasingly amoral and immoral, and saturated with violence and sadism. Many send messages laden with false hope and infer promises that engaging in activities that are in opposition to the universal law of perfection bring happiness rather than misery. As always, the evil spirits poison by degrees.

"The war-obsessed gaming industry is an extension of this mania. At first, video games were created as innocuous stress-relievers, ways to socialize, and as mediums for learning various literary and other skills. But they morphed into another genre, just as cinematography and television. Gambling, lotteries, addictive games and sites all followed suit, promising happiness a click away.

"Humans have generally abandoned the right course of attaining peace and happiness, as well as sound wealth, as counseled by the Supremos: to work hard with our hands; to pay a tenth of our profits for building the kingdom of the Supremos; to freely give help to the poor and needy, the widows, and the fatherless; and to continually give thanks and honor to the Supremos, the providers of all good things. When humans follow such counsel, they have been promised blessings of untold peace, guidance, wealth, and plenty to spare.

"What you are about to witness in the next and last cave will surprise you," the unfailing mental messenger said.

I left the third chamber and entered the fourth through a short corridor as instructed. I was surprised to see what seemed to be an elite group of evil spirits in reasonable numbers seriously engaged in some form of research. But for their evil eyes, one would never have suspected their nature. They were clad, not in black as their colleagues, but in fashionable suits, stylish attire, and expensive jewelry. Dressing modestly and adorning the temple of our body appropriately glorifies the Supremos, but robbing ourselves in exotic silks and extreme, attention-seeking garb devalues, and at the same time, inflates the self. Neither yields joy or progress.

I then noticed that they had a large stock of books, and were busily engaged in reading and discussing, occasionally arguing among themselves. They appeared to be unconcerned but curious about my presence. What I saw was this: Learning. Appearances. Pride. Knowledge is a ruby, if sought after for righteous purposes. Left to oneself, however, learning can lead to pride. My thoughts turned to another learned group--seminarians. Then the question rose in my mind: *Have you thought of the proliferation of religious sects on the planet and the miraculous powers displayed by most of them to impress and draw millions or thousands of souls after them?*

"Recall to memory the lifestyles of most of the priests in your youthful days, before you were called to this work, and you will come to see now the false ones who deceptively relied on evil forces for the miraculous works they performed. There have been millions of such sects since the creation and population of your planet. They generally started as simple, community-based, scripture-studying organizations. But these rapidly underwent a metamorphosis into complex, sophisticated organizations.

"They are deceptive organizations which operate without authority from the Supremos. In reality, their founders are instruments of the evil religious angels, as these group of spirits are called. Initially they are not recognized as such by their chosen greedy and receptive agents. They craftily pose and imitate miracles that convince thousands. After winning a large following and making their agents wealthy, they reveal their true identity. Governed by greed and a desire to maintain and make more wealth, these agents willingly submit to the angels' control and operate the organizations as churches with their usual founders. The agents adopt a pious attitude and minister to their congregation with a pretense of humility; they lead with pride and a show of affluence and pomposity. They eventually develop these quasi-religious bodies into commercial enterprises, a medium for further enriching themselves at the expense of their impoverished yet faithfully ignorant congregations. Their agents dress in the most fashionable attire, drive the most modern and expensive vehicles in their day, and live in the most coveted homes. They do so while their congregations wallow in poverty or struggle to make ends meet, yet donate their little resources to maintain the high lifestyles of their priests or pastors, hoping for a miracle to ultimately redeem them from their misery. Indeed, the shepherds who should risk all, including their lives, to defend the sheep of their fold, become instead the lords of the sheep to be worshipped, protected, and provided for by the poor and defenseless!"

Some of these leaders, wolves in sheep's clothing, employ the evil eye and, with incantations, prepare charms disguised as sacred emblems for their clients for various purposes. Their targeted victims easily fall prey to the effects of these charms, if their own spiritual development has been thrown to the wind.

"This final chamber in this second cave is, therefore, the source of all false and counterfeit authority, power, and miracles" the voice continued. "These evil essences are servants of the master of all evil and have been assigned to this work of deception. I was puzzled at why the Supremos would permit those true Agents, who were elected to come to serve in various ages, to be rejected and attacked by the humans who were under the influence of the evil essences, and to be tortured and murdered at the peak of their mission. *Why would the Supremos, who are all-powerful, permit the untimely death of their elected emissaries? What short lives they were permitted to live after all their obedience and honesty!*

"It is not how long you live that matters," the voice in my mind explained, "but how well you make use of the period you are permitted to live on the planet. Planetary life is only a brief probationary period in the eternal scheme of things. Some humans are allowed to live longer than others to impart to succeeding generations knowledge that will benefit them immensely. Others are mercifully granted an extension of life to change and live the true law. Those Agents who are permitted to be killed have completed their mission and are admitted, in their spiritual state after death, into a peaceful rest. Their innocence cries from the dust and witnesses of the sins and the bloodstains of a planet dominated by evil. They are in a state of peace, waiting for the day they will receive their reward of exaltation and joy. You saw this in the City of Light. Death is an inevitable and essential event for all humans and is part of the plan of the Supremos. It may come early or late. It is part of the continuum of life into the eternities. It also serves to define the limits of the period of probation."

I finally exited the second cave and was directed to move on to another: the last of the ranges of caves used by these evil forces.

CHAPTER 7

Third Cave

I made my way carefully toward the last cave and arrived at the entrance of the first chamber. I entered without calling attention to myself. I was surprised to find that the chamber was very wide and long. In fact, it was over ten times the size of any of the other chambers I had visited in this realm. I was taken aback that not one of the evil beings in this expansive assembly paid the least attention to me, though they knew of my entry.

Some were seriously engaged in drills, and others were issuing instructions that I could not understand. Their leaders could be identified by their smart attire and commanding stance. They looked proud, majestic, and authoritative in their different but very formal uniforms and brows topped with different models of caps or headbands. Commands were being issued from all angles, and it became momentarily difficult to sort them out. I, therefore, made a mental appeal for help from the Guardians.

"You are in the cave where dictatorship is spawned and unleashed onto the planet through converted proud and ambitious agents. This is the specialty of the master of all evil. Deception, usurped authority, the annexing of power, and dictatorship rooted in pride are the very vices that brought about his fall! The different uniforms with caps and turbans and armament identify the sectors of operation of totalitarian regimes and reflect the tactical methods adopted."

I studied the spirits and identified a group wearing military uniforms. Some wore insignia and medals identifying their ranks. Military drills were being conducted to try out maneuvers for planned operations. I surmised that a *coup d'état* or a war to annex a smaller country by a more militant, powerful, and well-equipped neighboring one, was imminent on earth.

My memory became activated and focused. A panorama of history presented itself. Dictators on various continents spawned atrocities. All were committed by egotistical men of unbridled pride. I grieved that I was unable to intervene in what I was observing in the cave. I could foresee the barbaric destruction of homes and the killing of masses of innocent humans of all ages.

Those who managed to escape death were often left homeless with virtually nothing to live on; yet, were pursued, hunted, and brutalized, and their defenseless women and children were forcibly deprived of their virtue. Some were cases of tribal or ethnic strife, in which one tribe deemed itself superior to another tribe and aimed to prove it by warring against them. I could discern clear cases of genocide being planned. Clearly this chamber was the location where all such atrocities were imagined, and where proud, evil-minded human agents plotted to execute the plan on the planet to destroy peace and to create unrest for the honest and the peaceful-hearted.

Then my view shifted to another scene, in which military personnel rose up against rulers and removed them as presidents of nations, often mercilessly killing them and their innocent families. Some of these ousted presidents escaped to seek political asylum in other countries. Many resorted to stashing the nation's wealth in their own foreign bank accounts and buying expensive properties in foreign countries. It was sad to observe that the officials of these foreign banks consciously and unashamedly received these monies in the name of doing business. They did so without regard to the masses who would be denied a decent living in the countries governed by these greedy leaders. The dictates of the perpetrators' consciences, even if they had not been taught fully the universal law of perfection, would provide evidence for their guilt during the judgment after this life.

I caught a glimpse of the possessed evil agents eating and drinking, laughing and strutting with glee and satisfaction at each dishonest transaction which they multiplied globally. The revelation that these evil spirits' success was imminent overtook me. I yearned to be released by my Guardians to intervene in future deception and oppression. It was disturbing to also discern the hatred that some of the ambitious junior cadets had for the high-ranking officers, though they obeyed every command issued without question. Outwardly they were compliant, but inwardly, defiant. I could discern their thoughts. Beneath their pretentious allegiance lay a deep resentment for their pompous officers. Their cloak of loyalty was thin, to those who had eyes to see. Occasionally, the junior cadets would strive to sabotage and undermine their superiors, in clandestine fashion.

It was mind-boggling to contemplate the fact that evil forces with a common agenda could not and did not work in unison. In fact, they would often would use some of their own kind to subvert and destabilize major plans of the prince of darkness. Then it occurred to me that each set of evil forces contributed to the chaos of both the spirit and the physical realm. As the chaos was mirrored on earth, it decentralized righteous agents, distracted them from their pursuits, and diverted their energy into attempts to restore order and the status quo. It became difficult to hear the voice of the Agents when they were dodging chaos.

The efforts I was observing in the spiritual realm became manifest in the physical through coups and counter-coups, so prevalent in developing nations. Who suffered in the end? Humans! The evil forces played their roles well, promoting pride and ambition and inciting wars or conflicts among nations and even among factions within the same camp. Once the damage was done, the evil spirits would withdraw, mocking the humans as they celebrated their own success. Each success spurred them to spread anarchy and insecurity among more and more nations.

Planet earth knew a history of wars and power struggles that had brought devastation and halted much progress. Some part of the earth always seemed in commotion. Some even blamed their mishaps on their creators, who they believed should have protected them. Many cursed the day they were born. The majority resorted to seeking protection from false deities whom they believed could keep them safe.

My attention then shifted to another group of dark ones. The leaders wore turbans and were dressed in flowing robes. A few of them wore long beards, and they looked deadlier than those in military uniforms. They were having what appeared to be a military rally—inciting one another with swords, knives and sophisticated guns. They were obviously being trained to invade other tribes, spy upon and set up plans to sabotage other communities, and prove their allegiance through extreme acts of terror and aggression. They saw these as legitimate acts against their hated communities, tribes, different religions, or nationalities.

These subordinates were fearless and seemed to hold a strong allegiance to their leaders. They fought with a frenzy that was almost inhuman and were widely feared. Here, in the chamber of this cave, all such plans were hatched and executed either by suggestion or possession of the bodies of receptive, proud, and power-hungry humans. There were other groups in small bands who were also attired like the military and looked tough and sharp. They were mercenaries, hired to destabilize governments and take over countries for a price. They were also fearless and wielded all types of sophisticated weaponry. I could see they were trained in guerilla tactics and were adapted to fight in any environment. Some of their kind seemed to operate alone and were seen simulating the aiming and hitting of objects from a distance. Then, incidents in history when lone operators had been hired to kill people of prominence registered in my mind. It was clear to me those I was observing were the snipers, the assassins who operated in secrecy or were in the military or played such a role in other subversive groups. All such evil and barbaric activities on the planet were truly influenced from this evil realm, as I had learned from my visit to this multi-dimensional and kaleidoscopic world.

A fourth group, who were yet to be identified, were going about their activities so quietly that I was not sure what they were up to. They worked and practiced so seriously and executed every action with tact and precision. They appeared to have no leadership but were bound together by common characteristics. These were the scholarly, usually found among the top echelons of public organizations and civil societies, I was informed. They were trained in the art of sophistry, deceit, falsification—the arts that promoted confusion, doubt, and skepticism in the minds of once-believing university students, and unrest and instability in civil societies and public organizations.

The Guardians explained to me that these evil ones were skilled in equipping their selected human agents with all the charisma and conniving needed to win favor with rulers of kingdoms, tribes, or organizations.

They were trained to gain their trust and pretentiously promote their own programs, while simultaneously telling lies and using their status as trusted emissaries to discredit and undermine their superiors. Once they created a discordant atmosphere, they would promote their own agenda, win the favor of the subordinates, and gain support to depose the incumbent leaders and seize their positions.

I walked farther down the large chamber and was able to identify a fifth group working together. They represented those who incited societal discrimination and promoted national, tribal, racial, cultural, and sovereign pride. They caused humans to confuse "different" with "inferior." Their work had brought a scourge on people of different color, race, culture, or habitation. Free humans of a particular color, forcibly taken from one continent to be sold on another continent, had suffered the most dehumanizing treatment as slaves. They were purchased as merchandise, branded with hot iron to establish ownership, and driven to toil under harsh conditions to cultivate large farms, build cities, and do all the menial work of their masters. They served and were poorly fed as beasts of labor, and yet the laws of the countries they served allowed them to be maltreated and even killed without restraint or punitive measures against the perpetrators. Other humans had also suffered their share of humiliation and had almost been exterminated for defending their land and sovereignty. For generations, humans had had reason to dominate and maltreat other humans as inferior due to the work of this last group working together.

Had they forgotten that the Supremos created us to be a diverse but united brotherhood and sisterhood? Think of the natural world—the endless variety of sizes, shapes, and colors to please and satisfy and contribute to the whole palette. We study different species of animals of a variety of sizes and colors, and different sizes of trees with different stems and shades of leaves. There are approximately 400,000 types of flowering plant species alone in the world. We rejoice in the delicacy of an orchid, the fragrance and velvety petals of a rose, the purples and deeps reds of petunias, the bright colors of sunflowers, the rainbow colors of baby snapdragons. We even appreciate variety in color, style, and dimensions of inanimate objects, such as cars and clothing. Yet, we discriminate regarding the most important creation, the offspring of the Supremos—and make snap judgments because of insignificant differences in color, physique, texture of hair, or shape of nose or eye.

The Supremos scattered the children of the Earth and placed them in individual posts on the planet. Each are identifiable by their language, culture, appearance, and customs. Each is a part of the divine whole.

Pride and ambition, which breed discrimination and hatred, were costing humans the greatest gift of life. The Spanish Inquisition and other religious persecutions were based on a claim of religious superiority and the desire to suppress others of different views, who were branded as heretics. Conflicts both within and among tribes were fought for dominance. Destabilization and bankruptcy of successful companies resulted from the infiltration of greedy and envious humans who sold to gullible owners false, ambitious plans for operation and expansion.

My mind returned to the present. I noticed that I had walked into the middle of the large chamber and could not locate the exit. I turned around full circle and managed to see a distant passageway that appeared to be the exit. I weaved my way through the evil crowd to the exit. It led into an open field. I saw a huge array of enclosures in the distance. I made my way to the enclosures, hangars adapted to serve as miniature factories.

I entered the first and confirmed that it was truly a factory, with a research and development wing where all kinds of bombs for warfare were being designed and built. I saw models of land mines, grenades, and medium and large bombs both for land and aerial warfare. These were designed, manufactured, tested, and released to willing agents to build physically on Earth. Over the years, research made possible the building of more complex and sophisticated weapons of war on the planet, and this factory was the otherworldly research arm and conceptual think tank.

The researchers and manufacturers, the scientifically minded evil spirits, were busily engaged in their work when I walked in. They paused for a minute and then continued their work as if I was not present. I moved on to the next enclosure, which was a gun manufacturing factory.

As in the one I had just left, the researchers were creating designs for powerful small arms, highly complex and sophisticated rifles, and large long-range rockets and launchers. They were also seriously engaged in their research on newer models and their appropriate bullets and rockets. Two processing divisions were at work here. In one division were a number of processing lines where the parts of the designed weapons were being manufactured and assembled, while the other division, with its own set of processing lines, manufactured the bullets and rockets designed for each weapon.

I had seen enough, so I moved on to the other enclosures. Three of them were still active, with evil spirits manufacturing a variety of simple weapons, like crossbows with up to twelve-arrow loading tracks, modern steel swords, light and aeronautically balanced spears and lances, machetes, crooked and sharp knives, and a host of other war implements. Another two were being used for the design and building of tanks and military vehicles. The last three of the enclosures appeared to be abandoned, but there were telltale signs of them having been used for fighting equipment that was now obsolete. An inspection revealed the designs of the ancient, outmoded fireball and rock throwers, ladders for climbing high walls, iron spears, and bows and arrows that were no longer used in warfare.

As new types of weapons were developed and tested successfully in these evil realms, the same weapons materialized through their agents, who made huge profits setting up factories and manufacturing and selling to dictators eager to seize power and overrun nations. History was replete with such experiences.

The wide field beyond the factories was strewn with various pieces of metal and empty bullet and rocket shells, as well as other items for weapon manufacture. These components indicated that the field was serving as a weapons trial or testing range. I was beckoned to move further down the field and to descend into a valley beneath it. I obeyed and walked for about three miles, during which time the terrain gradually improved; I sagged through marsh first, then loose dirt, then, sandy terrain. The sandy, even path gave way to a gentle incline of about twenty degrees, continuing for two miles, before flattening out into a walking surface of sand layered with rugged, solid rocks.

I looked up to see that I was at the bottom of a very deep valley that stretched for miles. I was encouraged to venture further, until I arrived at a township of coral buildings. I was met by four scantily-attired women who escorted me cautiously. Their eyes revealed both fear and suspicion. They guided me, to a coral throne on which sat a big, shapely woman with very long hair. Behind her throne was a bevy of similarly clad girls, her subjects, baiting her next command.

The queen of the coral kingdom was equally scantily attired. Piercing me with her venomous eyes, she asked why I had come to her kingdom without invitation. Just as she posed the question, her long black hair stood erect to reveal more of her nearly nude body. A hissing sound revealed that the hair that appeared woven into small strands was actually made up of a large number of live, deadly snakes.

I felt embarrassed and repulsed both at her nudity and the snakes who adorned her. I dropped my eyes and attempted to politely apologize for invading her territory, as taught on planet earth. I quickly realized, however, that embarrassment was construed as a sign of weakness. The queen and her bevy of evil subjects unhesitatingly threw large quantities of a sticky, corrosive black fluid at me. Once again, my new spirit body responded intuitively. It not only repelled the corrosive material but propelled it in the opposite direction, towards the attackers, at high velocity. Again, I had failed to keep my eyes on the enemy and almost paid for this neglect.

As they were spirits, the fluid could not corrode their bodies but inflicted such great pain that they writhed and wailed. The queen, who was closest to me, suffered the most. I could not figure out what this effective sticky chemical was, but then, under the instruction of the voice in my mind, I moved farther into their city to a large coral building in which different manufacturing processes were in progress— my question was attracting its response

"You are at the last sector of your training in this dimensional world. This evil spiritual kingdom is beneath the sea. In the spirit state, you cannot feel the water around you. The sand, the rocky terrain, and the buildings of coral are indications of the location of this kingdom. This ruler of this kingdom of women is the evil queen, who has taken her residence in the sea and has enticed thousands of seafarers to shipwreck and death.

"The main duty of the numerous females in this abode is to focus on women on Earth and design provocative dresses, eyelashes, artificial nails, extreme eye shades, enticing lipstick, nose- and ear-piercing tools and rings, tattoos, and other similar beauty artifacts for extremists to artificially enhance the beauty and attractiveness of women to excite the desires of weak, sensual men.

"In the name of fashion, indecent dresses, intended to scintillate men's lustful desires, are produced in this realm. They are seductively marketed, sold, and worn in your societies, promoting whoredom." I entered the large coral factory and observed the workers, all women, busily overseeing their chemical blends and the design and production of other items for creation on the physical planet by their converts.

"You have traversed the full length and scope of the source of all types of sin, or violation of the laws of the Supremos, on your planet. From this dimensional world is spewed the entire evil, destructive arsenal developed to derail humans from the true path. Humans are tempted to disobey by refusing to do what the Supremos require of them or choosing to do things contrary to what is taught by the Creators— committing sins of omission and commission. These are the two classifications under which all sin may be defined. You have observed that all the efforts of the master of evil have been focused on enticing humans to succumb to the sensual desires of the flesh—including greed and pride. All sin stems from fleshly desires placed over godly ones.

"Equipped with this knowledge and the authority and power that you have been endowed with," the voice in my mind continued, "you are now about ready to leave this dimensional world to the real one to complete your training."

The next moment, I found myself again back in the Dome. The leader of the Guardians was waiting with refreshing drink and food to nourish me. I returned to my emaciated physical frame, which I had left in the Dome for my trip to the dimensional spirit world. My Guardian then issued further instructions to me and left as usual.

CHAPTER 8

The Peaceful Kingdom
Beneath the Sea

After I had rested for about three hours—time enough for my physical body to be fully rejuvenated—I approached the panel that opened the portal to my last training assignment. I had been told that in my final assignment, I needed to visit a kingdom that was very old and located beneath the sea. Its existence was unknown to the human population on Earth. Unlike my earlier trips, I needed to inhabit my physical body to meet the leaders and to be finally equipped to begin my duties to the human race. The leaders of the kingdom, I was informed, would be my allies and would be very helpful to me whenever circumstances would necessitate their help. The kingdom had been of immense help to those who had preceded me as Wackida in earlier millennia.

I was told of a legendary Wackida, who later became ruler during the last fifty-five years of his assignment. He had removed a mysterious sword planted in a stone that he had actually placed there centuries earlier during one of his assignments. To the superstitious citizenry, this fulfilled an omen that he was to be their next ruler. The sword was formed from a hard, unbreakable metal called rhumbion, and was given to him as a gift by the ancient leaders of the kingdom. I was happy to hear that he ruled with wisdom and built a strong and powerful kingdom in the kingdom I was about to visit. He was greatly loved by his subjects until his death. He is still remembered today as one of the greatest rulers of the land.

I braced myself, touched the panel, and confidently stepped into the dark space inside. There was a sudden flash of light. In the next moment, my body was lifted, and I felt water swirling all around me. As I gasped for air but drew in water through my mouth and nostrils, I felt, for the second time, my spirit body's oxygen extraction system activated. I felt as comfortable as I'd been when I'd awakened to fluid in the biosynthetic machine. I relaxed as I effortlessly and calmly sank into the deep sea.

I could feel and yet withstand the pressure of the seawater on my body. I did not experience the painful nitrogen bends that I'd heard so much about. I felt full of energy and strength, and my vision improved, enabling me to see further into the depths of the ocean as I sank deeper and deeper toward the ocean floor. Different types of fish, marine mammals, and vicious predators—some of which were strange to me— were all around. I sank deeper, however, I encountered only a variety of flatfish before the animal population thinned out considerably. I sank about ten yards down, toward the ocean floor—a level the fish themselves appeared to be avoiding.

There appeared to be no life forms in this oceanic area. I'd believed that the flattened shape of the fish was an adaptation to withstand the high water pressure, to enable them to live on the ocean floor. So I was surprised to discover that even the flatfish were avoiding this area. Then I struck the defined barrier and sank through it onto the ocean floor. As I sank, I felt a sensation, similar to the flow of an electric current through my body. At that moment, the solid rock floor gave way beneath me. I now understood that the fish were repelled by the high electrical charge.

I fell for about a hundred yards onto another rocky floor and watched the area that had given way quickly seal up above me. I stood up on the rocky floor and looked far into the distance. It looked like empty space. Suddenly, a faint humming sound, like motors running, met my ears. It was then that I noticed that the water around me was swirling and moving in a number of directions and, at the same time, dropping in level at a rapid rate. I figured that a set of powerful pumps were sucking the water out of the space and replacing it with air. This continued for about half an hour until the water had all been sucked out of the space and had been replaced with oxygen-rich air.

A panel opened on the rocky floor on which I was standing, revealing a flight of well-constructed metallic stairs going down to another level. This was followed by a very bright light. By the time my vision adjusted to its intensity, I saw men and women in smart-fitting, shiny uniforms standing in front of me. They all looked so physically young, yet there was something about them illustrative of a high level of maturity, intelligence, and wisdom. The epidermal layer of their uncovered forearms appeared to be covered with almost imperceptible tiny scales, similar to my modified skin. The women were very beautiful and had long hair of various shades. In fact, it was somehow evident in their countenance and assembly, that they shared a common Parentage. They smiled at me and beckoned me to follow them. A touch on the rocky roof near the staircase closed the gap above and opened a doorway near the foot of the stairs. We descended the staircase and entered a large chamber furnished with very sophisticated furniture and equipment. From this chamber, I was led down a long, illuminated corridor into a large open field where a number of strange vehicles were parked in hangars. I recognized different sizes of spherical vessels resembling the mysterious flying saucers claimed to have been sighted on the planet in the past.

There were many workshops surrounding the large open field. Different types of machines and equipment were under construction in these workshops. One of my escorts gave each of us a device that we strapped to the base of each foot and locked at the ankle. A thin strap of strong, flexible metallic wire linked the lock on the ankle to an adjustable helmet at the back. My escorts demonstrated how to wear the device. I was later informed that the contraptions were called transporters and were designed to respond to the wearer's mental impulses for locomotion. I immediately thought about crossing the length of the field. I arrived in a matter of minutes. Initially, it was difficult for me to control the transporter efficiently, but I soon got used to it and floated along with my escorts to another distant range of buildings.

Up to this time, not a word had been spoken. All communication had occurred through gesticulations and signs. I began to wonder whether my benevolent hosts had any language at all. I was led into an enclosure with a large tower constructed from a crystalline material that resembled thick glass. The top was shaped like a mushroom, and the whole structure had a greenish hue. On the walls of the base of this huge tower were outlines of a series of panel doors. I was led into a chamber that opened to us at the touch of one of the panels. One of my escorts motioned me to sit on a heavily padded chair and to hold on to knobs on the arms. He pointed to a shiny helmet, gesturing that I should first put it on and firmly tighten the strap before holding the chair knobs.

As soon as I sat down and held onto the two knobs, one with each hand, a transparent flexible material quickly enclosed my body from the neck to the feet. Once again, I heard a humming sound, followed by the sensation of an electric current running through my spine. At the same time, a faint glow in the region of my forehead turned gradually to a bright pulsating light. How long this sensation lasted, I cannot be certain. I only recollect that the feeling in my body stopped as suddenly as it had begun, the flexible enclosure vanished, and I was left sitting on the padded chair.

One of the escorts spoke for the first time. To my surprise, I could understand everything she said even though she spoke in a dialect that was not familiar to me. Anticipating my curiosity, my escort spoke: "The cubicle you entered is part of a complex machine designed by our scientists to mentally implant our language, or any other programmed language of choice, into the memory of foreordained, approved leaders who visit us," " she said. "You have just gone through the designed program and can now understand and speak our dialect as if you have lived among us for years. In addition, you now possess an enhanced capacity to learn different languages after a few seconds of registering their phonetic memes. We shall now take you to our rulers. All other things you are required to learn for your mission shall be determined by our council of rulers and shall be imparted to you according to the will of the Supremos. There, any concerns or questions you have will be addressed."

I was taken to a large room where three men sat at the head of a long crystal table. They were gorgeously attired and were obviously of the noble, ruling class. On the sides of the table sat twelve other nobles, six on each side. An empty chair stood alone at the foot of the long crystal table. The room was empty save for the table and the chairs occupied by the twelve nobles and a number of healthy, beautiful potted plants, which lined the inner walls of the chamber. After I had been ushered into the chamber, my escorts departed. I was in the presence of the council that ruled this kingdom. I was instructed to sit in the chair at the foot of the table facing the three high-ranking rulers. I later learned that the rulers were made up of the Head Ruler in the middle, in whom all power and authority was vested, and two nobles who sat with him, one on either side, as advisors. They constituted the *Kimsuburu*, interpreted as the "great ruling head" of the whole kingdom. The twelve others were the councilors, or the *Samaviak,* each of whom was assigned the governance of one of the twelve cities of the kingdom. They met once a month as the Great Council and occasionally during emergency situations to deliberate on issues of the kingdom.

Two advisors assisted each of the twelve governors. Thus, each city was governed with love and justice by three wise and committed men, while the whole kingdom was ruled by the fifteen nobles seated at the crystal table. There was law and order because even the Kimsuburu, the most powerful of the ruling body, was subject to the councilor who ruled the capital city within which they lived as the city ruler's subjects.

"Welcome to our world within your planet," the head ruler began. "The laws of our kingdom of twelve cities, with a total population of one hundred and fifty million, are based on the universal laws of perfection. For that reason, we have increased in wisdom as we have sought knowledge and been enlightened by the Supremos.

"Our scientists have been blessed with knowledge over the centuries resulting in the elimination of disease from our society, construction of all types of machines and technical accessories to modify our genetic constitution, enrich our lives, and prolong our existence. We are often in direct contact with the surface of the planet, from which we draw electrons to neutralize released radicals. Radicals are responsible for rapid aging, and neutralizing them allows us to slow down this process within ourselves. Our scientists have determined that our average lifespan is about five hundred years.

"We have learned to respect, love, and adapt to nature. Our studies have revealed natural secrets we have adopted as the basis for the design and the building of simple as well as complex machinery, some of which you saw in the field on your way to the language chamber. Our research into all subjects, including physics, chemistry, human anatomy, neurology, physiology, psychology, as well as advances made in biological studies conducted on plants and animals, have empowered us to create an empire here and adapt to living beneath the ocean.

"This adaptation has occurred over decades, as our scientists have modified the constitution of our bodies by implanting special genes in our cells. The resultant genetic changes have made it so our bodies, particularly our breathing organs and skin, can withstand the harsh conditions of the undersea environment. Though initially our people came and left with the help of artificially designed breathing apparatus and had to be fully protected by diving suits, we are now able to extract oxygen from water and overcome the painful nitrogen bends triggered by exposure of the normal body to the high pressure of water in the deep.

"Our skins are able to withstand the high pressure of the sea water on our bodies while at the same time repelling all sea predators. Your skin, we have learned from the Wackida of old, is structurally more advanced and can also withstand underwater pressure. Additionally, it can absorb unlimited energy from the environment.

"We are generally omnivorous but live mostly on special seaweeds and other identified high-yielding, nutritious sea plants. These are scientifically cultivated by our agricultural scientists to provide us with the rich supply of antioxidants that we need to supplement our metabolic processes. In addition, a few nutritious berries as well as fruits, vegetables, and roots are cultivated on small, uninhabited islands in various parts of the planet. Our trained personnel oversee the planting seasons to ensure very high yields, which are then harvested, processed, preserved, and stored to prepare us for the next season.

"We also eat preserved lean fish, which we snare on our deep-sea fishing trips. We have created the ideal conditions—a replica of the planet's atmosphere— in which to plant food for the rearing of cattle, sheep, birds, and other herbivores from which we obtain milk and meat.

We eat meat very sparingly, however, as cautioned by all the teachers of the universal law of perfection.

"Each city has been equipped with facilities for the efficient storage of about three years' food requirement for the community. This is supplied to the citizens on a first-in, first-out basis to ensure we do not stock any products for over three years. In fact, we are a community where every citizen lives in contentment because we take care of the needs of everyone. There is no poverty among us. As leaders, our duty is to serve the people, not to lord over them.

"We see to the welfare of every citizen, and our service to them has created a bond of trust and respect for us and promoted love among all citizenry. The universal law of perfection, upon which our laws are based, has created a people who live in comfort, peace, and mutual trust and with love and concern for one another's welfare. It has contributed to our advancement in wisdom and knowledge, and our progression as a people. This is how it all began:

"Thousands of years ago, our race built a civilization on the surface of the planet, on the shores of a great ocean. Our leaders were taught and applied the principles of the universal law of perfection to enact laws with which we were governed. Seeking each other's welfare brought many blessings, and we were endowed with great knowledge and wisdom.

Our scientists discovered an ore that, when processed with other chemicals, created a special translucent metal that was very hard yet supple when thin. Fused layers of this new metallic substances formed a tough, solid block that could withstand the impact of any force at a very high velocity. No scratch. No dent. This was the perfect metal. It was employed in the construction of many of our vessels and instruments of labor. It could easily cut through stone, metal and any other materials of this planet's origin. This metal was named rhumbion.

"The principle of photosynthesis in plants also yielded great knowledge. Our ancestors fused billions of interconnected miniature photonic cells into rhumbion, in its liquid state and cast it in the form of tall tower of interlinked broad-based circular electric conductors of fortified aluminum and copper. The structure of the top section looked like a great crystalline mushroom when viewed from afar.

"It was from this source that our ancestors obtained unlimited energy to power sophisticated generators for all their lighting, heating, machinery, and vehicular operation, and to fill all other energy requirements. With this unlimited source of energy, the age of inventions was ushered in, and energy was produced in new and accessible forms. About a century after the erection of the energy crystal, our ancestors had improved to the point where they were able to become highly efficient in the trapping of energy from the sun.

"During this age, came the invention of artificial gills and a light, tough, flexible diving suit constructed from a thin layer of *rhumbion*. With this equipment, our scientists could spend hours in the oceanic deep, protected from the water pressure. It was during this period that the idea of a city beneath the ocean was born. The canopy of our current abode, with its tight-sealing entry and departure areas, was constructed in the deepest part of the ocean, disguised to look exactly like the rocky ocean floor and given a charge of electricity to keep away all living things. A habitational equivalent of twelve big cities was demarcated, and several years were spent constructing the second layer of *rhumbion* beneath the first, and to install powerful submersible marine pumps to pump out the water from the enclosure.

"This was followed by the construction of the cities, each with an improved version of the power crystal tower adapted to the ocean depth to provide lighting. These were equipped with special devices to carry energy in the form of electricity via nona-waves to receiver cells installed in all machines to reconvert the electric power back to kinetic energy, enabling the machines' function.

"Laboratories were thereafter constructed to produce a combination of gases comparable to the makeup of the planet's atmosphere. The creation of an artificial atmosphere similar to that of the planet, with an artificial sun, was also a success. Seawater was desalinated with machines our ancestors designed, and it was purified for storage in numerous overhead tanks for agricultural purposes and to cater to other human needs. The planting of select, genetically-modified trees and the rearing of genetically improved ruminants and birds began. The idea was to create a balanced, self-sustaining environment conducive to the survival of both plants and animals. No carnivore or animal with predatory characteristics that had not been domesticated was permitted in the new abode.

"After this, construction of homes began. Though the majority of the citizens were not aware of the inventions beneath the sea, their leaders occasionally spent some time with the scientists and their families in the newly constructed homes. They did this to ensure that the cities were equipped with the ideal environmental conditions conducive to human habitation.

"These were unselfish, sacrificial services and a demonstration of commitment by our leaders that earned them the continued allegiance and support of all the citizenry. They taught the universal laws of love and sacrifice, and they always were ready to demonstrate these laws by example. They would readily put their lives on the line to ensure the safety of those they ruled in love.

"Before your departure, you will be taken to one of the numerous forests and the breeding fields and farms for rearing useful domesticated ruminants to see the miracle performed by our ancestors. The rulers, then fifteen in all, twelve of whom were assigned specific duties and worked under the rule of the one ruler and two counselors, charged the scientists to construct premises for education akin to what existed in their societies. In response, schools, both technical and of the arts, and a host of technical workshops and additional scientific research laboratories sprang up in every city.

"With the success achieved in the ocean cities project," the ruler continued, "our ancestors shifted their attention to conducting research into outer space. Knowledge in astronomy was already far advanced among our people. They already had fairly accurate charts of our solar system and our galaxy. Space travel became the focus and challenge of the chief scientific minds.

"Physicists and astronomists persevered until they discovered the Trilliwave, which permeates the galaxy and which could serve as a channel for receiving and converting the energy beamed into space from the power crystal into waves. These waves were then transformed to kinetic energy to move space vehicles into space and beyond.

"They designed our first spacecraft with the least resistance to speed while traveling in the planet's atmosphere. The first unmanned spacecraft constructed in the form of one inverted saucer joined to another upright saucer at the wider circumference was launched into space successfully. It was guided by radio waves to return into a predetermined spot in the sea close to our city of abode. The first test, however, exposed some unforeseen weaknesses. The craft could not travel beyond a particular distance in space, delimiting the craft. Again, they proceeded to work on the powering, durability, and stability of the craft.

"The design was modified, the outer shell being constructed with layers of *rhumbion* embedded with a rich supply of the miniature photonic cells, to trap energy that fed and activated miniature generators installed in the crafts. These powerful generators provided electric power to run efficient jet engines for propulsion. The inner shell, which housed the pilots, was also constructed with *rhumbion* and was insulated and comfortably furnished on the inside. The space between the two translucent metals housed cameras, generators, jet engines, and other aeronautic machines, including a gyroscopic device that held the inner vessel in a horizontal position despite any maneuvers executed by the craft. Speed was also critically considered. After a number of modifications and rounds of testing, they succeeded in constructing the first ideal multi-directional vessel that was fast, tough, stable, and easy to control by touch buttons and programmed voice commands.

"Then teams constructed huge deep-space satellites and programmed them to track the sun and feed our space vessels with energy via the Trilliwave for deep space travel. Very thin, supple layers of *rhumbion* were lined with the appropriate fabric and converted into spacesuits, helmets of various designs, and other protective wear. Our ancestors then embarked on space travel and prepared more accurate charts to map out the galaxy, solar systems, and other planetary bodies. Since that time, there have been vast improvements made to the prototype to give us the efficient, comfortable, and almost indestructible vessels we have now. We now possess accurate maps of our galaxy and the distances of some nearby galaxies. You will be given a demonstration flight into space before you leave our city.

"Our civilization was at the peak of its progress when it was threatened by imminent destruction. We were a community of peace-abiding citizens, and violence against other humans was unknown among us. We had the technology but refused to create any destructive weapons against fellow humans. And yet, our scouts, who had been spying on other primitive, warlike empires not too distant from our cities, learned that they were planning imminent attacks.

"Our supreme intelligent leaders accurately predicted the time of the intended attack, so they evacuated all our inhabitants, our inventions, and our wealth to the cities beneath the ocean and manufactured explosives to destroy our cities on the shore. They did not desire to lose a single life or take the life of an enemy, so their scientists diverted the enemy by destroying the empty cities (assumed to be full of inhabitants) when the offensive armies, were about a mile from attacking the nearest city.

"The explosives were designed to implode and bury the cities in the ocean and deep in the sand, and this is exactly what happened. With the implosion, all buildings with their initial crude, land-mounted energy crystals sank into the sea to be buried on the ocean floor. The surface dwellers, our ancestors later learned, drew the conclusion that a natural disaster destroyed our cities and the whole population. Since new, improved, ocean-adapted derivatives of the energy crystal had been constructed by then to serve the cities beneath the ocean and were working more efficiently, and though they knew the location of the sunken energy crystal, no attempt was made to retrieve or deactivate it.

"Ever since that time, our existence has been kept secret from the surface dwellers on the planet, except the Wackida and others who became ensnared in the ocean tides and were in danger of drowning. We rescued them out of sympathy and, by their choice, our scientists adapted them to live among us. We have protected agents who live in disguise for periods of time among the surface dwellers to learn of their governments' plans. They bring messages to us so we can take countermeasures to stop any evil plans that might destroy the planet before its foreordained time. We have information that our females, who are occasionally seen swimming in their electronically propelled tail fins, are mistaken for legendary mermaids.

We still explore space and have had occasions to land in isolated areas on the planet on our return to conduct some research. A few of these expeditions to the surface have been spotted and mistaken to be the work of aliens. Our spacesuits easily support such a fiction. Some of our helmets were designed with antennae as sensors, and with two wide, convex visual ports where our eyes are located. Traveling from space, our spacecrafts must plunge into the sea to dock in our hangers and are occasionally seen by surface dwellers' scientists. As a result, government officials send crude underwater vehicles called "*submarines*" equipped with detectors, to search for the crafts on the seabed. Their attempts are usually unsuccessful, so they don't pose much of a threat.

"We are your only allies against evil on this planet. For this reason, many of the Wackida were sent to our ancestors in their time to be tutored and equipped with weapons beyond their genetically engineered defenses.

"You may now retire from our presence," came the command from the ruler. "After your body has been nourished, you will be given the opportunity to see the miracle performed by our ancestors and learn how to use some of our inventions."

With this statement, the chief of the rulers pressed a switch on the knob of the arm of his chair, and my escorts entered and beckoned to me to follow them. I was taken to another chamber, where my escorts gave me a meal of vegetables and fish and left.

As I ate the nourishing food, I could not help reflecting on what I had been told. This empire beneath the sea was at the peak of its civilization because it had lived the perfect law of the universe for so many generations, and every citizen was at peace. They were content and never in want. They would never be misled by the enticement of the evil one because generations upon generations had lived the law and known its value and benefits. Greed, covetousness, envy, pride, unrighteous desires, and all that promoted negative traits in humans appeared to have been eliminated in this society.

If only the surface dwellers would accept and live the perfect law, what great blessings would be bestowed upon all humanity! Such is not the case, however. Counter methodologies and tools used in generations past to deceive offspring of the Supremos are continually upgraded and used by evil forces to lead mankind to destruction. It was clear to me that rising generations had not learned from their predecessors.

My train of thought was interrupted by my escorts' arrival on the scene. They invited me to accompany them on a tour of the technical wing of their abode. Our first port of call was the hangars where space exploration ships of various sizes were parked. I was taken to a small craft designed for the exploration of our solar system. I was encased in a shiny spacesuit that was light, flexible, and comfortable. But for the front magnetic overlap seal, there appeared to be no other seam or joint.

I was strapped into a comfortable seat before a control panel of microphones and touch buttons inside the upper saucer of the craft, which constituted the cockpit. Two of my escorts, clad in similar spacesuits, joined me in similar seats for the trip. Three empty seats suggested the craft was designed for six. Large windows, equipped with changing positional maps of our galaxy, gave each occupant an unlimited view of the craft's location and the surrounding vastness of space.

When the engines started, I noticed that only the outer shell below the cockpit started to rotate. I felt the craft rise as the top of the hangar opened and the plates meshed tightly with layers of *rhumbion*. The shaft that was formed collapsed to seal off the lower barrier, while another opened above, through which the craft rose gently. When we rose to the correct elevation, the new shaft and the other layers of *rhumbion* fell successively into place, sealing off our exit. I felt the vessel rise smoothly and rapidly to the surface of the ocean. By a complex radar and closed-circuit system that revealed the identity of any object within a one-mile radius, we certified that there was no vehicle or sea creature in our path. I now came to understand that deep-sea creatures had been mercifully kept at bay by the permanent electrical charge above the artificial ocean floor. We paused at the surface for a brief period, during which I could faintly hear the jet-engine propulsion sound crescendo. Then we shot up out of the ocean and through the planet's atmosphere at an incredible speed—we were soon out in space. *How can a vehicle*

overcome the gravitational and frictional forces and move at this speed?
I wondered to myself.

My companions saw the bewilderment in my face and smiled at me.
"Earth's gravity, atmospheric pressure, and other frictional forces must
be overcome before a vehicle can move at this speed," they explained.
"Our scientists discovered ways to adapt our spacecraft to accomplish
this. They invented macro-atom manipulator valves and installed them
evenly at the top, the bottom, and around the circumference of the
vessels.

"These manipulator valves, when activated by the astronauts, disturb
the stability of all free molecules that are fifty feet in the direct chosen
path for the vessel. This initiates the transfer of electrons in range to
the valves to create a negatively charged head. The craft is then drawn
magnetically by the positively charged atmosphere of protons in the
immediate path of the moving vessel. The magnetic attraction created
between the negatively charged outer shell of the craft and the positively
charged proton-infested atmosphere works to create a frictionless path
through which the vessel glides without resistance.

"By successive, rapid activations of these valves, the vessel glides
through the frictionless atmosphere, and the craft is rapidly drawn
up into space. This mechanical charging system could also be used
to maneuver the craft horizontally or in any chosen direction in
the atmosphere at an incredible speed without encountering much
resistance. Creating the same magnetic effect all around the craft causes
the varied directional pulls to negate each other's effect, allowing the
craft to hover suspended at a stationary spot in the sky. Neutrons that are
only occasionally loosened from the protons offer very little frictional
resistance.

"We have not attained, or even come close to, the speed of light,
though. Our scientists correctly perceived that any effort to travel close
to the speed of light would result in the disintegration of our mortal, yet

imperfect, bodies. Only the Supremos and the Guardians, we were told, have the technology to utilize light in relation to corporeal travel. They can travel instantaneously, by thought speed. We were also informed that the knowledge and ability to teleport would be given to us when, through obedience to the universal law of life, we qualify for the gift of life after this life."

I watched with wonder at the orderliness and beauty of the heavenly bodies. We came close enough to observe the colors of some of the planets in our solar system, but not close enough to be in range of their gravitational forces. After some time in space, we came back to Earth and docked in the same hanger beneath the sea. Everything that I observed or was taught was retained in my memory, even though I did not yet fully comprehend each applied, scientific principle and imprint It was satisfying to learn that humans could develop to this almost perfect state on the planet through obedience to the great principles of the universal law of perfection.

The next sector we visited was the open field, with its artificial replica of the planet's atmosphere. It looked so natural, with trees, different types of birds, and herbivorous mammals. They looked so peaceful. Further down this field were farms for the cultivation of a variety of vegetables, food crops, and fruits to supplement what they cultivated and occasionally harvested from the planet's surface. A variety of grass, hay, and barley also grew here to be used for feeding the cows and goats to produce milk and meat.

I visited their canneries and storage for preserved food. I went to their manufacturing sector to observe different factories busily producing a variety of useful products. These included spacesuits; mechanized swimming tailfins; micro-suction tactile hand gloves for safe climbing of smooth surfaces and high structures; mechanical transporters, and other travel gear.

Other engineering sections focused on the manufacturing of heavy duty machines, such as spacecraft, ocean bed crawlers, sophisticated weapons, and, surprisingly, other simple weapons and tools. Among the simple weapons that I recognized were miniature crossbows that could shoot out, over a long distance, an unlimited number of high-voltage electrical bolts instead of arrows. I also saw energized javelins, energized swords and shields, and ray guns that could decimate any structure. Mechanized, serrated-edge machetes could double for saws.

I was assured that some of these weapons were meant for defense against unexpected attacks. They were used occasionally for the temporal immobilization of their assailants to enable escape. Sometimes, they came under attack on their trips outside the oceanic cities for research and snaring fish for food.

I was given a gift of a ray gun, a mechanical transporter, a pair of micro-suction gloves, a crossbow, an energized machete, an energized sword and shield manufactured from *rhumbion*, and a mechanized tailfin. I was instructed on the usage of these sophisticated versions of familiar and was cautioned to use them wisely. I was finally taken back to the council hall of leaders to thank the rulers and bid them good-bye. I was then guided out of their kingdom.

With the tailfin strapped to my waist, I propelled myself rapidly toward the surface. A look back toward the ocean floor revealed no trace of the inlet to the kingdom I had left a moment ago. With one final glance, I continued upward and was whisked instantly to the Sacred Dome of the Guardians the moment I struck the surface.

EPISODE II:
THE EMPIRE OF
ZAMUNSTRA

CHAPTER 9

The Lost Empire

I was received back to the Sacred Dome by all ten Guardians and was informed that I had completed all my training assignments successfully and was to finally be ordained, to receive the authority to embark on my sacred assignment. I had presumed that my foreordination, initial invitation, and preparation by the Guardians was authorized by the Supremos and, therefore, was adequate authority to empower me to start. The leader of the Guardians then gave me a lecture on authority.

"Magnus," he started, "being called and prepared alone does not constitute authority to embark on a divine mission. As past records of your planet's history attest, one must receive authority to act from one who holds it themselves. All authority must be traced back to divine authority, granted by the Supremos. This sets apart the true messenger from the false one.

"Your history has records of kings," he continued, "and appointed religious leaders who had no divine authority, imposing man-made laws to run religious organizations. The inhabitants of this planet still accept these false, man-made laws as the source of divine authority. They are ignorant of the truth. They are still under this illusion, to the triumph of Xoedikus. You have been a witness, in the world of spirits, to the state of the religious leaders and kings who were misled and those who rejected the truth as taught by the Agents in favor of what these unauthorized leaders taught them. You saw their misery in the Realm of the Noble and the Ignorant. There is, therefore, human authority and divine authority."

We continued on until we entered a well-furnished room behind one of the panel doors. He motioned me to sit on a padded chair. He was then joined by the two other Guardians I had seen with him in the forest. The three walked toward me and proceeded to gently lay their palms on my head. With the seven others looking on, and the leader as the voice, they conferred the necessary authority on me and blessed me to receive the power, strength, direction, and wisdom necessary to fulfill my millennial assignment successfully. I was ordained, or set apart, for the work to which I was called.

"This room will serve as your abode for the most part of your assignment. You may marry and live in any city of your choice, among humans, within the last century of your service. After you complete each one of your assignments, center your thoughts on this room, and you will be teleported home. And remember, we will always be available to offer any assistance necessary," he concluded.

With this assurance, the whole team of Guardians bid me success in all my endeavors and disappeared from view without further instruction.

I was left alone to figure out where I was to start. After feeling a kind of mantle descend upon me, and pondering its implications, I stepped out of the room to see that one of the panels was glowing. I knew that the passage beyond that panel door would lead me to my first real assignment. Equipped with a few of my new weapons, I stepped up to it and touched it. It slid open with a *whoosh*, and I stepped into the passage to find myself on the top of a high mountain overlooking a seemingly unending canopy of thick green foliage. As I focused, my memory took me back in time through the brief history of one of the greatest civilizations that had existed at this location. The empire had been blessed by the Supremos for centuries but, through the pride and uncompromising conduct of a young emperor, it was ultimately invaded by evil.

The ancient empire of Zamunstra, nestled in the fertile valleys of a range of spent volcanoes, had been ruled by a succession of emperors who had continually sought wisdom from the Supremos. Their vast empire was made up of six great cities, and it had only two passes for entry, both heavily guarded. One was on the south end of the empire, and the other to the east of the city of government. Access into the empire could be gained only through either of these passes. The position of the empire offered its people security from the barbaric tribes who lived on the surrounding plains.

The western border of their land was protected by the strong currents of a wide and fast-flowing river created by a great waterfall, which roared over a high precipice west of their empire. Tributaries of the river passed through the empire. They were tapped to create an effective irrigation system to sustain the cultivation of food year-round. Inhabitants of this land had lived in peace and advanced in knowledge and wisdom for so many centuries. They were far ahead of other civilizations of the same era, scientifically, agriculturally, and spiritually.

This civilization was envied by other ancient people on the planet. Newcomers were frequently disallowed; anyone hoping to settle among them needed to accept an oath to live by the laws of the land. This precaution was adopted in order to avoid contamination of seed and spirit of rule by intermixing with the evil citizens of the other known empires and their neighboring tribes.

However, this era of peace and enlightenment came to its close. There came a time when the eldest of the two sons of the ruling emperor, Aristarchus, was crowned as the rightful heir of the people, after the demise of his aged father. Xenos was hot-headed and arrogant and chose to retire the elders who formed the council of advisors. In their stead, he appointed inexperienced youths, against the advice of the wise elders and also his younger brother, Thordis. In time, the firm, age-old laws for settlers were relaxed, and strangers were allowed to settle among them without any commitment.

Before the turn of two decades, their population had grown considerably and was on the brink of upheaval. The peace they had enjoyed for centuries had been disturbed by acts of wickedness, greed, and intrigue, as citizens were attracted by profits from the rich gold mines and fertile valleys of the empire. Before long, violation of the laws of the land became commonplace, and control began slipping out of the naive hands of the emperor and his youthful advisors. Thordis, who had always walked in the footsteps of his father, persistently tried to persuade his brother to trust and rely on the wise elderly councilors to restore order. Unfortunately, however, he only succeeded in earning the recalcitrant emperor's displeasure. Xenos threatened to have him arrested and imprisoned.

Thordis's mysterious disappearance shortly thereafter raised suspicions of foul play on the part of the impetuous emperor. Efforts by a royal search party to find him proved futile, and although Xenos vehemently denied his hand in his brother's disappearance, he was suspected to have ordered his abduction and possible execution.

The mystery of the missing youngest son of Aristarchus was never solved and eventually faded from the minds of the people. In time, Xenos, who was without a child, was poisoned by a servant who had secretly sworn loyalty to an ambitious and wicked opponent of the emperor: a rich and arrogant settler named Draconis, who had a large following. With his younger brother given up for dead and no blood successor to be found, this wicked man seized power, and the empire fell into darkness.

The plunder of the rich gold mines became the focus of the

usurper. The Indigenes, once a peaceful people, were forced to labor in the expanded mines and farms. It was pitiful to see these peaceful subjects of the empire suffer so. They bore their burdens without hope of deliverance. Generation after generation passed in which a succession of wicked emperors reigned. These emperors protected the mines and evergreen farm lands with a firm fist. They falsely accused visitors of being spies and executed them. Zamunstra eventually became a feared and then a forsaken place. After three centuries, with the migration of many of the neighboring communities, the memory of its existence was lost to succeeding generations.

The cries of the true Zamunstrans, descendants of the righteous citizens of the empire, had reached the ears of the Supremos. The oppression in their own land was now beyond endurance. I had been elected to start my mission by going to their rescue. I stood quietly on top of the mountain considering carefully my strategy.

I focused my thoughts on the time the empire had enjoyed peace under the reign of the last righteous emperor. Detailed scenes of his reign flashed through my mind's eye, up to the time of his death. These were followed by scenes of the crowning of his firstborn as successor, as well as the events of his tyrannical rule. Then, an image of the younger son of the emperor, who had mysteriously disappeared from the community, came to my view. The strange events surrounding his mysterious disappearance began to unfold before my eyes.

As a youth, Thordis was fascinated by the fast-flowing river that ran through the empire and wondered about its origins. Curiosity led him and some of his very close friends to secretly investigate the source, and this led them to the vertical wall over which the waterfall fell into the valley. On one such occasion, the young man was investigating the misty rock surface under the waterfall and discovered a crevice wide enough to admit him. Against the advice of his friends, he forced himself through the tight passage and wormed his way forward until he saw a faint light ahead of him. As he moved further along, the passage widened, and he could move freely toward the light.

Finally, Thordis emerged to find himself in a large valley with rich fauna and a large pond of clear, fresh water with extending tributaries. It was formed by trickles of water seeping through from the river above through many tiny fissures in the rock wall. Other tributaries ran through the valley and meandered through subterranean passages to empty into others. The sky could be seen above the high rocky walls of the valley, which held more than enough resources to sustain life. For over four hours, Thordis investigated the virgin valley with its rich supply of fruit trees, birds, and rodents. He finally rejoined his anxious friends and swore them all to secrecy before recounting his miraculous discovery.

From that time forth, the group paid regular visits to the valley. They equipped themselves with tools to widen the hidden entrance for easier passage. They also created a slab of rock to fit into the passage and hide the entry point. By the time of his father's death, Thordis and his friends had constructed a few settlements in the secret valley and had introduced a variety of fingerings into the large pond and the other tributaries. They had also secretly smuggled foals, sheep, and calves into the location. When his brother threatened to arrest him, he decided that it was time to settle in the prepared valley with his trusted friends. They quickly gathered some extra necessities for the settlement and, at an appointed time, vanished from society.

Thordis became their leader, and in the years following, he reinstituted the old laws in their community. The community flourished and prospered by the hand of the Supremos who responds generously to all those who strive to obey his law. Occasionally, Thordis and his troupe disguised themselves to visit the old community for trade. While there, they observed the level of crime and wickedness that had permeated the government and lifestyle of their society until the death of Xenos and the seizure of power by Draconis. They sadly watched the plight of their kinsmen as they were forced to slave away in the mines and on farms. By this time, Thordis' group had become self-sufficient. They decided to avoid the risk of discovery by their former community, so they fitted the carved stone slab into place for what appeared to be the final time and sealed off their exit, severing any contact with past connections.

Thordis and his people lived happily and died peacefully in their old age, and the eldest son of this righteous ruler succeeded his father in leading the community. From generation to generation, they lived in a state of contentment under righteous rulers from this lineage. Over a period of many centuries, the knowledge of the old community became lost to the new community. Things would have remained this way had the current leader not stumbled upon ancient records of the history of his people hidden by their first ancestral settler and decided to investigate it. He located the carved stone and ventured, in disguise, into the old community to see for himself the plight and sorrow of the descendants of a people who had been their kinsmen so many generations earlier. This ruler then narrated the history of their people, of the old empire, to his subjects. In compassion, a collective decision was made by the people to fight to deliver their kinsmen from oppression, to reclaim their land, and reinstate their own citizens. They cried to the Supremos for assistance day and night. My assignment was to aid them in response to their mighty prayers of faith.

Having learned what had happened and what needed to be done, I decided that finding my way into the valley was the first thing I needed to do. I felt a prompting to look up toward the skies. I did so and was startled by the sight of a white object in the distance, swooping down toward me at a rapid pace. At first, it looked like a bird, but to my great surprise, a beautiful white stallion with wings and saddle landed in front of me, rearing up on its hind legs.

Before me stood a mythical stallion known from my favorite

childhood stories as Pegasus. He looked into my eyes and then whinnied loudly. Miraculously, I could understand what he was trying to communicate. He wanted me to mount him. *Had I been endowed with the gift to understand the languages of animals?* I had been assured in my youth that the flying horse was a myth, a creation from the imaginations of Greek writers, but here he stood before me, the beautiful stallion from those tales of adventure and glory.

I gathered my courage and mounted the flying stallion. As I clutched tightly to the short reigns, he soared into the air, darted toward the green canopy covering the land, and broke through it into open air. Below us was a rushing river, leading to a habitation near a waterfall. I supposed that this was the habitation I'd been summoned to visit and assist. Pegasus circled for a moment above the waterfall before swooping down into the valley, where he landed on a patch of grass near a pond of clear water.

This time I was alert and clearly heard Pegasus's message to dismount, which I did promptly. He then trotted up to the pond and drank his fill of water. When he finished, he reared up on his hind legs, flapped his wings, and was out of sight in minutes. I was surprised that the Supremos had provided me with this admirable stallion as transport. The stallion had a body and drank water, so I wondered whether he was mortal, translated, or immortal. I tried to appeal to the Guardians for an answer but received none. I decided then that, by the wisdom of the Supremos, it was not necessary for me to know at this time.

I stood by the pond and cast my eyes around, looking for possible observers. I saw none. Pegasus had made his landing well out of sight. I chose a footpath that ran under the shade of trees and followed it. Before long, I sensed I had company. I could feel that I was being followed on either side by unseen footmen. At an overgrown turn in the path, I quickly climbed up into a tree. After a few minutes, I saw a large number of young men dressed in hunting gear, armed with crossbows and long hunting knives, treading softly and emerging on either side of the path.

Realizing they'd lost track of me, they met on the path about fifty yards ahead of the tree I was hiding in and started accusing each other of losing me. They conversed in soft voices. Interestingly, I could hear them clearly from that distance. I rejoiced when I realized I could understand their language. After their small debate, the men decided to go home and report to their superiors. I came down from the tree and followed them closely, invisibly, until they broke into a clearing three miles down. Ahead of us was a walled city. They arrived at one of the guarded gates and gave a password to be admitted. I was close behind them, but they didn't notice.

The group of young men marched through well-constructed roads, which crossed other streets outlined by beautiful houses with planted gardens and lawns at the intersections. It was a big, beautiful city. As I marched unseen behind the young men for over an hour, I noticed that they were going up a gently sloping road where the houses were getting larger and more sophisticated and magnificent with each passing.

At the top of this hill stood a hulking, well-guarded edifice, much like an impenetrable fortress or castle. The high gates fit snugly into the equally high and thick wall surrounding the building. They were constructed with huge bars of bronze overlaid with thick sheets of embossed metal. Alert sentries were posted at the gates, and other sentries were held in special enclosures built at intervals on the top of the high wall. I knew by inspiration that we were at the residence of the chief ruler of the beautiful city. When we reached the top of the gentle slope, I looked around and was impressed to see intelligence and wisdom emanating from the ruler's residence. The whole city could be seen from this elevation. The ruler's residence stood in the center of a hill, in the apex of the community. This placement offered protection and allow him to see the city from his abode. The panoramic view of the city revealed its significant growth over the years. My escorts, oblivious to my presence, reached one of the gates. The youth who'd given the password at the city entrance made a sign at this gate and offered another password. The gate opened silently and slowly to admit us. I followed them, still completely invisible, into the compound. The gate closed silently behind us. A number of guards on the compound came over to search the youths for concealed weapons and to inquire of their mission. The leader of the group replied that they had come to report to the senate on an errand assigned them. A guard entered the residence and returned to usher them into the presence of the senate. Members of the senate were seated in a large, attractively furnished hall. They'd deliberating some issues concerning the city's involvement with the adjacent empire, but immediately stopped the conversation to give audience to the new entrants.

The whole group bowed respectfully, and their leader gave an account of their reconnaissance, depicting what they'd seen after five days of hiding in the trees not far from the pond. They recounted my arrival from the skies mounted on a white-winged stallion. The leader reported that they had tailed me quietly but then had lost sight of me unexpectedly. He said that they'd concluded that I was somewhere in the countryside.

The ruler questioned them, seeking a detailed description of me, smiled, and gave thanks to the Supremos for what he recognized in this retelling: The Supremos' agents, the senate, had long prayed for and anticipated a leader who would help them reclaim their lost empire from entrenched invaders. Some of them had been granted a vision in which they saw a conqueror mounted on a flying white stallion, who would come among them within a decade to lead them to victory. I was that conqueror.

After nine years and eleven months of preparation and waiting, the citizens were beginning to lose hope and to doubt the fulfillment of the prophecy. But he, their ruler, being of strong faith, had persisted and quietly assigned a group each week to look out for the mounted warrior up to the last week of the tenth year. Now he had been vindicated. The prophecy had been fulfilled two days before the end of the tenth year. He dismissed the young men, calling them to silence, and promising to honor them later. He straightaway engaged the senate in preparing for a fitting welcome for me, their long-awaited deliverer.

My description, as offered by the young men, fitted what the chief ruler had seen in his vision, so it was decided that my description be sent to the security men at the city entry points with a call to keep an eye out for my arrival at any of the gates. They were to accord me the respect and welcome that would be given to one of their rulers. I was to be graciously invited to accompany them in a coach to their chief ruler's quarters.

I'd quietly stood by and watched events unfold in the senate hall until the young men were dismissed. I listened to their plans for me and remained in the building unseen. I was torn between revealing myself to the senate and waiting to address only the visionary, faithful ruler. I opted for the latter. Meanwhile, I spent some time touring the premises of the building and familiarizing myself with its layout, entrances, and obscure passages. I was, however, careful not to do anything to raise the suspicion of the guards and service personnel inside and outside the building.

At last, I saw the senators leaving for their homes. I silently walked to the side of the ruler who was seeing them off. He seemed so excited, to the surprise of his guards. They had never seen him in such a blissful mood. As he turned into his living quarters, humming a song of praise, I went in with him. He closed and locked the door, then knelt down and excitedly offered a long prayer of thanks and adoration to the Supremos.

I stood at one corner of the room and made myself visible to him the moment he finished his prayer and opened his eyes. He was startled to see me standing before him dressed in military regalia. He stared at me, surprised, then confused. I could see a tinge of fear in his demeanor, and his brow creased with uncertainty. He strained to discern whether I was real and of the flesh or of the spirit, as a result of divine vision. Then, remembering that I'd been sighted in the countryside, he made a poor but dignified attempt to collect and compose himself. He finally spoke with a shaking voice: "Welcome to our kingdom," he started. "We have been waiting for you for a great many years, and we are grateful to have you come among us."

He then commenced to narrate to me what had happened to their empire and how the young son of the emperor had discovered this land and secretly settled in it and married. Over the centuries, their population had increased so much that the thought of reclaiming their legitimate land, as inspired by the records of the early settlers, was revisited scores of times in the senate. They were ill-equipped to directly confront their enemy. They feared exposing their kingdom—the existence of which was still not known to the wicked empire—to invasion and subsequent slavery.

I listened quietly until the ruler stopped talking and had calmed down. Then I spoke.

"I am aware of your history," I assured him. "Though my mission is to assist you, we need to develop a strategy to overcome the energy and restore the empire."

"I propose a meeting with the council on the morrow to deliberate this," he replied.

"We must avoid getting the citizenry excited by the announcement of my arrival into their midst. For that reason, I have chosen to come to the city unseen and to appear to you alone." The ruler then remembered to extend courtesies to me as his guest, so I was offered an apartment in the ruler's senatorial quarters. I was refreshed as two of his elderly personal attendants cared for me as if their own kin—which I was. They, likewise, had sworn an oath to keep silent concerning my arrival.

Early the following day, security men were dispatched with sealed invitations for the senators to attend an emergency meeting convening that afternoon. At exactly the twelfth hour of the day, all of the senators were seated and ready for the deliberations to commence. The chief ruler sat down and opened the meeting with a prayer, followed by an excited announcement of my arrival. He then went on to caution them to secrecy to prevent the citizens' overreaction. He afterward sent for me to join the senate of his land to formulate the crucial plan of action. I joined them and was graciously greeted. They happily welcomed me to their city, and I was invited to speak in order to outline our prospective course of action.

CHAPTER 10

The Modus Operandi

As the meeting commenced, it became apparent that these humble people were not familiar with the tactics of warfare and were looking to me for every instruction. Each generation had lived in obedience to the universal law of perfection and was more at home with extending love and promoting peace and justice than making war. *Why would they now decide to fight off the settlers who had occupied their land for centuries? Was there an ulterior motive driving such an otherwise peaceful people to war?* I decided to survey the situation more fully before formulating a plan of action I spoke at length to the senate about the need to exercise caution and restraint for a time in order to avoid bringing any undue hardship upon their people caused by a rushed and hasty plan. I needed a few weeks to conduct a secret reconnaissance of the old empire and to learn of their security, strength, methods of defense, habits, and areas of weakness. We also needed to forge better swords, shields, and other protective armor for the young but willing fighters, who must be trained in endurance, discipline, combat strategies, and focus.

The senate accepted my proposals and assured me that I would be offered all the help I would need to succeed. The senate went into recess with a commitment to wait until they were invited by the chief ruler to discuss further action. With the knowledge I'd acquired from earthly schooling, buttressed by lessons given me by my father on mining, I taught a few reliable citizens how to accelerate the mining of iron ore— deposits of which were found in modest quantities in some areas beyond their city walls. They smelted the ore and carbonated it to produce steel for the forging of swords and other armaments, as well as helmets and other protective armor. I gave them the design to forge the swords and shields with strong steel in the pattern of that which I received as gifts from the good people in the cities beneath the ocean.

Over the next few weeks, I mentally combed the past to learn from the military giants who prevailed. I learned of their war strategies, their weaponry, their successes, their frustrations, their weaknesses, and their failures. After I had finished organizing these affairs in the city, I went to visit the unsuspecting communities of the empire in the night. I witnessed the nobles wasting away their lives and strength, drinking heavily in taverns and fornicating with women. I listened to them swear and boast of their wealth and power, issuing threats and trampling upon the rights of those less fortunate. I learned about the indiscriminate conduct and cruelty of some of their offspring who followed their patterns of oppression.

Disguised as a slave, I visited the long stretch of shanties which served as the living quarters of the poor. I saw the extreme poverty and the appalling conditions of their homes. I saw the pale, sad, drawn faces of their malnourished children.

I also visited the mines and witnessed the brutality of the guards as they drove the toiling slaves with whips to work beyond human endurance. I saw the hatred and the venom in the eyes of some of the youthful slaves as the whips cracked and flayed their exposed backs. I worked among them unnoticed and listened to their whispered conversations. I heard them as they groaned and prayed for the day when they could rise up in revolution and pay back the guards in their own coin. If only someone would lead them in revolt to bring about a change, they lamented. I listened and made a mental note of their grievances, their hopes, and their secret plans.

I next visited the farms and witnessed the slaves laboring under similar ill treatment from the guards. It was appalling to see the harvest stored in barns while those that worked to produce it were issued very little food and looked as malnourished as their children.

The empire was fortified by its natural location near a fast-flowing, dangerous river to the west and two well-guarded exits; its hedges made it almost inaccessible to any invader. Paradoxically, it also made it impossible for anyone to escape. I had seen a young man put in the stocks in the public square because he was caught eating an apple during the harvest. He had been in the stocks for three days without nourishment and was emaciated and faint. I broke into the stocks during the night while the drunk and sleepy guards dozed, and I carried him, unconscious, to the safety of the new habitation. Initially, my compatriots were alarmed, since no one from the empire knew of their existence. I assured them that the rescued man was unconscious when brought in and would recover without knowing where he was. He was now a fugitive and would not dare go among his people again. He would also be a source of vital information to us when he recovered fully.

The next night, I returned to continue my espionage. I soon learned that a great number of furious guards had conducted a search through the slave camp to find the escaped prisoner. Some people, including his aged parents, had been interrogated, mistreated, and threatened in vain for information. I learned from the excited slaves that the guards responsible for his escape had been locked in prison to await charges that could carry a verdict of death by hanging. The emperor and his cohorts were at a loss as to how the escape could have occurred. This was unprecedented. It was clear to observers that such an escape could not have been executed by any normal human. They were bewildered by the incident and slightly shaken.

I next focused on secretly observing the daily routine of the emperor and his senate. There were days in which I invisibly observed their meetings. Other times, I went from home to home to spy on their living conditions and eavesdrop on their conversations. They were considered the noble class; they lived lavishly and pompously, unlike the general population of commoners—made up of inter-bred indigenous people and settlers. The settlers served as the working middle class in their factories—as guards, as entertainers, and as fighting forces. The indigenous, on the other hand, served as the slaves in the mines and fields. My visits to the senate meetings were occasional, and it was on one of these visits that I witnessed something that shocked me and kindled my anger.

It was the first Friday of the month, and members of the senate settled down for the meeting to commence. One of the senior senators opened the meeting with the usual commendations to the emperor, after which he announced the need for consultation to seek protection from their deity as had been the custom every first Friday of the month. They responded spontaneously and, led by the emperor, moved in a line down a flight of stairs to the basement of the building.

I followed them, unseen and quiet, to the basement. I was surprised when we arrived at a strong metal gate, which opened to reveal a spacious area under the basement of the senate hall. I saw, mounted at the farthest northern end of the basement, an altar of some sort. Behind this altar was a huge effigy of a strange creature. It possessed the head of a snarling lion with long fangs and a long flowing mane. The bust resembled that of a very powerful human. The chest, part of which was covered by the mane, was broad and muscular, as were the human arms. But the hands had stubby fingers with long, curved claws like those of a cat.

The strange creature held a trident in the right hand and a human skull in the other. The lower part of the body, from the waist down, was very hairy and resembled the hind legs of a powerful bull, but with the tail of a lion. It walked with a vertical gait, as humans do, judging by the setting of the thighbone and the pelvis. Behind the altar were passages with fortified metal gates, which led to a labyrinth of tunnels. I noticed a thick layer of a substance that resembled coagulated blood drying on the altar.

"Ritual sacrifice…," I thought to myself, stunned. "Horrific…" There were no words to match the scene. References by spiritual historians came back to me. The Word depicted such sacrifice and detested it. Innocent virgins and children were offered as sacrifice to this strange effigy at midnight on the first Friday of every month. The dead bodies of the victims, after spilling their blood on the altar, were left at its feet. Strangely, they were gone by the next visit. The corpses' disappearance was a mystery to them, though not to me: I knew that the bodies were feasted upon by the real creature living in the labyrinth. It registered powerfully that the slaves were not only serving as beasts of burden, but that their daughters and children were being offered as the sacrificial lambs to this evil creature, the god of the invaders.

I now understood the motive and unflinching determination of my compatriots to wage war against these depraved invaders, even at the risk of defeat or enslavement. Their chief ruler had sensed evil in the land when a warning was given him in a dream after a three-day fast. He learned in the dream that the time was approaching when evil and carnage should visit his realm if a deliverer was not sent to their aid. I was aroused from these thoughts when a little human, a midget in a raffia skirt, emerged from the small opening of the only tunnel on the eastern wing. He sprang close to where I was standing unseen, and shot into the center of the chamber. He barely missed bumping into me.

As he danced before the senators, he picked up a wooden brush from the altar. After reciting some incantations, he dipped the tip into the thickening blood on the altar and drew an eight-pronged star with a circle around it on the forehead of the emperor and each of the eighteen senators. I was surprised when he stood still, shaking a horse tail vigorously in his other hand, before calling out. In a deep booming voice, uncharacteristic of a human his size, he said, "Beware! Beware! There is one among you who will rise to vanquish all. He is protected by a power that is greater than that of my master. He does not desire power but will restore the rule to the ordained. Beware!" Then, as quickly as he had appeared, he rushed back into the tunnel from which he emerged.

The emperor and his senators stood aghast. They looked at each other, wondering what the soothsayer's words meant. They had never experienced such an utterance in the many years they had ruled the empire; neither had there been any record of such an occurrence in the annals of their ancestors' rule. They filed back to the senate hall mute and with heads wagging in disbelief. They were the only people in the basement. Who among them was plotting the emperor's downfall and to take over the government? I was the only one who understood the meaning of the soothsayer's words. The warning had been issued by the evil spirits whose realm I had visited some time ago. They knew I was in the basement and had tried to expose me.

I slipped out as soon as possible and left the premises of the confused emperor and the senate. I had discovered the source of evil power that infected the covetous emperor, his senate, and the corrupt nobles. I had also found out the secret threat to the chief ruler and the senators of the new settlement that was motivating them to take the risk of fighting for their land. The ruler had narrated his dream to the senators, and though they did not fully understand its implications, they were convinced of impending evil. It was obvious that an attempt at negotiations would have fallen on deaf ears and ended in disaster for them.

As I reached the public square, I was met with another surprise. Gathered together in the square were all the slaves who worked in the mines and the planting fields. Erected in the north corner of the square was an effigy similar to the one I saw in the basement of the hall of the senate. I'd noticed it near the gallows the night I freed the slave in the stocks, but now I could see it clearly for what it was.

Surrounding this idolatrous structure were huge basins containing a liquid into which the slaves, their guards, and all the middle class workers filed past and dipped their hands, before smearing on their foreheads. They then knelt and bowed to the effigy and went to continue their labors. I later learned from the man I rescued from the stocks, that this was the system of worship and a way of swearing an oath of allegiance to deity, the emperor, and his senators.

In the past, those who had shown any sign of rebellion or disloyalty had suddenly vanished from society or died mysteriously. For this reason, the citizens lived in great fear. I learned that similar ceremonies took place in the other cities of the empire on every first Friday of the month under the supervision of appointed high-ranking nobles.

I paid secret visits to their food and technical factories to assess both the range and the level of sophistication of their arms. I realized that while the food preservation factories were progressive enough, their weaponry was modest. For centuries, they'd not encountered any threat of invasion, so they likely had little impetus to build advanced weaponry. They were still manufacturing normal wooden bows and wooden arrows with cast-iron heads, as well as cast-iron swords, which were cumbersome and broke under heavy impact. I saw spears and crude armors and helmets cast with the same brittle material. They were thick and heavy and would hinder the free and quick movement of any combatant.

I had taught the chief ruler and those newly settled in the area, how to combine the right ratio of carbon to molten iron with small amounts of manganese, chromium, and nickel to produce strong steel. They now habitually used this formula to manufacture better arms. Prior to this, they had been manufacturing swords and other tools out of bronze, an alloy of tin and copper which were abundant in their territory. They had also discovered other minerals and were finding ways to use them when I arrived to tutor them in metallurgy. Additionally, they had advanced from riding on horseback in the old empire to riding in carriages pulled by a team of horses on well-constructed paved roads. Horseback riding remained popular, however, in the settlement.

I'd finally learned all I needed to know to formulate the modus operandi for the assault. The upper echelon of society in the empire was evil and corrupt and needed to be destroyed. The working middle class were of mixed blood and were seemingly loyal to the nobles. Some, however, had been overzealous in performing their duties and had maltreated slaves, but could be taught a lesson and permitted to live.

It was obvious that if we were able to secretly arm the slaves and start an insurrection, they would become incensed enough to fight for their freedom and destroy their enemies. Given their numbers, the likelihood of overtaking the government was high, and nobles in the other regions of the empire would inevitably surrender if such occurred. Having the guards surrender would spare their blood. Leaving vengeance to the Supremos would be paramount, even in the face of the guards' prior egregious crimes. I would have to distill this thinking among the slaves who had known brutality at their hands. I felt that was do-able. One formidable challenge, however, was how to vanquish the evil creature the citizens worshiped. I had learned that the midget soothsayer who had warned the emperor and the senators of the conquest of their empire, was the priest of the deity. He had served in that capacity for over sixty years. He, as his ancestors for generations, was initiated into this duty. He considered his duty an emblem of his prominence. Through it, he felt he had a hold over the senate who were desperate for protection against their enemies.

The soothsayer's abode in the labyrinth was not linked to that of the creature's abode, but rather opened outside into an area within the community that off-limits to citizens. This location was safe because the abode's internal entrance was too narrow for the creature to penetrate. The night before the first Friday of the month was the period set aside over generations for the creature to vacate the chamber in the basement in order for its sacrifice to be brought to the altar. These arrangements were observed for generations. At other times, the creature had periodically been fed with livestock that had been raised purposefully for feeding it.

The creature had to be destroyed, along with the soothsayer if need be, and I needed to have a plan. It was now time to call for a meeting of the senate, so I made this known to the chief ruler. The invitation was sent out, and all the senators arrived at the designated time. As the meeting commenced, all attention was focused on me with high expectancy. I laid out my plan in no uncertain terms.

"It will be necessary to incite an insurrection," I said. "We are going to use the bitterness of the slaves against the nobles and the guards, but we need to avoid much bloodshed. Our first order of business must be providing arms for the slaves. It will be difficult to arm them while they are laboring in the mines and the fields. It will be my duty, therefore, to sneak to their homes and supply them with their weapons in the night. "While in their midst, I learned that slaves' homes are never visited by the guards or the nobles at night.

I then informed the senate about the evil creature that was being worshiped and my intention to slay it.

I inquired about the buildup of weaponry. I was assured that the forgers had worked day and night to produce a great number of sturdy steel swords with scabbards, shields, helmets, crossbows, spears, and plates to cover other vital parts of the body. They had also produced a number of long sharp knives with leather sheaths.

The youth were taking their training seriously. They were fearless and eager to go to battle to rescue their own from the cruelty of the settlers and wrest the land out of the hands of the accursed invaders.

Their mothers had instilled in them unflinching faith in and reverence for the Supremos. They entertained no doubt regarding the ability of the Supremos to aid and protect them in their righteous endeavors. They were not afraid to die for an honorable cause. I expressed to the senate my desire to help prepare the youth well. I explained that the youthful force that was being prepared should serve as a contingent force and be used only when it was absolutely necessary. They would be organized under appointed leaders and trained to obey every instruction with precision.

At last, it was time to reveal my identity to the warriors—to boost their morale, to embolden them, and to end the weeks of speculation, uncertainty, and doubt concerning my promised arrival in their community. The senate listened to my plan silently. They followed up with questions about how to destroy the beast of the labyrinth and public square. It appeared to be a formidable creature whose destruction would not be achieved easily. In my preparations for this assignment, I had not physically seen it, nor had I learned much about its actual size, habits, speed, or strength. I also reflected on the fact that I had been detected by the priest of the creature in the basement. It would, therefore, be difficult to keep myself unseen by the beast. I told the senate that they did not need to worry, but instead, should exercise faith in the ability of the Supremos to aid me in vanquishing my formidable opponent. With that assurance, they went into recess again to await the time when I would inform them of the completion of the first phase of the operation, and the date and time of the insurrection.

Over another six weeks, I assisted in the training of the young men. They were about two thousand in number. They became highly motivated once they were certain that I was truly in their midst. They trained with determination, seriousness, and zeal. Basing procedures on information from my mental studies of past warlords, I divided them into contingents of 250 each, and each unit was put under one strong adult leader and a deputy as its commanding officers.

153

I instructed them on tactical warfare to the best of my acquired knowledge. The initial training was carried out with wooden weapons, but by the end of the fourth week, the young men were ready to wear their protective armor and use real weapons for practice. A few weak enlistees could not cope with the rigorous nature of the training and had to be discharged, but the majority were tough and strong-willed, and made the grade.

With the young men in good hands, I shifted my attention to my nighttime visits to the slave shanties. My intent was to outfit the slaves with weapons and to instruct them in matters of combat. Initially they were frightened, but I was able to soothe their fear and convince them of an assured victory. This would come with an unexpected revolt and their resultant release from the debasing torture of slavery and bondage. Once pacified, the slaves were organized into groups of fifty, each headed by an appointed leader. They were assigned specific areas to target and informed of the overall strategy. I assured them that during the night, I would smuggle large quantities of foodstuffs from the farms to the slaves' homes to reinforce them and their families.

Since I was working alone on the distribution of arms and instructions, it took me almost four weeks to accomplish this task. The slaves were sworn to secrecy about the revolt. I promised that I would notify them of the day of insurrection in due course. We would start to engage our opposition as early as five o'clock in the morning, to ensure a surprise attack. After I had successfully equipped the slaves with supplies and instructions, I settled down to determine how to kill the beast.

In order to lure the beast out of the maze of tunnels, we would need human bait and fresh blood (signs of human sacrifice). But to lure them without endangering anyone seemed impossible. Who would willingly put himself in that kind of danger? I needed counsel, and I knew where to get it. I needed the Guardians.

CHAPTER 11

The Insurrection of the Slaves

My longing for the Guardians' support was met with their immediate response. The voice of the Guardians' leader provided timely perspective:

"Your fight is not only against the formidable beast, but against the horrors of the powers of darkness," the voice stated solemnly. "A contingent of the evil spirits from one of the caves in the dimensional world, one that specializes in possessing human bodies, controls that beast and has a firm hold on the senate, the emperor, and the nobles. They are their devotees, and they can possess their bodies at will and control them. These rulers have sworn a permanent oath of allegiance and servitude to the evil lord of dark forces in exchange for fame, wealth, and power. They have enjoyed these privileges for a long time, as generations of their ancestors. In times of threat to their well-being, they will resort to calling on these hellish forces to aid them.

"These forces will go to great lengths to defend their subjects, but will rely on the subject to make requests for aid. Only then will these spirits descend and wreak havoc on those disturbing their minions or hosts. *Why will evil beget evil, you wonder?* Here is the answer: One irrevocable law applies to every human in the universe. What we seek and desire, we will attract, whether good or evil. In other words, there are forces of good and of evil which will respond according to these desires. No good or evil can be imposed on humans without their willing consent and without their direct participation, or indirect fulfillment of a required condition. Just as obedience to the universal law of perfection opens the way for the fulfillment of righteous desires so does obedience to carnal and sensual laws open the way for the fulfillment of unrighteous desires. One course develops a charitable character and serene disposition; the other invites a contrary character and disposition to evil," he concluded.

"Now, to respond to your request for a plan to enable you to destroy the beast. Our duty is to educate you and to help you help yourself. We cannot take over, but we can assist with promptings and suggestions. We can give you some information that you may use as the basis for formulating your plan. Remember, Magnus, light dispels darkness and weakens the strength and power of evil, just as you experienced in your visits to the dimensional worlds. You can defeat the beast only by fighting it in broad, bright daylight.

"The shield you received as a gift from the cities beneath the ocean has the insignia of the noonday sun embossed in the center. The insignia is embedded with a number of photonic cells, which collect and store energy in a converter located at the center of the image of the sun. When a trigger on the inside of the shield is touched, the stored energy is released all at once, and the converter releases the energy in the form of white light. Your sword also has similar microscopic photonic cells embedded in it, but it is not as concentrated as your shield. Every stroke of your sword weakens your evil adversary."

He continued, "At noonday, it will take about fifteen minutes for the shield to restore its released energy. The day of the strike should be the first Thursday of the month, the day before sacrifices are to be made to the Homoleotaurus, the beast you saw in the cave. This is all we are permitted to tell you for now. Remember, the death of one who has lived according to his conscience, even if he is ignorant of the saving laws, is rewarded by the Supremos, who sees and assesses all events from the eternal perspective. The virgins and children who were sacrificed to the beast over the generations will be received into an abode of rest and learning to prepare them for their eternal progression."

Now that I'd been reminded of the powerful arsenal I had at my disposal, I sat down to outline a plan to defeat and kill the Homoleotaurus. I'd also been warned that the emperor, senate and nobles would be endowed by the lord of evil. I knew that the fight would not be as easy as I hoped and that lives could possibly be lost on our side as well as on the opposing side.

I sat pensively on the bed in the chief ruler's abode, seeking to cultivate a perfect plan. I finally settled on a day for the insurrection and finished detailing the strategy and positioning of the slave contingents. I called for a final meeting of the senate and briefed them on my plans for the insurrection. I also informed them of the revised role that contingents from the new settlement would be required to play.

After the meeting with the senate, I visited the training grounds of the new settlement's young men and was impressed by their progress within just a few weeks. They responded to every prior command with precision. They were practicing mock attacks, withdrawals, and counterattacks in new formations as they were commanded by their leaders. I knew that if we were to succeed, we would need some of them to participate in the initial assault on the precincts of the rulers and the nobles.

Of the eight groups of 250 boys each, I appointed two contingents that exhibited extreme bravery to join me in the initial assault on the rulers and the nobles. I then issued instructions to the remaining six contingents on the parts they were to play. I briefed them on the final strategy and the necessity for each group to perform its duties in time and with precision.

"Some of you could die," I said solemnly. "There is still time for any among you who is afraid to back out now. No one will condemn or judge you if you choose to do so. This is a dangerous mission." Not one of them flinched at the mention of death, but each stood at ease in rows. I was now sure that we were ready for the assault; we retired from the training grounds. Later that night, I visited the slave quarters to learn how their preparations were coming along and to give them final instructions.

The day of the assault seemed to arrive quickly, and I left the settlement with my two contingents at four o'clock that morning. They waited as instructed at the outskirts of the city of the seat of government while I went ahead to verify the last-hour preparation of the slave armies. The other six contingents had left with their commanders on horsebacks at two o'clock that morning to their various assigned cities. When I arrived at the slave shanties, I was happy to see that the appointed leaders had organized their men and instructed their wives not to go to the farms, ensuring that they and their children stayed indoors for the whole day.

They moved quietly to their assigned areas throughout the city. By five o'clock in the morning, all the slave armies were in position and in full fighting gear. Each community—occupied by fifty security personnel and their families—was surrounded by two groups of the slave armies totaling one hundred angry men hardened by years of abuse. Each community of the non-military, working middle class was surrounded by only one group of fifty members of the slave army. By this arrangement, with the exception of the slave shanties, all other communities in the capital had been surrounded by their armies.

Within the community of the nobles, the senate, and the emperor, each home was strategically surrounded by ten armed slaves from the groups assigned to that area. I strengthened them by bringing and assigning fighters from my two contingents of 250, totaling 500 trained young men, to the cadre. I did not forget the security posts at the two main entry points to the empire; I assigned a group of fifty to disarm the ten-member security team at each point. At about five-thirty in the morning, the security men and the guards, emerging from their homes to go to their outposts, were greeted by sword tips pressed to their throats. Heeding my warning to avoid shedding blood unnecessarily, the armed slaves disarmed, bound, and led each guard to a predetermined area to await further instruction.

The slave army was, however, compelled to kill the few guards who made an effort to raise an alarm or resisted arrest. The slave army then took hostage the families of the guards. This was necessary to prevent them from warning the nobles of the insurrection. The homes of the middle class workers were also taken over successfully, with a warning to keep calm and avoid bloodshed. By ten o'clock in the morning, the takeover plan had been successfully implemented, with minimal bloodshed. The time arrived for the nobles to open their gates for the usual activities of the day. The security personnel attached to each home were provided with living quarters near the closest gate and ran a rotating shift system to maintain twenty-four-hour surveillance. A trusted servant in the home of each noble opened the fortified gate at ten o'clock each morning.

It had been fairly easy to catch the security men by surprise. However, at ten o'clock none of the gates of the community of nobles or the senators had been opened. At this point, we developed a creeping suspicion that the plan had somehow been exposed to the nobles. I started to feel uneasy. I tried to conceive of the one who might seek to betray the plan to the rulers and the nobles. Then I remembered the soothsayer. I realized that I hadn't accounted for or dealt with him, prior to enacting our plan. I imagined that the soothsayer had somehow warned the nobles, and that the nobles were undoubtedly performing rituals to unleash evil forces upon us.

I suddenly realized the danger: The nobles in the other cities had likely been alerted to our attack as well. If this was so, then the contingents that had been assigned to go on horseback to each of the remaining five cities were likely to be met with resistance from the cities' guards. I could only hope that the faithful youth and their inspiring commanders could overcome this setback.

A brief mental analysis of the events within the empire over the last five hours boosted my hopes that all would be well. I was elated to learn of the success of my contingents when I later received a report on the campaign. Apparently, since they had gotten an early start, they arrived in time and took charge of affairs as planned. The evil spirits had indeed warned their nobles at the last hour and they made an effort to flee, but the contingents overtook them before they could escape.

The guards accompanying the nobles had surrendered without resistance, but the nobles had fought ferociously and with great power. After a brief battle, the nobles were finally overpowered and put to death for refusing to surrender. Luckily, there were zero fatalities among the young warriors and only a few were wounded.

Being encouraged by this triumph, I returned my focus to the events in the community of the nobles and the senate. The imperial court became apprehensive about two days before our planned assault. They hurried to alert the others of the impending danger, for they knew the attack could not be averted. The Supremos, the avowed enemies of their demonic ruler, were behind the danger at hand.

The members of the imperial court had all deserted their homes and sought refuge and protection in the cave where the Homoleotaurus resided. As I probed further, I saw them hiding in the narrow tunnels of the labyrinth that were inaccessible to the beast while their unknowing families were left in the open chamber with the effigy.

It was six o'clock in the evening. It had been thirteen hours since the insurrection began and there were still six hours to go before it was time to offer a sacrifice to the Homoleotaurus. *What would become of the wives and children of the emperor and the senate if the beast broke the bounds into the chamber?* The scene would surely be beyond detestable. The nobles and senators were selfishly sacrificing their families, who were ignorant of the danger, for their own safety. I needed to rescue the families of the ruling nobles despite their arrogance. They had not sworn allegiance to the evil lord of darkness, and therefore, stood a chance of changing their spiritual and moral posture. They could yet choose to follow the universal law of perfection. Time was running out. With the special climbing gloves I'd been given by the sea people, I climbed the high wall of the emperor's home where the senate met occasionally. Easily breaking a few of the cast-iron spikes on the top of the wall, I jumped into the compound and broke the heavy padlocks on the gate with a single stroke of my sword. I then summoned some of my contingents and moved with them down to the basement.

The gate was open, and the defenseless families were cowering in the chamber. They started crying out loudly, calling to their husbands and fathers to save them from their attackers. Notwithstanding their pleas, the selfish leaders moved in on them. I and my team of armed men sheathed our swords as a sign that we were not there to destroy them. I raised my arms, inviting silence. Though perplexed, they complied, and within a few seconds, only the crying of the little ones remained. I then spoke to them and explained the danger to which they were exposed. I pointed to the statue of the Homoleotaurus. I explained to them that the statue they saw standing there in the chamber and in the public square was a horrible creature that lived within the labyrinth of tunnels before them. I promised them that we meant them no harm, and we needed to evacuate them to a safe place before the creature broke loose into the chamber to kill.

They appeared horrified by the news and fearfully glanced at the tunnels behind them. I told them their sires knew about the savage beast and had selfishly deserted them to seek protection from the soothsayer, who was a priest to the beast and performed rituals to protect their husbands and also grant them power, riches, and fame.

After I finished speaking, there was a heavy silence. Even the children had stopped crying. I informed the wives that their husbands had left them here to die. Unless they came with me, their fate was sealed. With resigned and drawn faces, they began to move forward, signaling that they would allow me to lead them to safety. Relieved by their cooperation, I gestured toward the basement and ushered them in that direction, out of harm's way. I then instructed those that had accompanied me to take the families of the deposed leaders to safety, that they were not to be harmed. After returning to the cavern, I realized I could destroy the evil emperor and senate at the hands of the beast. I quickly entered the chamber and cut through the barred gates of the entrance from the tunnels of the beast. I moved out and locked the thick main gate to the basement from the outside. Afterwards, I joined my team of armed soldiers and slaves stationed at the community of the nobles and rulers. I was assured that though some of the armed slaves had desired to kill the nobles' family members, they were duly restrained. I commended them for preserving life, reminding them that the new order would need everyone. All were aware that all wartime casualties would be examined, and perpetrators of any unjustified acts would reap consequences.

Next, I organized some of my men and instructed them to collect dry wood and freshly cut branches with leaves. I asked them to place them in separate piles close to the exit of the tunnel, near the working-class community adjacent to the emperor. This marked the exit route of the soothsayer that all had been forbidden to enter under threat of death. In about two hours, those that were appointed to supervise informed me that my instructions had been executed according to command. I was satisfied with the results.

I quickly organized the workers and gave orders for them to arrange the dry wood for a bonfire about four yards into the tunnel. Atop every tier of four of the dry branches, they were to pack a pile of fresh branches with leaves, then another four tiers of dry wood on top, followed by fresh, leafy branches until the exit was totally blocked by the pile for the bonfire. At about nine o'clock, only three hours to midnight, the bonfire was ignited. As the fire from the dry wood gradually reached the layer of fresh branches, the smoke was pushed into the tunnel by another team using the remaining leafy branches as fans.

This strategy of smoking out the nobles was sustained for the next four hours. During this time, I mentally revisited events in the tunnels from nine o'clock—the hour the bonfire was lit and smoke fanned into the tunnel. Though I'd received firm directives to destroy the nobles who had sworn allegiance to the evil prince of darkness, I could not fathom killing anyone who did not raise a weapon against me. I had plotted to achieve the same results by inducing their destruction by the horrible beast: I hoped that the Homoleotaurus would carry out this task for me.

As the billows of smoke filled the tunnels, the soothsayer had led a line of gagging nobles into the basement chamber where the air was more bearable and the smoke wasn't as thick. The nobles had been persuaded by the soothsayer to rush quickly to the chamber to join and protect their families and to sit out the storm of the insurrection. The soothsayer had assured them that none would dare come to the basement and that the beast could not break through the strong, heavy gate at the entrance of its abode.

Upon the nobles' arrival, though, and to their dismay, the chamber was empty; their families were gone; and the main fortified gate to the chamber was locked from the outside. They cried out in desperation to their master, the prince of darkness, to come to their rescue. It was at that time that a deafening roar filled the cavern. They turned in fear toward the horrible sound, but before they could focus through the blinding smoke in the chamber, the horrible beast was upon them.

With one sweep of its mighty arm, six of the nobles lay dead at its hoofs. A second blow sent another eight nobles flying into a nearby wall, immediately killing them. The remaining nobles screeched as they were torn apart like old rags within a few minutes. The only occupant of the chamber who escaped the massacre was the soothsayer, whose duty it had been to listen and ensure the beast was not close to its gate before quickly and noiselessly collecting the remains of the virgins and children offered as sacrifice.

Many years of serving as the priest of the beast had helped the soothsayer develop an unbelievably fast response to danger. He shot like a cannonball into the safety of his abode at the first sound of the beast's roar. He wondered how the beast had managed to get through the fortified gate. Within ten minutes, the screams turned to silence as every one of the nobles lay dead or dying in the sacrificial chamber. In all, over thirty-five souls, including the eighteen senators and the ruler, perished at the hand of the false deity they and their ancestors had worshiped for decades.

Such was the way of the power of evil. The prince of darkness always deserts those who worship him at the time they most need his help. He grants his faithful subjects riches, fame, and power during the initial stages of their devotion to him, to entice them to put their trust in him, to make them feel that he has the power to fortify and protect them from any other power. This trust increases as he remains true to his initial and short-lived promises. Ultimately, however, they are left to themselves, with no resources but their own. These never prove enough. His servants come to the realization that he has deserted them to face their destiny alone, sealing their fate.

Millions have similarly fallen victim to the adversary's enticing offers, only to learn of the deception too late. Deception usually involves a surprise ending for captives. Who would have thought that the beast would attack its own subjects? Who would have known their term of usefulness would expire. The nobles had indeed exhausted their utility to Xoedikus. It was important to him that they should die in their wickedness and remain his subjects forever. This is a type and shadow for all who live in this probationary state.

But back to our plan. The beast had destroyed the nobles and saved me from that unpleasant responsibility. Now I needed to focus on destroying the prime target: the beast.

The beast had fed well on the dead bodies of the nobles and was satisfied. With the gate into the wide chamber destroyed, it was free to visit the chamber at will. I now needed to entice it into the open in order to destroy it without exposing the citizens to danger. I also needed a well-lit area to fight, instead of the dimly lit basement chamber. I recalled that it was, indeed, a big and ugly brute, standing about ten feet tall with a large, muscular build. Despite its huge, solid, hoofed legs, it moved with great agility and unbelievable speed. It was a formidable opponent to face. I also remembered the soothsayer who had escaped from the beast and back into the safety of his tunnel. Had he survived the choking effect of the smoke, or had he also perished? Though he was small in stature and was physically of no threat to me, he was sneaky and could pose a problem. I decided that I first needed to deal with him in order to prevent him getting in the way of killing the beast.

It was now about seven o'clock in the morning, and there were only five hours left until noon. The sky was clear, and it promised to be a sunny day. The Guardians had counseled me to fight the beast at midday, and I had to get to work in order to entice it out into the open public square, where no foliage blocked the glare of the sun. It must be accomplished by noon. I was determined to succeed in the first assignment after my training tour of the spirit realms. I could not fail.

CHAPTER 12

The Battle of Wits

I began executing my plan by posting a few slave soldiers at the only external exit for the soothsayer. They were instructed to capture him if he attempted to escape. They were also to enter the tunnel for safety in case my plan should fail and the beast should break free. I then sent a message to the citizenry and the remaining members of the slave army; they were to remain indoors with their families until a trumpet was sounded signaling that it was safe. The captured security men were released without their weapons to join their families. With the exception of my contingents' leaders and a few soldiers, the others were dispatched to go back to the new settlement. I was now ready to face the formidable beast alone. I made my way to the senate house and opened wide the main gate to the compound. I needed to move fast to avoid being in the range of the Homoleotaurus until we arrived at the public square.

As I moved toward the basement chamber, I made sure that every door was opened and every passage cleared of impediments. I arrived at the fortified gate to the chamber of sacrifice and death. Here I stood quietly to inspect the dim chamber and listen for signs of life before opening the strong gate. On the floor lay the dead bodies of the nobles.

There was no sound or any sign of the beast. It was then about ten o'clock, and I had only two hours left to accomplish my task.

I realized that I would have to sneak into the labyrinth to locate and entice the beast out into the open. The risk was high, but it had to be done, and I was the only person who could do it. I stood quietly at the opened gate and cast my mind back into time to learn of the beasts' activities over the last few hours. I saw the beast feeding upon the bodies of three of the nobles, including that of the emperor. After it was filled, it lifted one more body onto the left side of its broad shoulders and went back into its lair. Within a matter of minutes, it had fallen into a heavy sleep. I could mentally locate it deep in a tunnel within the labyrinth. The linked passages that I had to pass through to reach the beast had many twists and turns, and I realized that I needed to keep a mental note of my path in order to retreat quickly. I studied the route for a while and felt secure. I finally went back to fetch a little pot of bright green luminous dye developed for protecting fruit trees, and to emit a glow during the night for easy passage by slaves who came home late from the fruit farms. I carefully made a hole in the bottom of a little pot of the luminous paint to allow the dye to trickle out, then plugged the hole with a piece of cloth.

Back at the chamber, I tied the little pot tightly to my left ankle and entered the tunnel, where I removed the plug from the pot. It was dark, and it took a little while for my night vision to activate. I was surprised at the beast's ability to find its way in such a dark maze. Obviously, it possessed keen senses of smell, sight, and hearing to be able to live in such a place. I looked back and was glad to see a luminous trail behind me marked out by the dye. I had moved about halfway to the location where I had seen the Homoleotaurus sleeping when my own keen senses of smell and hearing warned me of danger ahead.

I had not anticipated the beast waking up so soon. It was foolish of me not to have mentally located the beast just prior to my entering the labyrinth, and after spending some time to fetch and install my tracking pot of paint. It was now too late. I turned and ran toward the exit with the beast close behind me. Despite my stealth, its sensitive senses alerted it of my intrusion. Had it not been for the pounding of its hoofs before an attack, I might have walked right into its hands—and disaster. I reached the chamber only to find that the gate I had left open was closed and locked from the outside. I was trapped! Out of desperation, I put on the cloak of invisibility to try and stall the beast for a moment, but this did not work. The demons that possessed its body could not be deceived with physical invisibility. It repeatedly made attempts to swipe at me with its powerful claws. I escaped his crude sweep by a hair's breadth.

As I jumped over a heap of dead bodies left on the floor with the beast at my heels, its foot caught on the clothing of one of the bodies. It tripped, crashing to the ground with a thud, giving me enough time to reach the gate and deal a mighty blow to the cast-iron lock, throwing it wide open. My Rhumbion sword sliced through the lock with ease and gave me confidence that it was the weapon destined to deliver the *coup de grace* to this horrible creature and personification of evil.

I made the turn and shot up the staircase from the basement to the senate hall with the beast a few yards behind me. I grabbed my shield at the entrance of the hall and shot through the gate of the emperor's compound, accelerating toward the public square. It was then that I saw the soothsayer running ahead of me as fast as his legs could carry him. I caught up to him and then continued past him. Surprised, he stopped briefly and looked back only to see his master, the beast he had served for almost sixty years, right on top of him.

His screams told the story of his fate at the hands of his master. Another devoted subject had been sent home without favor to the spirit world to serve his evil lord in misery forever. He had also been denied a chance to learn of an alternative way to live and One to worship. I learned later that the soothsayer had attempted to escape when the burning cinders finally died out. However, upon discovering the post I had mounted to capture him, he decided to check the main outlet through the chamber of the beast. He saw the locked gate open and, guessing correctly that the intruder might be in the labyrinth, went out through the gate and locked it to trap me for the beast to kill. I was glad the crafty midget had not died at my hands. Our brief encounter had again slowed down the beast and allowed me to gain a few more yards. I finally arrived at the deserted public square under the glare of the noonday sun. Events had turned out in favor of my plan to destroy the Homoleotaurus. I took a deep breath and turned around, waiting for it to come at me.

The furious beast arrived at the public square and stopped charging when it saw that I was no longer running. It howled and started circling me with an ugly snarl. I could see that it was surprised that I was not running. It was intelligent enough to size me up for some time before attacking, though. I stood my ground and waited for its attack, my sword in my right hand and my shield in my left. Then, as if satisfied that I was not a threat, it pounded its hoofed legs and charged at me with both hands raised to deliver a killing blow. It was fast for a creature of such size, but I was ready for it. I sidestepped and ducked under the powerful blow it swung at me. As its giant arm swished over my head with power, missing me by a sliver, I dealt it a blow with the sword, wounding it on the hip. As it turned with a roar of pain and made a second charge, I activated the power of the shield, and the energy of the glaring white light sent the brute reeling backwards. It fell heavily on its back.

I rushed forward to plunge the sword into its heart, but it sprang up and swung another deadly blow that caught me on the shield, hurling me about fifty yards away. I crashed heavily to the ground. That blow could have shattered the head of a bull, but I easily bore the heavy impact without pain or damage. The Guardians had indeed done marvelous work on me. My confidence about my indestructibility grew with each dueling moment. Then, suddenly, I saw the sky darkening as if night was setting in.

I looked up and saw what looked like a wide stretch of thick, black clouds floating to blot out the bright noonday sun. It moved so fast that, within minutes, the area was covered in semi-darkness. The evil forces were coming to the aid of their puppet.

Before my eyes could adjust to the darkness, the beast, which had lived under such conditions in the subterranean labyrinth, was on me and had grabbed me with both hands, lifting me toward its open mouth, its long, ugly canines dripping with saliva. As it lifted me to bury its fangs into my neck, I thrust the sharp point of the sword up into its throat. In a hellish pitch, it moaned deeply in anguish, and instantly dropped me. I stumbled forward to put some space between the beast and me, and as I ran from its presence, I focused to activate the glow of my body. I looked back to see that the beast had gone mad and was close behind me. I arrived at the position where its statue had been erected and, stopping, I lifted and hurled the heavy statue at the beast. It saw the statue coming and met it with a devastating blow that shattered the massive idol like glass. By this time, the glow of my body was piquing. White light exploded to fill the whole square. Just then, I saw the Homoleotaurus stop in its tracks and turn toward the gallows. It charged toward the gallows and dove under the high platform, breaking some of its wooden supports and bringing the whole structure down upon it. Just at that instant, my body discharged the power-laden white light, missing its deadly effect on the covered beast.

How had it known about the power of the white light from my body? It had craftily avoided the effect by covering itself with the rubble. Then it occurred to me that the evil spirits were the real opponents and knew of the power within the Wackida. They had obviously encountered the weakening effect of the white light on their kind from other Wackida in the past and had craftily avoided exposing the beast to it.

The beast may have escaped the emasculating effect of the white light, but something else could not. Just about the time of the light's release, I saw a strange phenomenon in the skies. The black clouds covering the sun were frantically clearing. Then, as the light glowed brightly around me to fill the public square, I saw what appeared to be the cloud plummeting downward as a sheet. As I watched it get closer, I came to see clearly what it really was. I saw thousands and thousands of vultures and magpies falling to the ground. It then dawned on me that the evil spirits had possessed the bodies of these birds and used them as a means of blanketing the noonday sun to prevent the sword and shield from gathering needed energy to weaken the Homoleotaurus. *Would the cunning of the evil realm ever outdo the wisdom of the Wackida?* With the sky cleared of the black cloud, my sword and shield started again to draw energy from the sun while my body's lethal brilliance gradually phased out. Suddenly, I saw the Homoleotaurus emerge from the rubble and make a dash for me. I needed to delay it from making any contact in order to allow my shield and sword to gather enough energy and draw the beast further out into the open. I turned and ran with the beast close on my heels. When I was certain that my shield was fully charged, I quickly swerved away from a devastating left swipe by the beast and veered sharply left again. The momentum of the rushing beast as it missed its target, and its attempt to change direction, made it lose its balance and fall heavily to the ground.

Again, it was up with amazing speed and agility and was rushing to destroy me. This was the moment I'd been waiting for. As soon as it reached out to grab me, I pretended to lose balance and fall down on my back. As I looked into the eyes of the infuriated beast, I saw hatred and a look of triumph, and I knew that had I been an ordinary human, it would have torn my body into shreds with its long, sharp claws. As it bent down to grab me again, I lunged at it with great force and buried the long blade of my sword deep into its heart and, at almost the same time, released the energy of my shield. The energy from the white light hurled it away from me as it clawed at the sword buried in its chest and roared in pain. I stood up quickly and rushed toward it with the intention of dealing it the final, fatal blow, but found on arrival that the beast was twitching and breathing its last breaths. To ensure that it was totally dead, I pulled out my sword and smote off its head. Suddenly, a gust of wind with a faint but distinct wailing sound started swirling around the beast, and I thought I saw face after face carried through the wind to fade away into nothingness.

I had finally triumphed over the beast, eliminated all that was evil in the land, restoring freedom to a once-hallowed community. I raised my head toward the heavens and, with a loud cry filled with emotion, expressed my gratitude to the great architects of the universe for their unfailing support and defense of all who put their trust in them and obeyed their will.

I looked around me and was surprised to see the team I had left at the exit of the soothsayer's labyrinth rush to the public square with cheers. They informed me that after waiting at the exit until the cinders had died out with no sign of the soothsayer, they decided to investigate by entering the labyrinth in an attempt to capture him. After hours of fruitless searching, they emerged to find me and were surprised to see me battling the beast in the public square. They had seen us early enough to avoid being seen and had hidden behind a building to watch the outcome of the duel. When I fell, they had feared that it was the end of me but were surprised and relieved when the beast was forcibly hurled away from me with my sword in its chest. They saw me rush to decapitate the beast and were elated at my victory.

As the agreed sign of victory, I instructed them to fetch a trumpet and to sound it to bring the citizens out from their homes. One of them hurried to the nearest guardhouse to secure the instrument and blew it hard and loud. Within moments, the public square was teeming with people as the message of victory was sent far and wide to all parts of the city. I then sent two young men to the new settlement to announce to the chief ruler and the senate the success of the campaign, the slaying of the formidable beast, and the complete retaking of all three cities of the empire. This provided an appropriate opportunity for the chief ruler to address the people in the capital city and to assure all that there was nothing to fear. As the crowds cheered, I worked my way in the direction of the dead Homoleotaurus. Standing at a respectable distance around it was a throng formed by an inner circle of some of my faithful young warriors, the citizens pressing in to catch a view of the monstrous beast whose image they had been compelled to worship for generations. Many of the women wept uncontrollably as they remembered their young maidens and children forcibly taken from them and sacrificed to this evil idol of idols.

While waiting for the rightful descendant of the rulers of the empire to arrive, I assigned some of my young warriors to construct a small, elevated platform from the pieces of wood that had been part of the collapsed gallows. My desire was for the chief ruler to stand on the platform in view of his people and to address them.

After a short while, I saw the chief ruler and his senate arrive on horseback dressed in ceremonial robes, led by the two young men I had sent. The surprised citizens looked upon them in silent awe as a pathway was quickly opened for them to ride in—first to the site where the body of the Homoleotaurus lay and, after viewing it, to the area where the temporary platform had been erected. The chief ruler assured me that emissaries had been dispatched to the other cities of the empire to inform them of the good news and to assure all citizens that the legitimate ruler of the domain had proclaimed peace and descried fear.

The crowd suddenly broke into cheers as the chief ruler mounted the makeshift platform. He then raised his hands for silence, and when the noise finally died down, he introduced himself and traced his lineage to the legitimate rulers of the former empire. He spoke with power and authority, thanking the great rulers of the universe for their love and for the redemption of the empire from the hands of all that was evil. He thanked them for fulfilling their promise in sending a warrior into their midst to lead them into this great victory.

He announced that all evil had been purged from the domain and that the laws of their forefathers would be reintroduced to ensure peace and prosperity for all. Henceforth, he continued, slavery was abolished and there would be no class distinction. Every citizen was a free man. All citizens would perform their duties as assigned and would be allocated adequate food and raiment according to their needs. Each was to be his brother's keeper.

He narrated plans to provide decent housing for all and to set up manufacturing industries to make more durable tools and weapons of defense, as well as carriages for traveling in comfort on the well-paved roads that were to be constructed. He assured them of establishing learning centers of various levels to educate the citizenry to develop their full potential. He spoke of strengthening security to ensure the safety of every citizen. Any stranger who wished to be admitted into the empire would have to enter into an agreement to abide strictly by the restored laws. Being a man who was well-acquainted with the universal laws of perfection upon which the laws of the land had been based, he described to the citizens the blessings to be earned in adopting and living according to such tenets. He ended his speech promising like rewards.

The speech was greeted with cheers of joy from the crowd. Just at that moment, we saw a group creating a passage and escorting some people toward the platform. When they got closer, I realized that these were the families of the nobles. I saw deep fear in their eyes. They sensed the hatred in the faces of the former slaves as they made their way toward the platform.

I stepped up onto the platform with the permission of the chief ruler and addressed the crowd as the children and wives of the nobles were brought before the chief ruler.

"Citizens of this blessed land," I started, "today marks the beginning of a new life in your redeemed land, a new era when each one of you can breathe the air of freedom. It is a day when the masters of the universe, through their grace, have provided all with freedom. In return they expect you to cherish every living soul and to forgive where you have been offended. Standing before your ruler now are the wives, sons, and daughters of your former nobles. They were born into families and were taught to look down upon you and to treat you unjustly. You would have been misled to behave in the same manner if you had been in their position.

"The supreme powers of the universe admonish us to love our enemies and to do good to them that despitefully use us. If we desire to live by their laws, then we must bury the bitter past, forgive, and embrace each other with love, and all old wounds will be healed. Our preparedness to do this and look forward to a brighter future will be the sign of our desire to be part of the new order."

When I finished speaking, there was a blanket of silence over the crowd in the square, followed by deafening cheers. As I stepped down from the platform, the eyes of one of the young ladies among the family of the nobles met mine. I was shocked, surprised, and then confused to see what appeared to be an exact replica of Jane, my spouse-to-be in the last hundred years of my service to humankind. Her poise and the air of confidence she carried about her—even under such an unfavorable, uncomfortable situation—baffled me. Her eyes glowed with intelligence, and I wondered why she had been born so early. She kept her focus on me until I began to shift uncomfortably. Then suddenly her face softened as her lips spread into a gentle smile. *What is happening to me? Is this really Jane?* I wondered. *If so, why is she here now, in the first assignment of my millennial service?*

A gentle touch on my shoulder shook me from my pleasant trance. It was the chief ruler. He had introduced me to the citizens and asked for the dispersal of the crowd to their homes, for the body of the beast to be cremated, and for all effigies and emblems of the evil apparition to be destroyed. The homes of the nobles were to be consecrated and dedicated for the habitation of those who were to take up senior public responsibilities, and the families of these nobles were also to be well accommodated.

We headed to the new settlement, where the citizens celebrated their freedom throughout the night, but I could not get the attractive lady out of my mind. I posed a question to the Guardians concerning her early birth and what that meant for my future. The response was another shock to me: "You have just delivered the ancestor of your future wife. Her resemblance to Jane is uncanny, and she is equally attracted to you. However, you know who she is now, and you must be careful with her."

During the last few days that I stayed among the liberated people, I saw the chief ruler crowned as the emperor. At his coronation, he honored me with a banquet. I saw the working class organized into an effective working force. I saw the renovation, consecration, and dedication of the old premises for all citizens. Settlements were also allocated to those appointed to serve in positions of leadership and trust, including the families of the nobles. I saw the sealing off of the tunnels to the labyrinth beneath the senate house. I saw plans drawn for the erection of beautiful housing to replace the shanties of the former slave camp.

I saw other plans for the reconstruction of roads, building of factories, construction of tools and armament, and creation of coaches for travel to distant lands for trading. I saw the passing of laws to protect the liberty and honor of all citizens and plans for the establishment of special meeting houses to worship the Supremos and to learn the universal laws of perfection. I toured all the six cities to see if the fever of freedom had caught on, brought joy, and promoted a desire for industry among the citizens. I was captivated by the enthusiasm of the people. During the period, I had occasions to meet and pay my respects to the ancestor of my future spouse. She tried to convince me to stay, but I told her my duties required that I should move on. Someday in the future, I said with a chuckle, we might meet again.

I had finished my work among the people of this blessed land. The guards and the former slaves had accepted the change and were now living in harmony. The families of the nobles had blended with the community, and old wounds had been healed. The contingents of faithful young men were honored and offered places within the defense forces created for the land. The two main entrances into the empire were broadened and fortified with high, strong gates of steel and efficient changing of guards. Peace now reigned under the rule of the faithful emperor, and I knew that the Supremos were happy with what had been achieved. I now had to wait patiently for the call to another assignment.

The call to return to the Dome came shortly. The time was fixed for the early morning of the Tuesday of that week. I was to wait in the public square. I bid my good-byes to the new friends I had made. They looked sad, and some shed tears as they came to the public square that Tuesday morning to see me off. Suddenly, out of the cool morning sky, the magnificent Pegasus glided down. It landed in front of me and, as usual, reared up on its hind legs. This time I clearly understood the message for me to mount it.

I climbed into the saddle and waved as the flying stallion soared into the skies, circled, and glided off at a terrific speed. Within moments, we were at the mountaintop from where I had been lifted six months earlier. I dismounted, and the stallion flew off, leaving me alone on the top of the mountain. As I focused on the Dome, I was instantly whisked there.

I was again met by the Guardians and congratulated by them for a job well done. I was told I needed to rest for a few days before embarking on my new assignment.

As I lay on the soft bed, thoughts of Jane's ancestor flooded my mind. I wondered how she was faring under the new government. The few times that I had occasion to be in her company had ignited something within me and had me wishing that it was Jane by my side. I had been assured that great care would be taken of her, and I had no reason to doubt the promise of the emperor.

I lay on the bed for a long time, feeling so lonely and yearning for the company of Jane, yet I knew the timetable of the Supremos would make this possible only within the last one hundred years of my mission. That was centuries away! A feeling of disappointment and emptiness filled my soul with grief. *Why did I have to meet Jane's ancestor?* I thought to myself in frustration. I tried so hard but could not get the image of Jane out of my mind.

Then, suddenly, standing by my bedside, was my future bride, Jane. She was radiant and wore a gentle smile that gave prominence to her pretty dimples. She was wearing a beautiful white flowing dress, and her feet were bare. Her long, thick brown hair hung loose and shone with a brightness that was heavenly. She stretched out her hand, held mine in hers, and said to me, "Come." I felt a wonderful sensation run through my body, and in the next moment, the two of us were in a valley.

The valley seemed to have been preserved and left untouched by the pollution that had degraded most valleys on the planet. It looked more like a new creation or something otherworldly. Everything was so green and full of life. The trees were very healthy, and a variety of birds with colorful feathers sang enchanting melodies among the branches. The greater part of the valley was covered by smooth, low-growing grass that was soft and hugged our feet, welcoming us as we strolled in it. In the middle of the beautiful greenery was a lake of crystal-clear water in which could be seen fish flashing by and other creatures endowed with awesome, colorful designs. I could also see plump, healthy-looking rabbits scurrying in the grass and among the trees. I wished I could stay in this enchanted valley forever with the woman I had come to love and admire so much.

We sat on a flat outcrop of rock on the bank of the lake, holding hands. Then she began to speak.

"The Supremos have seen your grief and permitted me to be by your side to keep you company and to comfort you for a while. I may come to you occasionally after an assignment or on special occasions when serious challenges confront you and you need to be encouraged to persevere and overcome. I am also permitted at this stage," she continued, "to reveal to you a few events from your preexistence.

"You and I loved each other's company very much prior to your departure from our former home. Before your birth, we were occasionally sent here on brief errands. One such occasion was when a three-year-old girl strayed from her parents' camp unnoticed during a summer vacation and was happily chasing butterflies. She strayed too far and was heading toward a fast-flowing and dangerous river not too far from the camp. We were sent to intervene and save her from falling into the river by distracting her with a white rabbit that she followed to safety. The alarmed parents discovered her missing and were searching for her. They were relieved when they finally found her safe and happy. She told them about her new friends with the white bunny, pointing to us and smiling broadly. The parents looked in the direction she was pointing and were confused. They could not see us, though the child could."

She went on. "At the time your foreordained assignment was revealed to you as a spirit essence, your countenance changed. There was a tinge of sadness in your demeanor. Our all-knowing parents knew your thoughts and assured you that I would, at a future date, be clothed and born with a physical body on this planet and be united again with you, to raise a righteous family that would live eternally. I was equally saddened by your departure and missed your company very much. I was, however, permitted to observe your progress from your birth up until the time you attained the age of eighteen and were ready to be conditioned for your assignment. From the day of your birth on this planet, we continued to communicate with each other occasionally until the veil of forgetfulness was drawn over your memory. I remember one occasion when you were five months old and I was by your bedside conversing with you. Your mother came into the room to feed you. She found you chatting excitedly and smiling broadly. To her, as with most mothers, she saw you as a baby making incoherent sounds. She was happy that you seemed happy. What she did not know was that I was there with you the entire time, and that you were talking to me.

"Though you could have been permitted to see me when you were a young child, your memory of me was gone when you were about a year old, and the veil was drawn over the memory of your preexistence. I, therefore, chose to stay away and watch your progress. A spark of my memory was, however, permitted to linger in your subconscious mind, and the vision of me that was given to you in the Sacred Dome awakened the affection that had existed between us, causing your instant attraction to me."

She then went on to narrate some other experiences that we shared together in our former home and on errands to this planet. She described to me the beauty of our exalted home where we lived with loving parents. "The peace, the love, and the careful nurturing that was fostered to us there was soul-satisfying beyond your present recollection," she concluded.

I felt so content in her company as we hugged, held hands, ran among the trees, and watched the rabbits scurry to us without fear and the song birds alight on branches nearby to sing us love songs. I wished it could go on forever, but alas, it was time for her to leave. She held my hand gently, and in an instant, we were back in my room in the Dome. She leaned forward and placed a gentle kiss on my cheek, and with the assurance that I would see her again in the future, she bid me good-bye. She blew me a final kiss as she receded from me and was gone.

I woke up with a start to realize that it had all been a dream. Or was it? It had felt too real not to be true. I knew then what had happened and was sure she would visit again in the future as promised. I had slipped into a light slumber while thinking of her in my sadness, and Jane had come to take me on a spiritual journey to the enchanted valley to share those precious moments together. I understood that the contact with my hand had drawn my spirit to go on that journey, as had happened to me on my journey to the spirit realms during my training. By the time reckoner in my room, I realized that I had dozed off for only one minute, and yet the time spent in the enchanted valley with Jane had seemed like hours. I felt highly motivated and rested for one week, with a heart full of gratitude to the Supremos for their magnanimity toward me in my period of loneliness. After I was rested, I came out of my assigned room to see another panel glowing and flashing, announcing that it was time to embark on my next assignment. I donned my weapons, touched the glowing panel, and stepped into the unknown for a new adventure.

EPISODE III:
THE DREADED CURSE
OF KUNTURAMNI BIO

CHAPTER 13

The Visit to the Tribal Settlement

I stepped through the portal of another tunnel into the unknown, as was becoming the pattern. The brief reunion with Jane in the spirit had greatly boosted my morale. A number of thoughts, however, were resting heavily on my mind. This was my second assignment after my training, and I felt uneasy. *What was I to expect?* I had no reason to doubt the assistance of the Guardians when necessary. I felt they were closely monitoring my progress as before, and I was gladdened by that knowledge. Moreover, I had now built some measure of confidence after testing my arsenal of resources and some of the armaments given to me by the people who lived in the cities beneath the ocean. Because of my encounter with the Homoleotaurus, I was certain I could face any foe with the supernatural aid of those who had called and ordained me to this work. I concluded that I did not need to worry.

Prior to my touching the panel, however, I had updated my memory concerning current events in the planet's history through the memory machine. What surprised me most was the number of births on the planet in the last few decades, rising steadily. With advancements in medical science, the rate of safe births increased exponentially. It set me thinking about the factors that determine the location and time each human's birth. I received an answer.

It was impressed upon me that each offspring is precious to the Supremos and that the conditions and locations of birth and upbringing are unique to each and optimal for their soul's development. Their pathways in life, however, vary according to circumstance, character, agency, disposition, and talents. For some, the road may seem consistently rugged and thorny; others may find life easy or accommodating; others blissful and fulfilling—yet each has their own respective challenges, heavy tasks, and trials tailored to them, to mold them into who they need to be. No one knows what an individual soul's journey is like; no one can tell simply by looking at outward circumstances, however dire or dynamic they may seem to the natural eye. Everyone will have the opportunity to grow into godhood, I was taught.

I thought back to the youth in my time and the gullibility of my peers. I recalled how easily they were enticed by the next new thing, the sensational, the seductive, the scintillating. I was connecting the dots. The accelerating rate of birth meant a youthful population in a few decades. I knew the youth of this millennium should be my greatest concern. I had to start early to protect them from being stained and corrupted by the lies of silver-tongued Xoedikus and his evil hordes. I knew how intelligent the youth in the last few generations were. I knew of their reasoning power and creativity. I felt their energy and power and enthusiasm to put their intelligence to good use. I was certain that, given the right direction early in life, they would be able to see through the wiles of the adversary, reject his enticing offers, and put their energies to good use. I needed to convince them, through whom future generations would be born, of the true source of knowledge and life. I hoped with all my heart that their hearts would be softened to receive the message I had for them.

Suddenly, I found myself at the foot of a very large oak tree after exiting the Dome. Stretching for miles all around me were tall, large trees of a variety of species. It was indeed a very dense forest with a lot of weak, flexible stems of creepers. Long, thick, strong vines filled the floor as undergrowth and hung from the branches of the tall trees. I wondered what I was required to do in a seemingly isolated area such as this. I decided to look around for a little while to get my bearings. As I trudged through the undergrowth, I came upon a river that churned its way from the north, southward. I followed it for a while toward the south and observed that it had a tributary carving its course westward. Further down, a second tributary was winding its way eastward while the boisterous main river continued to flow south through the dense forest.

By all indications, there was no human habitation close by and this forest had not been accessed by humans for decades. I needed to find out about its recent history. I focused and relied on memory to learn of the recent past. Images flashed through my mind and began to arrange themselves like a jigsaw puzzle.

Located about seven miles away on the plains of the western sector of this forest were the tribes of Namumba and Kakumba. In the eastern sector, about six miles out, dwelt the tribes of Koazilla and Bambuka, and lying five miles southwards was the tribe of Lumsaka, the most populated of all the tribes in the region. These tribal settlements were located not very far from the tributaries of the river; the river served as the inhabitants' primary source of water. These were peaceful tribes that spoke the same language and had lived and farmed on these plains for generations. The distances between the settlements clearly indicated that they were not too far from the thick forest. It was a mystery to me why the tribesmen had been avoiding coming into the forest for decades despite its abundance of game.

I traced the history of the peaceful tribes a few generations further back and was again surprised at what I learned. For generations, the tribes knew nothing about the sector far north of this dense forest. Moreover, events associated with the forest brought great fear among the tribesmen who lived on the plains. All tribesmen who had ventured to this sector or came too close to the edge of the forest had mysteriously vanished without a trace. For this reason, it had become forbidden among them to venture close or to even speak of it. These superstitious tribesmen had consulted their most powerful shrine, located in Lumsaka, and had not received a clear answer as to why the mysterious disappearances were occurring. The oracle had merely warned the tribes of "the Curse of Kunturamni Bio" without giving much information about who or what Kunturamni Bio was, who it was that was cursed, or why the curse was affecting the tribes living near the forest.

Legend had it, however, that a powerful witch doctor had lived in the land about a century earlier and had been the source of a blessing and also a scourge to their forefathers. He had on occasions healed their sick with herbs and, on other occasions, placed curses on people he claimed had offended him. Misfortune and death had been the bane of those that were cursed by him.

It was said he could talk to the trees and tell them to yield up their secrets, and had prepared potions with which all types of diseases could be healed and with which spells could be cast on humans. He was the only one who could enter the forest alone for days and return with new concoctions to prepare his potions for healing and spells. Indeed, he was very much feared and often avoided when he came into any of the communities. He was not indigenous. In fact, no one knew where he came from or even his name. One day he suddenly vanished and was not seen or heard from in any of the communities for decades. His disappearance created much fear and deepened the superstition and feeling of insecurity among the simple peasants in the settlements. They became sorely afraid of possible vengeance from the spirits they believed dwelt in the forest with the witch doctor, and of possible repercussions that might come upon the tribesmen over his disappearance.

Their fear was validated when, a few years after the witch doctor's disappearance, men, women, and youth from the settler tribes started disappearing at an alarming rate. It was learned that all the disappearances occurred when the victims ventured close to the forest. Since that time, the tribes had avoided the forest and resorted to traveling by the long route in large groups to trade among themselves on their individual market days, always making a detour around the forest by very wide margins. Even then, occasionally, some members of the group would be found missing at early dawn or dusk on some of the trips to the markets and back. The tribes lived in constant watchfulness and anxiety and cried to the unseen deity of their shrine to redeem them from the hands of this evil. But the disappearances continued.

I realized it would be necessary for me to gain the trust of the tribesmen and learn of their beliefs, the stories passed down to them by their forefathers, and their current experiences. That knowledge would allow me to discern truth from myth. It was easier to mentally access clear historical information on past events than current events of a people that had given in to superstition and paralyzing fear. I needed to be tactful in my approach, though, considering the existing pagan undercurrents.

As I sat under the great oak tree, the wind started blowing, and I heard a rustling noise amid the foliage. Then I heard the whistling of the wind in the trees as its rate increased. It was as if a thousand voices were whispering the same message to me. The tall trunks of huge trees started swaying from side to side, as if about to topple over, and then the wind suddenly ceased. The rustling and whistling resumed at a greater intensity and then stopped again. This phenomenon was repeated at short intervals, and on each occasion, the whispered message became clearer and clearer until, at last, I thought I could decipher and put together the message being conveyed to me.

Could it be that I had been endowed with the power to understand the plants? I sat down and reflected at length on what I thought I heard. I was being warned that danger and destruction were coming from the north and that I was to be careful. The moment I came to that realization, the wind ceased and the forest again became as calm as when I had met it. This truly appeared to be an enchanted forest.

I received my warning from the forest trees and had formulated a plan at the same time to pay a visit to the Lumsaka tribe. In the night, I followed the course of the river and walked the distance to the outskirts of Lumsaka. I arrived at a stony area over which a little shallow tributary of the main river flowed gently into a pond of clear water. I sat close to the pond, from which it appeared that the settlers regularly fetched water for their domestic chores. I sat still on a piece of stone with my legs and arms folded, looking in the direction of the footpath that led to the clear pond. It looked like it was about three miles west of the settlement.

Early the next morning, a group of women and youth were making their way to the pond to fetch water when they saw me. In fright, they dropped their water pots and took off running and shouting. The message soon got to the community and the elders of the tribe that a strange apparition had been seen near the pond.

After about three hours of waiting, a large number of settlers—led by people dressed in nicely crafted animal skins and amulets, who appeared to be the warriors—approached. With caution, the warriors surrounded me at a respectable distance. One of them, who apparently was the leader, spoke loudly in a strange nasal language, looking me straight in the eye. I stood up with a smile on my face and moved toward him. All the warriors raised their muskets and moved back, waiting for a command to fire at me. The leader was a brave man and did not move but instead raised his palm to stay the intended action of his warriors. Then he spoke again in a loud, commanding voice.

I felt an impulse, a prompting from the Guardians, to go on my knees and bend to touch the ground with my forehead, with my hands stretched out in front of me, palms on the ground. I had the impression that this was the sign of peace expected by any stranger who came into their midst. I then sat up into a kneeling position with my palms on my thighs, still smiling. My intuition was right. It worked. The leader smiled back and moved with an outstretched right hand toward me, the others still fearfully looking on.

I stood up and shook his hand, to which he said something in his language and beckoned to me to move in the direction he was pointing. I moved abreast of the leader and was followed by the warriors and the frightened settlers who had accompanied them. All the while, I was attentively listening to the hushed conversations of the throng of people following us at a respectable distance. I felt strongly that I was being taken to the tribal head and his council of advisors, the elders, who would have gathered by now to receive a report on my capture or destruction.

As we approached the settlement, I heard deep and light notes of sound from musical instruments coming from the direction of the settlement. True to my expectation, we arrived at an open area where canopies had been erected for shade, and I was surprised to see a chief, not a tribal head, dressed in his regalia and his royal elders seated. They were waiting with talking drums, horns blaring, and xylophones and other string musical instruments delivering mysterious and soul-chilling sounds. Almost the entire population had gathered in fright to have a glimpse of the dead body of the strange apparition in their territory. The death or capture of the apparition was hoped to bring an end to the riddle of their vanishing people.

I noticed that the settlement was a township with fairly good paved roads and a few other civil amenities. The muskets, canopies, and machetes were indicative of established trade with a civilized people.

The throng of frightened natives quickly parted to create a wide pathway for the advancing warriors and their strange prisoner. I was brought before the chief and his elders as the leader of the warriors gave a lengthy speech, after which the chief began to speak. As tradition demanded, the chief paused at intervals to allow the linguist to explain his response to the listeners. While they spoke, I continued to focus on the syllables of the language, and before long my gift of learning languages took over, and I could understand what was being said.

After I had been presented to the chief and his council of elders, the leader backed out to join his warriors in a semicircle behind me. I heard the chief instruct the leader of the warriors to strip me of my weapons, to which the leader responded that I had shown no aggression when they arrived to investigate me and that I had acted more as a friend than an enemy. He indicated that I must be shown hospitality rather than offense.

To their surprise, I then spoke haltingly in their dialect. "I have been sent here to help you solve the mystery behind the many disappearances that have brought insecurity and fear among your people. I am a friend and mean no harm to your people or the others who dwell on these plains. All I desire is to have your cooperation and assistance in solving this problem once and for all."

At my words, the chief and his elders welcomed me. The chief then instructed the head of the warriors to go with me to the shrine to consult the oracle and get the nod of the priestess, and then to bring me back to the gathering for a formal introduction to the people. I was led to the shrine and was admitted into the presence of a beautiful woman of about forty years of age. She had a large number of small, attractive beads strung around her neck and a light mauve silk blouse and a white skirt made of a thick, beautiful woven cotton material. Around her ankles and wrists were strings of large beads. On her beautiful hair rested a crown crafted from ivory, with a circular gold medallion dangling on her forehead. Her feet were bare, but she wore a ring on each first toe, as well as on each finger.

The beautiful priestess of the shrine was sitting crossed-legged on a red cushion. Another red cloth covered the wall behind her. In front of her stood a low table covered with a clean red cloth, in the middle of which stood a calabash with a fluid that looked like water in it. Around the calabash were cowries arranged into three concentric circles.

She looked steadily into my eyes without blinking and then into the fluid in the calabash.

"Stranger," she said in their dialect, "you carry a power that is greater than any other power we have ever known. You have been sent into our midst to solve the problem of the vanishing tribesmen, but beware—beware of the forces that support and sustain the Curse of Kunturamni Bio." With that, she relapsed into silence, and we were compelled to leave her presence.

My escorts brought me again into the presence of the chief, who asked one of his elders to formally announce the acceptance of my presence among his people and instruct them to give me any assistance I might need to succeed in solving the problem of the forest. Talking drums were used to send the same message of my arrival to the distant communities in the other tribal settlements.

I had succeeded in my plan to form an alliance with the troubled tribesmen. They would now talk to me freely to help me gather the information I needed to conduct investigations concerning the strange phenomenon in the land. Over the next week, I spoke to those of various ages in the community who had been present when relatives had vanished without a trace while going or returning from the market. Details of accounts varied, but the storyline remained the same: Many who traded were never seen again. They also told me that very faint humming sounds had been heard occasionally and had appeared to come from far away, in the direction of the forest.

I could not read any mystical disappearances in these events but suspected abduction by beings stalking the tribesmen while remaining unseen. Apparently they silently whisked their victims away into the unknown. For what purpose the tribesmen were being abducted, it was difficult to establish. I had been cautioned about the north, and this kindled my suspicion that the assailants may have come from the northern part of the area. I needed to travel through the forest in that direction in order to verify or dismiss my theory. Though the tribesmen believed the forest was unending and uninhabitable, they agreed that I should try and find out the truth for myself. None of them was, however, prepared to take the risk of venturing into the forest with me.

I bid the chief and his people goodbye, promising to return to them with my findings. Early the following day, I started out on my way into the forest. The tribesmen accompanied me as far as they felt safe to go and waved me off. I was on my own again in their dreaded forest. I needed to travel fast, but the undergrowth of creepers and vines would slow me down considerably. I thought of using the transporter, but again, the terrain was uneven and would offer me problems. Moreover, I did not want to disturb the untouched nature of the forest floor.

Finally, I decided to make use of the long, strong vines hanging from the high branches of the trees. It was a good decision, for as I swung from vine to vine, I realized that I was making very good progress. As I whisked between the trees, I occasionally saw on the forest floor a variety of small cats, porcupines, deer, and poisonous snakes, which would have slowed my progress had I traveled on foot. I noticed that the river ran all the way through the forest from the north. I traveled this way for about six hours without stopping and had covered a distance of about thirty miles when I saw that the forest was finally starting to thin out. With no more vines to aid me, I was compelled to walk the rest of the way.

After walking another three miles, I arrived at a clearing where I saw telltale signs of human habitation. I would need to be careful from this point on. Stretching for the next five miles or more were neat rows of a plant that I suspected to be *Cannabis sativa,* the dreaded hemp or marijuana, which contained the drug cannabis, a hallucinogen that was illegally sold to youth of many countries by the underworld. Planted on the other side, parallel to the hemp and over about the same distance, was another more deadly addictive narcotic-producing plant, coca. The river was on the western side of the farms, and channels had been constructed to irrigate the farms as far as I could see.

Cocaine and similar drugs had been known to have destroyed the lives of many bright and promising youth over the years. These hallucinogens had impelled violent crimes and perversion and had directly or indirectly led to deterioration and death of their victims. My suspicion was immediately aroused, and I put on the cloak of invisibility to search ahead. *Could it be that these illegal farms planted deep in the jungle in this isolated area were somehow tied to the disappearances in the peaceful tribes?* I needed to investigate thoroughly before drawing any conclusions.

As I moved further north, I saw that the farms stretched beyond the five miles I had anticipated. On either side of the path, I saw the two types of plants stretch for miles. Such a large farm would require machines or a large number of humans to plant and to harvest. After about another two miles of farms freshly planted with new seedlings, I came upon a clearing, which I guessed to be an improvised runway for small aircraft. On the left side of the clearing was a long stretch of makeshift accommodations built with wood and roofing sheets, while a little farther on the right side of the runway were small brick homes. Dusk had set in by the time I reached the outskirts of the farm. It appeared deserted, so after my initial rounds of the facilities, I decided to find a safe place to rest until nighttime, when I would prowl around for more facts to substantiate my suspicions.

Behind the rough structure of wood and roofing sheets was a tall mango tree with abundant foliage. It was an ideal place to wait for deep night, so I climbed the tree and found a spot where two of the high branches naturally ran horizontally, almost parallel to the ground and close to each other, to form a comfortable resting place. Here, I relaxed to wait for the night. As I lay there, I thought I heard a sound like that of a running generator coming from the area of the brick houses.

As darkness fell, I saw lights come on in the brick homes. I also heard some music playing loudly in one of the larger brick houses closest to where I lay. At about eight o'clock, I noticed that most of the occupants of the brick homes had gravitated toward the house from which the music was blaring. I heard laughter and loud talking coming from the direction of that house and guessed that part of it served as the dining hall for the workers.

The buildings made of wood and roofing sheets were left unlit and remained dark and silent throughout the night. At about an hour to midnight, I saw some of the people in the mess hall come out with lit lanterns, which they lined up on either side of the improvised runway. Then the droning of a twin-engine aircraft was heard, and at exactly midnight the craft touched the ground and taxied to a stop.

The two men in the cockpit jumped out and were hailed by their colleagues on the ground. They began unloading large plastic drums and cartons of goods and took them into a shed, which looked like it served as the warehouse. The aircraft was reloaded with bales and bales of goods, after which it took off. The lanterns were removed and put out, and the group returned to the mess. By one o'clock, everyone had returned to his own house, and the whole compound had become silent except for varied pitches of snoring from the drunk and exhausted men in their brick homes.

When I was sure I wouldn't be seen, I descended from the mango tree and quietly moved around the large wooden houses. I noticed that the doors were not locked, and on further inspection, I was surprised to see that each wooden house was occupied by about fifty poorly kept humans of various ages and genders. They lay prostrate on the bare floors, clumped together in what appeared to be a very deep sleep.

The majority were adults who slept by their dirty tools, including machetes and hoes. The three rows of wooden houses, about forty houses total, held about two thousand people used as laborers. I made my way to the warehouse and saw that the door was heavily secured with three strong padlocks. I took from my arsenal a slim, pointed pin with which I worked on the padlocks. In a matter of minutes, I had succeeded in picking all three locks.

I opened the door to the warehouse and was surprised by the immaculate manner in which the goods within had been arranged. Drums and cartons of different sizes and contents had been neatly stacked and differentiated, and the floor was free of litter. I took time to examine the contents and discovered that the cartons mostly contained canned and preserved food supplies, while a few contained polyethylene and other packaging materials. The drums were found to hold various chemicals for their work, while a few large aluminum containers held some well-packaged apparatus.

A door on one of the walls opened into a small, well-equipped laboratory that seemed to be set up for quality control on production-line samples. Beyond the laboratory was another door, which opened into a sizable storage space for the processed and packaged items produced from the factory.

I needed to locate the processing factory and learn about the security measures used to protect its operation, so I rearranged the items I had disturbed during my inspection and relocked the door after me. I combed the area for a while before locating a tall rectangular brick building in the middle of the four rows of brick homes.

The factory had high windows and four sets of double metal doors, each of which had two wooden cubicles, one on either side of the entrance. These cubicles, I felt, were normally occupied by personnel who served at the security checkpoints when the factory was in operation. It became obvious after looking around that the security personnel who worked at these checkpoints were usually armed.

The doors were strong, and though I could have torn them from the hinges, doing so would have created a stir. At the right time, I hoped to identify those running the factory and controlling the laborers, and to help the poorly treated laborers in the wooden housing. I postponed touring the factory until it was open and working.

I continued my investigation by walking the length and breadth of this drug-processing community, taking note of everything that attracted my attention. By dawn, I had become fairly familiar with the lay of the camp. I had barely settled down in my hideout amid the dense foliage of the mango tree when I saw some men approaching the door of the first wooden structure. They opened it and shouted at the occupants to march forth and get to work.

I saw the occupants file out in an orderly line to the furthest side of the farm, where planting was in progress. The occupants from the other sheds were similarly called to their various duties, which included harvesting, carrying the harvested hemp in sacks to the factory, carrying finished products from the factory to the storage room in the warehouse, and clearing more land for hemp planting. No whips were being used on the workers. However, a guard would occasionally fire gunshots into the air to goad the workers on.

As I observed them working, something about them appeared odd to me. They seemed to almost be in a trance. They worked without complaining or even resting, and their eyes looked glazed and empty. It was as if they had been programmed or were under some hypnosis. My suspicion was confirmed when, at noon, at the sound of a loud horn, they put down their tools in unison and shuffled to their sheds to eat some cooked tubers and herbs that were provided. Then, at two o'clock, they shuffled back to resume their work and closed at six o'clock, just before dusk.

Each, however, knew where he or she should sleep and stretched out with his or her working implement by their side. I had seen enough to understand why this pitiable team of forced labor never complained or conversed while working side by side, or even made an effort to escape. They had no control of their minds and only responded to programs fed them from an external source. Their actions were all at the behest of their masters.

Was this hypnotism or some kind of magic? It reminded me of the possessive spirits in the dimensional or kaleidoscopic world I visited, who had mastered the art of taking over the bodies of weak-minded, receptive humans and who'd used these annexed bodies any way they pleased.

My anger was kindled against the drug lord and his team of heartless officers for denying humans the right to live individually and freely. Exploiting others and using them to destroy others' lives—those to whom these mind-damaging drugs would be peddled—was wrenching. I needed a plan to redeem these exploited natives and to destroy the farms and equipment.

My major challenge was going to be restoring the memory of these induced automatons. *How were the captors able to put them into this state where they lost their individual identities?* My mind then focused on something that was revealed about the witch doctor who could access the secrets of the plants and trees in the forbidden forest of the natives.

I was determined to give it a try, and I felt divine forces would aid me in finding a solution.

Having arrived at this decision, I started out from the camp in early dawn under the cover of partial darkness and arrived at the edge of the thick forest when the sun was just about to emerge from hiding in the east.

CHAPTER 14

The Secret of the Vanishing Tribesmen

After traveling by the vines in daylight for a while, I stopped for a moment and sent my thoughts back to the time the witch doctor lived and occasionally dwelt amongst the natives. I was desperate to find a solution to the problem affecting the indigenous people. Moreover, I was curious to learn the reason behind the witch doctor's disappearance. A hazy vision of him began to clear.

I watched as he carefully picked up a variety of leaves in the forbidden forest and began pounding them together. I took mental note of the types of leaves picked and combined to obtain different potions. I watched as he added water, coconut oil, and small quantities of smoothly ground ginger and pepper to the pounded leaves, boiled them, and strained the concoction to extract liquids which he then allowed to cool. He administered the resultant potions on trapped rats and mice to see their effect. He was able, through these trials, to develop a variety of panaceas for a variety of diseases.

As I watched, I observed one type of potion that appeared to kill the rat. The muscles twitched continuously for the space of approximately two minutes, then stopped. The rat lay motionless. Then, after a while, rigor mortis seemed to be setting in, and the motionless rat became very stiff. Then, strangely, after the witch doctor poured an additional potion into the rat's mouth, the rat was slowly restored to full activity. It was if the witch doctor had imposed a temporary paralysis on the critter, which he then reversed. After the second dose, the rodent began running around the enclosure frantically.

Could this be the product administered to the laborers on the hemp farms? How could the owners have learned about the potion?

As I continued to observe the witch doctor, I noticed that he often traveled far into the forest in search of special leaves and roots for his potions. On one such trip, he encountered a group of foreigners who appeared to be exploring the virgin forest. Communication with them was initially difficult, but through hand gestures and broken communication, he was able to gather that they had come to farm and produce tobacco for their employer. The tonnage demanded was great, and they had been searching for a sizable piece of land for the project.

An agent who had ties with the government had referred them to this unexplored area to see if a portion would be suitable for the tobacco-development project. They asked for the witch doctor's assistance, and he designated the present site of the forest as the most suitable for them. After some tests were carried out, it was concluded that the land would be most suitable for their endeavors. The company was delighted with the discovery. The land was purchased from the government, but labor would be difficult to come by because there were no villages close to the selected area. The nearest settlement was about forty miles away. The company was eventually able to hire workers from distant townships and bring them to the site by helicopter to clear the land and to begin planting. The workforce was provided with the wooden structures to serve as temporary accommodations.

Brick homes were later constructed for the officers of the company, and a rough runway was built for bringing in supplies and transporting the tobacco. Because the witch doctor had become a regular visitor to the site, he began to acquire friends who shared their foreign liquor with him. In time, the secrets of his potions were craftily extracted from him and documented by the company chemist. The locations of the five other tribal settlements in the south were also discussed casually, and the foreign company kept tabs on them.

For almost six decades the company prospered. The tide turned when chewing and smoking tobacco were found to adversely affect human health. Heightened awareness of tobacco's impact on health, in the form of negative media campaigns and advertisements, led to a decline in tobacco use. Smoking was banned or discouraged in public areas in many countries on the planet. With the later link established between lung cancer and tobacco smoking, the tobacco industry gradually collapsed—and with it the contract for the supply of tobacco from the farms.

By this time, the old witch doctor hadn't been seen in any of the communities for years, but the compiled list of potions and drugs and their methods of preparation remained in archived records of the company laboratory. The new generation of officers of the defunct tobacco company became desperate and called a meeting to discuss new ways to survive. They agreed that they would go into the planting of hemp and coca and find a market with pharmaceutical firms that might need it for medicinal purposes.

They managed to find a few pharmaceutical firms in the city that needed small quantities of hemp and coca for legalized drug preparation. Filling that need provided some revenue but not sufficient to allow the company to break even. The head of the firm then serendipitously met a very influential philanthropist. The two quickly became close acquaintances. While discussing business one day, his new friend learned about the rapidly growing hemp and coca farms—and became intrigued by the business. He offered to finance its processing secretly on the farms and have it delivered to an agreed-upon location for a very attractive price.

Back at the farms, the officers were excited at the turn of events, but most of the workforce had been paid off and lifted to their townships and could not be persuaded to return to the isolated farms. In desperation, they searched for labor and remembered the five tribal villages south of the farms. Hence, the plot to kidnap people for labor, using the witch doctor's potion, was born.

The chemist had searched through the old files in the laboratory to discover what his predecessors had compiled about the potions. He worked and experimented on rats until he had recreated the potions that caused partial paralysis and restored muscular activity without full consciousness.

An armed team from the farms ventured deep into the forbidden forest and located spots that were fairly close to the tribal villages. With the money provided by their new financier, they purchased a few more helicopters, and each of the three spots was sufficiently cleared of trees to create a landing pad. Thus began the mysterious disappearances.

These abductors would lie in wait until a tribesman would come close enough, and then they would shoot the isolated victim with darts dipped in potion. Paralysis was almost instantaneous, and the helpless tribesmen would be dragged into the forest and carried to the helicopter. In the initial stages, large numbers of tribesmen from the five settlements could be captured per trip, until the frightened tribes got wise to the danger of going too close to the forest. The captors then resorted to laying ambush before dusk and pouncing on those that strayed from the large group—going to the neighboring markets at dawn and returning the following dusk. It was the noise from the distant helicopter that the tribesmen described as the occasional humming sound heard coming from the direction of the forest.

Back at the farms, the paralyzed tribesmen were injected with the antidote to restore them to activity so they could then use them for labor on the farms. Parts of their memories were lost to the effects of the potion, and they were somehow programmed to respond to commands as if they were under hypnosis. They were fed on tubers and a few nutritious herbs, to which some of the leaves used in making the potion were added to keep them strong and secure their hypnotic state. They were an ideal and cheap source of labor for the farms, and multiplied fortunes exceedingly.

I also learned that back in the city, the philanthropist, Geri Karlvaski, who had now become the kingpin of the illegal drug industry, had set up secret agencies in many cities to recruit peddlers for the illegal cocaine, cannabis cigars, and cigarettes. Though the selling price was very high, business was flourishing in the underworld, especially at the expense of the ignorant youth.

Lives were being destroyed, and the crime rate was rising in many of the cities. Murders and rape, which were rarely heard of in times past, were the order of the day in the cities affected by the drug craze. Law enforcement officers who were investigating the source of the proliferation of these dangerous drugs were targets of the secret agencies and the peddlers.

Some law officers lost their lives on duty, while some consciously turned a blind eye to the activities of the drug agencies and peddlers for attractive purses, having sold their conscience for filthy lucre. It was a desperate situation that required a rescuer. I could demolish the program by destroying this farm and its central and outlying processing centers, but first I needed to find a way to free and heal the zombies who worked on the farms. Many of them had died over the years and had been buried by their colleagues in shallow graves. Others who were fairly advanced in years had less time to live, but quite a reasonable number of them, both male and female, were young and strong. Moreover, each was a child of the Supremos and deserved a free, decent life in the environment in which he or she was born; each deserved an opportunity to learn of the universal laws of life or love and make a choice to obey or reject them.

I sat quietly among the tall trees of the forest and started meditating, in search of a solution to restore the tribesmen and reunite them with their relatives in due course. As I focused on seeking divine intervention, the rustling of the wind in the trees started again and increased in intensity. Just as before, I thought I heard whispered instructions through the wind to look for three herbs, flashing a purple color on and off. To this instruction was added the mode of preparation of a curative potion.

Had the witch doctor truly been endowed with this gift of communicating with plants to learn of their secrets, as I had learned earlier? The phenomenon of the wind rustling and whispering in the foliage continued, and the message was repeated until I became sure of what I was required to do. Then it stopped as suddenly as it had started.

As if directed by some unseen force, and after combing through the area where I'd sat to meditate, I was able to find the recommended plants in abundance. It was obvious from the plethora of plants in this area that they were common and could be found throughout the forest. Nature had revealed and confirmed some of its secrets to me; now I was sure as to how to seek help from the plant kingdom when required. The universal wave linked all living things, which were designed to support each other to progress in this life. If only we could learn how to treat and relate to one another, and to the natural world, in love and concern for the divine ecology, we'd be lightyears ahead of ourselves. Each plays an important part in the progression of all life as instituted by the Supremos.

I'd been divinely guided to unravel the secret of the vanishing natives, their whereabouts, and their current state. I'd been provided with the antidote for reversing the effect of the potion administered to erase their memories. I'd also been educated regarding underground agencies in various cities that were peddling mind-destroying drugs. I knew they were produced in this factory deep within the forest and far from the knowledge of law enforcement. I now had to visit the processing plant and formulate a strategy to destroy it, the hemp farm, and the products—without destroying human life, if possible.

I also needed to find out the secret behind the Curse of Kunturamni Bio. The priestess of the shrine at Lumsaka had mentioned it but had not hinted further about its nature. I made up my mind to visit the processing plant first and learn about its operations and anything else that might throw extra light on the whole operation.

I took off in the direction of the illegally operating farm and arrived at midday, when the factory was at the peak of production. At the edge of the hemp and coca farms, I put on the cloak of invisibility and walked the distance to the factory along the path between the plants, and through the workforce in the field. The doors of the factory were closed, and two guards armed with guns were posted at each door. The guards were used to their routine, and because their location was so remote and they had never experienced any attack by rivals or law officers, they were casual in their duties. I knew that before long, the opportunity would present itself for me to gain entry to the factory.

Waiting for chance was taking too long, so I decided to distract the guards. I went to the isolated outer housing of the generator that supplied power to the processing plant and flipped the power switch off. The reaction was instantaneous. The engineers on the plant threw the doors open to investigate the cause of the generator's failure, which had brought the whole factory to a standstill. They were followed by some security men who were inside the factory, leaving one exit door ajar with the attendant guards' attention focused in the direction of the generator. I took advantage of the opening and slipped inside the factory. Soon the generator was restarted, and processing resumed. After I entered the facility, I observed the whole production process, from the placement of raw materials to the packaged products. There was a laboratory staff that collected samples at some stages in production to test the purity of the products on the line. The company was indeed a more lucrative venture now than it had ever been.

Then, as I was moving forward to inspect something else that had caught my eye, I accidentally tipped over a white substance in a beaker. It fell and broke, and spilled the contents all over my feet. I instinctively moved away from the spot, only to leave the traced outline of my feet made by the white substance on the floor. One of the security men close to the spot turned in the direction of the noise from the broken jar and saw the footprint on the floor. He immediately raised an alarm, and the whole factory was thrown into confusion.

A siren blew as armed men were brought in to search for the intruder, while more security men were posted at the exits to ensure that no one left the factory unnoticed. I was in a fix. I quickly climbed the wall with my micro-suction climbing gloves and perched on the sill of one of the high windows. Scores of officers and security men were afoot, with guns cocked. I stayed on the windowsill to avoid any collision with the search team. After a long while, the tempo died down considerably. The outline of the feet on the floor was still a mystery to them, but in time, work resumed until the factory closed down at seven o'clock in the evening. As the workers left for their homes, I quietly followed them under the cloak of invisibility. Meanwhile, I had acquired enough knowledge to know the operation's points of vulnerability.

I made my way to the wooden sheds under the cover of night to find the laborers lying on the filthy floors as usual, as if in a trance. The drug was very potent, and I needed to neutralize its effect to wake the tribesmen out of their hypnotic trance. I needed to go back into the forest to collect a large quantity of leaves in order to prepare the antidote.

For a week, I worked at this in the forest until I had produced enough for my needs and stored them in some empty plastic drums I'd found in one of the unused sheds next to the laborers' wooden habitations. I then collected more of the four types of leaves I used for the potion and kept them stored for future use. When I returned to the outskirts of the farm, I waited until night fell and then silently entered the camp. I picked the lock of the storage shed and took out several syringes without needles. Since I did not have the facilities to refine my potion through scientific extraction, I needed to administer it orally with the syringes.

It was deep in the night when I entered the shed in which the tubers and herbs used to feed the laborers were kept. I replaced most of the herbs with the extra leaves for the antidote that I had collected, but left some of the originals to disguise their appearance. I hoped that those assigned the responsibility for the daily preparation of the herbs to feed the laborers would not notice the substitutes.

For the next week, I substituted the leaves and monitored the supervisors in case they discovered the switch and raised an alarm. But, as time passed, there was no indication that the alternate substances had been detected. After all, the new additions were not too different from the old leaves, and it would take closer scrutiny to know the difference. Moreover, those in charge neither had cause to suspect any sabotage nor cared much about the quality of food, as long as the laborers remained healthy and strong and were available to work.

For yet another week, I watched and noticed some signs of consciousness as the antidote began taking effect. It was now time to put my final plan into action. On the last night of the second week, I waited until the unsuspecting supervisors were all asleep and the camp was quiet. Then I slipped into one of the wooden accommodations for the laborers. I was surprised to see some of them sitting on the floor holding their heads, as if trying to remember who they were. It was dark within, but thanks to my improved vision, I could see them.

I began to speak in their language, alerting them to my presence.

"Hello," I said slowly so as not to frighten them. I could sense their alarm and tried to allay their fears. "My name is Magnus, and I have been sent by our mighty creators to deliver you from captivity. I have not come to hurt you." I could tell that their superstitious minds wondered if they had imagined me, or if I, the unseen speaker, was a vengeful spirit. Their fear was actually encouraging, however, because it let me know that the antidote was indeed working—they were waking up after their long slumber.

"You have been captured by a foreign force that has been illegally drugging and exploiting you as slave labor. Because of the mixtures they have been feeding you, you may have trouble remembering who you are and where you're from. I am here to help." I could see the shock on their faces as I explained their condition to them. They began looking around frantically, as if noticing their surroundings for the first time. I went on, "You all belong to tribes that surround this settlement, and you have families and friends anxiously waiting for your safe return." I saw tears begin to well up in some of their eyes as they began to remember their former lives. "I know that you are eager to return, but for now I need your cooperation if we are to escape safely. For the past few days, I have been lacing your food with an antidote to the drugs you have been given. It is imperative that you continue to take this antidote in order to fully restore you to your former selves." They mumbled quiet responses, which further confirmed that the antidote was working. "But," I continued, "more than anything, you need to continue working with the same diligence as before until the time is right. The guards cannot find out about your recovery, or all is lost." My final words hung in the air with solemnity. I watched as they continued to look around and even talk to one another and noted that these people were far from the automatons that had worked without rest and responded to commands without question. The herbs I had added to their diets were doing wonders and gradually neutralizing the effect of the potion initially administered by injection. The neutralizing antidote was now being unknowingly administered through their food.

After a while, I repeated the instructions regarding the need to drink the antidote in order to make a full recovery. They responded affirmatively. I then personally administered the first dosage to each one of them, since it was dark and visibility was very poor, and then moved on to the next wooden habitation to deliver the same message. By dawn, I had succeeded in administering the antidote and winning the confidences of those within three of the wooden shelters.

It took me another forty days to work—even at an accelerated rate—in administering the first dose of the potion to the rest of the natives in the remaining wooden sheds. I was happy to observe that none of them rebelled or resisted, and all continued smoothly as planned. When almost all of them had fully recovered, I began choosing leaders from the various working groups and gave them instructions regarding Operation Freedom. Though they seemed largely recovered and could reason, I noticed that they got up on time as before, worked and went on break for meals, and closed at the given time, as if they were still controlled by some outside force. Though this behavior was favorable to the cause and aided in keeping suspicions among the supervisors at bay, it appeared abnormal to me. I began to have a nagging feeling that there was something I'd overlooked.

CHAPTER 15

The Last Stand and Freedom

T he plan was now complete, and I was just waiting for the appropriate time to kick into action. The opportunity came during the time of the next airlift of goods. I managed to sneak onboard the aircraft loaded with bales and bales of cannabis and coca products as it was being loaded. It took off, and after three hours, it landed on a little airstrip close to an isolated canyon at about five o'clock in the morning.

Trucks were waiting to convey the goods into the city. The trucks were loaded and kept in waiting for the night. I lay on top of the lead truck, still under the cloak of invisibility, waiting to see where the trucks were headed. During the night, I heard the engines start and felt the trucks begin to roll forward as they continued toward their destination. They were driven under escort to a big warehouse in the city, and the goods were unloaded and stacked alongside a large stock of similar bales of goods.

The warehouse was advantageously located a few miles from an intercity railway station, a vantage point for transporting the goods to other cities beyond. Not far from the warehouse I approached were similar ones, housing various goods, provided with railway tracks and cars that linked with engines to convey loaded goods to other destinations.

It was obvious that I'd chosen the right time to arrive at this big warehouse. In fact, it proved to be the main center of distribution of the illegal goods. The large stock was an indication that the stock released to the agencies for distribution was now low and that the agents would come here to replenish their goods. This would most likely require that Geri Karlvaski come to supervise and personally collect the money that would accrue from the sale to the agencies, and to receive reports on events in the sectors of the agencies.

It was now daytime, and the area around the warehouse was quiet, with no indication of recent activity. I had allowed myself to be locked in and was spending the whole day setting small fires to a number of places. The large stock of jute sacks used in packaging the illegal products provided adequate fuel. The moment sections of the goods burst into flames, I opened the latches of the four high windows on either side to make my escape and allow the inflow of oxygen to accelerate combustion. After a while, the conflagration was noticed by some owners of adjacent warehouses, and the fire service was called in. By the time the fire service arrived and was able to break into the warehouse, though, everything had been totally destroyed.

News of the disaster traveled far, and by the following night, the area had burst into activity again. Karlvaski arrived first by helicopter with four armed security men. Not long after his arrival, the custodians of the goods also arrived, shaking with fear. They had secured the warehouse very well, as they had always done. The suspicion arose that a carelessly dropped cigarette butt by a goods transporter had been the cause of the destruction of the total consignment worth millions of currency.

The open high windows were noticed but did not raise any suspicion, since they could have been left that way by the firefighters. Geri was furious but also relieved that there was no evidence of the type of products that were kept in the warehouse, and thus he had escaped being investigated and caught in his illegal activities. The drugs had been destroyed, and tragedy had been averted.

Out of greed and desperation, Geri called the aircraft team to return to haul in an emergency consignment to restock the agencies for distribution. He would personally have to fly over to the farms to inform them of the disaster and to negotiate a delayed payment for the drugs that had been destroyed under his care, and for the release of a new consignment to him.

Messages were sent to the agencies to postpone their arrival at the rendezvous until a week later. The frightened warehouse custodians were warned to be more vigilant the next time and to hire labor to clean up the mess the following day. As the drug lord and his security men boarded the helicopter to fly to the farms, I hitched a ride by sitting on one of the landing skids.

After about three hours, we arrived at the farm, and about an hour later, the other aircraft also arrived. The stage was now set to put my next plan into action. I first took advantage of the darkness to immobilize Karlvaski's helicopter's tail rotor by removing critical parts. I did the same thing to the rotors of the others' crafts that were used for kidnapping the tribesmen. In addition, I drained the fuel supply of the helicopters into plastic containers and hid them at vantage points throughout the broad cultivated farmland, as prearranged with the workers. I finished about an hour before dawn and went to my hiding place to wait for daytime.

The following morning was a busy day for the officers. The presence of Geri Karlvaski on the farm was regarded as a great honor, for he was the source of their income. He was led on an inspection tour of the factory that he had loaned funds to build, as well as of the residential facilities provided for the officers and laborers. They inspected the large stock of products that were packed into storage bays and were ready for shipment. Karlvaski was then led to the farm. He stood at the edge of the wide expanse of fields to look at the long stretch of cannabis and coca plants in various stages of development. He was pleased by the large number of laborers working on the farm.

There were areas where the plants were matured and were being harvested, while other areas had plants that had recently been planted. He viewed these with lustful satisfaction, probably calculating in his mind the wealth they represented. The quantity lost in the fire was only a fraction of the goods matured for harvesting, and there were additional finished products in stock. The stages of maturity of the hemp gave the indication of a continuous supply of the goods for a long time.

Finally, late in the evening, the touring team retired to the officers' mess hall for negotiations. The discussions were long and frank, and after initial disagreements, the farm officials finally agreed to release the entire consignment to the kingpin the following day, as he had requested. He had been key to the farm's success when he loaned them enough money to set up the processing plant at a time when it would have been impossible otherwise. Though they had fully repaid the loan with interest, he was their only source of revenue now, as the primary purchaser of their products. Afterward, the company drank a toast to the success of their transaction and then relaxed and conversed about affairs of the globe far into the night. The Karlvaski later said his goodnight and meandered off to bed in his assigned guest room, with security personnel posted at the entrance.

I had quietly followed them throughout the day, observing and making mental notes of their every statement and plan. Deep in the night, I climbed up the wall of the factory and through a high window into the processing plant, and I permanently immobilized all of their machines. I then started from the matured crop farthest out from the camp and nearest to the forest's edge and began making my way through the settlement with my ray gun, setting the farms ablaze.

The fuel from the helicopters and the twin-engine aircraft had been planted at the vantage areas where I'd instructed the tribesmen to hide them on the farm. As the flames traveled to these locations and the plastic containers ignited, the plastic melted away and the fuel exploded, spreading the burning fuel throughout the surrounding areas, thus accelerating the destruction of the illegal crop. Only about five acres of newly planted hemp on the farm was deliberately preserved to serve as evidence.

After ensuring that the destruction of the rest of the farm would be complete, I turned my attention to the stock of finished products in storage. I picked the locks and entered with the intention to set the products on fire, but by this time an alarm had been raised and the officers and supervisors had come out to witness the destruction. They scattered in confusion, unsure of what to do.

Karlvaski was jolted awake by the commotion and came out to find his livelihood on fire. His first reaction on discovering that his million-dollar empire was being destroyed was to rush to the location where the stock of finished goods was being held in storage, to save it from being destroyed. I had originally intended to destroy the drugs but had been inspired not to, since evidence would be required to catch the kingpin in his dirty work.

I now saw the wisdom in setting a trap by picking the locks to the room where the products were being stored, making it easier, as anticipated, for his men to load as much of the finished goods as possible into the aircraft. The light twin-engine craft could carry only a sixth of the tonnage of finished products in stock.

Karlvaski then issued instructions to his two pilots to lift the goods to a spot near the canyon and arrange for its transfer to another warehouse close to the one which had burned. They were then to send messages to all the established distribution agencies of distribution with specific orders: They were to congregate at the familiar location in three days, instead of one week, to collect enough stock for the next two months. The aircraft was then to return to haul more of the consignment until all the sound stock was evacuated to the city warehouse. But three days was enough time to finish executing my plan and to expose the "philanthropic" drug lord for who he really was.

Karlvaski then left to see the state of the fire and to inform the company of the measures he had taken to ensure sufficient goods were sold to finance the replanting. After all, the period of growth was very short, and before long, the new plantings would mature and they would be back in full business.

It was dawn by this time. Daylight revealed a pathetic sight—the company staff and supervisors lamenting their great loss, their hope worn thin. The farm was totally destroyed. When the pilot tried to start the engine, he found that the aircraft had run out of fuel. Panic set in. However, the pilot had always deposited enough fuel in a drum at the storage onsite just in case of emergency, so the craft was quickly refueled. We experienced a smooth takeoff from the farm location—the craft having boarded an unknown passenger—me. Once again, I joined the moving trucks after they finished loading at the new warehouse, which was not too far from the one I had burnt down. While coded messages were being sent to the agencies from the security guards, I made my way to locate and inform the police authorities about the activities of Geri Karlvaski and the time and location that the drop was going to occur.

They desired to know of my identity, but I assured them that the information was good and that it was my duty to alert them. It was necessary that all who were involved be exposed and convicted according to the laws of that country.

After leaving the law office, I stopped by one of the shops in the city to purchase five portable solar-powered radio boxes. I then returned to the warehouse area to wait for the time when the aircraft would return with another haul of drugs and then send a message to the haulage trucks to return to the canyon to convey the goods to the warehouse. I joined the haulage trucks heading down to the canyon and snuck onto the aircraft on its return to load more of the products from the farms to carry them to the city.

On my return, the farm was in confusion. The discovery of the damaged processing machines and the fuel-less helicopter, as well as the damage to its rotors, had raised the suspicion that there was an intruder in their midst. In fact, it was suspected that a government agent had infiltrated their ranks and was in the camp.

Karlvaski, it was argued, had been in the business for a long time and would not shoot himself in the foot like this. After all, this was the source of his wealth. As for the tribesmen or natives, they were not in control of their senses and therefore were incapable of planning and executing such a complex plan. The suspicion fell on the personal security. They were the only ones who had been in the vicinity when both acts of arson were carried out, but they would have to be dealt with after the helicopters were repaired. One of the security men, a trained mechanic who had been enticed into working for Karlvaski with a handsome salary, had himself surmised that the disruption was an act of sabotage. He went so far as to identify the parts needed to rectify the problem. The kingpin ordered a new rotor for his helicopter and also enough fuel with extra drums to enable the other grounded helicopters to return to the warehouse and get the operation up and running again. The items were purchased, and as soon as the parts arrived, the mechanic got to work.

The other security man was inexperienced when it came to airplane and helicopter technology, so the greater suspicion fell on the mechanic with knowledge about aircraft. However, he also had a strong alibi provided by his colleague, who swore the two of them had been at their post throughout the night. Moreover, on the day the warehouse stock was destroyed in the city, the two security men were in the company of Karlvaski in another city on business assignments.

The cause of the mayhem was a great mystery to the officers and the supervisors, but not to the tribesmen who were still playing their roles—acting as automatons to avert any suspicion of conspiracy.

By the evening of the third day, the stock of packaged products I deliberately spared had all been hauled to the shed in the city, and the fuel and helicopter parts for the damaged helicopters had been brought to the farms. There was enough time for the mechanic to complete the installation of the rotor and to fuel it.

The drug lord needed to get to the city to supervise the final distribution of products to the agencies as promised. He assured the officers on the farm he would be back as soon as he finished in order to deal with the chaos.

Meanwhile, the ravaged fields needed to be prepared for early planting, so the tribesmen were organized to blend the ash from the burnt hemp into the soil for planting. The kingpin had left for the city on the night of the third day to fulfill his promise and—unknown to him—to face his capture, trial, and conviction. I had laid out a foolproof plan to get him arrested and had now only to look to the freedom of the tribesmen.

Security had been doubled on the farms, especially during the nighttime. There had been no need for tight security in the past, but recent events changed that. I rested for the whole day following the departure of the kingpin and prepared mentally for the following day. When night fell, I slipped into the dark sheds where the workers slept, doing my best not to startle them. When they heard my entrance, they began sitting up.

"I am sorry to wake you, my friends, but the time is soon at hand to win your freedom." I could see the sleep leave their eyes as I continued speaking. "We move at dawn, but for this to work I need your complete trust and cooperation." They all nodded their heads solemnly in agreement as I filled them in on their roles. When I had finished speaking, I could see in their eyes that they would do whatever was asked of them.

When I was sure that they understood what was expected of them, I left the last shed and started my rounds on the security personnel posted at various points along the residential quarters and the factory environs. As I came up behind them, I knocked each one out silently so as not to disturb the others and conveyed them, tied and gagged, to a spot behind the wooden structures. Their firearms were taken and given to some of the leaders among the tribesmen who had been trained in shooting while with their tribes.

After I had finished dragging the last guard behind the sheds, I broke into the armory and collected more weapons to arm others who knew how to use them. Preserving lives was paramount. Each member of the group was cautioned not to take any life needlessly. They needed these arms only as weapons of defense. I gambled on the officers and supervisors of the farm surrendering without too much resistance since they would be outnumbered. For each officer or supervisor, who together totaled about two hundred men, there were about eight angry tribesmen. Already a total of twenty-five of the men who were on security duties the night before had been overcome and bound, leaving one hundred seventy-five more men to be captured.

When the officers and supervisors awakened to tend to their normal posts, they were stunned to find that they were surrounded by the labor force armed with guns and machetes. They were also surprised to find that their armory had been broken into and completely stripped of weapons. Without weapons to fight, the frightened officers and supervisors had no option but to surrender. They were bound and taken into custody and guarded by the armed tribesmen. I was inspired to go to the office of the chief executive officer to look for other incriminating evidence. The leader was a cunning man and had not kept much information on file. I was, however, fortunate enough to stumble upon a list of coded information that I was able to decipher. It was a list of the names of corrupt officers who were on the payroll of the kingpin's organization in the cities where they operated.

Now that the major work had been done, the next thing to do was to organize the tribesmen in order to rejoin them with their tribes and to hand over the two hundred prisoners to the authorities. Although the parts removed from the helicopters could be restored, I was hesitant to attempt flying one of them. When it looked like we had reached a standstill, I recalled my super-natural abilities: I could teach myself how to fly the craft. I immediately went to the cockpit, retrieved the operator's manual, and started reading at super speed. I also delved back into my memory to watch countless numbers of pilots operate their planes. In just a few minutes, I had the knowledge needed to safely pilot one of the helicopters.

Within an hour, the parts I had removed from one helicopter had been fitted into place on another, and the fuel from the reserves brought in by the kingpin were used to fill it up. I then began interviewing the officers to identify which one of them was the pilot and took him on board the helicopter. He sat by me with hands bound as we took off for the city after informing the tribesmen that I would be back soon. We arrived in the city a few hours later, and with permission, we landed at a small field near the police office complex.

I handed over the pilot to the authorities and submitted a detailed report on the activities on the illegal farms, ending with the surrender of the farm personnel, who were now tied up and being guided by the exploited tribesmen. Next, I privately gave the list of the corrupt officers to the chief of police. I was, in turn, informed that an ambush had been laid the previous night to capture the kingpin and his customers. Karlvaski had arrived by helicopter at midnight, as expected, to wait for the managers of his drug agencies. They had all assembled by two o'clock that morning at the warehouse, which had been opened to admit four buyers at a time to collect their supplies, pay, and leave. As each agent left the scene, one by one they were followed and captured, about two miles away, by government forces. Because each had incriminating evidence of illegal drugs on them, all but the last four agents had been quietly arrested. The kingpin and the remaining drug agents were finally apprehended after a shootout with the remaining security guards. They had been arrested with the remaining drugs, and the drug money was confiscated as evidence.

The kingpin had been shot in the thigh after attempting to escape. When he realized that he was caught, he attempted to shoot himself in the head but was disarmed and bound. By interrogation, the locations of the remaining drug agencies in the other cities were revealed, and measures were being taken to shut them down as well. The arrest of the kingpin was to be kept out of the news to enable the security forces to clean the system of as many of those involved in the drug business as possible. The kingpin and his team had all been taken into custody under heavy surveillance to await trial and conviction.

It was good news to learn that one of the largest drug suppliers in the country—and probably beyond, into other countries—had finally been eliminated.

Samples of the seedlings cultivated on the farm were collected and photographed. Forensic data was also captured from the fields, the factory, the filthy and cramped residences of the tribesmen, the homes of the officers, and the processing factory. The exploited tribesmen were interviewed and tested, adding kidnapping, slavery, and abuse of human rights to the list of charges against the agents and Karl.

Everything had worked out as well as I could have hoped for, and the last thing that needed to be done was to resettle the tribesmen. The government was cooperative. They advocated that tribesmen who wanted to return to their settlements should be relocated to join their families, while those who wanted to remain on the farm could do so, continuing their agricultural labors for the government. All the aged men and women—and some of the younger ones as well—chose to remain and their requests were granted. The helicopters were confiscated by the government with a promise to send them and a few more back for the evacuation of those who had opted to go back to the settlements.

All seemed to be well, and I felt that I had been successful. There was only one unresolved issue. I noticed a subtle but odd behavior in the tribesmen. Even after obtaining their freedom and receiving an allocation of brick homes for their housing, when the time came that they had previously retired from their labors, they would shuffle to their old wooden shelters to sleep. They behaved as if some unknown forces were still controlling them. Since I had agreed to hang around until the tribesmen who desired to be reunited with their families were evacuated and those who desired to stay were properly settled, I decided to conduct further investigations to try and solve the mystery.

While looking around, I felt strongly that I should search the now-vacant homes of the former officers. I managed to search all two hundred homes without finding any clues, though. As I was about to chalk my feelings up to paranoia, I suddenly remembered that only a portion of the building that had served as the mess hall had been in use, and it was the only building that I'd not bothered to investigate much. I entered the building the following morning after the tribesmen had awakened and shuffled to the fields. I then started a thorough search. For a while I yielded no results, but then I noticed something odd about the wooden shelf behind the counter used to display various types of liquor. After reaching up and feeling around in it, I detected a hidden latch on the wall, just below the second shelf, and pulled it. To my surprise, the shelf quietly swung inward on hinges, revealing a dark room beyond it. I slowly walked through the entryway, and upon seeing a latched window,

I opened it to reveal a strange spectacle. Seated on the ground with his legs folded under him was the figure of a withered man who appeared to be very, very old.

Initially I thought he was a mummy, but then I saw the lashes of his eyes move slightly as he winced at the light that abruptly flooded the room. Around his neck he wore a metal ring, on which hung a broad metal plate that covered his small naked chest down to the lap. He seemed to have no clothing on below his waist except a number of stringed beads and the black cloth on which he sat. A rectangular table covered with a similar black cloth stood before him, on which rested a human head with the flesh dried and with eyes equally shriveled in their sockets. Hundreds of tiny pins were stuck fast in the dried parchment of skin covering the skull. He was surrounded by a number of gourds, which I assumed contained various potions. He gazed up at me with weak, tired eyes and uttered in a feeble voice something I couldn't quite make out. I knelt down to hear him properly as he whispered again, "I am tired."

He was silent for a long time after that, as if saying as much had taken a lot out of him. When he gained more strength, he continued in an almost imperceptible voice, "I am Kumaziri, the roaming herbalist in these parts." He paused, caught his breath, and muttered, "I was naturally gifted in the art of healing. I could hear and use the secrets of the plant kingdom to achieve any end. I became very powerful and was feared throughout—." His body shuddered under the strain of speaking so much, but he continued with his tale.

"With my success came pride and arrogance. I was invincible, until one day, as I was walking through the forest, I came upon a strange and evil apparition that commanded me to serve him so that he could give me wealth and power, greater than any power on earth. He said he could give me wealth beyond my dreams. All I had to do was to win souls for him in exchange for his offer.

"Pride and wicked ambition overcame reason and drove me to carelessly accept." At this point, the old man began shaking, and I could see tiny drops of sweat start to bead on his forehead. "In the initial stages, my desires were fulfilled, and I lacked nothing. I was happy as I walked among humans, enticing them to submit to the power of the one I served. I won many souls for him, but as I grew older, I began to feel a void that power and wealth could no longer satisfy. I was empty.

"I was feared and shunned wherever I went. I became so lonely, and I desired to stop serving him but realized that I had gone too deep. I had sold my soul to him and would be destroyed if I broke our agreement. I went on to meet the men who had arrived to cultivate tobacco in these parts and befriended them. I worked among them for a long time to have company. I even shared my secret with some of them, but none had the power to help me." Tears began to spill from his sunken eyes and roll down his weathered cheeks as he finished his sad story.

"I finally resolved to face the consequences rather than continue in his service. For my rebellion, he placed on me the Curse of Kunturamni Bio, which inflicted upon me a strange weakness and then partial paralysis that finally left me trapped here. None of my potions could stop my body from gradually wasting away and becoming the living dead that you see before you now. I have lost count of days, and I no longer know how long I have lived. I do not eat and cannot sleep, yet I do not die. I would give anything to sleep. I am tired."

He finished on that sad note and then went quiet. Stunned at what I had just discovered, I, too, sat silently as I gathered my thoughts. "Are you aware at all about what's going on in the outside world, or even just here on the farm?" He looked at me with a puzzled expression and shook his head no. "It's over. The entire business. It's gone. We stopped Karlvaski, and he is currently in custody." The old man's eyes lit up slightly at this.

"What about the tribesmen? I lured so many over here, and it eats at me every day. So many lives ruined. Are they alright?" I wanted desperately to tell him that they were fine and all was well, but the image of their entranced faces and their mindless shuffle flashed across my view. "Well, you see, that's the last mystery. We were able to get them off of the drug that allowed them to be controlled, and their taskmasters are all gone, but they continue to labor mindlessly on the farms as if they are still under some kind of spell. That's why I'm here. I'm trying to figure out why."

He listened intently to what I was saying, but he was still very tired from speaking so much earlier. He closed his eyes and sat still for a long time without uttering a word. Finally, after what seemed like forever, he began to speak again.

"I think I know why your tribesmen are still in a trance." He then gestured to the disembodied head lying on his table.

"Evil energy is housed in this talisman and emanates from it," he continued quietly. He hit the metal plate hanging from his neck, which emitted an almost imperceptibly high-pitched sound. "I am forced to ring this at dusk, midday, and dawn. I never knew why, but I believe that this is how your workers are kept under control."

He then beckoned me forward and gestured at the head. "Take this. Take it away, and burn it. Do not allow one piece to remain." I quickly ran back into the mess hall to find something to start a fire with, and I found some matches tucked away in a drawer behind the bar. I ran back into the room, struck the match, and ignited the head. I watched as the pins began to fall out, the head aflame. "Each one of those pins represents a person. A tribesman. As long as they remain in the skull, they are under its spell." We watched as the last pin fell to the ground, as the skull was completely consumed. He then instructed me to fetch some particular herbs and bring them back to him. I did what he instructed me to do and hurried to gather the supplies. On my return, I was forced to stop from entering the chamber by a thick, tall, shadowy apparition. The dark figure had no body, but I could feel evil emanating from it. While it struck a chord of fear, I knew it had no power over me because I was the messenger of the Supremos.

As it breathed out threats, I focused my mind and energy on the power and authority I had been given and was rewarded as I began to feel my body fill with light. Suddenly, a powerful burst of energy shot forth, and the entire room was bathed in white light. With a dreadful and soul-chilling scream, the apparition dissolved before me.

After the apparition had completely faded, I ran in to find Kumaziri sitting calmly, with a faint smile on his lips. He looked up at me, and with a faint sigh of relief, he closed his eyes. After a moment, he opened them again and instructed me to prepare the herbs. When I had finished, he brought the bowl to his lips and began drinking in the potion. After a small sip, he informed me that this was how he would regain his strength and be restored. He thanked me profusely and asked me to leave.

As I walked away, I thought of the frail man who had been trapped in that room for decades and felt pity for him. He had followed the evil one in his youth and had enjoyed the wealth and power and recognition he earned from his service. But, over time, he had regretted his actions and desired to quit, without success. He was now worse off than the automatons or zombies I had worked to free. He was a living mummy under the Curse of Kunturamni Bio, which left its carriers half-dead for centuries. No memory of such persons was left in the sands of time from the day the curse was placed on them. I wondered what his fate would be when he died and was received into the spirit world. *Will he be assessed as an ignorant heathen and given an opportunity to learn and live the true law? Will he suffer the punishment of the damned?* It was all at the discretion of the Supremos, the righteous judges of all.

Just before dusk, I went to the field to observe the tribesmen. I was relieved to see that their behavior had become normal. They did not all stop work as before; some stopped earlier and went to their allocated brick homes, and some later. The dreaded effect of the talisman had been lifted, and the others who opted to return to their settlements were now free to go. I owed it to Kumaziri for revealing to me the solution to the problem, and I prayed that he might be pardoned despite his ignorant submission to the evil one. "After all," I thought to myself, "he had regretted it and had ultimately defied evil." Moreover, despite his personal suffering, he had been concerned about others enough to reveal a way to free them. That was a good deed. I remained hopeful for him.

I went back to the secret room, where Kumaziri had stayed in seclusion for years in his suffering, to express my thanks to him. I opened the secret door, and to my surprise the room was empty. All that was left was a little heap of ash, some beads, and the metal ring and plate. The herbal remedy he had instructed me to prepare for him was right where I had left it, but the liquid was all gone.

I now understood what had happened and was happy Kumaziri had at last gone to rest.

In the week following, the government fulfilled their promise to evacuate all the indigenous people who had expressed a desire to rejoin their families at the settlements. Having fulfilled my assigned duty, I had the opportunity to join the helicopters used for the evacuation of the workers to meet the chief and people of Lumsaka again, as I had promised, and to celebrate our success. The riddle of the Curse of Kunturamni Bio and the vanishing tribesmen had been solved. The settlements were assured that the forest was safe and could now be visited without fear.

For three days, I remained and taught the people of Lumsaka the perfect laws of the universe and encouraged them to live them and to teach them to their children for generations to come.

"The greatest oracle, the Supremos, assigned me to come to your aid when you cried for help," I told them. "As long as you remain faithful to them, your prayers will be answered. For as long as you remain faithful to the Supremos, you will be protected from evil. If you should eschew pride and greed, you will be protected from the Curse of Kunturamni Bio."

I had sown the seed and was hopeful it would take hold and bear fruit in the community. I knew that in the future, some of their youth would travel to distant lands to acquire knowledge and return to teach them in their own language the teachings and uplifting messages being given in our day by the true Agents of the Supremos. I sought permission to visit the four other tribal settlements and teach them also. I left with each settlement a wireless radio box.

On the sixteenth day after the resettling of the tribes, I returned to bid the people of Lumsaka farewell and departed to the base of the oak tree. A moment after my arrival, there was a flash of light, and in the next moment, I found myself in the Sacred Dome. I was met, as usual, by the Guardians. They were happy with my success and congratulated me. I was given a good meal to nourish my physical body, after which I asked to rest to prepare for the next assignment. As I sat reflecting on my last adventure, I wondered what would be next. I glanced at a map of the planet in an attempt to guess where my next call would take me and what I would be required to do. I focused and reflected long without success and eventually gave in to sleep. Obviously, the Supremos did not desire for me to know of my assignments and their locations in advance for a wise reason, and I appreciated it.

Four weeks later, I stepped out from my room, under inspiration, to find another panel glowing and flashing with red light—a signal that the time for the next deployment had arrived. Equipped with my weapons, I stepped forward and touched the panel. The door slipped open, and I stepped through for a new adventure.

EPISODE IV: THE TRIBE AT EARTH'S CORE

CHAPTER 16

The Strange Tribe

As I emerged from the Sacred Dome of the Guardians, I was surprised to find myself in a land that was completely covered in snow. A heavy blizzard threw snow everywhere, and visibility was very poor. Even with my improved vision, I could not see very far. I started forward in what I hoped was a northward direction. I trudged over the icy terrain for miles, but there appeared to be no habitation or shelter in sight. And, thanks to the Guardians, while I still felt the sting of the icy air, the freezing temperatures had no adverse effect on me.

After what seemed like hours of dragging myself through waist-high snow, the blizzard abated, and I began to see this world of snow and ice more clearly. After travelling a few more miles, a high cliff covered in snow came into view. It was almost completely vertical and went on for miles. When I arrived at the base of the cliff, I stood wondering for a moment how I was supposed to get around this large obstruction in my path. There appeared to be no other option other than to scale it, but even that seemed impossible because of its smooth face.

An attempt to use my micro-suction climbing gloves proved futile, as my weight caused the gloves to slide down on the slick surface of the ice wall. I eventually gave up trying to climb and instead began examining the cliff's base hoping to find an area where the inclination of the slope would enable an easier climb to the top. I had been walking along for about a mile when I came around a bend to my left only to notice a continuing bend to the right and again to the left. I had stumbled on an S-shaped pathway that would have been impossible to see by an observer walking perpendicular to the ice wall.

A strange, wide tunnel bounded by a wall of ice lay ahead of me. I entered the spacious tunnel and followed the path, and though it was dimly lit, could feel it gently sloping down. Beyond the first ten yards, the tunnel was lined with rock but continued to stretch ever downward. After what felt like hours, I finally arrived at a rocky, winding stairway that led me even deeper beneath the surface of the planet toward its core. Junctions along the route were marked by broad and deep excavations, and the floors were lined with a glowing reddish metallic substance. The temperature in these excavated areas was cooler when compared with that of the main tunnel. It was obvious these enclosures had served as caves or settlements that had been deserted a long time ago.

I noticed that as I progressed deeper from the freezing crust, the temperature began to rise; the air became warmer and warmer. I arrived at the bottom of the long, winding staircase to find my path barred by a high gate fashioned out of the glowing metal-like material. The solid gate and perfectly hewn stairway confirmed my suspicions that intelligent creatures had either dwelled or were currently dwelling somewhere beyond. This realization made my pulse spike. *What sort of intelligent creatures lived so deep under the planet's surface? What did they look like?* I wondered. *Was I sent here because of them? For what purpose? Why weren't the Guardians responding to my request for information on this assignment, and why can't I find anything in history about my location?* Puzzled and curious, I continued to descend the flight of stony steps down into the depths.

Though ravaged with curiosity about this strange place, I had learned not to pester the Supremos with questions about what they desired me to do. I knew I needed to submit to them and trust them absolutely in everything. They had not failed me so far, and I was confident they would never abandon me if I were submissive and teachable, and pursued my assignment in faith and diligence.

I reflected on how I would manage to open the gate and felt the prompting to simply knock. The next minute, the gate began to slide slowly open, and I was greeted by a strange layout. Stretching for quite a distance was what looked like a world within our planet.

I stepped onto a floor that appeared red-hot, yet its temperature was moderate and very comfortable. The rocky ceiling of this habitation could have been no higher than the total height of ten tall men. I was also surprised to see that the entire area was well lit and airy. The cavern was located deep under the planet's surface, where the sun's rays could not reach, and yet the air was clean and breathable. These observations set me thinking about how such an ideal living environment could have been created in such a place. I heard the gate slowly slide shut behind me as I waited and grappled with how to contact whatever creatures lived so deep within the planet's core.

Fortunately, I did not have to wait long before six large, hairy beings emerged, three from either side of two wide tunnels that opened close to the gate, and beckoned me to follow them. They, I presumed, were the gatekeepers. They bore the structural proportions and gait of humans, although their huge frames, height, facial features, and hairy bodies made them look more like apes than men. I was relieved that they had not shown any aggression toward me, so I meekly followed them.

Along the way, I noticed rows and rows of shelters constructed out of rocky pillars and a combination of rock and the metallic substance from which the gate was fashioned. In between a pair of settlement segments—each segment comprising of about fifty units of shelter— were a series of open-ended pipes made from the same glowing material that were bent into an S-shape at the terminal but rose vertically to penetrate the ceiling. These pipes were linked by a series of horizontal pipes lying against the rocky ceiling. At the base of the vertical pipes was a transparent dome from which was emanating a humming sound; I guessed it might be that of running motors. After passing by a number of the shelters, we came upon a great lake with dozens of branching streams that had been created to supply the various settlements with water. The water looked clear, and though it was a lake, it had been designed to flow by creating a series of barriers over the brim of which the water fell from one level to the next level into the artificial tributaries.

Above the lake and protruding from the rocky canopy, clad in the glowing metal, was a series of pipes that were also interlinked. From the open ends of this large collection of pipes, water fell in drops into the lake in a regulated and orderly manner. It appeared that all the horizontal pipes between the residential segments converged to link up with the vertical pipes over the artificial lake.

At the junction of each tributary was a number of medium-sized transparent domes from which could be heard the humming sound of what I presumed to be motorized pumps. I speculated that these domes were responsible for providing safe water to the inhabitants. It was a well-planned settlement, and it further confirmed the intelligence of the beings dwelling there.

After walking for a while along the bank of the wide lake, we arrived at another series of settlements. My escorts led me into a shelter that was bigger and taller than the rest. It had a number of stories and rose almost halfway to the rocky ceiling of the settlement. The internal design and furnishing was far more beautiful than I anticipated, given the rough, stony outer view of the shelter. I looked around me in awe at the intricate designs on the walls and the plush seats and other furnishings. The inside was also cooler than outside, as if a cooling system had been installed to create a comfortable living environment for the residents.

I was led to the foot of a beautiful throne carved out of a beryl-agite type of translucent, precious stone and lined with a soft, leather-like material that shone. As we continued forward, four of my escorts departed to resume their duties at the gate. Meeting our anticipation, an elegantly robed man appeared with four escorts of his own from behind a curtain with pearls woven into it in patterns. As he sat down on the throne, I saw that he was a tall man with extremely handsome features. He was by all measures a perfect human, and so were his four escorts. The one sitting on the throne captured my surprise and appeared amused. He smiled and, in a language remotely familiar to me, issued some directives to one of the two remaining escorts from the gate, after which the beast started pulling off the front pieces of its huge skin upon touching hidden fasteners.

A well-built man, about my size, emerged and jumped down from the huge frame that had been formerly been one of my escorts. This was another great surprise to me. The large frames of my earlier escorts were actually protective suits with intricate engineering mechanisms for internal control, and not the real beings themselves! *How could they move with such agility and ease in this bulky shell? Why did they don those suits while living in this safe abode?*

After waiting for some time, allowing me to get over my surprise, the man on the throne, who I presumed was their leader, addressed me this time in the same ancient language as before. "Hello. My name is Zadok Yochanan, and I am the head of these people. Do not be surprised to find humans like you living and surviving in a location deep inside the planet," he began. "In the beginning, we were twelve tribes from common parentage, and we lived under righteous kings who loved to serve the Supremos and live the universal law of perfection.

"We became a nation dearly loved by the Supremos and were nurtured to become a delightsome race, favored by them. Our land, a gift from the Supremos, was flowing with sweet wine, milk, and honey, and we were protected and strengthened against barbarians who attempted to invade our territory. For generations, our empire fought wars and was victorious, allowing us to expand through the conquest of the territories around and beyond us. We grew to become a rich, powerful, and highly feared, yet respected nation.

"The beginning of the end of our kingdom began after decades of righteous rule by two successive kings. The youthful successor of the last king, who was highly favored by the Supremos in the beginning, became proud and conceited, married idolatrous women from heathen nations, and began polluting the pure worship of the Supremos by worshipping their wives' and concubines' idols. The general populace was thus led into idolatry. They violated the sacred laws of perfection and indulged in the frenzy of riotous celebrations. They abandoned brotherly love and became envious, greedy, covetous, proud, and contentious. They thus rebelled against the Supremos and the true path to happiness. We lost favor with the Supremos, and with it our protection from the barbaric nations around and beyond our territory.

"The first sign of disintegration and disaster was an internal rebellion that caused the splitting of our beloved nation into two, the North and South, each ruled by a wicked and proud king. Our plight worsened when the next successor of the northern kingdom placed the citizens under heavy taxation. The division and the heavy burden of taxes weakened the kingdom enough so that when the heathen nations attacked, the kingdom was overrun and vanquished. Our ancestors were part of the conquered kingdom. A large number of our citizens were butchered, and many of them were taken captives and marched as slaves farther north.

"Along the way, the captives, numerous but unarmed, revolted against the captors. Although some were killed and some recaptured, a large number of them managed to escape and find their way to other unknown nations. Our ancestors appointed leaders and traveled far in a northwest direction to avoid recapture.

"For a period of over a century, they traveled by land in nomadic fashion until they reached an ocean. This forced them to take to the water in strong and well-stocked boats to escape barbaric tribes that roamed that territory. As time passed, old generations gave way to new, who followed in the footsteps of their ancestors. Along their nomadic trek, they survived on roots, wild fruits, fish, and snared animals. The skins and fur of these animals were preserved to provide protective clothing and shelter against the weather.

"An entirely new generation of our ancestors finally arrived in this cold, mountainous land. The climate was wretched and the land was blanketed in snow soon after their arrival, but they were grateful to possess it. They carried with them a written history including our origin and the events that motivated our travels. They also had in their possession a faithful record of the laws of the Supremos as given through inspired Agents on our former land. Repentant of their rebellion, they began crying to the Supremos for forgiveness and help throughout their journey. It was under their inspiration that they began the laborious construction of a passageway toward Earth's core, safe from apprehension and enslavement.

"As they ventured deeper and deeper, they discovered iron, magnesium, nickel, and other rare and unknown elements and compounds. Revelation guided them to mix some of the unknown elements with iron and nickel. This formed a tough alloy that glowed and that could, even in its thin foil, insulate anything against excessively high temperatures, while maintaining a far lower temperature on the outside. This discovery turned out to be one of their greatest blessings. Using this alloy as an insulator against the hot environment enabled them to dig deeper into the boiling depths of the planet's core than they would have been able to otherwise. They created numerous safe areas to dwell in as they progressively dug further down, deep into the planet's bowels.

"Finally, at a level our ancestors considered safe, they began digging and building horizontally to create what you see now for future generations. At intervals of fifty meters, vertical columns were dressed and strengthened with thick layers of the alloy and decorated to support the rocky ceiling of the settlement. The molten alloy was also poured to form rigid insulating and protective layers on the floors of each dugout. This protected abodes at each level from the heat that emanated from the lower depths of the planet. The same alloy was formed into thicker plates to fashion the sliding gate, and was used, as well, in constructing rocky columns, basements, and the comfortable shelters in which they dwelt.

"The reddish glow that provided a little illumination was, in time, replaced with chemical light obtained by experimentation with other compounds. Generations later, they discovered how to utilize the heat from magma to produce power; this involved the use of special conductors. This, in turn, led to the production of unlimited power to run efficient power generators to provide more light and to power the pumps that processed clean water and fresh air. Plants that could survive in artificial light were planted to help filter the air and bring an ideal balance of gases to their habitation.

"Vertical, metallic, tubular shafts were laboriously passed through the constructed and vertically-created passages over very long distances. These opened into the rocky parts of the planet's crust, from which drafts of air, saturated with water, were sucked by powerful pumps into the habitation. The vapor condensed in the cooled pipes, and the drops of water that fell were collected into a wide, deep basin, lined with the alloy to form a lake. The lake waters cascaded over the brim into lower concentric channels. From these, artificial tributaries were created, allowing the water to flow and undergo treatment before supplying various sectors of the habitation with needed moisture.

"Treatment of the condensed water from the planet's surface became necessary when various varieties of high-yielding fish were introduced into the artificial lake; these had to be fed with organic matter. Fish that they were able to culture in the lake, vegetables that they were able to cultivate in specially designed structures, and large seasonal tubers dug from the surface, including a few varieties of fruits, became our ancestors' staples. They still form the bulk of our diet in this age, but due to the rapid increase in our population, we've supplemented these with fish caught in the surface seas during our periodic expeditions, as well as animals trapped on the land some miles from our abode.

"Because of these trips to the surface, we were at risk of discovery and harm. Thus we created those suits you saw the guards wearing, as disguises. To the surface dwellers, we appear to be a part of the ape family adapted to the cold climate of these parts. Made from the same alloy as the rest of our settlement, these suits effectively hide our identity while giving us the advantage of size, strength, and agility over almost any opponent. This allows us to overpower other creatures and use them for food and clothing. Our carrier mechanized suits are made up of different furs, but mostly that of polar bears. Surface dwellers rarely spot us, and those that do usually freeze to death, so our identity largely remains a mystery."

I then remembered the numerous stories of the elusive abominable snowmen that had been sighted near the Arctic Circle and the northern part of Canada by explorers and other research scientists. *Was this the explanation for the legend of the yeti or Bigfoot?* I now understood why no capture had been recorded, though a few photographs had been obtained of this elusive creature.

I now understood that each carrier mechanized suit was designed from one, two, or three different kinds of leather and fur, the most common of which was polar bear. The shape of the head, space for the eyes and nose, and the shape of the ear also varied slightly according to the designer. It was amazing how these intelligent settlers had managed to elude surface-dwellers by wit and design over so many centuries.

Musings paused as Zadok continued, "Our ancestors covenanted to live by the universal law of perfection and thereby established learning centers to teach this and impart other technical and secular knowledge to their offspring. We have been beneficiaries of this vision. With the faithfulness of our ancestors, they and we have been blessed and often inspired to innovate and improve our society.

"Many, many generations before our settlement here, about two thousand years ago, our history recounts a miraculous encounter with a member of the ruling Head of the Supremos who was the architect in the creation of this planet. He taught the Law of Perfection and assured our ancestors that he would establish a kingdom of peace and love, which our people would be part of —if we remained faithful to the Supremos and were obedient to the laws we had been taught.

"This wonderful message of assurance has been passed on from generation to generation and reiterated by Agents raised from our loins from time to time to be the mouthpiece of the Supremos. We have carefully avoided any interaction with the population on the planet's surface and are thus ignorant of their level of development or deterioration, but we have faithfully lived by the law and have enjoyed peace, prosperity, and progress ever since.

"We are a peaceful people and gladly welcome all who come to us in peace. We only use weapons and violence if we are acted upon, and only then to defend ourselves, our families, and our homes. We look forward to the day when this kingdom will be established on the surface of this planet as promised. Your coming has been known to us for generations, and we have counted the days until the fulfillment of this revelation. The purpose of your visit, however, was not revealed. All we knew was that you would be sent to bless us, so we prepared ourselves for your arrival.

"Now that you know our history, we wholeheartedly welcome you into our domain and appeal to you to tell us of your mission in this secret abode of ours."

When I realized it was my turn to speak, I began in a halting version of their language, still wondering how my coming among them had been revealed and known in generations past, even before I was born on the planet.

"Thank you for your warm welcome and your generous hospitality." No sooner had I spoke those words when I remembered what Jane had told me about preexistence and foreordination. Enlightened by the memory, I continued: "I was led here for a reason that I have yet to learn from the Supremos," I continued. "I can appreciate your desire to keep your location a secret and assure you that I will do all in my power to ensure it remains that way for the duration of my time here." They nodded and smiled in approval at my words as I continued. "I ask that you allow me few days to scout around your settlement and prepare to receive any directives that the Supremos may have for me. My only concern is the rest of your settlement. I fear that because they do not know me, they will view me as a threat and act accordingly. I would appreciate it if you would allow me to have escorts, or if an announcement of my arrival could be made," I finished humbly.

Zadok smiled widely as he stood up from his throne and began walking toward me. When he reached me, he stretched out one of his powerful arms and pulled me into his side in an embrace. "Your coming at this time has been anticipated by our people for the last four decades, and the predicted time has been accurately fulfilled. You were known to them before your arrival," he stated. "You are a special person sent to us by the Supremos, and every household has prepared and will gladly receive you as an honored guest. Have no fear of an assault by any group of citizens. We are a peaceful people, and all are anxious to accommodate you in any way that they can. All we ask is that you spare some of your precious time to dine in our households."

With this assurance, Zadok instructed two of his attendants to take me to a well-furnished suite, where I was given a nutritious meal of fish and vegetables. A comfortable bed was available for me to rest and to seek further instruction from the Guardians. After eating, I reflected on how to conduct a survey of this strange land and where to start. I desperately needed the Guardians' direction, but strangely, I drew a blank whenever I made the effort to contact them or access my memory bank. Finally, I decided to start my investigations from the source of what I had identified by his description to be electrical power and the water supply system. With that decision, I lay down to rest and prepare myself for the next day.

CHAPTER 17

Threat to the Settlement

That night, I fell into a fretful sleep and was greeted by a strange dream. The dream was so vivid. I was convinced it was more of a vision or a revelation than a dream, and it had something to do with my assignment in this strange habitation.

In my dream, I had seen two of the earth's plates that had previously been separating at a gradual rate over the centuries suddenly change direction and begin moving toward each other. When they met, the one that was denser merged under the other. I could not understand what forces had brought about this sudden change, but the result was disastrous. I saw a series of earthquakes at the points of collision and sudden malformations of the planet's crust above them. At the points of impact beneath the ocean, waves of extraordinary height hoisted and buried nearby cities, destroying everything in their path. In other areas, landmasses folded, with some parts sinking and other areas rising to create deep valleys and ranges of high mountains with volcanic eruptions spewing hot lava and deadly gas. The commotion and destruction it caused was immense. The surface was thrown into chaos, structures were splintered and destroyed, and lives lost in great numbers.

I pondered the clarity of the dream and responded to the promptings to start my investigations early. *If this could happen to the crust of the planet, what then would be the fate of a settlement in the bowels of the earth?* I got to work immediately, starting with a survey of the periphery of the habitation.

For hours and days, I searched untiringly for any clue of a threat to the habitation—without success. I pleaded with the Guardians to respond to my request and reveal to me my mission in this strange land, but I continued to be met with silence. I carried on my search. I investigated next the areas of power generation, where the glowing metal had been used to insulate the residential areas from the heat of the magma. I also examined the transparent structures that housed the pumps and other equipment for water treatment. I was unable to find anything that could be responsible for the possible destruction of the settlement.

Frustrated at the lack of answers, I sat down and began thinking. *Was the dream that I had really just that—a dream? Maybe it was the product of a tired mind. Why am I not receiving answers? Where are the Guardians when I need them?* For the first time since I had received my call to protect humans, I was disappointed and felt my confidence waning. I felt abandoned by those I had learned to reliably consult in my earlier adventures, and I could feel my faith wavering.

Dejected and deep in thought, and thinking back over the month of fruitless investigations, I heard the voice in my mind speak to me for the first time since my visit to this habitation.

"Have you really investigated everything in this land?" the voice asked. "You must come to understand that the Supremos, through the Guardians, will offer information and assistance where necessary but will leave you to use all your abilities to find out some things for yourself. It is through such personal efforts that you can build the experience and strength you need for the rest of your assignments in this millennium. You are still learning. Give all that you have."

I saw the wisdom in the counsel offered by the voice in my mind. It was the way of nature, and the best way, at that. The offspring of the mammalian class is taught the rudiments of survival and then permitted to build on lessons learned through experience— to survive and thrive on a planet full of trials, challenges, danger, misery, victory, and joy. The ultimate goal of this laboratory-like experience is to become more like the Supremos. I had been guided and assisted in my earlier assignments as a novice. I made some mistakes, but through them I gained enough experience to work things out for myself and leave the Guardians to direct or assist with the things that were beyond my endowed capabilities.

After I received this insight, I immediately went back to work. It occurred to me then that the only area I had not investigated was the pond. When I arrived, I surveyed my surroundings and then decided that I would need to search the depths of the manmade body of water. I dove into the deep and accelerated toward the bottom. Over a period of five days, I conducted a search for any clue to a potential threat. At the end of the fifth day, and after examining almost every inch of the pond, I noticed a very thin, almost imperceptible, fissure running from the eastern to the southwestern floor of the pond. Its discovery was made more difficult by the deposit of silt that had accumulated on the pond floor over the years. *Could this be the threatening problem to the habitation?* I needed to discuss this with Zadok to confirm my suspicions.

The meeting with Zadok was brief. Records kept over the years indicated a very slow but sure rise in temperature within the habitation. There had been recorded minor tremors in approximately fifty-year intervals, but they had not been considered seriously because of their once-in-a-lifetime frequency. Through the records of their ancestors, residents read about the destructive effects of earthquakes, but the reality of them was far-removed. They were long isolated from the populations on the planet's surface. Additionally, the knowledge regarding shifting continental and oceanic tectonic plates was born in modern times and was completely inaccessible to these isolated occupants of the inner part of the planet.

I made it my duty to educate Zadok and the other members of his ruling council on natural upheavals. I taught them about the structure of the planet and sketched a cross-section of it to explain to them in simple terms the structure of the hard inner core and the molten layer of the inner core surrounding it. Then I explained the inner mantle, and then the part of the outer mantle within which their habitation was located and which was part of the lithosphere. I explained that the lower part of the upper mantle, called the asthenosphere, was highly viscous and mechanically weak—the unstable base that was contributing to continental drift and the deformation of the planet's crust when the lithosphere was put under stress by the movement of the underlying continental plates. The highly ductile asthenosphere was the reason for the floating of the lithosphere's various continental and oceanic floors on what has been technically labeled tectonic plates.

They were a highly intelligent people, and it was obvious they were favored by the Supremos. My explanations of the fissure as the cause of the slight but progressive increase in temperature and of the periodic tremors as the cause of the fissure, were perfectly understood. After I'd finished explaining the science and cause behind the imminent disaster, we began discussing strategy. I cautioned them, however, to avoid creating any panic by revealing the findings to the populace. Everyone in attendance agreed that this was the wisest course of action.

As we continued our discussion, I understood the reason for my spiritual deployment. These faithful inhabitants were in danger, and they needed my help to map out a strategy that would save them. I felt that the Supremos had given me enough time to accomplish my assignment before the disaster struck, but I also sensed that we needed to hurry.

We decided to begin by looking through the old census records. The last census that had been conducted was about five years ago. At that time, it had revealed a population of about 1,455,000 people. It was decided that the first order of business was to conduct another counting, to be current. Census officers were immediately sent out to conduct citizen surveys and household tallies, including unborn, expected children.

In a period of five days, the census was completed, and the current population was about 1,936,000. Hunting and fishing parties were sent out on the instructions of the leader and his council of rulers to provide adequate food storage for any impending migration. Large quantities of fur and skins of animals were also gathered to provide shelter and to build different models of more carrier mechanized suits with compartments to house the aged, toddlers, and babies. Other models fashioned in the form of gigantic elephants, horses, and other carrier animals were craftily built and mechanized for easy control from within to serve as transporters to carry food, clothing, and other items for the trek. These huge models were dismantled and stored in the deserted caves in the upper levels to await the time to assemble them.

It was a labor-intensive crash program, but the hardworking citizens responded, and, in a few months, they'd zealously cultivated vegetables, dried meat, smoked fish, gathered tubers, and preserved fruits to keep in stock. Many carrier mechanized suits had also been built and allocated to families according to their needs. Progress was very impressive, but as yet, the purpose of these hurried preparations had not been revealed to the general populace.

I needed to know the terrain over which these underground dwellers would have to travel and how far they needed to go to escape destruction. Moreover, their movement needed to avoid attracting the attention of the surface dwellers so as not to incite a possible attack. I was at a standstill. *How would I be able to plan all of this without a good knowledge of the environment and the terrain?* The regular hunters knew part of the terrain and the settlements close to their hunting grounds, but they knew nothing beyond these areas.

It appeared to be a hopeless situation, so I again made a passionate appeal to the Guardians for help. *Please. I know that I have to do this on my own if I can, but I need guidance now. I've done all that I can think of to do.* I was delighted when the voice in my mind spoke to me, congratulating me for my efforts and faithfulness thus far. At long last, I had resumed receiving regular responses from the Guardians. It became clearer to me that though the desire of the Supremos was to teach and encourage humans to accept the universal law of perfection, they would never do anything that robbed any human of their free will. They would never dictate a course of action on any issue which that individual could, with effort, work out on their own. Each human was to apply the correct principles they had learned, seek guidance to understand and find solutions, and then pray for help to choose which of the planned solutions was the right one. Only under such circumstances would the Supremos inspire the faithful individual to the correct path.

In situations where one was on a special errand of the Supremos, as I was, the same principle applied. The Guardians would grace me in many unseen ways and then come specifically to my aid when there was an emergency, and I had no knowledge of what was ahead or could in no way find out about it unless taught. Direction and enabling power came often and as needed, and required me to do my part, even if that was asking in faith and trying my best to respond to impressions. Suddenly, the answer was made clear to me. "Magnus, the disaster will occur in the thirtieth month from your arrival. You must evacuate the habitation six months prior to the catastrophe." After hearing this, I realized that this meant we had sixteen months left to complete our preparation and move out for the six-month trek. The Guardians went on to explain that we would be led to a prepared habitation by a power from on high and protected from any threat or harm. "Magnus," he continued, "it is important that you understand that your protection and the protection of this settlement is dependent upon your continued obedience to laws that you have all been taught. We can only continue to direct you through your continued faithfulness. Remain steadfast, and all will be well."

After this final admonition, the voice in my mind went silent, and I knew what I needed to do next. I called for a meeting with the ruler and his council and relayed what had been revealed. They received it with joy, and preparations were immediately intensified to ensure that all requirements for a successful migration were accomplished on time. It was also decided that the time had come to reveal the impending danger and inform the populace of the plan for their preservation. Each household would be advised to put together only essential items and food for life preservation on the long trek.

One day, as preparations commenced, the hunters and fishers who had been busy bringing in game and fish to build stocks of meat, hide, and fur from animals returned from their duties with news: Poachers were spotted on the hunting grounds. Quite a number of bears and big game had been slaughtered and skinned, their hides taken away, leaving their carcasses scattered under overhanging rocks on the hunting grounds.

Their activities had been secretly observed at night by the hunting party. The poachers had easily overcome these strong animals using long muzzled weapons that spat fire, smoke, and thunder. I knew that was the best description they could give for rifles. I was glad they were sensible enough not to engage these night prowlers, but remained in hiding until they left at dawn in a flying machine, a type of makeshift helicopter. As worrisome as the encounter had been, it also blessed them with fresh meat of polar bear, musk ox, and caribou, in addition to those of the arctic wolf, mountain hare, and other small game whose bodies had been abandoned once their valuable skins had been taken.

Still, this information troubled me. The appearance of the poachers made these hunting grounds dangerous to the core dwellers. If the poachers were ever to see one of their people, they would mistake them for game and kill them on sight. Their identity would be discovered when they attempted to skin them, and then the news of their existence would be revealed to the world. Newsmen and researchers would likely attempt to capture them. The only way to avoid capture would be to stop the hunting parties from going out and to seal off the tunnel to their habitation, and with that would come an abrupt end to their preparations.

Realizing that the second option wasn't an option at all, I needed to figure out a way to stop the poaching. With this resolve, I sought permission from Zadok to travel to the hunting grounds to attempt to solve the problem. After I received the go-ahead, the citizens were commanded to remain in their habitation, and guards were posted at the entrance of the tunnel until my return.

I took my journey to the hunting grounds, ensuring that I traveled close to the ice wall in white camouflage to avoid being sighted from the air during the day. I arrived at early dawn after traveling for more than a day and sought out a cave that was not being occupied by any predators. I guessed that the former occupant had been killed by the poachers only a few days back because its scent was still very strong in the cave, which served to ward off other intruders from its territory.

For a period of three days, I waited patiently. Finally, on the afternoon of the fourth day, I was rewarded with the whirring sound of helicopter blades. I watched as two helicopters landed in an open area about two hundred yards from where I had concealed myself. The occupants included two pilots and six other persons who were outfitted against the weather and armed with rifles and other hunting gear. As they grouped to plan out their strategy and the direction each pair should go, I donned the cloak of invisibility and drew within hearing distance to listen in on their hushed conversation.

They were obviously making a lot of money on illegal trade, and the government was not aware of their activities. Rangers were occasionally assigned to patrol the area by air in the daytime, so these poachers did their hunting from dusk to dawn to avoid detection. By morning, all the animals that had been shot were skinned, some heads kept for trophies, and the carcasses concealed. In addition, the offspring of some of the animals were captured, after killing the parents, and were sold to private zoos in the cities beyond. If they weren't stopped, their activities would soon deplete the game in the area, especially if other poachers became aware of the spot.

While the two helicopter pilots waited in their vehicles, two of the poachers went east, another two went south, and the last two went west. I followed two of the armed poachers toward the east for about a mile and watched them conceal themselves under a frozen outcrop of rock. I followed at a good distance to avoid being detected by my footprints in the snow. They laid down in their protective clothes to wait for the falling of dusk.

After a few hours, their muffled conversation died off, and a quick glance in their direction confirmed that they had fallen asleep. I crept close to them, reassured that they were sleeping by the sound of their soft snores, and began hiding their rifles and all of the other hunting gear. I then cautiously tracked the men that had taken the southern direction and found them fast asleep as well, next to their gear.

I was busy planning how to get their gear away from them when I heard the sound of a helicopter above us. After quickly moving their weapons beneath one outcrop, the poachers moved to hide under another nearby outcropping. This was the opportunity for me to act. I waited until the helicopter turned northward to avoid being seen and then quickly moved to collect their gear.

The poachers were so focused on the helicopter that they didn't notice me gathering their belongings. After I had finally gathered everything together, I vanished behind an outcrop in the rocky terrain east of their position. Out of their sight, I moved faster and farther away from the spot and hid their gear in a shallow pit, covering it with snow. All that was left to do was sort things out with the last team that had traveled west. I was grateful that they had not brought any form of communication system with them so as to alert one another of my presence. It occurred to me that this precaution was to avoid detection by the patrolling law officers who were equipped to detect communication devices in their range of patrol.

It was now approaching evening, and I decided that it was time to go back to the area where the helicopters had landed to learn of any other developments. To my surprise, when I arrived at the place, both of the helicopters were gone. I hoped that this was an evasive action taken to outwit the patrol team, and that the poachers' helicopters would be back to collect them and their goods at dusk. From my hideout, I could see the eastern and southern teams moving toward the rendezvous point where the helicopters had initially landed.

Each team was arguing nervously among themselves about what had happened at their sites. As they arrived, they informed one another of the strange disappearance of their rifles and hunting gear and discovered that the other two teams had experienced the same thing. They wondered aloud if this was an action taken by the government to stop their illegal activities or if it was some sort phantom spirit that was angered by their unjust treatment of the animals. They concluded that whatever it was, whatever happened to their gear could have happened to them, but they had been spared.

As the evening wore on and dusk approached, we heard the sound of the two helicopters returning to the poaching grounds. The pilots landed to hear the strange events that had transpired. After assessing the situation and realizing that only the western team was equipped to carry out the poaching for this trip, It was finally decided that all should stay together until dawn to see if their colleagues would have any luck bringing in some skins and fur by then. The matter was settled, and all six personnel took shelter in the helicopters to wait for dawn.

It appeared that the teams did not bring any extra gear, and they didn't seem willing to risk moving around without weapons during the night. Because of this, I decided to go after the pair of poachers who had gone west. As dusk was just approaching, I was finally able to locate them. They were completely oblivious to what had happened to the rest of their team, since there was no means of communication between them. Because they were wide awake and preparing to move together for the hunt, I could do nothing but wait until an opportunity to strike presented itself. My chance came during nightfall, when the team's hunting lamps revealed a musk ox resting under a snowy overhang. The two poachers split up to get close enough to ensure that at least one of them could hit the target. I crept silently behind the one closest to me, and as soon as they were a reasonable distance apart, I leapt from my hiding place and knocked him out before he could utter a word. The dense sound of the poacher falling heavily to the ground was enough to alert the musk ox to our presence and sent him running. I heard a shot fired, which I was sure missed the animal. Disappointed, the poacher ran in the direction his colleague had taken and was met by a swinging blow that put him out cold.

The waiting teams in the helicopters woke up at dawn to find their two colleagues lying unconscious under one of the helicopters, stripped of their hunting gear. This was enough to send the remaining hunters running to get away. As I watched them take off, I smiled because I knew that my plan had worked. Just to be sure, though, I waited in the area for about a week afterward to make sure that they didn't return. They didn't.

After giving thanks to the Supremos for their aid, I started my journey back to the settlement with the rifles, ammunition, and other hunting gear, and I arrived within two days. After informing the governing body of my success, I showed them the weapons and gear that I had collected from the poachers. The leader and his council were amazed at the working principle of the rifle and its ability to bring down big game with little to no effort on the end of the handler. They assured me that their scientists would study it and build some for defense and hunting. I further warned that the hunters who went to the hunting grounds in the future needed to be very cautious.

Preparations for the evacuation of the settlement were continued without interruption from that time and into the following months. The carrier mechanized suits designed as beasts of burden were dismantled and transported to the caves in the area close to the entrance and assembled six months from the day evacuation was to start. Counselors supervised the loading of these huge carriers with protective wear, various implements, and preserved food for the trip.

Immense progress was made as the colony organized and prepared to abandon their beloved home. There was a hint of sadness in the air as they prepared to depart from the only home they had ever known, but they trusted their leaders' inspired judgment and cooperated in the preparation to leave for good.

CHAPTER 18

The Great Exodus South

It had been twenty-four months since my arrival among this intelligent and peaceful tribe at the earth's core. I had grown to love their honesty and industry. They lived as an almost perfect society, each resident serving for the good of the whole community. There was no want, and all appeared to be of one heart and of one mind. They lived in faith and sincere obedience to the universal law of perfection, as had been taught to them by the member of the Supremos who had visited their ancestors so long ago. Their community was a peaceful and harmonious one, and each citizen was his brother's keeper.

I mused at the contrast between this tribe and others. I compared them with the little I had seen in my earlier adventures among other societies on the globe—societies where acts of selfishness, greed, pride, jealousy, hatred, suppression, and exploitation of the poor, the ignorant, and less endowed was common. The evil forces reigned supreme and had captured minds to succumb to their every whim and cause mayhem that had no end.

No wonder these faithful people at Earth's core were so loved and favored by the Supremos and that I had been sent to their secret abode to rescue them from the impending disaster. I had enjoyed their unparalleled hospitality and absolute cooperation. We had worked hard together for the past twenty-four months to achieve the level of preparation that was desired, and we were finally ready.

The trek into the unknown started on the first day of the twenty-fifth month of my arrival at the settlement, as had been instructed by revelation. The people were organized into groups of ten couples with their children. All unmarried adults were classified as children and traveled with their parents. A leader and two assistants were appointed for each group of ten families to address the possible challenges that the group might face. Ten of the groups, totaling a hundred families, were also grouped as one large team under the leadership of a technological expert, a nutritionist, and a health expert to whom problems would be referred for a solution.

Leaderships of three talented men were set up then for each combined group of five hundred families, five thousand families, fifty thousand families, and so on until the whole population had been cared for. Any unsolved problems were to be referred to the ruling council to which I had been accepted as an honorary member. The decision or solution offered by the ruling council was to be accepted as final. Lastly, the carrier mechanized suits designed for goods, which were filled with preserved food and protective clothing, were put under the charge of appointed teams.

With all arrangements made for the little ones, the aged, and the few physically challenged persons to be carried in the multi-carrier mechanized suits, the exodus began. The ruling council took the lead and some guards were appointed to bring up the rear after ensuring the total evacuation of all citizens. The suits designed for goods were organized to move at strategic intervals between groups to ensure food and raiment was readily available to all. The suits for the aged and children were arranged to move along the sides of the long train of citizens. The majority, including the ruling council, chose to walk. The going was long and slow, but the people were cheerful and hopeful.

As we emerged from the tunnel that led from the settlement into the open crust of the planet's surface, we were surprised to see a strange wide tunnel stretching far ahead of us from the exit. It was bound by a thick green mist that defined the outer boundaries of our path during the exodus. We could not see through the greenish mist to know of our surroundings. Inside the tunnel, however, it was as bright as noonday, and the air was fresh. Far ahead of us, at the open end of the tunnel, we could see a pillar of clouds as if it were charting our course.

We traveled at a normal pace for a whole day until the internal light started to dim, indicating that night would soon come. Before darkness could fall around us, however, we saw the cloudy pillar begin to glow until it was very bright. The bright light that emanated from it filled the entire tunnel. Just ahead of the glowing pillar, we could see the tunnel gradually sinking into total darkness. It was a mystery why the brightly glowing pillar of light was filling only the tunnel with bright light, while everything beyond it was enveloped in blackness.

I sought permission, donned my transporter from the cities beneath the ocean, and rapidly moved toward the back of the long train of citizens. It was a long train, so it took me a while to arrive at the extreme end of it. My objective was to check on the welfare of the citizens. I was happy to observe that all was well and that, miraculously, the very end of the tunnel created for shepherding us out of the settlement at the earth's core was somehow sealed off by a barrier of the greenish mist after the last citizens had left their homes and joined the exodus. We were in the belly of the illuminated protective tunnel. The only open end far ahead of us was blocked by the brightly glowing pillar of light, which receded to maintain the same distance from us as we advanced on our journey. After confirming that all was well with the people in the rear, I rejoined the council and made my report.

With solemnity, we walked and watched in awe at the strange phenomenon that was unfolding before us. The leading groups spontaneously broke into appreciative songs of praise, and before long, the songs had caught on with the entire humbled throng on the move. Some were singing and crying softly because they were sad to leave their homes for good, while appreciative of the love that had been demonstrated by the Supremos in saving them from the impending catastrophe.

We traveled for a month without mishap—sleeping, eating, and resting as was determined by the leadership. We made good progress, and there was cooperation and good feeling among the citizens. We reached a point where, ahead of the pillar, there appeared to be a large body of water that resembled an ocean. Panic starting spreading among the council members who were leading the exodus, but I reminded them to put their faith in the Supremos and trust that they would not lead us away from destruction only to lead us back into harm's way. This realization humbled them, and they joined me in praying and exercising faith in the Supremos. Their example strengthened the citizens who had also seen the body of water in our path. Then a miracle occurred.

The open end of the tunnel suddenly started closing until it was totally sealed off. We were now fully in the belly of the strange tunnel and could see nothing ahead for a period of fourteen days. During this time, and despite the fact that we believed there were fourteen occasions of nightfall, it was never dark in the sealed tunnel, the air was constantly fresh, and we moved along on dry land. On the fifteenth day, the anterior end of the tunnel opened to reveal the pillar of light at the entrance and the night sky ahead of the pillar of light. Then, as the day dawned, we saw land ahead of us.

We had miraculously crossed that part of the ocean on dry land and were now moving again toward our unknown destination. We progressed into the third and then the fourth months of our travels without any major challenges, but by now our food reserves were dwindling. It had been revealed to me that we would trek for six months, so I knew we had two more months to arrive at whatever destination had been prepared for these faithful former residents of the core. Enough food had been preserved for the six-month trek, but the leaders for each of the one hundred families were immediately instructed to assess the food stock left for their group. We learned that while some of the groups had wisely rationed their food reserves, others had often given out more than was required, resulting in waste. On average, the remaining food would last for about a month and a half if frugally rationed. This realization sent some panic among the leaders as they wondered how their groups were going to survive until the end of the journey.

Somehow, rumors of the waste spread like wildfire through the whole populace, and attitudes changed toward the offending groups. Bad feelings were openly expressed, and accusations were leveled at them as being the cause of the impending starvation. This was a great test to a people who had lived in love and harmony for generations. The fear that generated selfishness and disharmony among them was palpable. I joined the leadership in ministering to the groups to allay their concerns and to remind them of the need for unity and support of each other in times of crisis. They were reminded of what the universal law of love had taught them. Those that had pointed fingers repented and apologized to the offended and embraced each other, and harmony was restored.

At the next stop for rest and eating, while the children were given their full rations. All the adults, meanwhile, agreed to have their rations reduced to save as much food as possible for the rest of the journey. Concern for each other's well being was lovingly expressed and demonstrated. This trial had, drawn them closer in support and concern for one another's survival rather than destroying the peace and harmony among these faithful people. The journey resumed, and songs of praise were raised to the ruling Supremos.

Soon after that event, another miracle occurred. As we continued to move along, we heard a strange noise that started faintly in the distance but began to get progressively louder. Unsure of what it could be, and worried that it was the sound of the earth preparing to shift, we stopped the company and listened. All of a sudden, as we stood where we were, we saw ahead of us an immense horde of some kind of animal moving toward us rapidly. At first, the people started shouting in alarm, but our fears soon calmed as we saw that it was a large number of rabbits. At this realization, we were amazed and excited. The Supremos had given us a solution to our concerns—concerns that had eroded and nearly ruined the good feeling and harmony that had been cultivated over generations. We quickly fetched our weapons and began capturing the God-sent rabbits for food. The preserved meat was reserved, and the rabbits were roasted and boiled to supplement our supplies. This phenomenon was repeated day after day, and we had an abundant supply of fresh meat until the end of our journey.

It was at the end of the sixth month of our exodus that the pillar of cloud by day and of light by night disappeared. This was an indication that we had finally arrived safely at our destination—a new abode chosen by the Supremos. It was in the hazy light of dawn that we saw the tunnel of greenish mist dissolving gradually as the people poured into a large fertile valley strewn with a variety of lush trees and rock-bound caves. A large number of the trees bore edible fruits, while others were good for lumber and construction. The undergrowth, it was discovered, was made up mostly of a variety of vegetables and tubers.

A spring of clear water and a river were found populated with a sizeable stock of edible fish in the southern sector of the valley. It was clear to us that this beautiful valley had been preserved and kept hidden from the view of the surface-dwellers for generations, for our sake, by the all-knowing Supremos.

By midday the next day, all the people had arrived in the beautiful valley, and the tunnel of greenish hue had all dissolved, leaving a misty canopy high above us that covered the whole valley. The leadership immediately began organizing and called for the next day to be observed as a day of rest and thanksgiving to the Supremos for their loving mercy and the great blessings bestowed upon us. From the morning of the next day until the evening, the whole day was spent doing only necessary work, or no work at all, and was observed as a day of thanksgiving and worship. It was made a law for that day in the week to be observed as a day of rest and worship for generations to come.

On the dawn of the day following, the leaders conducted a survey of the new environment and started the process of allocating residential areas and lands to the families. It was interesting to observe that the caves in the rocky deposits were many, and arranged as if designed especially for the occupation of a number of families. These were given to the older families to clean and prepare for settlement. The experienced craftsmen and young men were organized under my instruction to cut down trees and prepare logs for erecting residential accommodations and barns and for making furniture.

The valley stretched for miles, and there was enough space to convert part of it into farmland. It was in this area selected for farming that the cutting of trees and logging was organized. The people worked hard to construct beautiful log homes after the pattern that I had taught them. After about five months of this, the large workforce had built enough suitable and comfortably furnished homes to add to the natural caves so that each family could have their own.

The preserved valley was also found to hold a large variety of game further out in the woods that served as their main source of nourishment. The large number of small animals gave us the impression that there might not be any, or at least very few, dangerous carnivores in the valley that would threaten our safety. It was haven of peace and comfort, and there was plenty to eat.

The challenge that we now faced, though, was finding materials to generate power for lighting and machinery. In the meantime, we adapted by applying existing technology. The inhabitants had learned to chemically generate cold bright light by mixing and separating three chemicals found in deep-sea fish. This provided the necessary lighting during the night until their scientists could find a suitable material to generate power to run the machines. They had wisely brought along a large stock of these chemicals in a few designated carrier mechanized suits.

After things had settled down and a few months had passed, craftsmen were dispatched to search for useful minerals in different areas of the valley that seemed likely to contain them. Fronds trimmed from palm trees were prepared and used to manufacture storage baskets and mats, while others took to using clay from rich deposits in the valley to manufacture pots and cups and other useful utensils. They were an industrious people and learned quickly to use materials they found in their new environment to manufacture useful items. After a year, they were all comfortably settled and had begun tilling and harvesting the land for their needs. Fish were found in abundance in the river to the south, and natural spring water was located farther out in the rocky terrain to satisfy their needs.

As I observed their community and how they were adjusting and working together, it appeared that my role had been successful. I then made a reluctant appeal to the Guardians to learn of the time I would be required to leave my newfound friends. Their response came to me almost immediately. I was to leave in one week. I broke the news of my departure to the ruling council, and though they were sad that I had to leave them, they acknowledged my responsibility to serve others who needed my help under the Supremos.

I had been an instrument in the hands of the Creators to bring great blessings to these people, and they were very appreciative of the service rendered. I spent my last days visiting and bidding farewell to the families. The day of my departure soon came, and after my final goodbye to the ruling council, I walked away toward the west, into the rocky range of hills and out of sight. The next moment, I was whisked to the Sacred Dome and was, as usual, welcomed by the three Guardians.

The miracle of shepherding these faithful people to the choice valley pressed in on me. But I remained curious as to what had happened to their former abode. I made an attempt to ask, but before I could utter a word, the leader of the Guardians beckoned me to follow him. He led me to the memory machine and asked me to lie on the protoplasmic bed. As had happened in my earlier experience with the machine, I was sucked in with only my face left uncovered. That was followed by the feeling of a current running through my spine and the tingling sensation at the base of my brain. Pictures of events that had occurred in the history of the planet since my last updating on the machine flashed rapidly through my mind.

It began with minor events that had occurred between the last time I had stepped out of the machine and continued with my assignment in solving the mystery of the dreaded curse of Kunturami Bio. It continued on through my arrival among the people of Earth's core and through the preparation and final march out of the abode of these faithful people. I saw with awe the tunnel bound in green mist descending from the heavens as the inhabitants, led by the ruling council, approached the outside world. I saw the tunnel settle to link up with the main exit of the old habitation near Earth's core and create the continuously moving passage we had journeyed through to the new destination, led by the cloudy pillar by day and the pillar of bright light by night.

I noticed that wherever the tunnel passed, the atmosphere darkened as if heavy rains were about to pour down, and a whirlwind veiled its passage and kept the residents of the area indoors. It was now clear to me that our feet were not in contact with the planet's upper crust, as I saw the tunnel suspended about two feet from the planet's surface. The miracle of our being sealed in the belly of the tunnel like a cocoon and our fourteen-day passage over a long stretch of the ocean was also revealed as I saw the pillar of light appear to evaporate and fill our path just before the closure of the anterior exit of the tunnel.

I observed that as we approached the fertile valley, the misty cloud that we had seen on entering the valley stretched to rest on the tops of six distant mountains, forming a canopy that covered the whole valley and prevented it from being properly seen from the air. In fact, the shade of the green fauna of the land seen faintly through the misty canopy from the air created the impression that it was a sea or a large body of water. The Supremos had wisely shielded this promised land from the view of the surface dwellers for centuries to reserve it for their choice children at this time. I felt a deep sense of gratitude for their love and concern toward those who were faithful to them.

What went on under the canopy protecting the valley was shielded from my view, but of course, I had just returned from there and knew what was transpiring. My not being permitted to see below the canopy was an indication that it was the will of the Supremos to keep their existence from other inhabitants of the planet. I was permitted to know about the new location because I had been an instrument in the hands of the Creators to preserve the former dwellers of the planet's core and bring them to safety.

The events that followed the evacuation of the tribes then started registering in my memory. It was frightening as I focused and observed the area of the planet's crust directly above the habitation heave and turn as explosions occurred deep inside the earth. This started exactly six months after we left. Shockwaves were felt for miles, and the destruction was great. After a week of this violent seismic activity, the churning crust and water settled down, leaving a steaming swamp that stretched for miles. I had lived in the habitation for twenty-four months and could deduce what had happened to bring about this sea of swamp. I could link the incident with the revelation I had received in my dream. It was obvious the oceanic tectonic plate had finally submerged under the continental plate that supported the former habitation. This had sent violent earthquakes throughout the entire land, contributing to the destruction of the protective structures of magma that were their source of energy. In addition, it had resulted in the opening up of the fissure in the lake and the escape of large volumes of magma into the lake. The contact of hot magma and water had produced superheated steam that expanded quickly, resulting in explosions that rocked the area for days. The destruction and collapse of the supporting pillars and caves of the habitation had brought about the total submergence of the large area of crust above. The source of water that became the steam was not only the lake of the former settlers, but also water introduced into the area from the ocean by the submerged oceanic plate. The resultant volume of steam had churned and turned the crust into the hot marshland that was still bubbling and exuding steam—an area that would not be habitable for generations to come.

Had the former tribe remained in their homes, they would have been overtaken by these events, and not one would have survived the seismic destruction. The Creators were indeed all-knowing and mindful of the welfare of all those who submitted to their will. It became even clearer to me that all people who had faith in them and looked to them for direction would be guided, invited home, or supernaturally protected at all times. And while they have the power to avert disasters, they oftentimes permit such natural incidents to occur for the greater good of the planet and its inhabitants but further ensure the safety of the faithful who would be affected by it.

I smiled as I realized that I had successfully completed another assignment and learned much from that experience. I was instructed by the leader of the Guardians to remember the counsel to update my memory of events from time to time, preferably after each assignment. I then retired to my residence to await the signal for my next assignment. As I lay on the soft bed after eating a nutritious meal of vegetables and fish, I reflected on the events of my last adventure and felt a deep sense of gratitude toward the Supremos for directing my path and using me as an instrument in their hands to move a cherished, unspotted people to a safe haven. My confidence grew from day to day as I reflected on the goodness of the Creators and waited anxiously for my next call to come.

EPISODE V:
THE LEGEND OF THE
FORBIDDEN MOUNTAINS

CHAPTER 19

The Flaming Mountains

In the deep jungle of the remotest part of the western sector of the planet, along the equatorial rainforest where very few had ever ventured, lay a range of mountains with an incredible history.. Their past was marked by a series of events that brought great fear upon the ancestors of the natives who dwelled there and had earned the territory the name Abonsam Kurow, which translated to "the abode of the devil."

Among the people, it was taboo to mention that name without first closing one's eyes and partially blocking your ears with both hands, for it was believed that doing so would bring the wrath of the evil mountains upon the offender. The paralyzing fear that came upon the natives upon mentioning the forbidden name, and the recurrent violent thunderstorms and rainfall over the area, somehow lent credence to the longstanding superstition. Something had occurred in the mountains of that rainforest in the past, and whatever it was, it was still actively haunting the mountain range today.

Within the communities of the natives, tales of the mountains were often narrated at firesides. It was intriguing to see the listeners, as well as the narrator, cover their eyes and ears at the mention of the name given to the mountains. These stories kept their fear alive and the new

271

generations away from the forbidden mountains and the somber stretch of forest surrounding them. This caused the passage to the mountains to become overgrown and almost impenetrable.

The legend dated back to the rule of their first tribal chief, Kumbo Khandi, who had lived over a century ago. The myth involved two families banned from the village of the Sumankura tribe who had migrated to settle at the present location. Within a few years, their descendants had multiplied greatly to become one very large tribe. Others that had migrated from other tribes in the region came to settle among them. With the rapid increase in their population, Kumbo Khandi, who was a descendant of the senior of the two families who first settled the land, was made the tribal chief. The village was named Kokou Bhutto after the senior founder, an ancestor of Kumbo Khandi.

Kumbo Khandi was a wise chief. Soon after his ascension to the throne, he was faced with one of the greatest threats to the safety of his people. The tribesmen who lived on the periphery of the settlement were being attacked and killed in large numbers by wild animals from the forest. The attacks also came upon isolated food crop farmers, as well as some keepers of kraals on the outskirts of the village for rearing livestock. The attacks were becoming so frequent that panic began spreading among his subjects. Because the old wild animals were weak and could not compete with the younger ones for prey in the forest, they were starving. So they began feeding on humans as easier prey.

Timber was readily available in the dense forest, so Kumbo Khandi organized the building of a great wall, an impenetrable stockade around the large settlement, treating the wood with a pungent chemical preservative found in the region. The scent repelled the reptiles and wild cats in the area and helped to keep the inhabitants of the settlement safe. He also constructed posts at intervals on the wall and kept sentries posted in shifts along and inside the stockade to alert the people of any danger. The same method of treating the wood was used while erecting kraals for the isolated livestock keepers. Simple timber structures erected on high, crisscrossing poles with retractable rope ladders solved the problem for those living on isolated farms.

A tribal army armed with bows and arrows, spears, and shields was also put into action to protect the people from dangers that the walls couldn't. It was a formidable army, among whom were the bravest of the brave. They were trained so well in hand combat, camouflaging, and tracking that former raiders from distant villages were no match for them. Before long, he had instilled great fear throughout the other settlements within the region. No one dared attack his village for fear of earning a swift and severe retribution.

Things carried on this way for many years. Then, in the tenth year of the reign of Kumbo Khandi, a bright flare fell from the sky one dark night. Such flares had been seen before on many other occasions, yet every occasion of a falling flare was interpreted as a bad omen. To the tribe, each star seen in the heavens was a representation of a living person. As a result, the occasional light that hurtled toward earth in a brilliant flare and fizzled out was an indication that the person to whom that star belonged had passed on and that his or her spirit was now free to roam the earth and haunt the living. The bright light seen on this special night, however, was particularly large and did not die out as the others had done, but hit the land with such force that it sent a tremor throughout their village. The distant mountains appeared to be the site of the impact, and the fire from the fallen star could be seen burning, flickering in the night and on through the next few days.

Early the next morning, Kumbo Khandi called his chief warrior, Gawasi, to report at his residence. "Gawasi," he started, "what is this that I hear about a falling star? Is it true that it retained its light and lit the hills on fire?" The king's face darkened as his chief nodded in the affirmative.

"It is true, master. The hills have been burning for days, and yet the light does not go out."

At this, Kumbo Khandi stood up and said firmly, "Then we shall send twenty of our best men to investigate. Gawasi, we must make sure that this does not prove to be a threat to our people." Gawasi nodded his agreement, then turned to carry out the instructions of the king.

Three days later, Gawasi set out with his twenty warriors in the direction of the mountains. It should have taken the warriors just over two days to march through the thick forest and reach them, but after two weeks, Gawasi and his twenty warriors had not returned. The king suspected the worst. When one month passed, Kumbo Khandi called for his second-in-command to venture out with ten warriors to search for their colleagues. He cautioned them to take extra safety measures, and to look after one another.

The second search party also failed to return after a month. Rumors began circulating that both parties' disappearances had to do with the strange fire that had come from the skies. Others speculated that the men had been attacked and eaten by lions or some other ferocious beasts that roamed the area. Still others said some of the distant villages had captured and killed the warriors in revenge for atrocities meted out to them during past conflicts with Kokou Bhutto. Answers were not yielding. How could the tribal chief adequately pacify and console the families who had lost brave fathers and brothers? How could he stem the fear that was taking root and was rapidly spreading among his people because of these unsolved disappearances?

The news had soon traveled to the other settlements surrounding their village, and Kumbo Khandi watched as fear began to take hold of the people in the entire region. Many wondered how they could protect themselves from this threat, if even the most feared tribal warriors could not withstand the wrathful force of the power from the sky. The news traveled like wildfire to areas beyond the boundaries of the region, and exaggerated tales circulated abroad—accounts of strange beings that could burn with a touch and incinerate anything with a breath of fire.

As time passed, the fear continued to keep people away from the burning range of mountains. New generations were born, and the mystery remained unsolved. The other settlements that dwelt nearer to the mountains were eventually deserted as strange activities and frightening sounds stretched for miles across the land. All of this mystery was multiplied by the unexplained disappearance of a group of tribesmen two years after the fall of the flare. The area of the mountains remained uninhabited for almost a century, until the day a flash of light on one of the many panels of the Dome of the Guardians brought me to the domain on another adventure.

I had been resting for about a month when, one day, I stepped out of my room to find one of the panels of the Dome flashing. This was my signal that it was time to embark on another errand. I strapped on my weapons and stood before the portal. As I reached out and touched the panel, the door slid open as usual, and I stepped inside. I was almost immediately whisked away to a location close to the village of Kokou Bhutto. When I arrived, I stood still momentarily, allowing my eyes to adjust to the night sky as I searched my memory for the history of the area. I was, as usual, able to access as much information as I was permitted to know as scenes from the past flashed across my mind. Strangely, though, I could not see what had actually happened in the mountains on the day the huge flare had been sighted. I saw the great impact that had sent tremors throughout the communities and the burning field that consumed everything in its range, before the historical reel ended.

It appeared the stockade had been rebuilt since the first one was constructed by Kumbo Khandi, and security was still very good. I could easily have scaled the wall but thought it wise to wait for daylight to enter and announce my presence properly. Though a century had passed since the strange phenomenon occurred, my sudden appearance within their stockade could aggravate the fear that had gripped their ancestors, inciting an attack.

I spent that night in the forest trying to locate other tribal abodes close to Kokou Bhutto but found none. Though areas that were overgrown with weeds gave indications of occupancy many years ago. It appeared to me that all the villages between Kokou Bhutto and the mountains had been deserted, and new settlements were founded farther away from the accursed mountains. The nearest settlement was about six miles away to the east. Another was about eight miles away to the south, and a third, seven miles to the west. Beyond these settlements, numerous highly populated villages could be located near one another for miles.

I noticed that game was abundant in this forest, yet fear of attack by wild animals kept the indigenous people from using this as an opportunity to hunt for meat. Their weapons, wooden bows and arrows made with heated and hardened wooden tips or sharpened bones, were not reliable enough to give them the confidence to go deep into the forest to hunt game. They would have easily fallen prey to the wild cats that roamed the region. Because of this, they relied mostly on livestock and the small game snared close to the stockade for meat.

As I continued to roam the jungle, I often caught glimpses of green eyes watching me from the forest floor and from within the low-hanging branches. These, I guessed, were various types of cats, but for some reason, none made any move to attack me. Whenever I turned to look in their direction, they would quietly slink away and vanish into the undergrowth. I guessed that there was something about my body or scent that was repelling them or preventing them from attacking. Perhaps they sensed that I was able to relate to them as to every species of the animal kingdom. I drew no conclusion. Because I possessed the strength and agility to vanquish any creature of this planet's origin, I could only imagine the destruction that could be inflicted on any creature that would dare attack me. I knew now that the Supremos had wisely prepared and made my acceptance in the animal kingdom possible. I continued to walk along, and by dawn I had surveyed the large area surrounding the habitation and was ready to follow up on my plans to contact the indigenous people.

Daylight came as the sun emerged from the east, throwing its beautiful, scintillating rays across the canopies of the forest. The soft light that seeped through the foliage onto the forest floor gave life to the lower branches of the trees and the creepers and vines. I stood off on a high branch waiting for the stir of life in the enclosure of the stockade. Two hours after dawn, the village burst to life, and the main gate was opened for the farmers and livestock keepers to attend to their routine duties.

It was time to approach the entrance and make myself known to the people of this land. I emerged from the forest into the wide clearing surrounding the stockade. I was spotted instantly by the sentries on the wall, and a shrill alarm was sounded with a long oxen horn. Within minutes, every space on the high wall was filled with warriors armed with bows and arrows. A warning was sounded, but I did not understand it and kept moving forward. It was then that a hailstorm of arrows flew toward me, and although quite a number of them ricocheted off of me and fell to the forest floor, I felt no pain and remained unharmed. I kept a steady pace toward the main gate and saw the warriors scurrying frantically to close it. Most of the external workers who were close by had rushed back into the stockade, and the sound of the alarm had warned the people who were far off of the impending peril.

After fruitless efforts to shoot me down, I saw fear strike the warriors. The words *boglu nnatifa* were echoed over and over again. At the time I didn't understand, but I later learned that *boglu nnatifa* meant "he is indestructible." After realizing they were just wasting their precious wooden arrows, they stopped shooting. Unexpectedly, the gate to the stockade was thrown wide open, and eight big men emerged. At first I couldn't tell what they wanted, but as I watched them start to circle around me, I realized that they were hand combatants and had been sent to overpower me. I had no alternative but to engage them in combat. Since I could not understand their dialect, it was the only way to prove to them I had not come to harm anyone.

With the gate now wide open, I saw a great number of the tribe standing in the entrance waiting to watch their fighters grab me and tie me down. My focus was quickly brought back to the task at hand as each warrior took turns lunging at me to show off their prowess. It would have been a quick and easy encounter for me if they were really my antagonists, but because I had come to help these people and not harm them, I feigned to struggle for a little while. Each one moved deftly and grabbed me with swiftness, and on each occasion I pretended to get out of the hold with difficulty before finally throwing each one of them down on his back, signifying that I was the victor. The warriors were not disgraced. These were brave men. I saw the initial fear in the eyes of the people soon replaced by cheers as I wrestled with their favorite warrior. It was turning out to be a form of entertainment.

After all eight had tried and lost, I took each one of them by the hand and then hugged them in turn with a broad smile and a nod of approval, recognizing their bravery and strength. Each one then took turns introducing himself. The tallest one in the group introduced himself as Akachi. Next in line was a broad-shouldered man with a heavy- brow. "My name is Caedmon," he said gruffly. Next was a slender man with lean muscles and feline features. "They call me Taryn," he said in a soft voice. The next man wore a huge grin on his face and shook my hand vigorously. "My name is Felix," he boomed, "and thanks for the workout. I needed it." I smiled in return, and I could sense his good and kind heart. The last four stepped forward and introduced themselves as Eadric, Zaire, Rafa, and Gael. After the last one had spoken his name,

I signaled to the men that we should line up, face the stockade, hold hands, and raise them together as a sign of victory for all of us. Cheers echoed among us. The attitude of the people had changed toward me, and I was signaled by the warriors to follow them into the stockade. I was then introduced to their tribal chief. He was anxiously awaiting a report on the task given to the warriors and was highly disturbed by the cheering, not knowing exactly what was happening outside. I saw relief come over his face when he saw me and his men coming toward him with smiles on our faces.

Through signs and gestures, I was able to communicate to them my intention to visit the forbidden mountains. The chief looked incredulous. My new friends requested to accompany me, but though the chief agreed, I politely declined. I insisted that I go alone, so as not to expose them to the dangers of the unknown. After I assured them I would be fine, the chief and my friends reluctantly agreed. I went on to spend one month with them to get acquainted with their language and the area. With my gift of learning, I could express myself fairly eloquently by the end of that period.

I used my short stay to learn more about the environment. I discovered a modest deposit of iron ore and copper not too far from the stockade. With this I began teaching them metallurgy and how to design useful tools. They were fascinated by my sword, shield, and lance but were overwhelmed by the mechanism of the crossbow that shot bolts of electric energy. The advanced designs were not common even to the developed civilizations living on the planet. I then taught them how to make simpler tools, such as arrowheads, knives, machetes, hoes, and nails. With the copper produced from the ore, they were taught to manufacture metal utensils instead of earthenware. They proved to be keen learners and were very excited with the new technology. Their appreciation to me was immense, and they expressed it in many ways.

I enjoyed the opportunity to be of help to such good people. I taught them to use their new knowledge wisely for the strengthening of their defenses and improvement in their community life, but not for weapons of assault on any tribe. I was assured that for some generations they had been at peace with the nearest settlements, which were very far from Kokou Bhutto.

At last, the day I had planned to leave arrived. As the sun emerged in the east, I made my last preparation to depart into the forest on my journey to the forbidden mountains. My friends again tried one last time to persuade me not to go. "Magnus," Akachi began, "the mountains contain dangers that we cannot yet imagine. You should not go. Stay here with us, instead, and teach us more of your ways."

At this I smiled and clasped his shoulder. "Akachi, my friend, you know that I must go. This is the reason I've come here. I must protect you and your people, and the only way to do that is to find out what's on that mountain."

"Then let us go with you," he pleaded. "Let us fight with you and die with you if we have to, but let us go."

My face softened as I looked at the brave warrior who had become one of my closest friends during my stay. "Akachi, you have three beautiful children and a lovely wife who would suffer dearly and never forgive me if you did not return to them. Stay. Be with your family. I promise you that I will return, and when I do, I will have answers." Seeing that I could not be moved on this, he took a step back and nodded in resignation. I smiled and clasped his shoulder tightly before continuing my final preparations for my journey up the mountain.

When it was finally time for my departure, the community riddled the entrance of the stockade to bid me farewell. I assured them that I would be back, but saw doubt register on most of their faces. They were sad to see me go to my destruction. After all, from their historical accounts, none had taken that journey and returned. As I traveled alone toward the accursed mountain range, I thought back on the events that had taken place, as assessed through my memory store and the variations narrated as folklore. The falling of the huge star, the fire it had generated, and the strange disappearance of the two teams sent to investigate matched each other in the accounts. The versions of other events associated with the mountains, however, were so varied that it was almost impossible to know if they held any credibility. It was now my lot to find out the truth.

After two days of trekking rapidly through the dense forest, I arrived early on the third morning at what I believed to be the edge of the forbidden area. I climbed a high tree close to the edge to have a better view of the land before me. It appeared that the forest ended abruptly, and stretching before me was a flat land of about a mile to the edge of the mountains. The bare area looked as though something had incinerated every living thing, leaving the land barren for almost a century. In the middle of the area, far ahead of me, was the formation of a great crater, which I believed was the point of impact of whatever had come down from the sky so many years ago.

I proceeded forward with extreme caution. Whatever forces were responsible for the incidents were making sure that no one returned to tell the tale. *Had the thirty warriors of almost a century ago been captured and killed?* It was a question I needed to answer, and I was determined to find out what really happened to them and what had befallen in the area since. I decided to wait until nightfall before coming out of the forest into the open stretch of land before me. I needed to adopt the guise of invisibility to avoid being seen or detected in order to conduct the necessary investigation into the legend.

I waited until midnight before continuing on my journey. I donned the guise of invisibility and, with the help of my gift of night vision, carefully avoided the many shallow pitfalls that dotted the clearing as I threaded my way on firm ground toward the crater. I had not gone far when I heard a soul-chilling sound coming from the direction of the mountains. Then fire spurted out of each of the many pitfalls on the clearing. Within minutes, the whole field was ablaze! Any ordinary person would have been killed in an instant, but luckily I was resistant to the elements, and the flames instead became a source of energy.

I wondered if I had been spotted despite my efforts or if there was a sort of radar installed to monitor the field and detect anything that crossed any part of the field. The latter seemed more likely, and this gave the indication that highly intelligent beings were behind the events in the area. *Was it this blaze that had in the past incinerated the two groups of warriors who had been sent to find out about the flare?* I thought to myself silently. I managed to walk through the fires and arrived safely at the crater. The edge was elliptical and raised about six feet from the ground. I held the firm edge and lifted myself to look into the depths. What I saw would have been uncommon, considering the high rate of rainfall in the mountainous region, but under the present circumstances, it was very strange.

CHAPTER 20

The Mysterious Crater

I nside the crater, a few feet from the edge, was a pond of clear water. It was very still and reflected the sky above it so perfectly that someone might have mistaken it for a mirror or even a continuum of the heavens above. I myself needed to toss a tiny pebble into it to convince myself that it was truly water. As the pebble touched the surface of the pond, I saw the initial ripples start from the point of contact and spread toward the edge of the crater. Then, as the pebble sank into its depths, a vortex was created at the point of contact, and the next moment a spout of the liquid shot out, projecting the pebble high into the atmosphere and out of sight. Surprised at this reaction, I tried again using a bigger stone and was shocked to see the same result. *What would happen if something other than an inanimate object fell into the crater? Like an animal, or a human being?* Though I desired to discover the effect on something living, no living thing other than me was in sight.

I was baffled by this strange phenomenon. *Where did the projected items go? What mechanism could project solid items at such an incredible speed to vanish into the heavens? Who or what was behind these mysterious occurrences in the mountains?* I wisely abandoned my earlier intention to dive into the pond to find out what was beneath the water and instead took a walk into the mountain area to investigate the base and surroundings. As I explored, I stumbled on a passage at the base of the highest point of the mountains. It looked like a normal entrance into a shallow cave, but as I crawled through, I came upon a solid metal panel, which sealed off any further progress into the tunnel. It was a sturdy metal, but fortunately I was able to force it open and crawl inside, only to trigger an alarm.

Within seconds, bright lights filled the large area behind the panel, and a fearful wailing sound emanated from what were probably many hidden speakers in the enclosure. The floor was made of what looked like tinted glass, the center of which was a hatch that had a spiral stairway leading to lower levels. From my position, I could not make out clearly the area below. The roof was formed in a cone shape with a large base and was dotted with lights. The apex of the roof was directly over the center of the hatch to the lower level. The design of the apex appeared as though an antenna was mounted above it. As I ran rapidly toward the hatch, a continuous stream of electrical current, like a ray of lightning, shot down from the apex of the roof onto a small revolving disc in the center of the hatch on the floor. Many small passages suddenly opened on the walls of the enclosure, and thousands of large, buzzing, ferocious wasps emerged and attacked me. I instinctively threw myself down on the floor, but before I could be stung by any of the venomous creatures, my defensive weapon, the burst of white light, came to my rescue.

In an instant, the floor was strewn with the charred bodies of the seemingly possessed wasps, and for many minutes, the bright glow on my body remained before it began to dim and then totally vanished. I had experienced this on a number of occasions while in the dimensional world of evil, but now I realized its effectiveness on the physical planet as well. *Were the wasps truly possessed? Is this why my defense mechanism was activated?* I remembered the large number of magpies that attempted to blot out the sun while I was battling with the Homoleotaurus in the land of Zamunstra and marveled. The evil rebel unscrupulously used the bodies of innocent creatures to achieve his evil designs. I was becoming more convinced that there was something sinister about this place.

I moved to the hatch and blocked the stream of electrical current with my shield as I tried to forcibly pry open the hatch. The stream of electrical current suddenly stopped, and I quickly dropped through the opening onto a circular platform that led to the staircase and the lower level of the enclosure. Beneath me was another wide floor made of the same type of tinted glass, with another hatch in the center. What was in store for me at this level, I could only imagine. It took me just a few minutes to find out. The moment my foot touched the floor, the hatch above me, which I had deliberately left open, swung shut with a loud clang, and other passages simultaneously opened on the walls of this new level.

Out of the passages emerged hundreds of poisonous snakes. I recognized among them the cobra, the puff adder, the rattlesnake, and the copperhead. There were other species unknown to me. As they began moving toward me, I felt prompted to stand still. As soon as I did, I saw the coldblooded slithering menaces, unable to detect my position by the vibrations, turn on themselves. The bigger ones began attacking the smaller ones, and in minutes, the floor was strewn with dead or dying snakes.

When I was certain that the snakes were no longer a threat, I quickly moved toward the center of the room and opened the hatch to the next level, went down the spiral stairway, and dropped onto the floor. What was I to expect at this level? Again, it did not take long for me to find out. Out of open panels emerged huge ferocious cats, leopards by their shape and the black spots on their coats, but too big for the natural species I knew. These were giant ones, and they looked about three times the size of normal leopards, as if they had been produced through genetic engineering. They were twelve in number, and their snarls filled the chamber. I was their common prey, but they did not attack at once. They moved in a slow circle around me, stalking, almost mockingly. I realized I had a fight on my hands and braced myself, my shield fastened to my left forearm and my sword firmly held in my right hand.

Two of them suddenly pounced from opposite directions. I turned and met the charge of the one on my right, plunging the sharp point of my unbreakable sword straight into its heart while I parried the impact of the attack from the opposite brute with my shield and threw it off balance. It landed awkwardly on its head. The weight of the other dead animal with my sword in its heart threw me to the floor. I quickly stood up and realized I had slid on the smooth floor up to the base of the staircase. With my back to the stairs, I braced myself to face the beasts. The next two that attacked were met by the tip of my sword, and both fell heavily to the ground as I sidestepped a third, causing it to crash head-on into the solid spiral staircase.

Before the cat could regain its bearings, I quickly sheathed my sword and made an effort to remove my crossbow from the pouch on my shoulder. As I was struggling to get the latch undone, one of the brutes leapt toward me with its claws fully extended and fangs bared. I saw it coming, quickly sidestepped its powerful strike, and in one smooth movement jumped onto its back. It landed awkwardly, and before it could recover from the shock, I had already gotten both of my hands on either side of its large head and twisted, breaking its neck. The remaining six circled cautiously, but before any of them could make another attack, I was able to get my crossbow from its holster and sent its deadly energy rays straight to their hearts. The beasts were killed immediately, and I was left standing there alone. Before I continued on to another level, I shot both of the cats on the floor one more time to ensure that they were dead.

Oddly enough, I still felt strong and full of energy after the encounter with these giant leopards. I had triumphed over the ferocious brutes, and my confidence soared. I thanked the Guardians and praised the Supremos for doing such a marvelous work on my body. Because of my experience in the forests of Kokou Bhutto and the animals there, it was obvious to me that these animals were possessed by evil spirits. It was, indeed, more evidence confirming my suspicion that there was something wicked about this place and that sinister spirits were involved. I was a threat to the plan of their evil master to destroy the happiness of humans through any means, and whatever plan had been hatched through this strange establishment was being frustrated by my interference.

I was now more determined to get to the root of this threat to the human race. I opened the next hatch and descended to the next level, alert and ready for whatever would greet me on the other side. I was not surprised when from the opened panels six huge, gorilla-like beings emerged. Their huge heads, long canines, broad and powerful chests, hairy bodies, and long arms were those of the normal gorilla, but the structure and characteristics from the abdomen down to the feet were more like those of extremely powerful humans. Instead of short legs, they walked on long, sturdy ones that were finished with broad flat feet, enabling them to stand fully upright like humans.

I remembered the evil creature, the Homoleotaurus, that I had vanquished in Zamunstra. I wondered how scientists could meddle with nature to create such nightmarish creatures. They seemed to be sizing me up before they made an attack. I realized I was going to have a fight on my hands on this one and braced myself for whatever happened next. Suddenly, all six brutes rushed me with their canines bared and their powerful arms raised, ready to deal a death blow.

They moved so quickly that, had I been an ordinary human, I would never have escaped. However, a split second was all it took for my brain to calculate a timed strategy. It revealed the meeting point of their joint attack and then prompted my reaction to jump high above them to avoid contact. All six monsters crashed head-on into one another, landing in a tangle of arms and legs. I landed a few feet away from them, and before they could recover from their momentary daze, I raised my sword high above my head. In one deft movement, I decapitated two of them, swung the blade in arch, and thrust my sword into a third's heart.

The remaining three spread out and glared at me while screeching and hissing angrily. They feigned as though they were going to make another rush attack but stopped just before they reached me. In an attempt to evade them, I had jumped, hoping for the same outcome as the first time, but when I landed, they were instead waiting for me. Two of them simultaneously dealt me bone-breaking blows that sent me flying and crashing against the far wall. The third rushed toward me to tear me apart, but I surprised it by rolling in its direction and dealing a powerful kick to its face. The force of the impact sent it flying backward to crash violently into its cohorts. They picked themselves up and stood back a ways as they realized that I was also a formidable opponent. I knew that they would now exercise more caution in any subsequent attacks.

While they paced, deciding their next move, I took them by surprise by rushing them head-on. I ran toward them at full speed, with sword raised, then deliberately fell down and slid on the smooth surface the minute they raised their arms to grab me. I swung my sword, effectively cutting off one of the legs of the nearest brute. The creature yowled in pain as it lost its balance and fell on its colleagues. I quickly sprung to my feet and dealt another blow with my sword, severing an arm of another brute. Distracted by the wild fury that I had sent the monster into, the only unscathed one unexpectedly made a dash to escape through one of the passages they had emerged from. My attention was refocused on the task at hand, and I ran and jumped on its back and began trying to get a hand hold on its neck. It struggled and thrashed, attempting to throw me off, but I was able to work my way to the front of its neck and tore out its throat and windpipe with my bare hands. It immediately slumped to the floor, twitching and gurgling as warm blood oozed from the wound. I turned to see that the other two had managed to escape through their passages of entry and that the panels had sealed off all six entrances.

I sat for a moment to catch my breath and then began making my way to the center of the room, as I avoided the blood and strewn body parts that lay scattered on the floor. I went through the floor hatch to another level and proceeded to battle flying reptiles equipped with long snouts, rows of razor-sharp pointed teeth, and membrane wings that created powerful gusts of wind. The wings bore pointed, bony protrusions on the forearm, and feet with talons like blades with which they tried to slice me apart as they flew overhead. I managed to overcome them by ducking and dodging their powerful swipes and snaps and slicing through their wing-like membranes, jabbing up at them with my sword to pierce their soft underbellies. Those that managed to survive retreated quickly from my onslaught and, flapping their mangled wings, escaped into the corridors from which they had emerged.

The next level had me fighting strange creatures that appeared to have both mammalian and reptilian characteristics, with tough, bony bodies that looked as if they were clothed in armor. They stood on four strong, jointed legs like those of mammals but had long, powerful spiked tails and snouts. And they were fast. Their speed made it difficult to avoid rows of dagger-like teeth and long canines. In addition, they spat out a thick acidic chemical that dissolved any flesh it contacted. It was through speed and cunning that I was able to outwit and slay all of them. Unlike the creatures I had encountered earlier, these grotesque-looking creatures fought without retreat until all of them were killed.

I began to feel the effects of the almost nonstop fighting as I slowly made my way to the staircase that would take me to the next level. I didn't know much more of this I would be able to take and hoped that

I was near the end. The next hatch led into a chamber that was about six times the size of the earlier ones I had come through. There was no hatch on the floor of this chamber, indicating that this was the last level of the hidden arena. I breathed a sigh of relief as I swept my eyes around the room, ready to face the next attack. But nothing came. Arranged evenly along the smooth walls were multiple panels, which I assumed opened into other sections of the building. The ceiling of the room was lined with numerous lights that illuminated the chamber to the point that it appeared as if the noonday sun were present in this deep recess. One of the panels was extra wide and ran the entire length of the wall. It was designed with a sturdy convex glass that reflected a mirror image of the chamber. As I moved closer to the panel, I suspected that it was a two-way mirror and that I was probably being watched. I waited for the anticipated assault from whatever was waiting for me behind the panels, but for an hour, nothing came. I was beginning to get impatient when suddenly one of the many panels along the wall opened.

Out of the corridor emerged six handsome men of perfect structure, dressed and armed as the gladiators of old. They were all blond, and each was an exact replica of the others, as if they had all been spawned from a single fertilized egg or cell. Their haughty features were complemented with piercing, intelligent eyes and athletic builds. Their confident stances revealed that they were skilled fighters and had probably vanquished many opponent. After they had all entered the room, they eyed me with mischievous smiles and a cunning glint in their eyes. I could sense that they were ruthless and evil and that this would be my toughest battle yet. Without warning, they all attacked at once with incredible speed, but I was ready for them. I parried hefty blows with my shield and sword. The arena was big, and this afforded me the opportunity to move as I escaped swinging blows from swords and thrusts with spears and three-pronged lances by a hair's breadth.

Nets were cast with precision to capture me, but with strokes from my own sword, I cut them into shreds and jumped clear before they could trap me. Large, rough cudgels were used to bludgeon me, but I was able to sidestep each swing. Those that landed on my shield were broken and smashed into pieces. All this time I was so busy avoiding their weapons that I had not countered their attacks with any of my own. After sidestepping another precise swing, I broke clear of the assault and turned on them, using the large floor space to pick them off one at a time. I attacked each in succession with lightning speed. I bore the impact of two of their swords with mine, causing their swords to break and leave only the hilts in their hands. I began slashing at the exposed parts of their skin, marring their immaculate appearance with ugly wounds. As I fought, I heard footsteps approaching from behind. This time, instead of parrying the lances with my shield, I took the impact of the thrust directly and sent their lances flying out of their hands. As I continued to fight, I alternated tactics; I either knocked their weapons from their hands or twisted on impact, while blows with my shield snapped their bones. In minutes, all of them had been disarmed and bore some injuries, but somehow, before I could launch my final assault, they all quickly fled into the tunnel as if they had not sustained any injuries. The panel snapped shut behind them.

I had not rested at all when another panel opened to admit another set of six men, these with dark hair, armed with steel whips, who were also exact replicas of each other. This time they were mounted on steeds and shot into the arena one after the other. I did not wait for them to organize an attack. I surprised them by diving beneath the legs of the foremost steed, causing it to trip and fall to the ground heavily. The three steeds following the first then tripped over the fallen one, and all four riders were thrown off their mounts and hit the floor with great force. The impact dazed them long enough for me to sheath my sword and disarm them. With two steel whips in each hand, I met the menacing whips of the remaining two that were still mounted. Whips flying in opposite directions met and wrapped around each other. Then, with a mighty pull, I ripped the whips from the hands of the two attackers and began lashing at the legs of their steeds, sending them and their riders tumbling to the ground.

I then launched an assault on all six disarmed men and was surprised to see that though they appeared to flinch as the whips tore into their flesh, the wounds almost instantly closed. Just as I was recovering from my initial confusion, they sped with their mounts into the chamber and sealed off the entrance, leaving their whips behind. As I quickly tried to process this new development, I realized that I would need to behead my attackers or remove their hearts in order to defeat them. All that survived regained their lost limbs, and their wounds were almost instantly healed. I learned later that they were healed the moment they took shelter in their chambers behind the panels. *What sort of beings were they, and why did each set of sextuplets look alike as if they were the products of one cell?* While engaged with these thoughts, another panel silently opened behind me, and before I could turn, a bolt of energy hit me with great force in the back, throwing me against the wall in the opposite direction. Despite my strength and resistance to earthly weapons, I was shaken, though no physical damage was done to me.

I wheeled around and saw three two-wheeled chariots heading toward me at full charge, each of which was drawn by three fiery stallions. Each chariot was driven by a charioteer and another human replica of him wielding a device that spurted out streams of electricity. Exasperated at their relentless barrage of attacks, I ran in a circular manner around the arena to throw off their aim while I pulled out my own ray gun that I had received from the ocean dwellers. I fired the first ray in the direction of the leading chariot. I had never had the occasion to use this weapon and did not know how devastating its effect would be. In an instant, the two occupants of the chariot were reduced to nothing more than red mist. I turned and gave the same treatment to the occupants of the second chariot, but the third team had seen the fate of the first two and doubled back into the open tunnel, followed by the fiery stallions pulling the two unmanned chariots. The panel quickly snapped shut after them before I could aim and fire the deadly rays at them.

I paused for a moment, waiting for the next attack, but none of the remaining panels opened. Maybe those manipulating these attacks had been shaken by my skill. They now knew that I had the appropriate weapon to vaporize anything and that they would encounter more casualties if more antagonists were pitted against me. I abhorred destroying human life and had my regrets for vaporizing the occupants of the first two chariots, but I also needed to do what was necessary to preserve myself.

As I pondered the situation, it was impressed upon me that I had done the right thing and that those identical siblings were in fact inhuman. They had perfect human bodies, cultured from stem cells and genetic engineering and scientifically programmed to grow and house wicked spirits who were denied bodies by the Supremos. They were programmed for periodic occupancy by spirits of the dimensional world I had visited during my preparation and were used to wreak havoc among the human race.

Was my reaction to the attacks the reason for the break in the assault, or was it truly the final of the battles to be fought in this chamber? Why these needless battles anyway, and where would I be led after this? As these thoughts raced through my brain, I realized that I had to do something before they changed their minds and more of the numerous panels were opened by whoever was controlling them. The weapons were getting increasingly more sophisticated with the advent of each new threat, and I had no way of knowing what to expect next.

I had been surprised that these strange beings had wielded energy bolt–discharging weapons. *Was the technology now known to the surface dwellers?* That, I thought, was very strange. I turned and directed my attention toward the large glass-like panel that, I suspected, was hiding from my view those responsible for the events in this amphitheater. I aimed my ray gun at the glassy panel and pulled the trigger. Another bolt of energy shot forth, and a gaping hole was left where the glassy panel had previously been. The effect was more devastating than the energy weapons of my antagonists or even my crossbow!

I stepped inside to discover a large room equipped with a variety of sophisticated machines and control panels. In the center of the room was an enormous globe of the Earth, on which numerous spots of light were blinking. I noted that the blinking yellow lights were located only close to the large cities of developed and developing countries on each continent. Other spots on the large globe were marked with steady, dim red lights. A big television screen with a range of controls was mounted on one of the walls, with three padded chairs in front of it. Each chair bore an intricately wired helmet, but there was no one in the room manning it. I saw another panel ahead and approached it. Close to this panel was a button, which I hoped would grant me access into the next area. I gingerly pressed it, and it did indeed allow me into an extraordinarily large chamber separated into many spacious sections by transparent glass.

Each section was equipped with numerous glass capsules filled with some strange circulating yellowish fluid. Within each of the capsules, I could see what appeared to be embryos in various stages of development. Underneath each capsule was a transparent tubular conveyor that had a unidirectional passage through a wall into another area, which was totally sealed off. The conveyors from each section were of different sizes. I could not detect any passage to this other area where the conveyors led, but I observed that the extreme south wall of the embryo chamber had a large television screen mounted on it with a number of control buttons on a separate panel underneath, similar to the one in the previous room.

I saw the initial switch-on button and pressed it—From the exit of each conveyor was revealed a different category of creature, a wide range of life forms: insects, crustaceans, reptiles, and mammals, horrible beings of reptilian and mammalian origin, of mammalian and bird forms, of human and ape combinations, and then a range of *Homo sapiens* of different colors, sizes, and gaits. Each category of creature had a separate production line and was conveyed to be enclosed in special equipment for inspection, for acceptance or rejection. Those rejected were put on an exit conveyor and directed to an incineration chamber to be destroyed. Those that met the required standard were conveyed to selected chambers to be available for use in some way in the diabolical plan of their master, the evil rebel child of the Supremos.

So this was the source of bodies of all the types of creatures I had fought against on my way to my current position. Death meant nothing to them because the spirits only discarded one body upon death only to enter another readily conditioned body, just as humans do when they change clothes. The repair rate to those that lost limbs and other parts was so fast that it was not worth the effort to wound them if you were not able to deliver a killing blow. As long as the incubation program for creating this unnatural form of life continued, there would continue to be a supply of physical bodies to serve the evil rebel's followers and wreak havoc on the genuine humans.

I was so engrossed in watching what transpired in the chamber on the television screen that I did not see the ceiling above me open until I fell victim to something indiscernible. It locked my arms and feet against huge magnetized metallic pillars, which I discovered later were the legs of a robot. It was the metallic robot that had quietly descended from an opening in the roof to take me by surprise. I made an attempt to free myself and realized that I needed to muster more power to break free of the magnetic fetters shackling me to the solid legs of the huge robot. Then an idea occurred to me—to feign the inability to break free.

I struggled convincingly for a time and then gave up. Thirty minutes passed after my feigned submission before I saw the television screen on the wall move to reveal a secret passage behind it.

From the passage emerged a strange-looking middle-aged man. He looked structurally perfect and appeared strong and intelligent. His skin looked healthy, almost youthful, but his deep-set eyes belied his age and looked very tired. His curly hair was shiny, thick, and blond but looked strangely unnatural. He walked with a firm gait and wore a wry smile on his lips. He held in his hand a remote control device with which he closed the passage he had emerged from. He moved to the previous room where the map of the planet, the big screen, and the three padded chairs were located and sent signals for the huge robot to follow. He then sat down on the middle of the three seats and put on one of the helmets. I was positioned to face the big television screen. Into a mouthpiece attached to the helmet, he spoke with a husky voice in a language that was familiar.

"Who are you, and why did you come here?" he asked. "I have been monitoring your exploits since you entered the perimeter of my domain," he continued without waiting for an answer. "You seem to be a human of many talents and exceptional ability. You possess gifts that are not common among humans."

He pressed a button on the remote control, and the recorded history since my advent into what he claimed to be his territory burst onto the screen. As the events unfolded, he pointed and commented on every act he observed to be beyond human ability—my vanishing acts, my resistance to fire, my speed, the destructive white light from my body, my strength, the types and power in my uncommon armament.

"I am truly fascinated by you. You are quite the specimen." He paused for a moment as if thinking of what to say next and then continued in a level voice, "I have desired to have the privilege of coming face-to-face with you to inquire about the source of your unnatural gifts and power. I am somewhat like you, but while you were endowed with rare physical powers, I am endowed with rare mental power. I was to try and lure you into a secure location so that I could speak with you privately, but it would appear that you have taken care of that for me." He smiled haughtily as if he was responsible for my capture and then looked directly in my eyes. "Now, before you tell me or I extract the truth from you about your origin, I shall tell you a little about myself."

CHAPTER 21

The Child Prodigy

"I was born more than a century ago in a warring nation—a nation inhabited by a proud and ambitious citizenry who believed that they were chosen as the superior race. In turn, we believed that this gave us the right to rule over the other inhabitants of the planet. I was an exceptional child that possessed talents and abilities far beyond those of my peers. At the age of fifteen, I had obtained doctorate degrees in physics, mathematics, astrophysics, chemistry, biology, and the humanities. By the time I was twenty, I was a celebrated engineer and a medical giant who specialized in the fields of neurosurgery, anatomy, and physiology. I excelled in mathematics and propounded a number of mathematical theories and equations that would lead to invaluable advances in technology.

"I developed much interest in cloning, embryonic development, and guided growth, as well as stem cell manipulation to overcome the rejection phenomenon of transplanted organs and body parts in animals. I wrote theories on a variety of subjects, which included metallurgy, nuclear fission, electronics, the galaxies, and galactic distances and forces. I successfully defended my theories on space travel and wave motion and transmission. I conducted research into image and sound transmissions over long distances in the cosmos, and built prototypes of the equipment for image and sound transmissions over unlimited distances.

"Because of my many accomplishments, I became proud and felt that, as a member of the superior race, I should be one of the greatest and most celebrated humans on the planet. My ambition to gain this status drove me into other fields thought impossible by humans during my time: the production of spare human organs and the designing of programmable robotic machines, androids, and equipment for transplants and replacement of lost limbs and other parts with developed biological prostheses. I also succeeded in accelerating the healing mechanisms of animal bodies from years, months, and days to days, hours, and minutes. Healing became so rapid that in certain cases it appeared to occur almost in an instant.

"To escape the distractions of society, and in order to carry out my experiments without interference, I developed a map of the planet with the ability to set accurate and perfect coordinates to any chosen location on the surface of this planet. My intention was move to an isolated and unknown location. Soon after followed the development of my masterpiece, the teleporter. This machine could relocate equipment of any dimension to any chosen location almost instantaneously. It was based on the simple theory of electronically breaking up any object into its molecular components, transporting the molecules in the proper arrangement within a set magnetic boundary, and reassembling the object upon its arrival at the selected destination.

"I had surveyed the planetary surface and chosen this ideal site. About a century ago, I was able to successfully teleport, in an expandable magnetic capsule, all the tested prototypes of my mechanical equipment, which had been programmed for the construction of a scientific empire, to this location. As I viewed the trajectory of my initial teleport through the thermosphere on my tracking screen, I noticed that the high atmospheric temperature intensified the vibrations in the molecules and the area around the expanded magnetic boundary began to heat up into a flare.

"The beginning of the bonding of the molecules within their magnetic capsule prior to its arrival at the site resulted in the release of more energy. The added energy released during the bonding of the equipment to its original form then created a flare that was fueled by the high oxygen level in the troposphere up to the time it was buried deep in the earth at this chosen destination. The flare was so huge it incinerated every form of life within a radius of about half a mile around it upon its arrival. Within this radius, the buried magnetic capsule continued to discharge occasional energy for a period of about one year. The occasional phenomenon found outlets for the released energy through weak points in the upper strata of the planet, leaving interconnected shallow pits distributed around the entire half-mile perimeter that occasionally exuded fire and has prevented the survival or growth of anything living within it.

"Any living thing that came within the perimeter range was instantly incinerated. The equipment, however, was left intact, since it was protected within the magnetic capsule. Manufactured construction materials were afterward teleported for androids to construct the half-mile fortified tunnel from the crater to this area and to build this structure under the mountain ranges. I directed and supervised the construction by remote control from my abode in my nation of origin. The defense system for the perimeter was retained by programming the release of energy at intervals from the manufacturing machines and subsequent teleports as fire via the shallow, linked pits created in the perimeter by the first teleported equipment. Alarm systems and radars were installed to augment the defense mechanism. The heat generated often brought about rainstorms in the area. The crater was lined and equipped to serve as the teleport exit for the complex, and water from the rainstorms filled to cover the equipment in the crater.

"A decade later, I located another ideal mountainous area in the remotest part of the countryside of my nation and set up another underground laboratory and engineering workshop, where I perfected some of my inventions and teleported them to this site. My research into animal tissue replacement was very successful, and I was planning to use humans for further research when a young admirer of mine initiated a war that nearly engulfed all nations on the planet. He became a dictator and was feared throughout many nations. I was growing old and knew it. I also knew that if I didn't do something about it, I would soon go the way of the Earth like every other ordinary being. Fortunately, I am extraordinary. I had earlier accepted the proposal of my admirer to invent and manufacture war machines and ammunition on a large scale, so I began designing. As these destructive wares were manufactured, the wealth that accrued was used to purchase gold and set up a secret deposit and a bank.

"I became rich beyond my dreams, and when this tyrant was defeated after his ambitious plan to rule the world, I helped fake his destruction, gave him shelter, and continued my research in my underground laboratory. His reign of conquest and terror had given me many war prisoners for my experiments, and I was able, after many trials, to succeed in organ transplant and replacement to renew the bodies of deformed or aged humans with parts developed in my laboratories. I then designed the android mechanisms and equipment for these transplants. I succeeded in replicating skin tissue at a very fast rate and gradually replaced my aging skin with a transplant of young and healthy skin. I did the same for my protégé and an assistant who had worked with me all my life. The only part that I could not succeed in rejuvenating after many trials was the human eye, which has truly proven to be the window to the soul.

"Teleporting a human soul was another challenge. I tried programming the construction and teleporting of combinations of animals and then living human tissue in magnetic capsules, and I succeeded. I noticed that the reconstruction of organic matter after its teleport did not release as much internal energy as did metal and other inanimate matter. The temperature and the short period for the disassembling and reassembling of whole living cells was favorable to the living cells and caused them no serious adverse effect.

"Then the idea of genetically engineering live tissue and creating and refining the bodies of both animals and humans, in the glass capsules that you saw, was born. With my knowledge of physiology, neurology, immunology, and anatomy, I pursued the creation of other combinations of different species whose cellular and nervous coordination functioned like living things. I considered how I could empower them with the ability to learn, eat, reason, and respond to stimuli. I had studied the mystical theory of astral or soul travel outside the body, as well as the life link between the physical body and the spirit. I had also studied the period the body would remain alive without the spirit if they were temporarily separated. I found out that the time was within the teleportation period of my equipment. I had, however, failed in my attempt to teleport living animals. I could teleport living frames, but I had failed in uniting the spirit and the physical body again after their temporary separation at death. This consumed me, but as I slept one night, an impressive being appeared to me in a dream. He was a very handsome human and possessed strange and awesome powers. He had cunning eyes and a dark countenance. There was something eerie about him, and his presence inspired a feeling of total dominance, reverence, and fear within me.

"He told me he was my master and the master of all the proud who aspired to usurp authority and gain power to dominate humans. He said that I owed to him all that I had achieved and all that I possessed, and he was very pleased with my work. He planned to honor me by entering into a pact with me and covenanted to provide hordes of spirits to animate the bodies that I created if I would remain faithful to him. This was my life's dream, so I readily swore to serve him. I woke up almost immediately and saw him fade away.

"When I fully recovered from my hypnotic state, I rushed to the storage area filled with completed bodies of living tissue and was delighted to see that in each segment almost all of them had become active, living beings that had been born and bred to adulthood. It was a major triumph for me. Those that were in human form smiled at me, and I heard them converse in a universal language that was unknown to the planet. Since some of the bodies had been incubated from cells from the same source through cloning, those from a common source structurally looked like carbon copies of each other.

"From that moment, I knew that I was the conduit through whom they were being controlled, through the power of the master mahan. I knew they relished obeying his commands, imputed by me. At this point, I had a willing army at my disposal. I had nothing to lose. After all, I had succeeded in creating animated beings that reasoned and fought fearlessly for survival and self-preservation. It was to me a mark of great success. It was a fulfillment of my life's dream!

"I used my acquired wealth to build large and costly entertainment corporations. These highly sophisticated joints were manned by human converts and some of my own creations. They attracted the high and middle classes, who paid well for their secret indulgences in special, well-furnished suites. Dotted on this replica of the planet that you see before me, as indicated by the blinking lights, are the locations of all the businesses I founded.

"Gambling houses, strip joints, pornography, prostitution, were instituted, and we enticed millions to cave and participate. I reaped more wealth. I realized the rich and famous in society craved violence, so I teleported all the remaining equipment to this location, flew with my protégé and assistant to this range of mountains, and, with the blueprint of the empire I had programmed for building on this site, found our way to this secret abode.

"From here, I have incited and organized battles among my creations and telecasted the fights to screens located in my establishments to satisfy the insatiable desire of humans for blood and violence.

"I provided my audiences with specially designed helmets that gave them the impression that they were the protagonists as they viewed the conflicts. Each saw themselves as the hero in every conquest they observed on the screen. Large sums of money were paid for these experiences. The opportunity to feel like the gladiators of old excited people. They particularly loved *your* fights at every level, as you used your wits and expert fighting skills to defeat your opponents. They would pay a large price to see you fight again. You should see the amounts of money these rich people pay! And now I'm one of them!"

He paused his gloating to announce the entry of his special guests into the compartment. His assistant and his old admirer, the dictator whom the world believed to be dead, emerged from the secret compartment behind the television screen. They looked middle-aged and had healthy, wrinkle-free skin, though I recognized each of the new entrants was nearly a century old. Their eyes betrayed their ages; they looked tired and glazed. But each wore a sarcastic and intimidating smile.

They sat on the remaining two seats and wore their helmets. Up until this point, I had remained unclear as to what was expected from me. I knew the issue: the age-old submission of weak-willed humans to carnal desires and evil influences. My obligation would be to launch a campaign countering lustful enterprises and revealing the counterfeit of happiness and joy—unrestrained lasciviousness and carnal pleasure.

The next comment came from one of the new entrants, the dictator who had been pursued for trial for war crimes against humanity and was thought dead. What he said caught my attention. He boasted of an opportunity again to conquer all nations and bring the planet under subjection. No one, he repeated with emphasis, could stop him this time.

I could read vaulting ambition in his demeanor and smelled the threat of another world war and the devastating effect it would have on nations in this technologically advanced age. *What was his secret plan? How were they going to accomplish this?* I avoided inquiring vocally to avoid raising their suspicions. To them, I was a captured antagonist who would never have the opportunity to go free into the world. In their boastful pride, they never imagined the possibility of me obtaining freedom, so it did not matter what I knew.

My mind started racing as I pictured the rising hordes of these inhuman, unfeeling, and nearly indestructible beings serving in the private armies of the dictator. The evil and wicked spirits that would occupy these bodies and use the advanced war machines that this super-intelligent being had created would result in great, unparalleled destruction.. I had watched these evil spirits in the dimensional worlds practice their act during my training trip to that realm, and I knew what they were capable of. I needed to develop a counterplan to stop this threat at all costs, and I needed to do so quickly.

My fears were confirmed as I heard the dictator gloat about raising an army and posting troops at each of one hundred secret locations scattered across the planet. I guessed these locations were the dull red spots on the globe. These beings, he boasted, would pursue their programmed agenda without pity or favor. They were armed with the most devastating modern equipment and a special weapon, the Kangaroblaster, a multiple power-packed explosive launcher that was designed to hop from area to area, tearing apart all ten areas it was programmed to touch. All were remotely triggered missiles that could destroy the armories and missile armaments of all the powerful nations through teleportation to the selected sites. It would spell doomsday for the planet if this program were put into operation.

It was at this time that I learned that the crater holding water with the power to catapult any inanimate objects through the troposphere was the channel through which all the equipment and creations had been teleported to and from their secret locations. I also came to realize that the two teams of warriors sent out from Kokou Bhutto about a century ago to investigate the flare might have fallen victim to the fire that was periodically released from the initial teleported equipment and which, within the first year, occasionally engulfed the area around the crater. The first team of twenty brave warriors had arrived to find a barren field and had seen the crater faintly from a distance. Curiosity had led them to investigate the distant object, and while on their way toward the spot, the fire was released through the shallow pits to engulf the field and incinerate them. The next team of ten had suffered the same fate. Neither of the two teams had a chance. They were brave men and had died honorably.

I further learned that a half-mile underground tunnel had been constructed to link the teleportation crater to the developed complex. It was lined with a highly effective fireproof material and was sealed with a heavy fireproof door to prevent the excessive heat from the teleported metallic equipment from entering the residential complex. It also had fireproof labyrinths through which the metallic materials that arrived were conveyed and stored by heat-resistant androids until they had cooled down sufficiently to permit their use for weapon manufacture and transfer to the secret armories.

The additional confirmation I received was that the power to create independent, self-conscious, reasoning, living beings with the ability to learn and respond appropriately to stimuli was the prerogative of only the Supremos. The spirits that followed the evil rebel, the usurper, yearned for the physical bodies of the faithful who had been blessed with bodies and endowed with freedom of choice. These evil spirits were envious of humans and were happy to possess and temporarily animate the created bodies to enable them briefly have a feel of what they had lost through their rebellion. I realized that their time within the bodies was limited and ended with their eviction from the borrowed flesh. It was more like the clothing humans wore and took off to be worn at another time. Each of these created human bodies could be used for a time by numerous evil spirits who functioned with a group mind to fulfill their master's bidding, but none was permitted, by eternal law, to possess a body permanently as humans were endowed to. I also learned that the takeover was easy if the genuine human possessor of the body willingly submitted to or served the evil master. What these invaders of bodies feared most was the power of the Supremos given to the Agents. They would flee at the command of the bearer of this power.

Pride had indeed always brought about the downfall of humans, yet humans had not learned their lessons from history. Those that were naturally endowed with a high level of intelligence and should have known better had always been easy victims to pride's persistent, ego-boosting deceptions in all ages on the planet. The boastful prodigy and his equally haughty admirer had revealed much more to me than they should have. I now knew the purpose of my being sent here and began to plan out a way to stop their evil designs. It was obvious that the Supremos had endowed the prodigy with exceptional talents for the benefit of all humans, but the gift of individual choice had permitted the evil rebel to influence him to use his knowledge and power against humanity. He had chosen the path of evil, and it was now my task to defeat him before he destroyed mankind.

CHAPTER 22

The Final Confrontation

The three centenarians kept me fettered to the giant robot as they moved into the secret chamber behind the television screen. Strangely, they did not disarm me. I guessed that they were planning to put me back into the arena to fight for the entertainment of their numerous customers. I knew that now would be my opportunity to free myself in order to further investigate the weak points in the complex's infrastructure. I strained against my constraints until one hand came free, and then tore at the fetters on my other arm and then my feet. The huge robot that held me was a mechanical type and not an automated android. Without anyone to control it by remote, it did not offer any resistance, and soon I was free.

I focused on the prodigy as I delved into my memory bank. Images of his childhood and development to the genius that he had become flashed across my mind. I watched him develop incredible and terrible machines. I watched as he dissected and studied prisoners of war for his experiments. The challenging design of the teleportation machine and its testing was followed with the construction of more devastating missiles, which were teleported to secret bunkers constructed in mountainous locations away from society in all the developed countries. In these same bunkers were located thousands and thousands of possessed human bodies. There were also factories that produced materials to feed the factories located in this complex. I was able to identify the controls for the various machines and equipment located in remote areas, as well as the accurate locations of the missiles in the various countries.

When I had gotten what I needed from these memories, I shifted my attention to the complex. I familiarized myself with some of the machines on site and other secret cubicles and passages, as well as entry and exit panels and their touch-control buttons. I then began enacting my plan by destroying the nutrient supply system to the developing embryos and the mechanisms for the conveyance and grading of the different types of bodies produced. I next concentrated on the destruction of the secret bunkers and the possessed bodies at their locations by detonating the planted missiles that were to be teleported to destroy the armament of developed nations. As I observed the effect of the detonations, I saw on the monitoring screen mountains torn apart, and the bodies that had served as the physical vessels of the evil spirits were consumed in the fiery implosions. Tremors of high magnitude were sent throughout the countryside, affecting the distant cities but causing little damage.

After I ensured that the last missile was detonated and everything in those locations was destroyed, I shifted my attention to the manufactured bodies in the corridors of the complex. As I moved from one level to the next, I tore off the panels along the walls, entered, and incinerated body after body. When I arrived at the last level, to my surprise, I saw that the glass pane that I had destroyed earlier had been replaced. That's when I realized that the prodigy and his two cohorts had discovered my escape and were probably planning something unpleasant for me. Nevertheless, I needed to keep moving forward. Almost instantaneously, as I took my first cautious step forward, the huge robot from before rushed at me, its huge arms swinging. I knew the prodigy was manipulating it. The robot was fast and gave me little to no time to recover in between attacks. As the robot's powerful arms swung through the air, barely missing me, it became apparent that death or serious injury would be the result of any slip-up on my part. In a moment of desperation, I reached for the nearest panel and tore open the door to reveal a corridor. I had intended to escape into it at the soonest opportunity, but the prodigy, realizing my plan, deliberately blocked the entrance with the huge frame of the robot. Luckily though, this action briefly put a halt to the chase and offered me a moment of relief and time to launch an assault of my own.

I pulled out my crossbow and fired a series of electric bolts aimed at the robot's jointed neck. Because of these joints, the robot could turn its head 360 degrees, and I guessed that this had to be its weak spot. I guessed right. Spurts of electricity began shooting out of the entry points as the robot began twitching and flailing its massive arms around uncontrollably. Its huge frame smashed against some of the panel doors of the arena, tearing them apart and leaving the passages open. Suddenly, after one final jolt, the metal colossus slumped inert onto the floor. Unsure of whether it had actually died, I decided not to take any chances and severed its giant head.

A loud noise behind me caused me to swing around instinctively to a strange sight. A prehistoric carnivore was alive and bearing down upon me from one of the large corridors that the malfunctioning robot had ripped open. It was a *Tyrannosaurus rex*. Its massive head was low as it towered above me and accelerated toward me with its jaws gaping open, exposing rows of pointed teeth, dripping with saliva. Just before it reached me, I made a quick evasive dive to the side, sending it off balance, causing it to slip and fall heavily on the smooth floor of the arena. Though it was a hard fall, it was up and after me again almost immediately.

By that time, I had already moved toward the spiral stairway leading up to the floor above and started to climb up to gain a higher elevation. As the dinosaur came charging after me, and just as it opened its jaws to grab me, I used all my power to launch myself high overhead. As the monster turned with its head poised to snap at me, I thrust my sword downward with one great swing and plunged the blade into its right eye. The dinosaur let out a deafening roar as its tail lashed out in anger and pain. Before I reached the ground behind it, its thrashing tail caught me mid-flight with enough power to send me flying into a panel door farther out in the arena. Had I been a normal man, the impact would have killed me instantly.

Partially blinded, the prehistoric monster tried to locate me with its remaining eye as it lashed at me periodically. I kept running toward its blind side to keep it moving in circles. In its attempt to keep pace, it lost its balance again, fell, and slid on the floor toward the panel doors. I took advantage of one such moment, rushed on it, and before it could regain its composure, I plunged my sword hilt deep into its heart. It tried to get up, clawing at the buried sword in its chest, but eventually, after one final attempt, it lay still.

I climbed up onto its dead body and retrieved my sword, but when I turned back to climb down, I saw another huge creature that looked like an oversized crocodile coming toward me from a different corridor. Its armor of thick scales appeared impenetrable, and its long, powerful snout gaped open to display a set of ugly teeth. It was relatively slower than the T-rex, and that gave me the advantage to outmaneuver it. I jumped over it and grabbed a firm hold of its tail, and with a great heave, I raised the tail and hind legs from the ground. It tried frantically to flick me off, but I held on as I began running in circles. I gathered enough momentum to raise its body off the floor and spin with it. The centripetal and centrifugal forces on it kept it spinning in an orbit around me until I let go of its tail. It flew through the air and smashed into the helical staircase, bringing the whole structure to the ground as it fell on its back and exposed its soft underbelly. Before it could recover, I was already on it, plunging my sword into its heart.

To avoid any more such encounters, I ran through the corridor my last opponent had come from and emerged into what looked like a large cage. I saw a sizable hole on one of the walls and suspected that this was how the ugly creature was fed. I quickly squeezed through the opening into another corridor and continued through a series of metal doors until I arrived at what looked like a laboratory. The area looked like it housed what could have been the control devices for cloning and other genetic creations. I immediately began searching around until I found another concealed door. I broke it down and entered another control room. This room had a global map of the world similar to the one in the room where the prodigy had related his life story. The labels on the map corresponded to labels on control switches around the room. There were other concealed doors, which, I discovered, opened to other corridors and secret passages that linked this area to other confidential sections of the empire.

As my mind raced, I started connecting the dots. This chamber was another room from which the teleportation and detonation of missiles aimed at countries could be executed. I had already destroyed the missiles, but I realized there were more control buttons here than in the other room. As I swept my eyes around the room, looking for more clues, I noticed a hidden dial on the side of the control box. When I turned it clockwise, part of the wall slid smoothly to the side, exposing a wall-to-wall television screen on which was presented a segmented telecast of activities in all parts of this complex empire. *Was this the master control room that housed all the additional controls for this complex?*

I saw the crater and the mode of teleportation via the crater and their mode of storage. I saw the secured room in which the prodigy and his cohorts had taken refuge. I saw the activities in the tunnel from the crater and the secure door that prevented the excessive heat from destroying the empire. I saw the corridors in each level of the multi-level coliseum and the destroyed and living creatures each harbored. I saw that though I had incinerated all the cloned animals and human bodies in the first levels of the coliseum, there were other strange creations still alive in large cages behind more of the closed panels in the last level where I had fought the robot, the T-rex, and the crocodile-like creature. This was the central control chamber for the entire empire! I now understood why the entry and exit doors before me had been fortified, but I wondered why the passage through which I had entered was not. It then occurred to me that the passages I had traversed led from cages of dangerous creatures. No one would dare enter the control room through the cages. I guess it had been more fortified than I initially thought.

What I needed to locate, in order to finish my work, was a master switch that could destroy the entire empire. I didn't know if there was such a thing, but I was determined to look. Alternatively, if I could capture or destroy the prodigy and his lifetime assistant, I would achieve my objective just the same. The admirer was no threat to me, since he was totally dependent on the other two. Without them, he was defenseless. I read through the labeling on the control panel and pressed the switch that controlled the insulating door on the tunnel from the crater. It was thrown open instantly. Though teleportation had been stopped for some time with my destruction of all the manufacturing bunkers, the heat from the last materials that came in had not fully dissipated, and it sent a wave throughout the empire that began forcibly flushing out the prodigy and his accomplices. I watched them on one of the screens as they escaped its effect by running through some passages into the large coliseum. Their torsos were covered in protective metallic suits that stretched from the neck to the chest, and they wore thickly insulated black pants under soft leather protective suits.

After making a mental note of where they were located in the building, I quickly retraced my steps through the crocodile cage and emerged to face them. They were all armed with lethal weapons and started an attack immediately. I was initially taken aback by the speed and intensity of their attack. I had assumed that because of their age that their movements would be slow and sluggish, but I quickly realized that they had superhuman powers. Their rage was tangible: I'd destroyed their plans. My enhanced reflexes and evasive maneuvering enabled me to avoid all of their coordinated attacks. I countered them occasionally with deadly strokes of my own, inflicting deep wounds, but I was surprised and dismayed to see the rapid repair of the wound on each occasion. My only method for their destruction would be to reach their hearts or to decapitate them. They knew this and had worn the protective attire to thwart any such effort from me. I had other ideas. I moved quickly and tore open one of the panel doors to release one of the creations of the prodigy into the amphitheater.

It was an unsightly creature possessing a tough, armored body with two long horns on its nose and a cape of long, stout, sharp horns around its neck. It was the size of a young elephant and possessed the skeletal head of a rhino and the mouth and teeth of a hippopotamus. Its protruding eyes mounted on the sides of its head swiveled back and forth as it assessed the room. It was an ugly creature of fury and destruction. It charged us on sight, propelled forward on thick and powerful legs, with the speed of a cheetah. It didn't take long for it to attain the momentum to smash through any solid wall in its path. In an effort to hurry out of its way, the assistant and the admirer crashed against each other, lost their balance, and fell into the path of the charging beast. The hoofs smashed through them, crushing them completely. They were dead instantly.

The prodigy and I managed to jump clear just in time to see the brute smash into the opposite wall and destroy a large portion of the coliseum. Momentarily dazed, it recovered, whipped around, and charged again while behind it another strange, elongated creature emerged from one of the tunnels that the first creature had smashed open. The new monster, a hybrid of an anaconda and the mythical flying dragon, with a row of strong, razor sharp teeth supported by a powerful set of jaws, a deadly scorpion tail, and fiery breath, managed to slow down the progress of the rhino-like creature by rapidly coiling around it and stinging its unprotected underside with its poisonous tail. Meanwhile, the prodigy and I had quickly vacated the arena and taken refuge in two of the empty corridors to await the outcome of the combat.

The poison from the sting started to have an effect on the rhino-like beast, but it continued struggling in an effort to free itself from the tightening coils of its deadly opponent. Finally, it collapsed and began thrashing around until it finally lay dead. As my eyes searched for the other monster, I saw that the horned creature had achieved its purpose for rolling. A long, sharp horn from the cape of spikes around its neck had pierced through the body, and another from the nose region had totally impaled the head of the anaconda creature, inflicting fatal wounds. With the brain pierced, the innate effort of its body to regenerate and repair the wound failed, and, as had happened to the assistant and the admirer, in a few moments the anaconda was also dead.

I rushed to the corridor in which the prodigy had taken refuge, only to find him gone. I sprinted back into the earlier corridor I had taken to arrive at the control room. He was nowhere to be found. I quickly switched on the screen so I could have a view of the surrounding areas in the complex. I spotted him climbing up a long flight of stairs and quickly memorized the floor plan of corridors to get to him as quickly as possible. I took off after him, taking shortcuts through heated areas the prodigy had avoided because of the high temperatures, and closed in on him.

I got to the base of the staircase only to see him already halfway up the very long flight of stairs. I could see the sky beyond the top of the staircase and rightly guessed that the staircase was an exit from the empire. He arrived at the top, but I had almost caught up with him. He made a dash to board an old-fashioned helicopter mounted on a pedestal only a few yards from the top of the stairs. He jumped into the seat and started the propellers. By the time I got to the helicopter, it had started lifting off the ground, so I jumped and held onto the landing skids as it cleared the platform. As we soared into the skies and away from the crests of the mountain ranges, I heard the sound of explosions beneath me and looked down to see the whole area go up in flames. Billows of thick black smoke started filling the sky as more explosions went off.

The prodigy had detonated hidden explosives by remote control to destroy the empire—and me—as a contingency plan to obliterate any evidence of his evil creations. He had maintained and kept the helicopter fueled and ready to be used to get away from any pursuers as a last resort. He still had the creative ability for cloning and stem cell research for his personal longevity treatments, and he could set up other laboratories to resume his evil plans. After all, he had billions in gold and a bank to finance the rebuilding of another empire. I knew that his only desire now was to destroy me and relocate somewhere else to pursue his evil trade. I was the only threat to his future plans.

As soon as we cleared the mountain range, the prodigy started maneuvering the helicopter in the direction of Kokou Bhutto and began rocking the helicopter in hopes of dislodging me from its landing skids. He flew low, just above the tall forest, in an attempt to scrape the skids against the treetops, but I held on until he had cleared the airspace above the stockade and gone a little further out. Tired of this game, I knew that I needed to end this, and I needed to do it now. Holding one of the skids with one hand, I removed the vaporizer from my belt with the other hand, let go of the skid, and shot a bolt into the helicopter. There was a loud explosion as the helicopter was torn apart and its occupant burst into red mist. Though I had allowed some distance between myself and the machine before using the annihilator, the force of the explosion hurled me forcefully into the trees. I hit branch after branch on my way down and finally hit the floor of the forest. I lay there for a moment, exhausted from the day's events but glad that it appeared to be almost over. As I slowly picked myself up from the ground, I checked everything to make sure that I wasn't injured and was surprised to find that I was still in good shape. I had truly been protected from any serious injury.

I looked into the sky and watched as the black smoke continued to billow away from the wreckage and debris from the helicopter littered the ground around me. I thought of the prodigy and his astonishing intellect and was saddened by his bitter demise. The planet had truly lost a genius, but an evil genius, and was better off without him. Others would come to build and put to good use the theories he founded for the benefit of the planet as a whole. This was the only good legacy he had to leave behind, and he would be remembered for it.

In a few minutes, my friends and some of the other residents from Kokou Bhutto arrived on the scene with worry splashed across their faces. They had heard the explosions and seen the billows of smoke in the distance earlier and had raced here as fast as they could. They had followed the events transpiring above them and saw the flying machine as it flew over the stockade with me hanging on to it. They had then heard the explosion some distance from their habitation. They feared that I was dead and had hurried to confirm this. Their expressions of fear and anxiety changed to joy when they found me whole and well upon their arrival. They lifted me onto their shoulders and marched to the stockade, chanting war songs of victory. The whole community had gathered to welcome me. I had been away from the stockade for two weeks, and I had come back among them as promised. As soon as the tribal head, the chief, and the elders saw me, they and the waiting residents broke into cheers to express their joy.

Over the next few days, I was fed well, and in the evenings as we sat by the fireside I had the opportunity to narrate to the ruling class and the warriors what had brought about the mystery of the forbidden empire. They were surprised when I did not cover my ears and eyes as I mentioned the native name of the empire. I told them the cause of the death of their brave warriors a century earlier and assured them that the evil that existed in the range of mountains had been destroyed forever. They were very grateful and believed that I was sent by their gods to save them. I assured them that the Creators of the universe, the Supremos, the only beings to be worshipped, had sent me out of their love for them to destroy the evil that was responsible for all that had transpired in their area.

I lived among them for one more week and taught them about the Supremos and the universal law of perfection. One morning, however, the impulse to leave and prepare for my next adventure came clearly to me. As the sun emerged into the clear sky the following dawn, I bid the chief and his elders; my good friends, the warriors; and all the good citizens of Kokou Bhutto farewell. As I was gathering my things, preparing to leave, Akachi walked up behind me and began helping me to fill my pack.

"Magnus," he said softly, "you know you could always stay." He stopped and rubbed his head with one of his weather-worn hands. "Stay with us. Live here in Kokou Bhutto and be happy. Whatever it is you are running toward or running from, wherever it is you feel you have to go, don't. Just stay and find peace here with us." I looked at the face of my friend and saw nothing but goodness in his eyes. For a moment, I longed to stay amongst this peaceful people, but I was reminded that my mission was to bring peace to *all* people. If I stayed here, that plan would be frustrated.

"Thank you, my friend," I said with a sad smile, "but I must keep going forward. I am not running from anything except time. I have limited time to complete my mission, and staying here would use that precious time for my own selfish wants." He looked away, ashamed that he had asked me to abandon my duties. I grabbed his shoulder, and with an even bigger smile I said, "Don't worry, my friend. I will see you again. Whether in this life or the next, I will see you again. Besides, I need to beat you again the next time we wrestle." Akachi's face broke into a sad smile, and he nodded in agreement as he backed away to let me leave. Tears were shed as I paced out slowly into the forest, waving good-bye. As soon as I entered the forest, there was a flash of light, and the next minute, I found myself back in the Sacred Dome of the Guardians.

The leader of the Guardians and his two advisors were there to welcome me as usual. After congratulating me on a job well done, they allowed me to eat and rest before resuming my education. From them I received further education about the Supremos. They taught me that everything is constantly before them and that events, like a ring, are in one eternal round, so they are in control of every situation despite the gift of the power given to humans to choose for themselves. They rear each human spirit, their offspring, to adulthood and thus know each human perfectly inside and out—character, talents, passions, thoughts, emotions, all other attributes—and how each will voluntarily respond or react to different situations or stimuli. They schedule the time of birth of each human on the planet and know the susceptibility of each person to choose one behavioral attitude over the other when certain options are placed before them. They know the lifespan of each human according to the challenges he will be brought to face in the course of his life, and the choices he will make using his free will. They teach and desire and hope that the right choices are made, but in no way do they interfere with the choices voluntarily made by each offspring.

"In just eighteen years of your life with your mortal parents, your father and mother could fairly accurately predict your behavior and adopt precautions to prevent you from getting into any mischief or injuring yourself. The Supremos have raised their offspring as spiritual essences for eons and are all-knowing. Is it not logical that they should know how each person will behave under different circumstances?

They knew how the end of the prodigy would come about based on the choices he made, and so also do they know of events to come that will threaten to destabilize the planet. They are everlastingly patient and know the antidote for every preventable adverse event on the planet. They apply the irrevocable laws of the universe to intervene when the general conduct of the populace favors intervention. They will allow certain destructive events to take their course when the universal laws favor destruction. They are in control and will guide this planet until the time comes for it to fulfill the full measure of its creation. Past records reveal that there have been occasions when future events or future generations have been revealed to Agents by the power and knowledge of the Supremos. This is called prophecy." The Guardians concluded their lesson and then left me to ponder the things I had learned.

The next few days were spent quietly in my assigned room, musing over my experiences in the forbidden empire and the education I had received about the omniscience of the Supremos. On the morning of the fifth day, I was staring pensively at the ceiling when I felt a strong yearning for my beloved Jane. The memory of our last meeting flooded me with a marvelous warmth. She had been permitted to educate me on some aspects of my preexistent life as a spirit essence, and I missed her very much. The legend of the forbidden empire was my third assignment since we last met, but I knew when the time was right I would see her again. I turned onto my side on the bed and saw, standing at the far corner of the room, my cherished future partner. "Jane!" I called out excitedly.

She was radiant as usual and wore that enchanting smile of hers. She glided over to my side and touched my hand as before. The next moment we were at the site of the ruins of a great city. It was a bright, sunny day, and there was not a soul in sight. By the look of it, it had been deserted many centuries ago. It had obviously been a beautiful city before its devastation by what looked like the ravages of war. As I focused on the fallen pillars of stone as well as the ones left standing, the partly collapsed buildings, and the ruined paved roads, I had a feeling they were not unfamiliar. The wild, overgrown bougainvillea of a variety of colors growing in what appeared to have been well-kept flower gardens, the lawns that were overgrown with wild weeds, all triggered a strange feeling of familiarity. I knew the city so well, yet in my lifetime on the planet, before and after my ordination as a Wackida, I knew I had never come to this location. *Was it that I had lived here in a previous life?* I struggled in my mind for an answer.

Jane looked amused at my creased forehead and blank stare. "A dime for your thoughts?" She pulled me gently to sit by her side on the stony staircase of a ruined amphitheater. "This place is familiar to you, isn't it? Yet you cannot remember why you know it." She smiled wistfully as if remembering a pleasant dream. She looked away for a moment across the ruins and then back at me. "You know this city very well, Magnus. You just can't remember it because the memory resides in the veiled portion of your mind from your pre-Earth life as a spirit. This is the same feeling you felt when I was revealed to you in the Dome.

"This city is one of the twin cities that you and I were sent on many errands to. The citizens and their rulers were extremely faithful to the Supremos and prospered for many generations. They were inspired to create beautiful architectural designs and built two cities with paved roads and created agricultural machines to increase the yield of their harvest. They were self-sufficient cities and were protected from invasion from the barbaric heathens surrounding them. But, as usually happens, wealth and pride eventually overcame them, and soon after, the succeeding generations rebelled against the Supremos and began violating the saving laws. We were sent on many occasions to help avert disaster before it was too late, but over time, their stubbornness and recalcitrant disobedience of the true laws alienated them from their divine protectors. They lost favor with the Supremos and were conquered. Their cities were plundered and torn apart, leaving only sorrow and death. Those that survived the onslaught were taken into slavery. The cities were left in ruins and have been left desolate ever since."

I wondered if flashes of memory, like the ones I had of Jane and this place, lent to the belief in reincarnation. Was it possible that people had mistaken these brief flashes of veiled memory and pre-mortal experiences for experiences in a previously lived mortal life? Jane continued to clarify while we strolled through the deserted ruins hand-in-hand.

"As I explained to you earlier," she said in her gentle voice, "long before we depart from the presence of our heavenly parents to be clothed in physical bodies, we are permitted to gain some experience. We are sent on special errands to assist those of our siblings who have been blessed with physical bodies and have gone ahead into mortality in earlier eras. In addition to those of us who have not yet received our mortal bodies, righteous spirits who have served faithfully in mortality and shed their physical bodies in death, living humans who are faithfully serving their probation (such as you), and special Agents who have been permitted to regain their perfected bodies after death, may also be sent on errands to administer to those in mortality. We are normally referred to as ministering angels.

"Though the veil of forgetfulness is drawn over the minds of spirit essences who are born on the planet," she continued, "some retain a hazy recollection of their former life as spirits. Certain people and places seem familiar to these spirits without apparent reason. They would even swear that they had seen these places and met these people before. The truth is, they were closely associated with such people and places in the pre-life, and they have their images so deeply etched in their veiled memories that glimpses of recognition flash in their minds when they see them in this life. This is why some might believe in the idea of rebirth, or reincarnation. But Magnus, it is very important to understand," she paused and looked deeply into my eyes, "there is no second chance. This life is our time to fulfill our purpose and then return to our heavenly parents. We must use it wisely."

As she said her last words, she grabbed my hands in hers and squeezed them gently as if to make sure that I understood the importance of what she was saying. I came to realize and accept that there is only one opportunity to live and serve a mortal probation by each offspring of the Supremos and that each human must make the most of this opportunity offered. After death, the spirit world mercifully becomes an extension, for the period of probation, during which an opportunity would be given to those who did not receive the law in life, or were given only the adulterated law put together by uninspired men, to hear and choose the true law and life eternal—or choose endless misery.

As I let this new information sink in, Jane grabbed my hand again and motioned to me that it was time to go. Just as before, she took me back to the room in the Dome and was gone in an instant. I woke up suddenly to find myself lying on my back on the bed, staring at the ceiling. I looked at the time reckoner and realized again that another spiritual date with Jane had lasted only one minute. Happy and satisfied with the gift I had been given, I spent the next few days before my next assignment resting and musing over the great lessons I had learned.

After two weeks, I was prompted to step out of my room only to see another panel door flashing. It was time for another assignment: an adventure in another unknown location. Obediently, brimming with more confidence and joy as a result of my newly acquired knowledge of the omniscience of the Supremos and the brief meeting with my beloved Jane, I opened the panel door and stepped through its portals into the unknown for my next adventure.

I found myself on the flattened crest of a hill overlooking an exceptionally deep valley in what appeared to be late afternoon. A large campsite covered with collapsed tents, scattered camp furniture, clothing, and other hiking gear lay before me. There was not a single human in sight. It was clear that a struggle between the occupants and some assailants had recently taken place, yet there was no sight of any settlement for miles. I stood at the edge of the valley and looked down. Even with my improved vision, very little could be seen of the valley's floor. The walls were steep, and tall virgin trees filled the bowl. The broad canopies of the trees made it almost impossible to view the valley floor from this height, yet I thought I saw faintly through narrow gaps in the canopy a river winding its way southward. Whatever secrets lay in this strange valley, it appeared as if nature was protecting it from view.

I attempted to access information from my memory bank, but nothing came. The realization hit me like a wall—I had made the grave mistake of not updating my records of the recent events in the planet's history in the memory machine before taking off. I was in a fix. I attempted to appeal to the Guardians for help without response. Of course! I did not deserve their help after neglecting their instructions to me never forget to update my memory before each assignment. My last hope was my gift of discernment. I stood still and concentrated as hazy flashes of brief, violent activities in the night and frightened sounds coming from the direction of the valley greeted my ears for a moment and then stopped. Whatever happened here happened in the dark. The scenes were not clear, and I needed to get some more information to confirm my suspicion.

I looked around for anything that could serve as a clue and stumbled upon a small diary that looked as if it had been abandoned in the skirmish. It had to have belonged to one of the missing campers. Excitedly, I began flipping through its sheets. The entries contained names of the campers and described the events that led up to the night of the attack. The last recording was during the day, an hour before nightfall, and right before the camp was deserted. What I read set my heart beating fast. I knew what I had to do, and I needed to hurry. Whatever unknown danger lay before me, I knew that I had to face it. It was my calling to fight evil and to deliver my brothers and sisters from tyranny and oppression. With this resolve, I began my descent into the mysterious valley.

About The Author

M ichael K. Andam was born in Takoradi, Ghana, West Africa, where he and his three brothers were raised by his parents, Kenneth Sr. and Jane Andam. He moved to the United States after high school to attend college. He graduated from Brigham Young University in Provo, Utah with a degree in Economics.

As a teenager, Michael loved to read both local and foreign comic books. The heroic and action-packed stories always drew him in. Since then, he hoped to someday become a published author. While his novels are full of fantasy and adventure—features fueling his wonder-filled, comic book obsession, they also seamlessly tie in valuable life lessons and insights into human behavior.

Michael is also a sports enthusiast with a passion for fitness. When he is not busy writing the next great American novel, Michael spends his days working as a personal health and wellness coach at his gym in Orem, Utah. He is the founder of Zealous Training (www.zealoustraining. com), a privately owned elite health and fitness organization. Guided by his knowledge of nutrition and excellent understanding of body mechanics, he and his team of Zealous trainers specialize in assisting individuals as they embark on their healthy lifestyle journey. Whether it be a stay-at-home mom who desires to lose some baby weight or a professional athlete needing conditioning for the upcoming season, Michael has the know-how to help and has helped change many lives for the better.